W9-BJK-555

"ROUSING SUSPENSE . . .
FAST-PACED . . . SURPRISING."
—King Features Syndicate

The Stage Is Set for Terror

Gail Edens, classic beauty, Oscar-winning actress, who spends her time between performances advocating radical causes . . . *Jack Riley*, America's most gifted actor . . . *Robert Morrison*, celebrated Hollywood golden-boy and superstud . . . and little *Angela Tuck*, seductive teen-age starlet, whose terrifying talents can save—or kill—them all. . . .

They are all hostages—caught in the inexorable web of terror in which their lives may be forfeited . . . as Colonel Franz von Werten, son of the man who defied Hitler himself, plots his chilling revenge . . . as the terrorists of the world unite under the dark symbol of the Reborn Eagle, sharpen their claws, and prepare to rise . . . again . . .

TO THE EAGLE'S NEST

"A RARE TREAT . . . ONE OF THE MOST SUSPENSEFUL AND THRILLING WORKS OF FICTION TO COME ALONG IN MANY YEARS. . . . EXCEPTIONAL-LY WELL WRITTEN."
—*The State Journal Register*, Springfield, IL

BOOKS BY JOSEPH DiMONA

Fiction
TO THE EAGLE'S NEST
THE BENEDICT ARNOLD CONNECTION
LAST MAN AT ARLINGTON
70 SUTTON PLACE

Nonfiction
THE ENDS OF POWER (*with H. R. Haldeman*)
FRANK COSTELLO: PRIME MINISTER
   OF THE UNDERWORLD
GREAT COURT-MARTIAL CASES

To the Eagle's Nest

Joseph DiMona

A DELL BOOK

Published by
Dell Publishing Co., Inc.
1 Dag Hammarskjold Plaza
New York, New York 10017

Copyright © 1980 by Joseph DiMona

All rights reserved. No part of this book may be reproduced
or utilized in any form or by any means, electronic or
mechanical, including photocopying, recording or by
any information storage and retrieval system, without
permission in writing from the Publisher. For information
address William Morrow and Company, Inc., New York,
New York.

Dell ® TM 681510, Dell Publishing Co., Inc.

ISBN: 0-440-18944-6

Reprinted by arrangement with William Morrow and
Company, Inc.

Printed in the United States of America

First Dell printing—November 1981

To an unforgotten talent
Arthur Fields
publisher, editor, great friend

Excerpt from a speech, May 18, 1980, by Kurt Mueller, the Fuehrer of the neo-Nazi party in West Germany, known as The Reborn Eagles:

". . . As Communist Russia grows stronger and more dangerous, the democracies are turning once again for leadership to those citizens who are hard and strong, the Nazi patriots. The Reborn Eagles are building mightily in number each day as worried citizens flock to our banner . . ."

Kill one another, my children. Kill one another to your heart's content. There are plenty more where you came from.

—George Bernard Shaw

To the Eagle's Nest

Book I

THE TRAP

1

Adolf Hitler slipped off his bathrobe and stood naked. Eva Braun didn't even notice; she was lying on her side in bed, facing away from Hitler, reading an illustrated popular novel. She had borrowed the book from one of Goebbels' film stars, a tome that had somehow eluded Hitler's ban on "pornographic filth." It was called *Lady Chatterley's Lover,* and right now the heroine was draping wild flowers around a gardener's privates. Delicious!

Or so the bemused smile on Eva's pretty face seemed to say as a hand caught a bare shoulder and rolled her on her back. "You are a real slut, Eva," Hitler said. He removed the book from her hands and threw it blindly across the room. "You have the Fuehrer in your bedroom and you read manure."

Eva giggled. Adolf was *so* old-fashioned. She found that trait in him endearing. He slipped into bed. And Eva knew that soon, through her skilled ministrations, she would reduce this "god" whom Goebbels feared, before whom even the mighty Goering trembled, to an ordinary man writhing and begging in the same tones, and on the same level, as a common clerk.

The only problem was that this time, in a seeming transport of passion, the Fuehrer called her "Alice."

Excerpt from a letter to Kurt Mueller, head of the Reborn Eagles, from a gauleiter in Bavaria:

> . . . Baader-Meinhof not interested at all in Hitler's personal life. Their enemy is the German government of today. So why is Baader-Meinhof working with the traitor Colonel von Werten who *is* interested? And why do they both want to kill Americans . . . ?

2

In 1944 General Felix von Werten stood in a Nazi court. A tall man of innate dignity he was now clad only in an old denim shirt and beltless trousers three times too large for him, so that he had to clutch them in front.

The trial was brief, consisting of the prosecutor's charge and the immediate sentence of death by hanging.

One hour later, the General stared at black-uniformed SS men who adjusted a rope around a meat hook, then draped its loop around his throat. A moment later, with no prayer, with only a last memory of contempt seen in the eyes of three SS executioners, the General fell into space as a trapdoor sprung. His neck snapped and he hung there, head tilted grotesquely.

The door opened and a motion-picture camera recorded the sight for Hitler's pleasure and the public's edification in theaters throughout Germany. Others of General von Werten's associates were impaled bodily on the razor-sharp meat hooks—dying in agony, the points of the barbed hooks protruding from their chests as they dangled.

This, too, was filmed, but not shown in theaters. Some of Hitler's female guests at a private screening fainted.

Thirty-six years later the son of General von Werten held a portable drill in a mammoth cave in the Alps. The shiny bit whirred; flakes of stone flew. Three inches into the wall the bit stopped as Colonel Franz von Werten of Wehrmacht Intelligence Headquarters withdrew it.

He laid the drill on the floor. Around him were desks, telephones, and maps, in a World War II command post his father had designed but never used because of the betrayal. Franz was crouching on the floor. A metal box padded with sponge rubber contained a series of glass cylinders. Attached to each cylinder was a tiny, button-sized radio receiver.

Inside each glass cylinder was Tuflex-2 nerve gas, the latest formula of the most lethal gas scientists had ever produced. Instant death, and no mask could filter it out.

The Colonel took one cylinder with its micro-receiver, stood up, and gingerly began to insert it into the hole he had just drilled. The trouble was that the glass was extremely fragile; it had to be if the radio impulse were to shatter it when the time came.

And the hole was not smooth; jagged points could rupture the glass. Franz tried not to breathe as he pushed the cylinder slowly, slowly into its socket.

He finished, knelt down again, this time beside a tool chest. Out of it he plucked a large ball of a putty-like substance. Franz had invented it. He took a welder's torch in one hand, the "putty" in the other, and stood up again beside the wall. He placed the edge of the putty above the hole and carefully applied the tip of the welding torch flame to it. The putty melted and dripped slowly across the opening, hardening almost instantly into what seemed to be sheer rock.

The hole was now invisible, but that was not the secret of the putty. The secret was that, despite its smooth rock face, it was porous. The nerve gas, when the signal came, would be released into this cave to kill all of its occupants, and not one of them, even with a warning, could discover the cache of death.

Franz was methodical, cautious, cunning. He took no chances whatever. In five other places in the cave he drilled identical holes and planted the nerve-gas mines.

Then he gathered up his gear and took one last look around the cave. He and his associates had labored long and hard to prepare this secret World War II command post for the operation which would begin this night.

Now all was ready. He checked the offices, sleeping quarters, and auxiliary rooms in the cave. In one room, across from the prisoners' cell, sharp meat hooks with ropes dangling from them lined the wall. Beginning tonight—if all went as planned—five Americans would hang from these meat hooks exactly as his father and friends had, writhing in agony.

And Franz would be ready to utilize Tuflex-2 and his other weapons for a terror his father would have approved.

If not his allies. General Felix von Werten would never have consented to the use, as shock troops, of the unruly, uncontrollable Baader-Meinhof killers.

3

A young man lay on a mountain peak holding a Czech rifle with a four-power telescopic sight mounted. The scope was focused on Hitler's "Eagle's Nest" across the valley.

Magnified in its lens, men in work shirts could be seen on the balcony, along with some beautiful women dressed in 1938 fashion. Trucks and cars of modern vintage were parked outside the villa.

Filth, was what young Kurt Ollweg thought of the people he observed through the telescopic sight. Technicians and supporting actors in the film *The Secret Life of Hitler,* for which the villa had been re-created in precise detail, they were, Ollweg believed, a living pestilence that had infested this natural German paradise of mountains and blue lakes.

But the technicians and extras in his lens were not the victims the Baader-Meinhof terrorists were stalking today. Inside the villa were the individuals whose murder was planned: four American actors and actresses and an Oscar-winning director, all superstars in the motion-picture world.

A second young man crept up silently on his belly beside Ollweg and grunted, "Any signal?"

"Nothing," Kurt said. "He hasn't shown."

Baader-Meinhof had planted a spy in the motion-picture crew. This morning he had informed them that the five potential victims had finally decided to accept the invitation to a party this evening at the villa of Felix Bernhard, a rich industrialist. The house was five miles away on a sheer cliff above the lake called Königsee, inaccessible except by a private road guarded day and night by security specialists. Nevertheless, Ollweg's Baader-Meinhof superior, Helga Neff, had decided the party at the villa would provide their best opportunity to strike.

Ever since the beginning of the filming of the controversial movie about Hitler, the actors had traveled separately in well-guarded and bulletproof limousines. They were all aware of the terrorist threat in Germany. The theory behind the isolation was financial; if one actor was killed or kidnapped, the motion picture could still be made. If all four featured actors were eliminated, a thirty-two-million-dollar picture—now only two-thirds finished—could never be completed.

But Helga Neff had devised a plan that would get all the victims into *one* limousine. Kurt didn't even know how she was going to do it. All she had said was that there would be a "surprise" at the party tonight.

Kurt Ollweg strained his eyes through the scope. A stocky, bald-headed man wearing a green kerchief around his neck suddenly appeared at the door which led to the balcony of the Eagle's Nest. He pushed through the crowd to the railing overlooking the lake, then loosened his green neckerchief and dropped it on the floor. When he bent down to retrieve it, Ollweg said, "That's it."

The signal had been given. The operation was on. The actors and director were going to the party this evening. It would be the last night they would ever spend alive. And the movie that glorified Hitler would die with them—a thirty-two-million-dollar loss for the Americans.

Americans, Ollweg thought. How could you understand them?

4

Bernie Weller was an aristocrat of the motion picture world. The winner of two Oscars for direction, nominated three other times, he was treated with awe by his actors. Which was the way things should be, according to Bernie.

Where Bernie differed from most of his fellow directors was that he actually respected actors, including those he had chosen for the most expensive picture of his career, *The Secret Life of Hitler*. And why not? All four of the stars had won Oscars of their own, were part of the intellectual New Wave of performers who chose to live in New York and not Hollywood, and, with one exception, came from a background of the legitimate stage. And even the exception had an excuse. Angela Tuck, the incredibly beautiful and almost sinfully sexy child-woman star, was only fourteen years old.

"Fourteen going on *thirty*" was the acid-tongued judgment of all those on the set who looked into her green eyes and saw what was in their depths.

"Silence on the set," Weller said, and watched the still astonishing vision before him: Adolf Hitler in bed with Eva Braun. Why did it amaze him so? They were actors, Jack Riley and Gail Edens, playing roles from a screenplay he had approved. He had to keep that in mind or this whole picture would collapse.

But the actors were having trouble themselves. Jack Riley saying "Alice" in the first take. Who the hell was Alice? Collins had sworn he didn't even know a woman by that name. Now for the second take the camera, trundled gently by a technician, trucked into a close-up of Riley's face. Jack Riley said "Alice" again.

"Cut!" Weller shouted. "Dammit, Jack, are you playing games here?"

But even as he stormed toward the bed in the middle of the set, Weller told himself to calm down. It wasn't the actor's fault. All of them were oddly unnerved by this strange film on which they had so unwittingly embarked.

Weller had read the screenplay of *The Secret Life of Hitler* many times before accepting this assignment. A Jew who had been smuggled out of Germany by his aunt, leaving his mother and father to die in Auschwitz, he had wanted nothing to do with a picture, or anything, concerning Hitler. But the screenplay had convinced him. Other films had dealt shallowly with Hitler as a posturing military commander. None had delved into his personality. For the first time this film would do so and, in Weller's opinion, would reveal his evil psyche in a new and uniquely effective way.

And so Weller had accepted the assignment to direct the motion picture—and what had happened? Why was he now on the set of Hitler's bedroom talking to Jack Riley, who was stammering, "I swear to

God, I don't know why I said Alice again. I told you I don't know any Alice. The name just came out." The actor, handsome in an offbeat way, sandy-haired, blue-eyed—and now very nervous—paused, then said, "This damn picture is *haunted*. I told you that a dozen times."

Gail Edens agreed. "I'm telling you, I was lying in Hitler's bed thinking I was Eva Braun. I knew just what was going through her mind when the jerk actually climbed into bed with her forty years ago."

Weller managed to calm himself. "Neither of you believes in the occult?"

Riley and Edens looked at each other and shrugged no.

Weller said, "Then there is a rational explanation for the use of the word 'Alice.' I will find it for you if you can't do it yourself. And the picture is not 'haunted.' You are just tired. Now let's try it one more time, please." He turned to go back behind the cameras. "Clear the set. Fred, check the light off the wall. I think we might have caught a glimmer."

But while his mind considered the techniques of production, he was disturbed as he made his way back beyond the lights which illuminated Hitler's bedroom set. The picture *was* haunted. Every day Weller viewed the rushes and saw what was taking place. This anti-Hitler film was becoming a *pro*-Hitler film, despite the screenplay. Why? Was it something occult, as Riley and Edens hinted? Or was it merely a stupid directorial mistake of his own, his insistence that the film, to show reality, must deal with the truth: that the German people had fanatically supported, indeed loved, Hitler. And so they must include scenes of the great Nazi political rallies during Hitler's rise to power to contrast with the grimy reality of his personal life and feelings, which the film would also reveal.

Jesus, he had known it was a mistake even as the cameras were rolling on those scenes of surging crowds at that Nuremburg rally, deliberately filmed by Weller in the style of Leni Riefenstahl's masterpiece, *Triumph of the Will*. That soaring eagle, those lights stabbing the sky to form a towering wall of pure white around hundreds of young, healthy, eager German soldiers, emotion building—God, Weller had felt it himself. Heil Hitler, the roar and the roar. Heil Hitler!

Now, on a set called Berchtesgaden, Weller's hand dropped into his left coat pocket and emerged with a tranquilizing pill. He gulped it down dry, thinking of Marilyn Monroe's endearing question when she was caught in a film that was a disaster. "Who do I screw to get *off* this picture?"

Somehow he had to persuade Max Weber and the rest of the studio "numbers" men to scrap the crowd scenes that he had shot at great cost. But were those scenes alone the cause for the pro-Hitler feeling of the footage? Or was it something demonic in Hitler himself that was as hypnotizing on a motion-picture screen today as it had been in real life four decades ago?

Apparently, word had traveled throughout Germany of the changing viewpoint of the film. When shooting had begun, they were picketed by tough-looking neo-Nazis who called themselves the Reborn Eagles. But as the film had progressed, the Nazis suddenly disappeared and the police said that the dreaded left-wing Baader-Meinhof organization was now in the area, apparently to protest the pro-Hitler movie. Which was worse? Weller didn't know, although all of his instincts feared the Nazis the most. But Baader-Meinhof had a reputation for violence these days that was frightening. According to the police, all of the actors' lives were now in danger. Thank God, thought Weller, they had such tight security.

5

When the invitations to Felix Bernhard's party had first gone out, Helga Neff, the leader of the Baader-Meinhof terrorists, had scouted Bernhard's property. At first it seemed impregnable. The millionaire's mansion sat on the edge of a cliff which dropped straight to a lake. Only skilled mountain climbers could make it up that sheer face—and the industrialist had made certain even they couldn't reach the top by installing below his house a maze of barbed wire that jutted out six feet horizontally from the cliff.

On the other side of the mountain the private road was blocked by a gate with guards, and other armed security men patrolled the grounds in case someone got through.

So how to crack that impregnable fortress? Helga sent word throughout the university campuses, and a day later heard from a young man named Hans Ulbricht. Hans was a mountain climber who had grown up in the Berchtesgaden area and knew all of the hills there. "There's a flaw in that cliff," he had told her over the phone from Munich.

"A flaw?"

"An opening. Just a slit. And it leads to a tunnel that's been there for centuries. I'm sure the owner doesn't even know about it."

Helga asked why not, and Hans told her that it couldn't be seen from the ground or the top. It was just a small aperture in the cliff face that only someone who had climbed the cliff before, as Hans had done, would know was there.

Helga had asked where the tunnel led and was told that it came up on the other side of the mountain, about halfway to the top. "Right in the middle of the woods, as I recall. In fact, that could be a problem. The roots of a tree might have grown through it. Or a rock slide could have caused a boulder to bury it. Anything."

The next night Hans had arrived in Berchtesgaden and made a reconnaissance of the tunnel. When he returned, he had given thumbs up. "A boulder, all right. But not immovable."

It was then that Helga Neff had realized that this was, at last, their great opportunity. An ambush on a dark mountainside could succeed. But the actors and director would be traveling in five separate cars, convoyed by police, which still made it almost impossible. Was there a way to change that circumstance, to force them into a single car?

One impulse might do it. Fear, which would cause haste, and disrupt the orderly security routine. Perhaps a fire at the villa? A diversionary attack?

Helga Neff, sitting in a small room in a Berchtesgaden house, turned to look out of the window. The movement caused her long golden hair to swirl. Young Hans Ulbricht found himself admiring the sheer beauty of this legendary Baader-Meinhof killer. In a newspaper story, a police captain in Frankfurt had called Helga a "sadist, a death machine, not even human."

She looked very human to Hans. Wide-spaced blue eyes, lovely sculptured nose, and a body that—even when encased in old denim shirts, jeans, and boots—was vibrant and voluptuous. No one in the organization, he knew, dared approach Helga sexually, and she never once gave anyone cause. There were even whispers that she was a lesbian. But most Baader-Meinhofers knew that she had lived for three years with a German student who was eventually imprisoned for terrorist activities in Berlin. Three weeks later her lover had committed suicide after a hunger strike in his cell. It was then Helga Neff had thrown herself full time into the activities of the Baader-Meinhof terrorists, acquiring quickly a reputation for ruthlessness that frightened even her associates.

Her blue eyes now fixed on Hans. He turned away self-consciously as she said, "If the party goes forward, we'll use an electric boat to go to the foot of the mountain. You'll climb up with a line and when you reach the tunnel you'll throw it down and we'll attach a rope ladder, correct?"

Hans nodded.

"You know where to get a rope ladder without leaving a trace?"

Hans said yes. Helga told him they would meet again to discuss the plans and she would introduce Hans to his fellow members. "Now go."

And with that terse farewell Hans had been sent on his way, an anonymous young man in a brown suede jacket plodding along a small cobbled street in the lovely Bavarian village of Berchtesgaden, the blood

coursing through his veins. Small yellow houses with
brown balconies covered with geraniums rose on either side of him. Pretty female tourists smiled at the
Bavarian natives, many of whom wore colorful leder-
hosen and Tyrolean hats with large feathers. Hans
was too preoccupied to notice. He was actually going
on a Baader-Meinhof mission. His first—after all the
false starts, and last-minute refusals. And why wasn't
he backing out now as he had always done before?

Because the magnitude of the operation—and the
people it involved—thrilled him. If he was going to
imperil his life, it wouldn't be on the kidnapping of
some anonymous businessman or stupid politician.
Their targets were Gail Edens, the classic beauty
known as the "intellectual" actress who used her time
between films to espouse radical causes; Jack Riley, a
wisecracking, savvy fellow who gave powerful performances beneath a brittle veneer; Robert Morrison,
the redheaded actor whom women accorded the title
"the handsomest man in the world"; and, most interesting to Hans, Angela Tuck, the "child-woman" star
who was so incredibly sexy on screen.

These, plus a legendary director, would make a
group of victims to light up the whole world.

Hans stepped into a pastry shop for some coffee
and apple strudel. His mind was on Angela Tuck. He
couldn't stop himself. What he was thinking was rape.
He was visualizing, specifically, her bumptious little
body pressed against him, her young mouth ravaging
his in passion. . . .

In the room he had left, Helga Neff thought she
should call the Colonel in Munich. She needed Hans
Ulbricht to execute the mountain climb. But she could
see that he would be a problem in an operation with

two professional beauties searching for any vulnerability in their captors.

But then she decided to forgo the call to Munich. Without Hans, they couldn't even get the plan started. That was basic. But God, this operation was complex. Somehow she had to disrupt that party, and already she had discarded the idea of a diversionary attack. That would immediately alert the police, who would throw a cordon around the actors.

On top of everything else, her superiors had thrown her a curve. Earlier this week, Helga had received a coded message sent from the Colonel on a one-time pad. The message said:

Execute Plan Valkyrie II at scene of party, if all preparations checked and confirmed by you. Warning: take special precautions with Angela Tuck. She is extremely dangerous.

Angela Tuck? Dangerous? Those unexpected words absolutely astounded Helga. According to a dossier Helga had seen, the tiny actress knew absolutely nothing about politics and cared less. That file revealed a fourteen-year-old girl whose knowledge of world affairs—and men in politics—was absolutely nil.

So why that odd warning about a baby like Angela Tuck?

6

Angela Tuck awaited her big scene: she was to burst in on Hitler making love to her "aunt," Eva Braun. She kept reminding herself, "Don't appear too adult, don't appear too adult."

She always had to do that.

Angela Tuck had long, shining blond hair parted in the middle and falling softly over a lustrous white forehead, impish large green eyes, aristocratic cheekbones, an upcurving nose with flaring nostrils, and warm, generous lips—in sum, a mature face that for two years had seemed deliberately to taunt men to forget all civilized laws forbidding sex with minors and take the illegal plunge. And this sexual appeal even survived the offscreen photos of Angela in which she appeared to be an absolutely normal child playing innocently with her little schoolmates. Somehow, no matter whether she was shown in a pinafore tossing a Frisbee or playing hopscotch in a schoolyard, her eyes broadcast a secret message to adult men: "Let's get it on."

In real life, Angela Tuck did have secrets the public didn't know, some innocent, some not. She was fif-

teen, not fourteen, her name was Dilts, not Tuck,
and—what would be surprising only to naïve women
among her fans—she certainly wasn't a virgin.

In fact, she was exactly what men instinctively
guessed: a nymphet with a joyously erotic, even
kinky, past, thanks to her divorced father who had
spirited her away to Europe every summer. How she
had loved those summer vacations lately. Those tall,
blond Germans! She could twist them around her finger every time. And twist them other places, too.

Angela Tuck saw that cute young assistant director
waiting to cue her entrance, and smiled. She had
plans for *him*, too, before this film was over.

Her father, who was stationed in Berlin, certainly
couldn't object to a love affair with the assistant director—or anyone. Not after what she had done for her
father last summer. Involving her in his political ven-
tures was one thing, but murder? For that's what it
was, no matter what her father said now.

Abruptly, she shuddered. God, she must stop thinking of that dead German boy. That experience had
been sickening. A hand touched her shoulder. "Now,
Angela. Now." She ran to a door on the set and entered Hitler's bedroom.

7

The operation was on. Baader-Meinhof would strike tonight.

Colonel Franz von Werten tried to control his nerves as he flew by helicopter from the command-post cave on a jutting peak in the Alps back to the Bonn military air base. "Good afternoon, Colonel," a white-gloved MP said as Franz walked into the terminal.

Franz returned his salute and drifted into the building. Military clerks manned weather desks; the terminal bustled with activity associated with the NATO war games which were to commence the next morning.

Franz drove to his office in Military Intelligence headquarters, Third Army. An aide awaited him. "General Krønfeld wants to see you, sir."

Franz looked at the clock. 5:00 P.M. In a few hours the Baader-Meinhof people would go into action. Franz concentrated on the General's questions. The games tomorrow would feature a tank thrust against a position defended by small nuclear mines. The General said, "The damn magnetometer you invented is going to lose us the games."

The General's forces were on the "defense" in the games. A year earlier, nuclear mines had seemed an absolute defense against a tank attack—or any ground attack at all, for that matter. But then Franz von Werten, working in his little office, had modified an anti-submarine device used by aircraft, the magnetometer which detects changes in magnetic field caused by the presence of metal. He adapted it for the infantry into a portable device installed in flashlight tubes. And now foot soldiers could use the invisible electromagnetic rays to pierce the earth and detect the mines underground.

"You'll know tomorrow," Franz said. "Meanwhile you'd better keep me away from General Helldorf." Helldorf was the commander of the offense. "He still says I should be assigned to him."

"He won't even be able to find you, as we planned. You'll be on an intelligence mission and the rules of the games say that your position cannot be revealed. And meanwhile, you drop out of sight so I can't locate you, no matter how loudly Helldorf shouts."

Ten minutes later the Colonel drove to his home on the base, a faceless brick structure with a small lawn in front of it, typical of officers' homes on military bases everywhere around the world.

The Colonel went inside, took off his jacket, and placed it neatly on a hanger in a downstairs closet. He removed his brown necktie, too, and hung that up. Then he went upstairs. A ladder from the second-floor hall led to a trapdoor in the attic. He climbed the ladder, hoisted up the door, and made his way into the top room.

He flicked a button on the wall, lighting the attic, then closed the trapdoor. He was now alone in a windowless room containing a desk, chair, and two telephones, both with scrambling devices. The red telephone led directly to the cave, whose telephone had also been equipped with a scrambler.

He picked it up and dialed 7135341429. Far away in the empty cave he heard a telephone ring.

The communication line to the cave was working. He used the other telephone, which was green, to call another number, this one in Berchtesgaden. The voice which answered was mature, deep. "Colonel Hurwirth here."

"Franz. Do the Baader-Meinhof people have the special pebbles?"

"Yes, sir. And the ski masks, guns, and electric boat. Everything."

"The helicopter laid on?"

"It's ready, too, sir."

Franz thanked him, hung up, and went downstairs to make a bachelor dinner before returning on watch. Passing his bedroom on the second floor he paused, then entered the room and clicked on the light.

The picture of his late wife was, as always, on the table next to his bed. Franz glanced at it as he went to the top drawer of his dresser. Inside it there was a gold chain with a locket. The locket contained a rather handsome picture of Adolf Hitler's face.

Hitler was not smiling in the picture. And that strange fact, as much as anything, was what had driven Colonel Franz von Werten to steal sophisticated military weapons for his own use—and to plan the kidnapping and immediate execution of five un-suspecting Americans.

How Franz hated that picture, and what it repre-sented.

Book II

THE PARTY

1

Jack Riley looked around at the party. By the marble stairway was a 4.0 blonde in a green chiffon blouse and a long skirt slit up to the hip. Robert Morrison saw a glance pass between the actor and the blonde, and smiled. "Three-point-nine?"

Riley laughed. "The big four," he said.

Jack Riley had spent some time in the Navy as a Seaman First before gypsying his way to Hollywood. Perfection in the Navy was 4.0. In fact, the Navy had a saying, "There never has been a 4.0 person." But the Pentagon might make an exception for the chiffon girl, now twirling a glass of white wine, hair falling over her eye.

Riley decided to pass her up for the time being and joined Morrison as he walked out of the mansion onto the lawn. Striped tents, a polished hardwood dance floor, and people looking at them. Riley had grown accustomed to stares long ago, never noticed them unless they came from a particularly beautiful woman. What struck his eye now was even more fascinating than the blonde inside. "Jesus," he said to Morrison, "a tank."

"A real panzer," Morrison said. "Not those props we're using in the picture."

Gail Edens, the actress with large round innocent eyes, penetrating brain, and cool Radcliffe voice, came over to them. "How do you like that? We go to our first German party and find that our host keeps a Nazi tank as a shrine."

But Riley was not so sure. "I talked to some people. They say Mr. Bernhard isn't one of the boys."

"What do you mean?"

"He's one of the 'new' German businessmen, which means he doesn't kneel down beside his bed every night and pray that Hitler's body was made of asbestos."

Edens and Morrison laughed as they went over to the tank to examine it. A bulls-eye on its side fascinated them. "What do you think that means?" asked Edens.

"A little game," a voice said, and they turned to see their host advancing toward them. He was a stout, florid-faced man wearing a green alpine hat. The actors knew that he was president of the Ronken Steel Industry, the third largest in Germany. Riley had also been told by a guest that Bernhard was eccentric. "What we used to call a Bohemian. How his business makes a profit we don't know." Now Bernhard said, "You people work in the world of illusion. Some of us outsiders can do it, too."

"What's the illusion?"

"You'll see," said the host, but Gail wouldn't allow him to drop it. Her blue eyes softened—a trick she had learned to do on screen when required to adopt facial expressions of torrid passion. Once, when asked by

Mike Wallace how she simulated such eroticism, she said simply, "I just give it the old Radcliffe one-two."

"Come on, Mr. Bernhard, you can trust me. Some of my best friends worship Nazi tanks."

Bernhard didn't like that. He said quietly that he had spent a lifetime taking abuse because he was *not* "a fan of the former Corporal, Miss Edens."

Gail quickly apologized and Riley asked Bernhard if the illusion had anything to do with the bulls-eye. Bernhard decided to tell them. "I have a bazooka with rubber bullets. The guest fires the bazooka at the tank. If he hits the bulls-eye, a dummy of General Goering pops out of the hatch shouting in a falsetto voice, "Help me! Help me!"

The actors laughed. Gail said, "Why not a dummy of Hitler?"

Bernhard said that he used to have a reproduction of the Fuehrer, but he couldn't take the chance anymore. "There are too many people who say it's a sacrilege. One student actually was so angry he threw red wine over the tank and said it was German blood."

In another part of the garden, Angela Tuck was reluctantly performing her little girl act for a reporter, a sharp-nosed German woman from *Der Spiegel*. The woman asked, "Don't you think it's almost . . . indecent . . . to project such sex appeal at your age?"

Angela batted her eyes sweetly. "I don't know what you mean, Miss Ohlstahf."

"In your first big picture you had incest with an uncle. In your second, you were a child prostitute. In this one, you play sexual games with a Nazi official. It's sex, sex, sex, all the time."

The woman was a bitch, Angela decided. But she

said innocently, "They're just roles, Miss Ohlstahf. It's only playacting."

"Only playacting? I heard it's *real*, offscreen, too," said the reporter, surprising Angela, who looked at her more closely. Then the child tossed her hair in irritation. "You always hear lies about Hollywood people, Miss Ohlstahf. But I can tell you something if it's absolutely off the record. Promise?"

The reporter's eyes glittered. "Of course."

Angela said gently, "I'm too young to screw. I know because I tried it once. My pussy is just too small. I almost killed a friend." She paused, then trilled, "Now remember, that's off the record, of course." And she walked away, smiling.

2

Kurt Ollweg crouched in a pitch-black tunnel beneath a mountain.

Above him Hans Ulbricht and Georg Freund were wrestling a boulder away from the mouth of the tunnel. Kurt heard their grunts as the men strained; then there was a rush of cool air, and stars could be seen. The boulder was off. Georg hoisted Hans through the opening to check for the guard patrol.

The darkness inside the tunnel was clammy. A rat rushed past Kurt, causing him to recoil, its gleaming eyes a memory he would never forget. Then Hans dropped silently into the cave. "A guard's there," he whispered to Helga Neff, "only twenty feet away."

Helga said, "Kurt, you go with Georg."

Two minutes later Kurt Ollweg was out in the open, breathing fresh air. Immediately he felt better. Georg put a finger to his lips, then turned and crept through the forest. Kurt took a knife with an old leather handle from his pocket, and followed.

Georg suddenly stiffened, then blended into the shadow of a tree tunk. Kurt vanished also. In a moment a stocky man with a broad, pleasant face, a machine gun slung across his shoulders and a flashlight in his right hand, walked silently through the woods. Suddenly his flash beam revealed Georg. The security guard jumped back, pulling his gun up to fire, but George was on him like a cat, clamping his hand across his mouth. Kurt ran to the spot where two bodies locked and strained. His blade flashed briefly before plunging deep into the guard's back. Georg's hand kept its viselike grip on the mouth so no outcry could be heard as the guard, in agony, slumped to the ground. Kurt slit his throat.

A few minutes later the guard's body was covered with green bushes, and Georg and Kurt were inside the tunnel again. "Walkie-talkie?" Helga asked. She was worried that the guards had a routine of reporting by radio. Georg said, "No."

"Then they won't miss him for at least half an hour, and by then we'll have them," she said.

Helga Neff said nothing more. Now everything depended on an old panzer tank in the garden at Bernhard's party. Some of her associates had suggested wiring it with explosives.

3

9:00 P.M. The party in the garden with its multi-colored tents was swinging. A blonde smoked a joint, then passed it to her friend, a bushy-haired artist in jeans. Both of them, like all the other guests, were trying not to stare at the movie stars in their midst.

Then they heard Felix Bernhard, in the middle of the garden, announcing the game with the tank. "The first one of our Hollywood visitors to hit the bulls-eye will receive a case of Dom Perignon champagne. First, Miss Angela Tuck."

Flashbulbs popped as Angela held the weapon to her shoulder. For a moment she toyed with the idea of turning the bazooka around and letting that bitchy woman reporter from *Der Spiegel* have a rubber bullet in the face, but she quickly conquered the impulse. She squeezed the trigger, heard a loud bang, and the next thing she knew she was on her backside in the grass with everyone laughing. She scrambled to her feet and the host, looking concerned, apologized. "I forgot to warn you that the gun has a recoil."

Angela smiled and rubbed her bottom. "I'm just glad this isn't a sit-down dinner."

Gail Edens was next, and people immediately saw that she handled the weapon professionally. She stood in the approved infantry rifleman stance, one foot in front of the other, the weapon balanced lightly on her shoulder. In fact, Gail had found she was intrigued by weapons on a trip to Vietnam and had hated herself for it, wondering how a woman protesting for peace could appreciate guns. Now she stood firm when the gun recoiled—and missed the bulls-eye anyway. Smiling, she handed the weapon to the host.

Robert Morrison was third and, as always, there was an intake of breath among women when they saw this handsome redheaded male standing so close to them with a face that was not rugged, not "pretty," but infinitely pleasing in an all-American way. Sadly for his fans, it was rumored that he was only interested in his wife, whom he had married fourteen years ago.

Morrison had done some trapshooting so he, too, looked professional as he aimed the weapon and squeezed the trigger. But again the bullet bounced harmlessly off the tank and the host said, "Three down. One to go. Please, Mr. Riley, for the honor of America." But a murmur from the crowd warned him something was amiss. He glanced around and saw that Jack Riley wasn't there.

Bernhard leaned toward his wife. "Where's Mr. Riley, dear?"

"I don't know exactly where he is," said his wife, "but I know *what* he is."

"What?"

"Stoned! Furthermore, he disappeared upstairs with the wife of the Minister of Finance and I expect you'd better find him before the Minister does."

Bernhard restrained a groan. Out of the corner of his eye, he saw the cuckolded Minister of Finance chatting, all unknowing, with another guest. Christ, Felix thought, I'd better get this game finished in a hurry.

He said, "I've been told that Mr. Riley has been taken ill. Perhaps it was too much champagne. Therefore, I will shoot in his place. If I hit the bulls-eye, then every guest here receives a free bottle of Dom Perignon, instead of the actors." A buzz of approval rose from the guests as Bernhard raised the weapon to his shoulder.

Upstairs in a bedroom overlooking the festive garden, Gerta Randall, the wife of the Finance Minister, was experiencing the lovemaking of her life. Jack Riley might be intoxicated, but there was one very sober portion of his anatomy. My God, it was a ramrod. Everything she had heard about Hollywood studs was real. Riley was a super lover. Now she straddled him, and in the midst of her passion had to restrain a smile. Her husband and she had been to Bernhard's parties often. When the bulls-eye was hit by old Bernhard (no one else could ever seem to do it) everyone would be busy for half an hour laughing and queuing up for free bottles of champagne.

That half hour was all she would need. She groaned as Riley's hands moved to her full breasts, his fingers pressing her sensitive nipples. She was almost there. Almost. She started to utter little cries of ecstasy and forgot all about the garden and the game and her fat old husband. This was what life meant. This!

* * *

Felix Bernhard pressed the trigger, and the bazooka went "Crack!" Smoke floated from its muzzle as the rubber bullet raced toward the tank. Bulls-eye. A motor in the tank roared to life, and the hatch slowly opened. A grinning Goering appeared, rising lifelike from inside the tank. "Help me! Help me!" he trilled. And then, my God, the tank moved!

Bernhard fell back in amazement. The tank was rolling. Impossible! It wasn't supposed to do that—in fact, it *couldn't* do that. The engine had been disabled years ago, its gears removed. The tank was a prop.

Now, obviously, the gears had been replaced because that tank was moving. The depression of the button on the bulls-eye had activated not only the dummy but the repaired engine, too. And because the empty tank was pointed directly toward the house, Helga Neff had known it needed only to be started to create havoc.

Bernhard's expression showed the guests this wasn't part of the game. Surprised, they turned to observe the old tank rumbling right toward them. A woman screamed, then another. Husbands grabbed their wives' arms and pulled them out of the path of the steel monster that was gradually picking up momentum.

A buffet table was in the way. The tank hit it head-on, and plates loaded with stuffed goose, turkey legs, paté, roast beef, hams, and salads flew into the air and disappeared under the inexorable tank. And now someone was shouting, "Stop it! Stop it!" and the situation was becoming actually dangerous. The guests, caught by surprise, now fought to get out of the way as the tank headed toward the house, cleaving the crowd. In the rush, some people tripped and the tank threatened to roll right over them. "Jesus Christ, Bern-hard!" shouted one of the guests, *"Do something!"*

An eighteen-year-old boy, son of one of the guests, jumped on the hull to pull the dummy of Goering out of the way so he could get to the engine inside. But the dummy was immovable.

With people on the ground in danger, three men rushed the tank from the front in a foolhardy hope to stop it. Instead, they found themselves almost imme-diately being pushed back, and then one of them slipped. He fell, and his foot was caught under the chewing tread of a ten-ton tank. He screamed. The other two men tried to free him, but they were re-morselessly shoved backward by the machine. In hor-ror they watched the body of the man disappear un-der the heavy tread of the tank until his head crunched, and blood spurted.

In the bedroom above the garden, Riley heard the commotion but, hell, he couldn't care less right now. He was floating. Marijuana, scotch—and fatigue—had gotten to him, and he was determined to stay right in this comfortable bed until tomorrow.

"Holy shit!" a voice said at the window.

Riley looked over—and there was a naked blonde. What was *she* doing here? Riley couldn't remember anything since the middle of the party when he sud-denly started feeling woozy from the lethal combina-tion of scotch and grass. But before he could collect his thoughts about the woman, she suddenly screamed so loudly that he jumped, "My God, Jack, it's killing people."

What the hell, thought Riley. He leaped out of bed and made his way unsteadily across the room to the window. Then he just stood there, staring at the terrifying sight below. The panzer tank was grinding through the crowd.

Riley observed a boy on the tank wrestling with the dummy, and then he saw nothing more because the machine suddenly struck the house under his window, the floor buckled, and Riley pitched forward into space. He landed on the aft end of the tank.

Curses, cries, and wailing were all around him, and the tank had stopped moving. It had hit a vertical cement foundation wall, and its motor roared to no avail. Jack Riley crouched, half-naked, on the hull of a Nazi tank with fresh blood on its treads.

4

The guard in the front seat of the limousine was angry. The actors and directors had emerged from the chaos at the party and told him they were leaving right now. But instead of taking separate cars—as the German police had instructed them to do in order to lessen the chance of an all-out terrorist attack—they had told all their other chauffeurs to assist the wounded at the party and to use their other limousines to take them to the hospital.

Now the guard, a chunky, meaty-faced man with a Uzi machine gun on his lap, was worried as they rolled down the mountain. All five Americans were his responsibility, and Baader-Meinhof could blow him away in a second.

Headlights blinded them as an ambulance approached. The limousine driver pulled over on the grass to allow the ambulance room to pass. He was about to start up again when still another siren was heard from below, and he cursed. "We've got to move on. We're sitting ducks here."

Jack Riley was clad in a T-shirt and a pair of khaki

pants he had liberated from the host's closet on the way to the car. He said, "You guys are paranoiac. Relax, will you? You're making me nervous."

But the guard's angry stare quieted him. "I'm hired to protect you people. That's my job. And you're in real danger right now."

"Why?"

"The tank, Mr. Riley. The tank. It didn't have gears."

"What?"

"I've worked parties up there before. The panzer tank was a shell, a prop. Now it moves. Now it has an engine with gears." He paused. "Who put gears in the engine of a prop tank? And why?"

Riley was stunned. Until now, he had thought the tank just went haywire. But if someone had installed gears in the engine, it meant that the accident was created on purpose. As the guard had asked, why? To create a diversion for the guards?

Great, Riley thought. Here we are alone on the middle of a German mountain at midnight in a country where every college kid is a practiced killer.

"Hey, man, I'm sorry," Riley said. "Protect us. I'm all yours."

No one laughed. They waited as a second ambulance rolled past them, siren howling, then started driving again slowly down the mountainside, headlights brightening overhanging trees and boulders and throwing into relief the bushes along the road.

5

The guard's hand struck the chauffeur's shoulder. "What's that?"

The chauffeur slowed. In the headlights in front of them pebbles gleamed on the asphalt road. "It's nothing," he said. But the guard was staring through the front windshield at the pebbles. "Stop the car! Now!"

The driver braked the car so hard it skidded. "I think they're right about you," he said. "You're paranoiac. What's a few stones on the road?"

"They're not stones. Bernhard sent a fire truck up here before the party to wash the road clean just so we could see if anyone monkeyed with the road."

The guard nervously held his gun pointed outside the window. "Everyone get down. I think they're out there."

Gail Edens said, "You're kidding," but all of them crouched down, even the chauffeur, who was irritated and said, "What's the hell's wrong with you, Mike?"

"I've been to school and studied those terrorists. And I just realized what that might be out on the road," the guard said in a low voice. "They look like micromines. If they are, the car rolls over them, every tire blows, and you're stalled while they surround you."

"Oh, for God's sake. You're dreaming," the chauffeur said. Abruptly, he shifted into gear and started the car rolling. "Stop!" the guard shouted, but the chauffeur replied hotly that they had self-sealing tires and could roll right through on the rims, even if the guard's fantasy was real.

He pressed the accelerator and the limousine raced toward the "pebbles," traveling at thirty miles an hour—a dangerous speed on that narrow cliffside road but one that the chauffeur knew could get them through the suspect area so fast they would be safe.

CRACK! CRACK!

Smoke gushed as the tires blew into shreds; the limousine skidded toward the edge of the cliff, then slewed back onto the road.

"Jesus! Keep going!" shouted the guard. "Ride on the rims!" But the windshield exploded in front of the guard's face, blinding him. Something struck the front seat, smoke billowed, and the guard began to choke.

In the back of the limousine Riley shouted, "Let's get out of here."

They piled outside and landed on their stomachs in the grass. Riley saw leather boots walking toward him at eye level. The boots stopped and one of them kicked his ribs, painfully. Riley rolled over onto his knees and looked up into the snout of a machine gun.

Ski-masked terrorists held guns pointed down at them as a man with a grenade launcher checked the limousine. Riley saw the guard and chauffeur lolling unconscious. So much for them. The actors stood up shakily with their hands raised. For a moment all was silent, and then little Angela broke the stillness by saying quietly to the terrorists, "You'll get yours."

Riley almost jumped in surprise. The child star had sounded . . . tough. He was even more startled when a ski-masked terrorist said sharply to Angela, "We've been *warned* about you. So just relax, or we'll put your problem away with a bullet in the head."

One by one the victims dropped into the earth. Flashlights from behind lighted the way; huge shadows preceded their bodies through the tunnel. A guard said, "Follow the people in front of you and listen for directions. Keep your heads down."

Riley crawled through the dark tunnel under the mountain. The enormity of what was happening was numbing his mind. They had been kidnapped by Baader-Meinhof killers. No question about it. Even in their ski masks, Riley could tell by their voices and physiques that every one of their captors was in his twenties. And what did Baader-Meinhof do with their kidnap victims? They usually issued demands asking that every one of the Baader-Meinhof terrorists in prison be set free. And what had happened in every case before? The German government had refused to comply with the demands, and the victims had been shot in the head and their corpses left in car trunks.

I'm dead, Riley said to himself, echoing the thought in every one of the hostages' minds. Robert Morrison remembered his wife and son; he had just begun really to get to know his ten-year-old boy lately. Now he might never know him at all. Gail Edens thought of the man she had met four months ago in New York, the one with whom she was in love. Bernie Weller remembered his mother and father, dead at Auschwitz.

And little Angela tried to recall everything her father had taught her in those delightful summers in Europe.

Now, in the hands of Baader-Meinhof killers, they were suddenly not actors or superstars or celebrities but ordinary people doomed to die. Riley edged forward, bumping into Morrison's feet every now and then. My God, was it all ending this way? he thought. The lucky metamorphosis from sailor into movie star? The success he enjoyed with such exuberance that it charmed everyone? And now a corpse for a political cause he didn't even understand?

Riley emerged from the tunnel. In front of him great mountains soared above a pristine lake graced by a white moon, a landscape that even now, when his blood was pumping fear through his body, impressed him with its beauty.

Below, a boat waited for them at the foot of a rope ladder. Riley hoped that when the engine started, someone might hear the noise, but the motor turned over silently. Weller saw Riley's expression and smiled resignedly. "Electric boat. That's all they allow on this lake."

"Why is that?"

Weller explained that no gasoline engines were allowed to pollute the air, and no houses were permitted on the shore to destroy the natural beauty of the Konigsee. Which meant they were all alone with no chance of witnesses.

Silently the boat carved its way across the moon-washed lake, and now they could see the lights of the chateau recede behind them, growing dimmer as they moved away. Weller was nervous. A wave rose over the bow and inundated them; Weller hardly seemed to notice. Arms cuffed behind his back, he huddled next to Riley, who said, "We'll get out of this."

"You might. I won't," said Weller.

"Why not?"

"I'm the wrong religion."

Riley observed the guards holding guns on. them. They had taken off their ski masks and Riley saw what Weller had instinctively realized. Physically, if not mentally, they were stalwart blond young Germans right out of Nazi lore and legend. And the blonde woman was a Hitler maiden come to life. Left-wing, right-wing, the race remained, Riley thought. Nordic, beautiful, and frightening, not only to the Jew!

The boat sliced blue water, rounded a bend, and ahead was a helicopter on the opposite shore. They would be flown so far from the kidnapping site they would never be found.

He became aware of Gail Edens sitting beside him in the boat, spume from the waves splashing her. She was saying something to herself. Jack Riley leaned over and heard the name "George." That must be her lover in New York, Jack thought. George Williams. A hell of a lot of good a lover in New York was going to do for her now.

Book III

THE DEMANDS
ARE IMPOSSIBLE

1

The U.S. Air Force Captain on the witness stand fidgeted. For a moment the light from the chandeliers in this old federal courthouse in New York City caught the high shine of his shoes and actually flashed, as if reflected from a mirror. The fidgeting Captain, John Draper, had much to be nervous about, George Williams thought. Williams didn't trust that Captain.

"In the grapefruit juice bottle, sir," the Captain said. He was replying to a question put by United States Attorney Jake Nettles. Nettles asked permission to introduce the grapefruit juice bottle into evidence, as prosecution exhibit 14. He held it up, and the spectators at this highly publicized espionage trial craned forward to see the bottle which had once held government secrets. Or so the Air Force Captain said.

George Williams sat in the first row of spectators behind the prosecution desk. As Assistant Attorney General in charge of the United States Department of Justice, Criminal Division, he had flown to New York from Washington to consult with the attorneys on the case. Justice was troubled. Some months ago, the Captain had come to the FBI with a story that he had been contacted by Soviet agents, and the FBI had "turned him around" and used him to plant false and specially made-up classified material of no importance on the Soviets. But something seemed wrong. Why had the Soviets approached this particular Captain, whose accessibility to secrets was limited at best? Yes, he could put his hands on some NATO material, including the disposition of a few special weapons. But the limited intelligence available to him was, according to Defense Department experts, "not valuable to the Soviets."

Nevertheless, the case seemed clear-cut. The two Soviets who sat at the defense table were officers assigned to the USSR delegation at the United Nations. The CIA people at Langley had told Williams they were KGB, which was absolutely normal. Two thirds of the Soviet delegation in New York were intelligence agents.

When the trial session was over, Nettles joined Williams in the attorney's conference room behind the courtroom. Nettles was looking feisty. A small, sharp-nosed man who was considered to be one of Justice's best in the regional offices, he strode up and down the room, as if winding down from the excitement in the courtroom. "One, two, three, we've got them," he said to Williams. "No way they're going to get off the hook this time."

"The bottle is funny," Williams said.

"What?" The attorney stopped and turned to stare at Williams. He saw a tall, handsome man in a conservative gray suit and blue tie, half sitting on the edge of the desk, leg swinging calmly. "Why use a bottle?" asked Williams.

Nettles was irritated. "That's what the Soviets told him to use, that's why. What's so funny?"

"Glass bottles break," Williams said. "They're transparent and fragile. They're unlikely containers to use to carry secret documents. In espionage cases, they use fail-safe containers." He paused. "I don't like the grapefruit juice bottle. Among other things."

Nettles sighed wearily. He had been over this whole case ten thousand times with those Justice types in Washington before it began. Again and again they had tried to steer him off it, but finally he had leaked some of the evidence to the newspapers—if Williams knew *that*, Nettles would be finished—and the Justice Department hierarchy had crumbled before the outcry. And now, after all that, they still sent Williams to harass him right in the middle of the trial.

Nettles knew all about Williams. The "legend" in the department, moving up from job to job through both Republican and Democratic administrations. Used by Presidents as a consultant behind the scenes on internal crises of national importance, in addition to the normal federal cases that came before him as chief of the Criminal Division. But Nettles was fed up. He was winning this case clean, two Soviet goons were going behind bars, and this quiet man was nagging him about how fragile a bottle was. So the Soviets were stupid. So they should have used something else. The fact was, they hadn't. They told the Captain to place the information in a grapefruit juice bottle and that's just what he had done, no matter what Williams said.

Williams said, "Relax. I've studied the evidence. I don't think there's any doubt the Soviets are guilty."

Once again Nettles was stunned. Finally he asked Williams why all the bother about the bottles if the Russians were guilty.

"Bottles don't seem professional. The KGB is professional." Williams paused. "The question that bothers me is: did the Captain—not the Soviets—*initiate* the deal from the beginning and call all the shots?"

"Jesus," said the lawyer. "Don't pull entrapment on me. They're still guilty if they took the information and paid for it—"

Williams said he was just wondering what the Captain would be up to. "Why is a junior officer in the Air Force initiating an international case of espionage?"

"Okay. Why don't you tell the FBI to bird-dog the Captain day and night? If he's playing a double game, I want him caught as much as you do."

Williams lighted a cigarette. Nettles thought, they're right about this guy. He's frightening, somehow. You never know what he's thinking.

Williams said, "He's *been* followed day and night, Mr. Nettles. For months." His blue eyes seemed chilly to Nettles. What a package he was, the overwrought attorney thought. But Williams surprised him by patting him on the shoulder. "Proceed with your case, Jake. Only, tomorrow, don't wave that glass bottle in the air any more than you have to."

2

As four kidnapped American actors and one director flew above the Bavarian Alps under guard, George Williams rode in a taxi uptown to the 21 Club. Charles Casey, the FBI Director, had telephoned him in the middle of the afternoon and arranged the meeting.

Williams had been inside the 21 Club only twice in his life, each time at the insistence of a woman: Stephanie Spaulding, now married to a Spanish banker and living in a castle in Marbella, and Peggy DuPont, who had left Williams for someone, as she put it, "My God, lighter. Someone who likes to live. All you exercise is your brain."

In a way, Williams had loved Peggy for a while. Her background was impeccably shallow Palm Beach, Newport, and all the ski resorts in the world. So when Williams discovered that she had a very down-to-earth sense of humor, he was charmed. Even so, their romance hadn't worked, because Peggy's lifelong habits had triumphed. Peggy, who had all of the money in the world, or so it seemed to government servant Williams, considered it absolutely appropriate to spend all of her life sunbathing on exotic beaches, skiing in far-off plush resorts, playing tennis in between, and making love every night. That was what someone did who "liked to live." And many times Williams had thought she was right, and even given some thought to being Mr. Peggy DuPont, floating on millions doled out by a loving wife.

Williams smiled when he thought of Peggy, as he always did. She was, in a way, outrageous, but considered herself perfectly normal, which she also was in the context of her background. But then it all became academic anyway when Williams had met Gail Edens.

From the moment Williams came to know the actress, Peggy DuPont was forgotten. For Gail Edens not only had Peggy's sense of humor but she saw life as Williams did. It was a struggle, yes, but also an opportunity—as William's lost idol, Bobby Kennedy, used to say—"to contribute."

In one way Gail was the quintessential Hollywood star of the seventies. She lived in New York, not Beverly Hills, made one movie a year, thought Burt Reynolds was funny, and even spent some nights in Elaine's with what she called "the troops." Where she differed was in her "other life." Almost from the first moment she appeared on screen, she told Williams, she had realized what enormous influence actors could have on public affairs, but all were afraid to use it. Only Jane Fonda, years before, had led the way courageously, particularly in the anti-Vietnam War effort when her visit to Hanoi had evoked storms of outrage from the Congress and the American public. But Fonda, Gail Edens's idol, seemed to have retired from much of the political speechmaking in later years.

Now it was Gail Edens's independent forays into political causes that inspired a constant burn in politicians' hearts on both sides of the Congressional aisle. Williams knew she was actually hated in Washington political circles, which resented "shallow" movie people using their "tinsel" celebrity to influence serious issues.

But, surprisingly, neither the Washington politicians nor its skeptical press had been able to stem Gail's appeal to the public. For one thing, Gail was in appearance—and real life—the "girl next door." Her countenance was wholesome and open; her family in St. Louis was solid middle-America; her social life was conservative. And what America saw was a "nice girl" with the guts to tell off Washington politicians, no matter what party they were in. Nothing could be more popular with Americans in the late seventies than that trait.

Or so Gail Edens had explained away her popularity to Williams on their first date. The date had come about when Williams had been told by an FBI agent in New York that Gail Edens had information on a terrorist bombing that had taken place in New York the week before. "The lady will speak only to you."

Williams had decided to see her even though he doubted she had knowledge of the bombing, which the FBI said was "perpetrated" by the Puerto Rican FALN, a cause not favored by American liberals. But Gail had also mentioned to the FBI agent that Peggy DuPont was a mutual friend.

Gail Edens lived in a surprisingly modest flat on East 61st Street. Her living room contained a maroon couch, an oriental rug, comfortable chairs, a few sculpted figures in unexpected niches, and a Juan Gris painting, signed. The actress looked fetching in an India-print blouse, denim jeans, and high-heeled boots—and seemed genuinely pleased to see him. "I didn't think you would come," she said.

"Why not?"

"Peggy DuPont said you're all business, and I suppose you think actresses are flakes."

Williams smiled and said he didn't know any Hollywood actresses so he couldn't make a judgment.

She said, "Well, you're going to be certain I'm one when I tell you I don't know anything about that terrorist bombing."

To her surprise, Williams showed no reaction. He just looked at her calmly. She actually faltered a moment under his gaze before saying she thought she needed something like the bombing to persuade Williams to meet her personally.

"So what's up?" said Williams quietly. He was sipping a scotch and water and seemed relaxed. She said, "Is this routine for you? Interviewing a person who tells you right away she lied to you?"

Williams smiled. "I knew you didn't have any information on the bombing, so why should I be surprised when you tell me it's a ruse?"

"You know who did it?"

"The FALN," was all Williams replied. No further data. Gail was beginning to feel really shaken. She had expected a typical Justice Department bureaucrat, no matter what Peggy had said, and here was a surprisingly handsome man who—let's admit it, she thought—started her heart racing just a beat faster for reasons having nothing to do with law.

"I'm sure I'm wasting your time. It's just one of those crackpot things, but still it worries me."

Williams asked if someone was following her on the street and Gail shrugged no.

"Telephone calls?"

"Letters, but I know as soon as you read one of them you'll say it's normal crackpot stuff. And in a way it is. I get dozens of letters from hatemongers after every speech I make. But these are different."

She went to a graceful Chippendale desk in the corner and returned to Williams with a handful of letters. She opened the first one quickly and extracted the letter. "Here's one little goodie." She handed it to Williams who read:

> You Commie pinko whore. The next time you come into our state you'll get a .45 slug up your Commie cunt.
>
> A Patriotic Oklahoman

Gail said, "Oklahoma heard from. Now, a letter from New Jersey." Williams read a second letter:

> You Commie pinko whore. The next time you come into our state you'll get a .45 slug up your Commie cunt.
>
> A Patriotic New Jerseyan

Williams said quickly, "All the letters are identically worded? And all from different states?"

"That's right. As if it's an organization or something, all over America. I even got one from New York, and naturally that worried me most of all because I live here."

Williams asked when the one from New York had arrived and was told yesterday. "That's when I got panicky and contacted you."

Williams didn't like it. "An isolated crank letter is

one thing, but identical letters mean planning and organization. That's unusual." He paused. "I think you'd
better move out of this apartment. Bunk in with some
anonymous friends. I'll take these letters to the FBI
and see what we can run down. Someone may have
slipped up and left a fingerprint. How many letters
are there? Fifty?"

"Forty-nine. Hawaii still loves me," Gail said, looking worried. But in the next moment Williams learned
it would be almost impossible for Gail Edens, a famous actress, to "hide out." An actress's life had to go
on. Career decisions had to be made. In a few moments Gail's agent called and said he absolutely must
meet her at the Four Seasons immediately. She asked
him to come to her apartment instead—but there was
a producer at the restaurant whom Gail must absolutely see—and the producer was leaving in an hour
for Europe.

Williams found himself on the way to the Four Seasons with a woman he had just urged to go underground and hide. The dimensions of her danger were
becoming apparent to him. Going to the restaurant
now was risky enough; what was worse was that she
would be making motion pictures—and her where-
abouts would always be publicly known if someone seriously intended her harm.

At the Four Seasons Williams met Arthur Corum, a
thin, alert young man in hornrimmed glasses who
turned out to be her agent, and the producer, Max
Weber, a more normal representative of what Williams
expected from show business. Paunchy, balding, nervous, he drummed his fingers on the table as he told
Gail what an opportunity for her this film would be,
how it would advance her career even higher. In

doing so, he never mentioned the subject of the film, a bit of verbal legerdemain which Williams had to admire.

Instead it was "points" and "weeks," and "extra weeks," and "travel accommodations," mostly conducted on a steady, serious plane by the agent and the producer. Then, like magic, the producer was gone and the three of them sat there. The agent turned to Williams who had been introduced simply as "a friend."

"I think we can squeeze a little travel money out of those cheapos to get you to Europe to join Gail, if I play it right."

Williams laughed. "I won't be going," he said. "I'm just a business friend."

But the agent said with a smile, "I saw Gail looking at you."

Williams turned to Gail, who said quickly, "I'm innocent, judge. I was just analyzing the curve of his ear."

But afterwards, back in her apartment, Gail said "Corum was right. But then again, maybe I'm brainwashed."

"What do you mean?"

"Peggy DuPont said you were the sexiest man she ever slept with. I keep thinking about that, somehow."

"I hope you didn't write those letters yourself," Williams said, and Gail laughed. "It would have been a good idea, but they're real." She paused. "Anyway, you'll have to keep in touch with me now, right?"

"I'll do that—but you can't go running to restaurants for meetings, making movies, and appearing on television to plug the movies or whatever you do"—and this stopped Gail, who said, "But I just can't drop everything and live like a mole because some . . . worms write letters like that? I'm surprised you would even suggest that."

"Why?"

"I thought you would do just the opposite. Dismiss the whole business as a normal crackpot deal."

"A nationwide organization sending identical hate letters from every state to one person? This is different from the usual, and 'different from the usual' always means it's serious."

Gail pondered this. She did so by resting her lovely chin on a fist, elbow on a bar in the corner of her living room. "Well," she said, finally. "Fuck."

Williams smiled. "Oh my God," Gail said, "I've shocked the man."

Williams said, "I use the word often enough. But it just . . . doesn't seem to go with your face."

And it was true. Gail Edens had such wide, innocent eyes, Williams thought, you just didn't expect. . . . Gail was around the bar, kissing him. "Hey," Williams said.

Gail said, "Peggy told me the only thing to do is rape you. Otherwise a woman might wait forever." Williams smiled. But he became very serious as she led him to the large maroon couch. Why this beautiful young actress, whose blue eyes were now inches from his own, as his shirt came off and her soft body pressed against his chest, why she was doing this he did not know. But somehow he found himself in her bedroom, his lips on her breast, and her hand tantalizing him below, and Williams mounted her feverishly, and Gail said, "Kill me, George, kill me," which seemed to fuse several thoughts in Williams's mind, and he destroyed her with pent-up passion, causing her to explode in a shattering hail of flailing arms and long shapely legs and small sounds of ecstasy.

Afterwards Williams was smiling. "I like long courtships."

Gail lighted some grass and smoked away contentedly, sitting against the headboard, before answering. "You know the male chauvinist motto, if rape is inevitable, etcetera."

"Yes."

She laid the joint down in the ashtray, slid down in the bed and, cheek against his chest, looked up at him. "Well, I have a saying of my own. If a real love affair is inevitable, why wait?"

"Are we going to have a real love affair?"

Gail's lips browsed on his chest. "I'd like to consider the previous performance as the introduction scene. In Hollywood they call it 'meeting cute.'"

"You did that, all right," George said, and didn't bother to tell Gail that he hadn't been with a woman in the year since Peggy DuPont left him, had decided after one wrecked marriage and two ruined love affairs that he was a failure at romance, didn't have the intelligence or sensitivity or drive, whatever women craved and needed. And if he was going to be hurt or, worse, to hurt others, it simply didn't make sense to try again.

But Gail? How could you turn down Gail, who was not only intelligent but funny, and who now said, "Look, if you think I was a little too . . . precipitous, you can always call the New York rape control center. You'll be their first man."

3

The next morning Williams awoke to find a famous movie actress wandering around the room. When she saw he was awake, she leaned over and kissed him. "Peggy DuPont was right," she said. "But I've got you now."

Later, Williams asked her about the movie that had been discussed at the Four Seasons and she told him it was the life of Hitler. "We're going to scald the little housepainter," she said. "Show what a personal pervert he was, really get inside the monster." She paused, a chunk of grapefruit in a silver spoon. "At least that's what old Max Weber, the producer, says."

Williams was immediately alerted. "Has that fact been publicized?"

"What?"

"That you're going to star in an anti-Hitler movie. That could account for the letters from the right-wingers."

But Gail put the idea to rest when she said, "I wasn't approached for the movie until yesterday morning. And the letters started coming in weeks ago." She paused. "No, the American nuts aren't after

Eva Braun, they're after Gail Edens. But there's one good thing about it."

Williams said, "You're shooting it in Europe? So you won't be here?"

"Right. I leave in two weeks. And maybe while I'm away you can get a clue to those people in this country who want to kill me."

But she didn't leave that soon. The start of shooting in Europe was delayed, and Gail came down to Washington to be with George, and their romance soon became a subject for "Ear," the gossip column in the Washington *Star*, and Rudy Maxa in the *Post*, and smiles among Williams's prosaic friends in government who could not conceive of their man romancing a movie actress, no matter how many socially conscious speeches she uttered . . .

. . . and all the while he had grown to love her, was sure he loved her, when she finally went off to some place in the Bavarian Alps two long months ago to make a movie.

Now, two months since Gail had left him, he entered the 21 Club to talk to the FBI Director. About what? Gail?

4

Jack Riley came awake on a bumping floor. He shook his head and looked around. Holy Christ! He remembered. He was being kidnapped.

They were in a helicopter. Around him, the other actors and the director lay in the middle of the floor, while the young, blond German terrorists sat on aisle seats with machine guns on their laps.

The fog lifted from Riley's mind. In the helicopter he had been sprayed with gas from a pistol that knocked him out in seconds. Now he started to sit up and realized his hands were cuffed in front of him. The muzzle of a machine gun stopped his movement. "Keep quiet and don't move," a voice said.

Ten minutes later the helicopter dodged through snow-peaked mountains to arrive at a plateau that jutted slightly below the crest of one of the mountaintops. Expertly, the pilot landed the machine on the small ledge. The other hostages were awakened with jabs from machine-gun butts and in a minute they were being herded off the helicopter into the dark night. They waited in front of the mountainside, a portion of which slid aside. Fantastic, Riley thought.

The sheer mountain face, with its shrubbery, had revealed absolutely no hint of door edges.

Inside they expected to find a dank little cave; instead an immense, high-ceilinged room carved out of stone confronted them. Desk after desk stood in rows down the room. Cubicles leading off the main room were entitled: SIGNALS, INTELLIGENCE, OPERATIONS, COMMUNICATIONS, TRANSPORTATION, SUPPLY. War maps lined the walls. Riley realized they had been ushered into a military command post.

But there was something strange about the room, Riley thought. And then he noticed that everything in the room was antique. The telephones were the old stand-up types, not handsets. The typewriters were vintage 1940 models. The desks were small metal jobs, not the commodious desks which graced offices today. What the hell was this? thought Riley. A World War II command post, forgotten for years? Riley tried to remember what he had read about World War II. Hadn't General Eisenhower constantly worried about a last stand by the German Army in the so-called Alpine redoubt. Yes, but that had turned out to be a fantasy. At the end of the war captured German generals revealed they had no plan to make a last stand in the Alps.

Riley whispered to Morrison, "Ike was right. We're in the middle of the Nazis' last hurrah."

Morrison shook his head. "It's not the Alpine redoubt Eisenhower was talking about. Look at the main map."

At the far end of the room was a huge World War II map. Bloodred color indicated the extent of German occupation of foreign territory. It included all of

France and, in the east, a large slice of the Soviet Union. Morrison said, "This post was operational way before D-Day. It's not a command post for any last stand."

"Then what the hell—" Riley started to say, but he found himself shoved by one of the young Nordic guards. "Into your cell." Riley and the rest of the hostages were taken to a metal door with a chin-high grille and ushered into a large room with five cots widely spaced around the wall. A metal pitcher of water and a glass were beside each bunk. The blonde woman, who was apparently the leader, said, "First, line up side by side."

They shuffled into position, and then the blonde, with the guards behind her, shocked them with her order.

"Strip."

The movie stars looked at each other. Gail Edens even attempted a joke. "Not at these prices." A hand slapped her face so hard her cheek tingled with pain. The blonde stepped back and said, "Take off all your clothes. We must be certain you're not armed."

"Oh, for God's sake," said Gail. But she began removing her dress. The men glanced at her and then started self-consciously unbuttoning shirts and unbelting trousers. Only little Angela Tuck seemed unconcerned as she slipped her mini-dress over her head.

Gail pulled off her dress and stood in panties. One of the young guards behind the blonde apparently couldn't resist staring at the bared flesh of the beautiful actresses. Gail made a mental note to concentrate on him later. In how many movie scripts had she seen the beautiful heroine seduce a young guard and help her friends escape—

RRRIPP! There went her panties. The blonde dyke was tearing them off. "I said strip."

"Easy," said Gail angrily. "You'll get your treat."

But the panties were gone. Down the line, Angela stepped out of hers, and the men slipped off every last garment, too. Four famous young movie stars stood in line naked. Only Bernie Weller, the director, looked out of place, old, trembling, and fragile. But the actors were now angry. "God damn peep show, that's all you want," Morrison said.

"Get dressed," the blonde said, her eyes crackling. What was she so angry about? thought Gail, slipping into her dress—her ripped panties gone for the duration; maybe that young guard would take them and start thinking. The blonde said directly to Gail, "You, I am disappointed in. But not surprised. You're a phony, which means you're the worst traitor to the working class."

Gail was on the blonde's mental wavelength now, and she blazed back at her, "Showing a sense of humor when some perverts force you to strip isn't a sign of treason to any working class. We're trying to act civilized."

"You're a slut. Nothing more." But then, to Gail's surprise, the blonde turned her attention to Robert Morrison. "You strike me as the only one of these degenerates worthy of addressing. One of the hostages will die at midnight." She looked at her watch. "Twenty-three hours from now. I would like you to select the first."

A stunned silence in the room. Gail was absolutely numbed by the words. Was anyone really going to die? Really? They weren't kidding?

Morrison stammered. "But—but don't you have de-

mands? Money? Ransom?" He paused. "Surely you're
not going to kill us for no reason."

"We have our reasons, Mr. Morrison." She turned.
"Take them to their bunks."

The guards shoved the actors to their various cots,
where they were placed in a sitting position with one
wrist shackled to the wall, leaving the other arm free.
The blonde was about to pass through the door when
she turned to say to Morrison, "Oh, on the selection,
don't choose Angela Tuck. She dies last."

With that she left. The door slammed behind her,
the face of a guard could be seen through the window
grille, and Gail realized she was in a cave in the Alps
so secret it had not been known since World War II—
the furniture and the maps showed it had not been
touched since 1944—and my God, this was serious.
The Alps were a mountain range of anonymous peak
after peak stretching to the horizon; who could find
one cave in one peak? It would take days, weeks—and
at midnight tonight one of their small number was to
be executed.

Except for Angela Tuck. What in the world was
going on with her? Gail had heard a guard say to Angela earlier that they had been warned about the little
actress. But if Angela was in some crazy way a threat
to them—and how could that be?—why didn't they kill
her first?

Gail Edens closed her eyes. In moments of panic,
when she became anxious and frightened, she had a
mental trick which helped. She would shut her eyes
and think of something lovely in her past. A rose in a
sunlit garden, its petals opening, in Mexico City. An
icy Mai Tai in front of her as she sat on a beach in
Bermuda. A particularly memorable slice of pizza on

a high-school date when she was eighteen in Webster Groves. She started to breathe easier, to think more clearly.

They had to escape, some way. All of her instincts so far had been to "go along," as everyone had always told you to do, if you were kidnapped. But if the terrorists really intended to kill them, they had better start trying to get out of here. But how?

The lineup of hostages from left to right was Angela Tuck, Jack Riley, Gail Edens, Robert Morrison and Bernie Weller. Gail suddenly heard Riley whispering to Angela. "What is it with you?" he said. "Why are you so special?"

But Angela only smiled. She was thinking what a shame that she was stuck with those four hostages. Oh, they were all nice enough, even funny. It's just that they were so . . . naïve. How could they be so old and yet so dumb? They actually didn't believe that the Baader-Meinhof terrorists were really going to murder any of them. And it was so obvious to Angela, who knew all about Baader-Meinhof, that it was exactly what the kidnappers intended to do. Murder all of the hostages one by one, stepping up the pressure on the Government each time. And if the Government absolutely refused to yield, all five would be executed.

Well, they wouldn't do it. Angela would rescue the hostages, despite themselves. But that order to strip had given her a shock. Thank God those young Germans had no training.

5

The FBI Director was chunky, cigar-smoking; in appearance a throwback to J. Edgar Hoover. Some said he lacked the late Hoover's shrewdness, but on the plus side, he also lacked Hoover's passion for political intrigue. No tape recordings circulated through Washington echoing Martin Luther King, Jr.'s grunts of passion. No letters coined by crewcut agents came to the Oval Office with veiled threats. Charles Casey, the new Director, was smart enough to avoid the intrigue which had cast a shadow on the fine record of the FBI. Williams liked him.

But seeing him at a table in 21 brought a smile to Williams's face. One thing that all FBI Directors seemed to have in common was a penchant for expensive saloons. Hoover used to "live" in the Stork Club in the forties and fifties, swapping stories with his pal, gossip columnist Walter Winchell. Now, years after Hoover's demise, FBI Directors had apparently continued their patronage of elegant cafés.

Was there something in a policeman's psyche, Williams thought, that craved what you would have thought it would despise: poshness, style, the so-called beautiful people?

In the necklace of diners around the curving lounge, Casey was the one uncut stone. He waved at Williams, who went over to his table and sat down.

They ordered drinks and Williams noticed the covert stares of various customers directed at the FBI Director. The diners seemed to be mostly rich businessmen. Casey seemed to make some of the customers uneasy, although not so restless as the Commissioner of Internal Revenue might have done.

Casey seemed to know all of the 21 owners, managers, and maitre d's; a steady procession stopped by his table to greet him. Men named Jerry, Pete, Sheldon, Terry, Bruce, Walter, were all introduced to Williams as fires flared under brandied dishes and red-jacketed waiters moved beneath toy trucks, planes, and ships suspended from the ceiling in deference to the corporate clients. Finally Casey decided to talk some business. "How's the trial going?"

"The Russians are guilty as charged," Williams said. But he told the Director of his conversation with the prosecutor about the glass bottle, and his opinion that the Air Force Captain might have initiated the deal with the Russians.

Casey shifted in his seat. "You're right to worry about that Captain. I saw the President this morning. And he told me to hightail it to New York to see you."

"What's the urgency?"

"We're finding out more than we want to know about the Captain."

"Such as?"

"You know he comes from Columbus, Georgia. Now we have an informant who tells us the Captain and his father were in the Ku Klux Klan down there. And the bone-headed military people missed it when they made their original security check."

Williams thought it over. The Soviets could go to town with that information. He asked Casey what else they had found.

"His high school papers, copies of which were furnished to us anonymously. Essay after essay, filled with right-wing fanatical stuff." He paused. "In college he leads the Conservative Union, and then he moves to England for a year and starts going to neo-Nazi meetings."

Williams was stunned. "And security missed all of that?"

"Not the neo-Nazi meetings in England. But security in the Air Force isn't that worried about right-wing stuff, Williams. Hell, if it was, they wouldn't have any Generals. Security just checked to see if there was any Communist connection." He paused. "And because of that we have this trial—and even you questioned a God-damned grapefruit juice bottle."

Well, hell, thought Williams. The waiter was before them, taking orders for dinner. The chatter of conversation around them was like a shield of privacy. Casey must have been reading his mind. "Nothing to hide. The Soviets already know it. We're thinking of suspending the case." He looked up at a waiter holding a telephone who said, "Call for you, Mr. Casey." The waiter plugged the phone into a jack on the wall behind them.

Casey said into the phone, "Casey here . . . All right, how urgent? We're just starting dinner . . . Okay." He hung up. The noise level in the restaurant seemed to rise and surround them. Williams felt somehow out of place, as he had since the beginning of this meeting. A trial which could escalate into a crisis being discussed over a telephone now nestled between plates of duck *a l'orange* and carafes of gleaming red wine, Chauvelot 1974.

But Casey surprised him. "The phone call wasn't about the trial." He was signaling the waiter for the check. "The New York regional office wants us now. It's an emergency."

"What's up?"

"Some American movie stars in Germany got themselves kidnapped. It's on the teletype from Munich."

HOLD HOLD HOLD
MUNICH . . . RADIO STATION MLDV HAS RECEIVED THE DEMANDS FROM THE KIDNAPPERS OF THE AMERICAN MOTION PICTURE ACTORS. THEIR NOTE READS:

Our demands are as follows:

1) All 58 Baader-Meinhof prisoners now held in German jails like dogs to be released within 24 hours, and flown to Algeria; only upon their safe arrival in Algeria will this demand be considered satisfied.

2) Ulrich Kandrof, the President-elect of this Republic who is so adored by the German people, to resign his office and reveal to the nation the secret facts of his treason;

3) the scandal of the motion picture, *"The Secret Life of Hitler,"* to be resolved by burning all existing footage in a public ceremony and destroying all sets from Berchtesgaden to the Chancellery to the bunker.

If our demands are not met within 24 hours, the first American hostage will be executed by hanging at midnight. Each day thereafter without complete capitulation to our demands, another American hostage will be executed. We will show no mercy.

THE ICE HOUSE MOVEMENT

Voices hummed in the long room, shirt-sleeved FBI agents talked at paper-strewn desks; through the windows of this new FBI building, Williams saw the World Trade Center climbing majestically toward the sky, and Gail Edens's voice was in his mind, her lips at his ear on that last evening in bed when he had told her once again she shouldn't be making this movie, shouldn't even be appearing in public because of those threats. "The letters came from right-wingers in America. I'm safer now in Europe than I am in this country."

But now Casey was talking reality. "The demands are impossible. The President of Germany to resign? Every one of those Baader-Meinhof killers to be let out of jail to start all over again with bombs and machine guns and kidnappings? No way."

Williams said to Casey. "The movie doesn't make any sense."

Casey asked him what he meant, as Williams leaned against a desk, studying the teletype in his hand. Williams said, "Gail Edens told me the movie was anti-Hitler. Why would left-wing Baader-Meinhof types object to a left-wing antifascist movie?"

Casey plucked an illegal Havana cigar from a pocket and lighted it. He looked uncomfortable as he said, "I might have to take a rap on that movie deal myself."

Williams said nothing, and Casey went on. "The movie company called me from Germany a few weeks ago and said there was trouble on the film. First the neo-Nazis in the country were trying to sabotage the movie because it was anti-Hitler. Then something happened during the shooting—I don't know what— but the neo-Nazis backed off and the left-wing students began to protest the movie because it was *pro*-Hitler."

Williams asked him why the movie producers called, and Casey touched his cigar to a tray and watched its ash tumble off. "The company's representative in Germany, a woman, telephoned from Europe to ask if I could help guard the actors and crew. I told her the FBI was domestic, so we couldn't operate over there even if we wanted to." He paused. "That was bull, of course. In effect, I told her to blow it out of her behind, and now this happens and she'll be telling every reporter in the world."

Williams said, "You didn't alert Interpol?"

"What was there to alert? No crime had been committed. Interpol isn't a bodyguard agency either." He looked away from Williams. "Yeah, well, maybe I made a mistake. I should have taken the damn woman more seriously."

Williams stood up. "Relax. It's all ancient history, anyway."

"What do you mean?"

"They're caught. We've got to stop worrying about the past and think in terms of the next twenty-four hours." He paused. "Because that's all we have. Those

Baader-Meinhof terrorists are going to execute the hostages. No question about it. At least one of the hostages will die tonight, just as they say."

Casey was staring at him. "What makes you so sure you know what they'll do? They've changed their deadlines on killings before."

"They never had five hostages before. With one hostage like the Italian politician, Aldo Moro, the terrorists had to delay their deadline because if they executed their hostage, they lost their bargaining chip. But five gives them flexibility. They can build the terror and raise the pressure from Americans who don't want their sons and daughters murdered just because of European politics." He shook the teletype which held the threat. "So the demands sound impossible? One corpse in a car trunk will start making the demands seem a little less impossible, two may make them look even desirable, and three dead hostages will be unbearable."

An agent was tugging Williams's elbow. "Telephone, sir. It's the President."

The President's voice had a hint of a tremor in it. The spectacular kidnapping had placed him in a difficult position. If American citizens were murdered while he didn't intervene, there would be a public outcry.

On the other hand, he would be criticized just as severely if he persuaded the German government to yield to the terrorists. It was exactly the type of classic ball breaker the White House feared and hated the most—a no-win proposition for the President. And for once a floor full of image makers bolstered by polltakers couldn't help. The President said, "George, we have to do something. Any ideas?"

"It's a quagmire, sir," Williams told the President. "We're only involved in one part of the demand. We can burn some fake film and blow up the movie set, but the Germans hold the hole cards. Did you talk to Ulrich Kandrof?"

"Five minutes ago. The President-elect says Baader-Meinhof hates him because they consider he betrayed them. Kandrof was originally elected to the Bundestag as a liberal, then helped sponsor repressive measures against the terrorists."

Williams said, "The Ice House bothers me."

"What?"

"The name. What does that name have to do with Baader-Meinhof? In their other kidnappings they called themselves the Red Army Faction. Why didn't they sign this demand with that name instead of the Ice House Movement?"

In Washington the President noticed his right sock was slipping. He was sitting in the Oval Office, leaning back at his desk, his feet on the edge of an open bottom drawer. Across from him sat five men, three Cabinet officers plus the CIA Director and a NATO General. The President suddenly felt a hundred and ten years old. A million decisions to make to keep this country—and his own career—going, and everything thrown into turmoil by a handful of goons in a foreign country. But, my God, they had been smart this time. Movie stars. Pop celebrities. Each of them more famous and loved than any President anywhere. No terrorist coup could possibly generate a more sensational spotlight on their movement.

"The name is the last thing that's worrying me, George," the President said over the phone. "Look, I want you to fly to Germany to be our liaison with

their investigative people. I've got a Phanton coming
up to La Guardia to pick you up and you can be in
Bonn in three hours. Nine A.M. their time."

Williams said, "I'll go—but I'll be operating in a foreign country. I won't have much leverage."

"Those are American citizens kidnapped by Germans," the President said, his voice sounding firm for
the first time. "You'll get one hundred percent cooperation, I guarantee you that." Then he surprised Williams by saying, "Jim Hirsch has a lead for you."

In New York Williams waited for Hirsch, the CIA
Director, to take the line. In the old days Williams had
been a bitter enemy of the CIA when he had discovered they were wiretapping and engaging in break-ins
and other illegal domestic activities. But since that
time, the CIA had straightened out its procedures, under congressional scrutiny, to control the huge, un-
wieldy intelligence organization. Hirsch was a good
friend of Williams's. He said, "George, one of the hostages, Angela Tuck, has a father that's ours."

Williams was stunned. "Her father is in the CIA?"
He was trying to absorb the implications of that fact
when Hirsch continued. "Divorced. He's her real father and never gets any publicity. We helped him
make the deal with the mother when they separated."

Extra alimony from the CIA. Nothing like unac-
countable funding, Williams thought, as Hirsch went
on. "Now get this. Jim Dilts, her father, is in Berlin
right now, our cultural attaché there. We're flying him
to Bonn to work with you. But that's not the big
news."

Williams waited and Hirsch went on. "Angela
Tuck's father was afraid some terrorists might kidnap
her in Europe for ransom, so he gave her a beeper

that can be traced. If she still has it, there's a radio impulse transmitting from the hideaway, and if we can get close enough we can pick up the signal."

"What's the range of the signal?"

"Five hundred yards. The Germans are already flooding the Alps around that lake with helicopters. And we may find their hideaway in minutes."

But Williams wasn't listening. He knew as well as Hirsch how investigators homed in on a beeper. Now he was simply experiencing a surge of joy. It had seemed so hopeless only two minutes ago—now there was a real chance that the hostages could be rescued. If only Angela Tuck could protect that beeper from discovery in the next half hour, he might get Gail Edens back.

6

Young Hans Ulbricht sat against a wall outside of the hostages' cell. Across the length of the room, Helga Neff was monitoring the radio. Hans knew she was in touch with the Colonel in Munich who had planned this operation.

But while his eyes took in the vast room with empty desks between him and the other terrorists, Hans's mind was on something he should not think of. Hans had been the guard who stood behind Helga Neff when the actors disrobed. He would have had to be made of steel not to be moved when Gail Edens and Angela Tuck, two of the most beautiful women in the world, stood in front of him, naked, so close that he could touch them. Then he had seen Gail Edens look into his eyes—and know! She knew he wanted her. He must stay away from her.

"Hans!"

So deep was he in these forbidden thoughts that he hadn't even heard his name called. Now he looked up and saw Helga gesturing to him. At her desk, Helga said, "I saw how you looked at Gail Edens. This is stupid. It gives her hope. It gives her ideas."

Hans said, "I couldn't help it."

"She's a pig," Helga said.

Hans thought it best to go on the offensive. "I think you're making a big mistake, anyway."

"What do you mean?"

"You tell us the little girl is the most dangerous. Yet you intend to kill the other hostages first."

"Our orders are that Angela Tuck will be last."

"Why?"

"I queried the people in Munich on that myself," Helga said. "It seems she has a father who's an American government official. They want him to suffer the longest."

"He's an enemy?"

"An American Central Intelligence agent. CIA."

Hans froze. "Then he's a bastard. You won't have to worry about my sex drive any longer, comrade." He went back to his seat against the wall. So the little bitch had a CIA father. Hans hated the American CIA. His brother Carl, who had joined Baader-Meinhof, had been murdered with the help of the CIA. Some woman had lured Carl into leaving his hideaway to visit her in a hotel room. A hotel room, for God's sake, with all of Germany looking for him! His brother, ambushed by waiting police, had tried to escape down a hotel hallway, and fell before a shattering blast of machine-gun fire.

The guard inside the prisoners' cell looked through the grille when he returned to his post. He said, "The little one wants to go to the bathroom."

Hans crossed the prisoners' room to Angela Tuck. She was sitting against the wall looking adorable in a torn mini-dress, but now he paid no attention. He unlocked the handcuffs which bound her to the wall, then pulled her roughly to her feet. She walked meekly in front of him out of the room.

The lavatory was twenty feet down the side of the main room. The door closed behind her, and Hans waited. There was nothing to worry about in there. No windows, no openings of any kind, just a niche hollowed out of a cave, with plumbing.

In the little stone lavatory, Angela waited. The guard, who obviously hated her, might burst in the door just to check. Nothing happened. Quiet outside. Her right hand slipped inside her white bikini panties, and foraged between her legs. The hand emerged with a metal cylinder half an inch wide and two inches long. The question was the plumbing. A military command post must have a septic tank. She dropped the cylinder into the metal toilet and flushed it. Rusty water gushed in the bowl and Angela Tuck smiled.

The electronic beeper was now buried in a septic tank, impossible for the kidnappers to find.

There was now a chance. Helicopters with radio receivers could hear that signal from beneath the cave. And her father *knew* she had a beeper, so he would alert them.

The guard was knocking on the door. Angela said liltingly, "Just one minute." She prepared to leave, patting her hair, reminding herself to appear humble and childlike.

She turned the knob on the door and instantly it was flung open. Hands clutched her throat and snapped her head back, smashing her against the wall. Pain shot through her brain. German guards were all around her, shouting, "What did you do in here?"

"Nothing."

"We heard you."

"Heard me do what?"

"Drop something down the toilet." The blonde leader pointed above the doorway and Angela saw a small opening. A microphone must be embedded there. The whole cave must be bugged, and the mike had picked up the sound of the metal clinking down the bowl. She said, "I don't know what you're talking about."

"You'll be the first to die," the blonde blazed at her. "I'm changing the orders. You hang first." Angela was shoved back to her cell by two of the guards while the blonde remained behind with one guard. "What could it be?" Helga said to Georg. "What would she want to throw down there?"

"I don't know," said Georg, "but we'd better find out fast. Get Hans and tell him to bring some hammers and wrenches from the tool room."

In a few minutes, the two Germans were hammering at the base of the toilet. There was no way to recover the metal beeper Angela Tuck had dropped inside without going down into the septic tank itself.

"Oh my God," Helga said. The two men working in the lavatory looked through the open door. Helga was by the World War II radio set, her hand on the knob, scanning frequencies. A beeping sound pulsed loudly through the room. Helga said tensely, "She planted a beeper down there. The helicopters can pick it up on their radios and trace us."

7

While disaster struck in the cave, General Erwin Rommel did not notice. He stood on the lip of a sand dune, green glasses reflecting the sun's glare. Around him three German officers waited for the word from the military leader on which direction his next tank attack would roll. Sand blew off the dune; in the background, three panzer tanks could be seen with soldiers sitting on their hulls.

Colonel Franz von Werten loved that picture. It was a family legend that, at the age of three, the great Field Marshal had once held him on his lap. That was when von Werten's father was a Brigadier General in Rommel's desert army, and the two officers had been in Berlin on leave in 1942.

Decades later Franz was in the Army himself, but he would never be a Rommel nor even a General. His career had been side-tracked just when it was about to reach its zenith and pass him into the Generals' ranks.

Not that the Army didn't respect—and utilize—Franz's talents. Indeed, they called him a genius. This was in recognition of his engineering achievements which had resulted in sophisticated devices of every kind.

Franz was a hybrid. His mother had early noticed his mechanical aptitude and sent him to Göttingen University's engineering school. It was thought at that time that Franz wouldn't even enter the Army; after what had happened to his father, his mother wished that he wouldn't. But the call of generations of von Wertens was too much, and after graduation Franz had enlisted. And there, it was soon found, he had another genius: this one for tactics and strategy.

Within a few years it was known in the Army that this officer, with a unique talent for both command and use of sophisticated weapons, was the best new prospect in the officer corps. There was no doubt that he would eventually become a General, and perhaps even Chief of Staff.

And then, in 1975, five years ago, he had thrown it all away by marrying a Jewess from Vienna, a reporter for the Vienna *Zeitung* who had come to interview him on the new German Army. Anti-Semitism was officially a ghost of the past, and yet it had not died in the Army officer corps. Not by a long shot, Colonel von Werten found out. Very swiftly he had been moved out of the career promotional ladder and shunted aside to the technical branch.

And the sacrifice of his career had all been for naught. Just last year his wife had died, killed in a three-car crash on one of Hitler's great autobahns that still tie Germany together with a constant reminder of the past.

Now Franz von Werten was in his attic office in his

home in Munich, his mind on a World War II command post where five Americans were being held prisoner. He had found that cave by accident two years ago while going through his father's papers before transferring them to the Bundeswehr Military School Library. A map of the Bavarian Alps, with one peak marked with the name Valkyrie, code name for a World War II conspiracy against Hitler. Franz had flown by helicopter to the mountain peak, and found nothing but sheer rock face—until he had set off some explosives, and a hidden door, sealed for decades, had emerged. His father, and the few other officers who knew about the secret command post for the conspiracy, had been executed before they could tell anyone.

The last call from the cave had said that everything had gone smoothly, and the American hostages were secure. But now the red telephone rang again. Von Werten listened as Helga Neff hurriedly hold him about the beeper.

"What frequency?"

"What?"

Von Werten said, "Calm down, Helga. Calm down." He deliberately paused to impress her with the need for cool, deliberate thought. "Tell me the frequency of the beeper."

"Thirty-seven point two kilocycles."

"All right. I'll handle it."

This time Nelga Neff was silent. Then: "You'll *handle* it? How? The beeper is pulsing right now."

Franz was irritated. All he said was, "Just sit tight," and hung up. Then he was on the telephone again to a Colonel in Berlin, and even that professional military man started to panic. "Do as I say," Franz said, "and everything will turn out all right," and hung up again.

Afterward he went over to the window to look out at the grounds which stretched before the Army building, formal green lawns with isolated elm trees. Germany, he thought. My God, Germany. What is your sickness?

8

September, 1975

The young woman had surprisingly fair skin, blue eyes, shiny black hair, and an English accent—yet here she was telling Colonel Franz von Werten she was Jewish. "I was born in England, you see." Her blue eyes seemed opaque to Franz. "My family settled there after Herr Hitler moved into Austria." She stirred her *café au chocolat* slowly; as if hypnotized, Franz watched the chocolate froth. "I grew up in a little town in Middlesex and didn't come to Vienna until four years ago. What a waste."

"What do you mean?"

"Vienna. It's so lovely. So haunting. Everything my father ever told me about it turned out to be true. And I spent all those years missing it."

"But England is beautiful, out in the country," Franz said.

"Yes, but it's . . . austere. Cold. Vienna is romantic, musical, warm."

Amazing, Franz was thinking, I feel jealous of a city. He had met Sharon Stael for the first time when he agreed to do an interview for the Vienna *Zeitung*.

The subject was the new German Army and the old Prussian guard still in it, including Franz, whom the editor referred to as "a rising star."

General Mohlner, Franz's superior, chuckled delightedly when he heard that phrase. "Rising star? Your father would turn over in his grave."

"Should I tell them to forget the article?"

"No. No. We need some good public relations for a change. Lay it on thick."

And so the interview was arranged at a coffee house in Munich, and here Franz was sitting, not with the owl-eyed pot-bellied reporter of the type he knew and had expected, but a slim, graceful, beautiful young woman who spoke in clipped tones, dazzled him with blue eyes, and had a way of absently trailing a fingernail across the table cloth—one could imagine that fingernail trailing lightly across one's shoulder, if one were not a Colonel and a "rising star." Franz smiled. "Well, enough about Vienna. Let's talk about me."

Sharon laughed. "You're not . . . humble."

"I have my moments, but my General told me to lay it on thick, by which I suppose he meant to show a certain confidence in the Army and its officers, including me. Our PR people call it 'image' in their press releases that no one prints."

Sharon lit a slim cigarette, then turned to signal the waiter for another *café au chocolat*. She said, "But you're not kidding. You really aren't humble."

Franz wanted this beautiful woman to like him. He knew she wanted him to say yes, I am shy, modest, insecure. But if Franz, at that stage of his life, did have a virtue of which he was really proud, it was that he never lied unless forced to. And the truth was that in September 1975, this son of four generations of von Wertens in the Army was enjoying life. His career was advancing, even in the face of those few in high command who hated, rather than revered, the memory of his father. He loved the Army, as his ancestors had, and it looked as if he was going to make an even greater contribution than his forebears, perhaps even be chief of staff before he retired. He saw that Sharon was smiling. "You don't have to answer," she said. "My word, he loves himself."

Which wasn't quite true because, by the time the interview was over, Franz believed he was in love with Sharon. Which was silly, of course, and made no sense, and was only a passing sensation which would have died in a week after she left him except, when they were outside in the street, hailing a taxi, the wind suddenly rose and she gripped his arm softly in a sort of proprietary fashion that was so . . . warming, so . . . loving, that he could imagine this beautiful woman to be his wife, dependent on him for support. . . .

He asked her to dinner that evening; she couldn't make it because she had to fly back to Vienna. But a week later when she returned to interview another officer—this one an Air Force General who, she told Franz later, "frightened me; he was so much like the Generals out of the American World War movies—" she agreed to see him and he took her to the Schwabing district, to the Osteria Italiana restaurant with its old oak beams and heavy tables. She loved it. "It looks so old."

"It was Hitler's favorite restaurant," Franz said, and heard her quick intake of breath.

"He used to come here? Right here?"

Franz pointed to an alcove with blue faded murals, half obscured by a green curtain. "He would sit right over there with his cronies," Franz said. "And occasionally, a beautiful woman. He met Unity Mitford in this very restaurant. You know of her?"

"Of course. The English girl who was in love with him. Did she have a *real* affair with him?"

"No one knows for sure. My parents knew a woman who was a friend of Unity's at the time—and my mother says simply it was all talk between Unity and der Fuehrer because Hitler was impotent. In fairness to Hitler, I have to say my mother hated him."

Later they danced at a nightclub on the Marien Platz; Sharon in a light blue dress that floated and swirled in the revolving colored lights, and later still, in his car, she said, "Don't kiss me."

"Why not?"

"You're nice, that's why."

Franz didn't understand until she said, "You're German. No matter what, I don't intend to get involved with a German. One anti-Semite mistake in a lifetime is enough."

He had drawn back, wondering what she was talking about and heard the story of her young life. Her mother was Jewish, her father an Austrian Protestant. A year after Sharon's birth her mother had died, and Sharon had been reared by her father and his second wife, both Protestants. "So," she said, "I fell in love with an American in London when I was eighteen. He asked me to marry him. Unfortunately, I had heard him make a few anti-Semitic remarks. I didn't know what to do so I asked my father. He said, you don't practice the Jewish religion, so why tell him? Believe me, I was agonized, but I was young, too. In love. So I didn't tell him. He thought I was a good old one-hundred-percent Protestant. And then we had the baby."

"What happened?"

"Well, that was too much. Religious roots have a strong pull, you know. I had to tell him the truth. The baby had Jewish blood. And you know what he did? He beat me for an hour, then packed up, moved to a hotel, flew to America, and got a divorce. That," she finished, "was my first love. Great story, right? I play the liar, my lover the heel. Hollywood should bid for the rights."

But she wasn't smiling. Franz didn't find the story so terrible. Even today, decades after Hitler, German Jews kept as quiet as possible about their religion, even though anti-Semitism was officially dead. And who could blame them? And meanwhile, she was so lovely . . . he kissed her. Her lips opened grudgingly, then hungrily, and her breath came fast but not as fast as his, and in the sweetness of the moment Franz knew he was going to marry this woman. So she was Jewish? So what, as long as she didn't practice her religion? This was 1975, not 1935.

Two weeks later he met Elise, her four-year-old daughter with the lively eyes of her mother, and Franz fell in love with her, too, took her riding on his big shoulders, she grasping his forehead and screaming in delight, and vowed to buy her a pony when she was big enough to fit a saddle . . . and eight months later Sharon left her beloved Vienna to marry him, and moved into a faceless brick house on an Army base in Stuttgart where he was stationed, and soon she started turning it into a home—and she was just the wife he had always dreamed he would find, self-reliant, intelligent, yet warm and loving . . .

. . . and it was all too good to be true, and within weeks the first realization of what had truly happened in his life struck him when he and Sharon came home from the grocery on the base, laden with two heavy shopping bags, laughing as their little spaniel, Erica, raced out to greet them—and found on the door of the Colonel's house on a military base in 1975 a small angry sign in white crayon:

KILL THE JEWISH PARASITES!

9

The cave. Gail Edens looked at Angela Tuck, who was sprawled on her bunk, a bruise on her cheek. All of them had heard the shouts and commotion outside, and then little Angela had been flung into the cell and handcuffed to the wall by cursing guards.

Ernst Hinkle, a muscular young guard who wore a T-shirt revealing heavy, hairy arms, stood over Angela as if to make certain she couldn't get away. What impressed Gail and the other hostages was that Angela was handcuffed, helpless, to the wall—and still the guards worried.

Jack Riley said to the guard, "What are you afraid of?"

Of all the guards, Hinkle was the most frightening, thought Gail. His blue eyes appeared to glitter with hate; he seemed to walk with a swagger; his appearance was vintage SS. Now his icy blue eyes turned on Riley. "Keep your mouth shut or you're going to join this bitch on the meat hooks."

Everyone in the cave was stunned. Meat hooks? What were they? Angela, who had appeared absolutely expressionless even when she was being thrown headlong into the cell, said, "I'd take it easy on the threats if I were you, including the butcher bit."

Gail heard her say "butcher bit," and wondered where Angela learned to talk that way. It almost seemed a trade expression among fellow ruffians. And yet this was little Angela Tuck who read comic books on the set. Hinkle said, "I mean what I say, bitch."

Angela said, "I'm only trying to help you. When the police find this cave through that beeper, I'll tell them who was the most violent of the terrorists."

In response Hinkle slapped Angela's face so hard the imprint of his hand was carved in red on her face. "You won't live that long to see any police. The first helicopter that gets near this cave, I'll shoot you, personally, ahead of time. Right in the mouth."

10

In his office the Chancellor of West Germany stood with his back to the German Republic flag furled on a standard. Nearby hung a photograph of John F. Kennedy speaking in Berlin in 1963. The Chancellor faced the Director of the BFV, the German equivalent of the American FBI, and the Director of the BND, the Intelligence Service. The three men were tense.

Paul Leuschner, a stocky bürgermeister type who headed the BFV, said he thought the kidnappers were still in the vicinity of the lake, so he had assigned helicopters at that location to search for the beeper. But the intelligence chief, Wilhelm Sartoff, crossed his elegantly tailored legs and smiled wanly behind a thin cheroot. "I know you're in charge, Herr Leuschner. But I must say what I think. The criminals would know the lake would be searched at once, so they wouldn't remain there. They would go elsewhere."

"But how?" asked the Chancellor. "There are just a few roads from Berchtesgaden through those mountains, and all of them were blocked within minutes. They'd need a helicopter."

The intelligence director brushed an ash off his

cheroot and said that if the terrorists required a helicopter, then they somehow acquired access to one. He
reminded the Chancellor that the police had found
marks that appeared to have been made by helicopter
skids on the far shore of the lake. Sartoff, the BND
Director, thought they *were* skid marks.

His words were depressing to the other two men in
the room. If the kidnappers had utilized a helicopter,
they could have gone anywhere in Germany—or even
to another country. The beeper on Angela Tuck
would be useless because no government had enough
helicopters and police cars to cover all of the great
mountains, dense forests, and crowded cities of a vast
continent inch by inch. One of the four telephones on
the Chancellor's desk rang. The Chancellor picked it
up and said, "Miss Heinstahl, I told you not to inter-
rupt us—"

But his secretary burst in to say that it was an urgent message from the police commandant.

The Chancellor told her to put the commandant
through, and the voice on the other end had the best
news the Chancellor had ever heard. "We've found the
beeper, sir! We're homing in on it right now!"

The American businessman, a vice-president of U.S.
Steel, waited eagerly in Room 1703 of a Berlin hotel.
He had telephoned a special number as soon as he
checked into the room fifteen minutes ago, and now
Madame Olga had arrived.

She carried an overnight bag. A tall brunette in a
simple green frock, she grunted one word as she entered the room and closed the door behind her.
"Down," she said.

Herbert Kallandrus was already nude. He obediently got down onto his fat knees on the carpet. Olga, who had a headache and wished she hadn't taken this damned job, took black stockings, garters, and a scanty black leather uniform out of her bag. A cat-o'-nine-tails emerged from the case next, which she daintily placed on the bureau.

She was only halfway into her uniform, the fat businessman so romantic he was kissing her toes in preparation for further pleasure and pain, when the door burst open and two policemen charged in with guns drawn.

"For Christ's sake," one of them said.

They saw a beautiful brunette putting on a leather costume, a pudgy, naked man at her feet, staring at them in horror, and a whip nestled on the bureau.

The second policeman said, "Olga, what the hell are you doing here?"

Both policemen knew Olga well from her prostitution record down at headquarters. Fined and let go, as all prostitutes were in all countries this side of the Iron Curtain. But what did Olga have to do with a beeper in a kidnapping? The policemen had expected to find five cowering American hostages and some gun-happy Baader-Meinhof terrorists. They had feared death when they charged into this room and instead they faced a prostitute and a degenerate client.

"Where's the beeper?" one of the policemen asked.

Olga's answer was blunt. "What the fuck are you talking about?"

But the policemen were already moving around the room, tearing open bureau drawers, ripping sheets off the bed, and upending the mattress. Then they saw a small plastic device on the bedspring.

The policemen whirled on Olga and demanded an explanation for the beeper, but all they heard in reply was, "Hey, man, this John called me for a job. Period. I don't know anything about the room—or him!"

And now all eyes were on the fat businessman who had climbed to his feet and was struggling to get into his trousers. "Oh my God," he was saying over and over again.

The first policeman went to him and grabbed him by his bare shoulders, his fingers sinking into fat flesh. "You're in the middle of a national crisis, Mister. How did that beeper get into your room?"

But the businessman cared not a damn about any national crisis. His lips opened, weakly, and the words came out so faintly they were like bubbles, each one exploding with little plops in the air. "I . . . I . . . can't . . . have . . . my . . . name . . . involved."

Then his head snapped as the policeman shook him violently. "To hell with your name. Where did the beeper come from?"

The fat man's head was now lolling as the full horror of the situation enveloped him. His name, his job, his family, his career would crumble when news of his assignation with a sadistic madame got out. He started to cry. "I . . . I don't know. I swear. I rented the room just fifteen minutes . . . ago. You . . . can check with the desk. I've . . . never been in this room in my life before."

The two policemen looked at each other. An amazing dead end, if the fat man was telling the truth. Someone had obviously slipped in here and planted the beeper under the mattress. But why?

❋   ❋   ❋

In Bonn the Chancellor knew at once, and the knowledge depressed him. The kidnappers had reacted to the discovery of a beeper in the hideout by planting one with the same frequency in Berlin to send the investigators off the track. The Chancellor looked at Leuschner. "And I suppose you called off all helicopter searches elsewhere when you thought you'd found the beeper in Berlin?"

The BFV Director shifted his feet. "Well, not exactly . . . but all the pilots knew about it, so why risk their lives dodging around for nothing?"

"Well, don't chastise yourself, Paul. It's all over anyway. The fact that the kidnapping gang planted a decoy with the exact frequency shows that they already knew about the real beeper—so there's nothing to trace anyway."

All three of the men in the room were so bitter they could hardly speak. A transmitter in the pocket of a kidnapping victim—and they had wasted the opportunity. When the German public heard that news, the government would be savagely ridiculed from one end of the country to the other. The phone rang and the Chancellor heard static. His secretary cut in to say that a Mr. George Williams was calling on a radiotelephone from an airplane. The Chancellor was surprised. The President of the United States had telephoned earlier to say that he was sending Williams and an FBI aide named Fred Jarvis—two bureaucrats, the Chancellor thought, who would muddle around and get in everybody's way. But the man didn't even have the decency to wait until he hit the ground. The Chancellor said, "Yes?"

Williams said, "Any luck on the electronic beeper?"
The Chancellor was irritated. Williams must be

some kind of a maniac. From a plane fifteen hundred miles away he was already starting to direct the German police. Trying to keep his voice calm, he told Williams that the beeper lead had come to naught. The criminals had planted a decoy beeper in Berlin, so it was obvious they had found the real one.

"Exactly the opposite," Williams said, his voice distorted by static.

"What?"

"If they *found* the real one, they would simply smash it, and that would be the end of the problem. No signal. But the very fact that they went to the trouble to plant a decoy shows they haven't found Angela Tuck's device."

The Chancellor's mind was whirling. "I . . . I don't understand."

"What must have happened," Williams explained, "is that Angela Tuck hid the transmitting device where they can't find it. So they planted a fake one elsewhere to buy some time. Did you call off the helicopter search in other parts of the country?"

The Chancellor pulled a crisp white handkerchief out of a coat pocket and patted his forehead. Christ, the American was right. And the three of them had been sitting in this room while the helicopters should be in the air right now.

The Chancellor was a fair man. He had misjudged this flying bureaucrat. "You're one hundred percent right, Mr. Williams. We did call off the helicopters elsewhere. But they're going up now. And, God help us, we'll find the real thing if we have to cover every inch of ground in the entire country." He paused. "When do you reach Bonn?"

"Nine A.M., your time."

"Our man will meet you," the Chancellor said. He hung up and issued the orders to Leuschner, but Leuschner had heard the conversation from this end and was already on the telephone. In a few minutes, helicopters were rising again over the Bavarian Alps to find Angela Tuck's transmitter. But were they too late?

11

In the night, Gebhard Beck flew a helicopter west through the treacherous updrafts and downdrafts of the Alps toward the cave, more than once seeing a sharp snow-clad peak rise abruptly in front of him, and swerving just in time to save his life.

The moon cast a pale glow on the dangerous mountaintops around him. Gebhard Beck was unaware that he was heading, unevenly and perilously, right toward the mountaintop hideout which held the hostages and an electronic beeper. One more mile and he would be in its range.

Hans's flashlight probed the interior of the septic tank, whose floor was covered with lichen and caked filth. The odor which rose was almost unbearable.

"Where the Christ is it?" Hans said angrily. "It ought to be lying right under the opening."

But Georg pointed out that the water which carried the beeper down could have washed it to any corner of the tank. Now, on their hands and knees in the muck, they searched the tank.

A voice from above startled them. Helga said, "The

girl tells me it's a cylinder two inches long that's metal, so it should shine."

But when the two men flooded light all around the tank floor, nothing glittered.

Above them, Helga Neff told Kurt Ollweg to take binoculars and a machine gun outside the cave. If a helicopter or mountain climbers approached, he should call out—and not be afraid to use his gun.

Kurt thought about that order. "If I have to use my gun, we're finished, aren't we? Maybe we should leave now while we still have time. Hide the hostages somewhere else."

"We'll find the beeper. The tank is small," Helga said. "Now hurry and go outside."

After the young man left, Helga looked down on the two flashlights playing across the floor of the dark tank. Suddenly, by chance, both lights turned toward her, and she saw two white circles like eyes that blinded her. Then the lights moved, and Helga was staring into darkness and remembering the white eyes of Herr Golden, the Minister of Justice.

December 6. Two years ago. The German Minister of Justice trembling. "Don't. Please. Don't. I'll do anything."

The deadline for the reply to the demand for ransom had passed. Helga said, "Your friends don't think you're worth much, liebchen."

"Oh my God," the frightened cabinet minister said. He was a balding, fragile-faced man, with spectacles now missing one glass. Its absence gave that eye a sharp clear image. "I have a family, a wife, three children."

For some reason Helga always remembered the

gaily colored bedspread on which the Minister of Justice lay. The contrast was so great. Bright colors below, and the pale man of top, beseeching her, drool flecking his lips in desperation.

"We do what we must," was all Helga said. She raised the revolver and at that point the Minister went crazy. He leaped off the bed, crying and pleading, and sank to his knees before her, hands clasped as in prayer.

"No, please. In the name of God—"

Helga shot the Minister in the forehead. His skull burst open and his brains spilled on the brightly colored spread. But what she would always remember was that his eyes rolled up in his head, showing only the whites, and he did not fall. He looked up at her with half a head and round white eyes bulging, mouth beseeching, oh God—

It was Helga Neff's first killing. The Minister of Justice had rejected the legal appeal of her imprisoned lover. He had killed Helga as a human being when he did that. Now both her lover and the Minister of Justice were dead, while she was alive to suffer.

But still—those two white eyes—horrible.

In 1963, Herbert Neff, her father, came to Helga's bedroom. "A coat for you, liebchen. Special."

He held up a little brown cloth coat with a fur collar. "You must look nice today."

Helga was ten years old—her father's favorite among three daughters, and she adored him. A Wehrmacht Captain in the war, he had been decorated three times and survived the Russian Front. Now he sold hospital insurance, mostly to fellow veterans, and did very well indeed.

Today, June 26, 1963, they were going to the Rudolph-Wilde Platz to see the President of the United States, John F. Kennedy, speak. Excitement in West Berlin was intense. The Berlin wall, the abomination of all, had been built in 1961—and Berliners were eager to show their defiance and anger.

Helga would never forget that day, so bright and sunny, and the feel of a festival in the air. They pressed through the crowd seeing everyone in high spirits, and Helga wondered why this American was the inspirer of so much joy. Who was he but a politician? And her father disliked all politicians.

But even the politicians had stood up to be counted when the Berlin wall rose, brick upon ugly brick; demolition started on buildings, and barbed wire soon coiled across the top of a wall thirty feet high that split mighty Berlin into two bleeding halves. The monstrosity of it. To divide this magnificent city and place a wall between families.

Now more than a hundred thousand Berliners were massed in the Platz to signal their indignation when the American President would arrive—and her father said, "Up this way."

He half pushed them through the crowds on the pavement toward an office building. On the rooftop the superintendent, a large-bellied man in a vest with a gold watch chain across his stomach, welcomed them. "Don't go near the edge," her father said, but his words were drowned by the sudden shouts of one hundred thousand voices. From where she stood in the middle of the roof little Helga had a perfect view of the Platz before them, with a speaker's platform mounted in front of the hated wall. Black limousines, led by motorcycles with sirens wailing, had just appeared in the square. The limousines stopped and security men ran to the back doors. Out came a stocky old man with graying hair, and a plump woman in a brown dress. A cheer greeted Konrad Adenauer and his wife, then Mayor Willy Brandt and his spouse. Finally a tall, freckled young man with short brown hair emerged from a limousine and held out his hand to assist a strikingly beautiful brunette woman out of the car: John Kennedy and his wife, the famous Jackie. The American President stepped to the podium, a tall man, confident, radiating appeal, and ten-year-old Helga Neff, for the first time in her life, felt a sexual pull. Others in her class were already talking about boys, but Helga had never joined in. But this man was *so* handsome.

She could not make out what he was saying because he was speaking in another language. But she could understand when he hammered the podium and shouted in German, "Ich bin ein Berliner. Ich bin ein Berliner. Ich bin ein Berliner."

On the rooftops all around her everyone was cheering and shouting, and Helga suddenly felt herself swept up in her father's arms. He held her in front of him so she had an even clearer view of the scene. "Liebchen," he said, "don't ever forget this day. Don't ever forget the Americans. They are our only friends."

Now seventeen years later in a cave in the Bavarian Alps in which five American "friends" were doomed to die at her hands, Helga remembered those words of her father and how exciting that day had been, and how everything had changed, Kennedy assassinated, Adenauer dead, and from the ashes politicians rising to take this nation down a traitorous course, and the blood of so many young people spilled in vain. . . .

. . . And now, for the first time, the young people had a plan to overthrow the rotten government . . . not just another terrorist incident that would lead to nothing, but a logical, methodically computed program that would succeed with what Helga considered the cream of Germany's old families behind it, beginning with the Colonel.

Colonel von Werten had found Helga through her father, who had served under General von Werten in the war. Her father would never have revealed her hiding place to the police—but to the son of his old General, yes. And Helga had met the Colonel, who told her that Ulrich Kandrof, who officially authorized the movie, was the traitor responsible for the shameful Berlin wall and told her more besides, opening Helga's eyes to a rot even she hadn't known. And here they were on the brink of success, the hostages captured and secure—and a two-inch radio embedded in filth could destroy everything.

Outside the cave, Kurt Ollweg shouted and ducked into the bushes. A helicopter rose over the mountain ridge to the west, within range of the beeper's pulses.

But two minutes before its arrival, in the dark, dank septic tank, Hans Ulbricht had swung a hammer down on the little metal device, breaking its electronic components—and silencing the transmitter.

They were safe. Helga Neff wasted no time. She telephoned the Colonel and said that she wanted to execute Angela Tuck now. She was too dangerous to be allowed to live.

The Colonel said no. The operation must go on exactly as scheduled. The Colonel must be present at all executions to film them in such a way as to project a special message to Ulrich Kandrof, the President elect.

Helga hung up, bitter, even though she realized the Colonel was right. Still, she must somehow deal with the little bitch, Angela Tuck—by some method take the heart out of her if she was going to be in that cave with them for five days. She said to Hans and Georg, "Take Angela into the hanging room."

A few minutes later Angela was being manhandled into a room across from the prisoners' cell, and she gasped. Along the right wall was a row of gleaming, sharp meat hooks—with rope nooses hanging from them. Below the ropes were platforms with trap doors. This was the execution room.

Helga couldn't hang Angela now, but she could torture her. How to do it? She directed the guards to tie Angela's hands to two widely separated hooks. When they did, Angela's body sagged in space, all of its weight pulling on her stretched arms. Suspended under glistening hooks, she looked as if she were being crucified. The pain was obvious in her tortured expression. Helga directed the guards to place cuffs around Angela's ankles.

Outside the room, Helga told the guards, "Let her hang like that long enough and we'll have no more trouble with the bitch."

Helga posted guards on watch, then lay down for a few hours' sleep in a room that had once been a conference room, off the main cave. A map of Berlin *circa* 1944 was on the wall, faded and yellow but still legible. War must have been so simple compared to peace, Helga thought as she began to doze. But she couldn't sleep; her mind was too cloudy with images.

A Cabinet Minister's white eyes after she killed him, a little terror named Angela Tuck dropping a transmitter into a tank, a Colonel meeting her for the first time in her hideaway flat in Munich. What a plan he had unfolded before her. It was mind-boggling, beginning with the attack on Ulrich Kandrof, the politician so beloved by the German people, so charismatic that he was called "the German Kennedy."

In the hanging room, Angela Tuck's body swayed in the dark. The pain was killing her.

Book IV

DEATH COMES EARLY

1

9:00 A.M. Fifteen hours before the hanging.

A crowd at the Bonn International Airport watched anxiously as a silver slip of a plane touched lightly on the runway and rolled to a stop. Aboard it were the U.S. investigators.

News of the kidnapping had spread throughout Germany during the early morning hours, electrifying the people. Baader-Meinhof again? This time kidnapping American movie stars? Reporters and television crews crowded the airport terminal along with hundreds of German citizens, among them throngs of teenagers who held signs: "Please, Mr. Williams, save Jack Riley," and "Don't let Bob Morrison die."

The Phantom bomber in which Williams and Fred Jarvis, assistant director of the FBI, had traveled boasted no creature comforts other than metal seats. As they made their way out the door, the pilot gave Williams a thumbs-up signal. "Go get them, Mr. Williams."

Williams stepped out on a small metal stairway into a country in which he had never been, that "strange, brawling, dangerous, industrious, neat, organized, ef-

ficient, neurotic, schizophrenic, egomaniacal, unpre-
dictable" nation called Germany. In his cramped seat,
under a pinpoint light, Williams had been reading
books on modern Germany during his flight over the
Atlantic, and all of those adjectives had been used.

And now this nation had spawned terrorism that
had spread throughout Europe, perhaps the most
frightening terrorism ever seen because it had no
stated goal, no announced program, nothing but an
iron determination to overthrow "the system," with
nothing to replace it.

What did the German people expect of him, Williams thought, as he walked toward a little podium on
which microphones had been placed. Was he—a for-
eigner—expected to solve a German crime committed
by Germans in a country he didn't know? Was that
why all these people had come to the airport? He
didn't even speak or understand their language, had
never visited their cities, knew nothing about their
criminals' haunts, habits, or past patterns of behavior.

He was really helpless, in a way, and only his personal ties to Gail Edens had prompted him to accept
this mission from the President so quickly. The German people must know he could not really assist them
in a concrete way. So why were they looking toward
him so hopefully and expectantly?

Then he saw some people in the crowd waving
newspapers with his picture on the front page. No
doubt his previous cases in America had been cited
and expanded into heroic proportions. Wasn't he
known in America as the man who had stopped a terrorist from exploding a nuclear bomb?

As he stepped to the podium, Williams was thinking
that the Baader-Meinhof terrorists must read the same

TO THE EAGLES NEST 127

newspapers. Perhaps he could make use of his newspaper image. He faced the television cameras and said, "I'm here to assist the German government in dealing with this terrorist crime. I have utmost faith in your government to do so efficiently. But now I would like to address a personal message to the terrorists. I have been sent here by the President of the United States for one purpose: to rescue the American hostages unharmed from you. I intend to do so. I will do so." He paused, then said firmly, "Because of the mistake you made in Berlin this morning, I believe I will be successful."

The crowd fell silent, astonishment on every face. What mistake? They had read that a beeper had been planted in Berlin, but the police had said that was a decoy and the trail was a dead end. Now this American bureaucrat was saying the terrorists had made a mistake?

In the limousine, on the way to Bonn, Paul Leuschner, the BFV Director, was furious at Williams. "With all respect, that was a stupid thing to do," he fumed. "We don't have one shred of a clue out of that hotel incident, and now you've got the whole world thinking we're on to something—"

Williams sat silent. Jarvis, a tall man in a tweed jacket, took out a pipe before gently advising Leuschner to relax. "George knows what he's doing."

But Leuschner said Williams had made the German investigators look like fools by broadcasting a grandstand announcement raising everyone's hopes, and then the German police would have to come along later and make apologies.

Williams said quietly, "They *did* make a mistake in Berlin."

"There were no fingerprints, nothing. And the desk clerk saw no one go to the room, other than the two people found there."

"A telephone call was made," Williams said.

The BFV Director stared at him. "A telephone call?" He asked Williams if he thought the BFV tapped every telephone in the country.

"No need to tap. Long distance calls go over microwave towers. Which means that satellites can find the telephone call that set up the Berlin incident."

The BFV Director said, "But there are a million calls to screen and that could take forever. Besides, the terrorists would know enough not to say anything other than in code."

Williams looked out of the limousine window. God, he was tired. His back hurt from the airplane trip. What was Gail Edens doing? Were they mistreating her? Torturing her? Ahead of him the solid, gray government buildings of Bonn, the capital of the West German Republic, rose beside the broad Rhine River, dominated by the Bundestag tower. He said to Leuschner that the discovery of the beeper presented the terrorists with an emergency, which meant they had to communicate instantly with their people in Berlin. In such a hurry there was no time for coding and decoding, and something might have been said in the clear. If it had been, computers could find it.

He paused. A white-gloved traffic cop waved the limousine into a road which led to the Chancellery. "Anyway," he said, "that wasn't the real purpose of what I said at the airport."

"What do you mean?"

"I want the kidnappers to start worrying a little—and preferably about me, personally."

Leuschner stared at the American. Was this some new form of arrogance? A hero created out of newsprint who believed his own headlines? Williams said, "Because of the beeper in Berlin we know they have people on the outside of the hideout coordinating with them."

"So?"

"If we can't find the hideout, maybe we can make one of those people nervous about the American investigators—so nervous he'll come out into the open."

"And do what?"

"Attack *me*." Williams paused. "The idea is we'd be prepared and capture him before he succeeded."

Leuschner was so surprised he could only grunt, then sit back. This Williams would take some getting used to. But Leuschner could say this for the American. He shook up the scenery, and that little speech at the airport might hit the terrorists as hard as it had him.

2

Colonel Franz von Werten sipped tea from a thick mug as he watched the arrival ceremony of the American investigator on a television set at a special "safe house" near Munich. After a moment he stiffened. A mistake, Williams was saying. What mistake? Everything had gone efficiently as ever; his man in Berlin had slipped into the room unseen, using a special key von Werten had issued him that could open every hotel room door in Berlin. It was typical of von Werten's methodical mind that he had issued such a key without knowing just what it might be used for, and therefore had it ready when needed.

So no mistake. But the American, a man named George Williams, seemed *so* confident. What could have gone amiss? Franz thought over the whole beeper incident. It had begun with a telephone call from Helga Neff to him—Franz von Werten smiled. He sat back, sipping his tea, the television news now an unalloyed joy to him. Of course. Satellites. Williams would have guessed that the kidnappers found the beeper, then had to make an emergency call from the hideout to someone on the outside who set up the Berlin operation. And he would know that the Baader-Meinhof kids only used makeshift codes—if any codes at all—so he might pick out something unusual in the clear, such as a frequency number, isolate the call, and track the telephone which received it.

But what Williams didn't know was that sophisticated military scramblers had been installed on every "Ice House Movement" telephone from the Bavarian Alps to Berlin.

So much for Franz's "mistake." But Franz kept staring at the screen even after William's speech was over.

Williams could be trouble. According to the Munich newspapers, he was considered an investigative genius in America, and his words at the airport reinforced that reputation, as far as the Colonel was concerned. Yes, the mistake Williams mentioned was not a real one, but only because Williams didn't yet know that military men were involved. But if Williams's past history was a guide, he would not be long in catching on to that fact, too. The police had already found the marks of helicopter skids along the lake shore, and an intelligent investigator like Williams would surely wonder how Baader-Meinhof youngsters got access to a helicopter.

Franz pressed a button. A television recorder cut into the TV screen and the picture ran backwards to the beginning of Williams's speech at the airport. Franz ran it again, searching for every nuance. "*I* intend . . . *I* believe . . . *I* will be successful. . . ." Williams was deliberately provoking attention to himself. And the Colonel smiled again. He knew what Williams was doing.

Franz faced a decision. His associates in the Ice House Movement didn't know he was playing a lone wolf in the most important phases of this operation. They had been told nothing about the nerve-gas mines, nor what Franz intended to do with the hostages on the meat hooks in the cave. They had gone into his venture with him—as angry as he at the events which forced them to risk their lives and careers. But Franz, because he wanted to protect them, had told them only of the kidnapping and the demands that he would issue. Nothing more.

Now Franz had another idea that he would keep to himself. He had planned a demonstration to divert the investigators away from the true identity of the Ice House Movement. How much more effective if he combined it with the death of Williams?

If the American wanted an attack, he would get his wish, but not the sort of attempt he would expect: an ambush on the street that waiting police in plainclothes might surround, or a shot by a sniper trying to melt into a crowd who would get caught. Williams would die Franz von Werten's way. By remote control, helping to mislead the investigators, and thereby sealing the doom of the American hostages.

Five minutes later Franz was thinking not of Williams but of Ulrich Kandrof. The reason was a call from his Ice House associate in intelligence. The associate said, "The Chancellor just pulled Kandrof's security file."

Franz hung up and swivelled his chair so that he could look out the window. The Chancellor would get nothing. Kandrof was a bastard; the files were shit, tampered with all the way. The very first "fact" in the file about Kandrof's father was a lie. Franz's research had shown that Kandrof's father was a Communist sympathizer, arrested in the Berlin riots of 1919. No mention of that fact in the files. Why? Because Kandrof had friends everywhere with the power to suppress facts. He was the most popular politician since the Americans' John F. Kennedy. His election to the Presidency, after Hans Leber, the incumbent, had been killed in an airplane crash, had brought the largest majority vote in the history of the Bundestag.

Franz von Werten sat on the windowsill, one leg swinging. For a moment there were tears; he wiped them away quickly with his sleeve. A woman walking beneath his window had glanced up suddenly, her eyes reminding him of his dead wife. So blue, so beautiful.

Then the intelligence specialist sat down at his desk and began to rehearse every step of the execution of George Williams.

Subject: ULRICH KANDROF
Ref. No.: 709 968 43215
Clearance: TOP SECRET

Facts of Record: Subject born in Berlin, 1920. Father, a physician at Frankfurt General Hospital; mother, schoolteacher. Politics, Social Democratic. Ulrich Kandrof attended University in Munich. Grades mediocre, only distinguishing accomplishment participating in university theatrical productions, including Shakespeare. Most students at the University joined Nazi party. Kandrof did not. War record shows service as enlisted man in Polish and Russian campaigns, a courier attached to General von Kraus's staff.

Post-war attended law school, Munich, became

aide to Supreme Court Justice Gottesburg, then entered politics as a Social Democratic representative in Bundestag, landsman in Bavarian region.

Made one trip to Moscow in 1972 with Chancellor Willy Brandt; no record of any other visits behind Iron Curtain. In Bundestag, played key role in passing legislation aimed at controlling terrorists.

OFFICIAL CONCLUSION: No clue in past history of any alleged "treasonous" activities of any sort, unless terrorists consider his legislation against them to be treason.

George Williams had once heard Bobby Kennedy say that his brother had admitted to being "carried away" by the Cold War setting in Berlin in 1963—and had delivered too "hawkish" a speech.

Now the picture of that historic moment hung in the office of a Chancellor who could save five lives, including that of the woman Williams loved, if he would yield to some demands much less frightening than those of Soviet dictator Nikita Khrushchev in Kennedy's day. But of course the Chancellor wouldn't yield, and Williams didn't expect nor wish him to, despite his personal involvement.

Bright, alert blue eyes that sometimes shifted rapidly in an almost furtive manner, and at other times disconcertingly stared straight through you, were a feature of the Chancellor's image—and personality. His figure was unprepossessing, small but so pudgy that his gray tweed vest seemed to bulge dangerously, with every button fighting for its grip. The Chancellor juggled coins in his right hand as he told Williams that Ulrich Kandrof was Germany's most beloved statesman. "Perhaps a bit too liberal for some tastes, but it isn't his liberal bent that bothers the Baader-Meinhof ruffians. It's the fact that Ulrich doesn't believe in violence, and he's had the courage to stand up for that belief."

Williams said he would like to speak to Kandrof, with the Chancellor's permission.

"Of course," said the Chancellor. "He seems to be the key figure in the demands. He's on his way right now." While they waited for the arrival of the President-elect, the Chancellor informed Williams that he had arranged for him to interview witnesses in Berchtesgaden.

"You have *eye*witnesses . . . who saw the kidnappers?"

"In ski masks only, Mr. Williams. The security guard and the chauffeur of the limousine from which the American were taken. We also have the mechanic who maintained the tank—" He stopped as he saw the expression on Williams's face. "You haven't heard about the tank?"

Williams said that the BFV Director had been too angry at what he said at the airport to fill him in on all the details of the crime. "I gave him good cause."

The Chancellor grunted and related the facts about the party until his intercom buzzed. The key figure in the demands, Ulrich Kandrof, was arriving outside.

Sirens screaming, motorcycles roaring, a convoy escorted a long black limousine to the Chancellery building. In a few minutes Ulrich Kandrof, a gray-haired handsome man, stepped briskly into the room accompanied by an aide. The Chancellor greeted him warmly, taking his hand and pumping it. "Chin up,

Ulrich. It's only one more attempt by those maniacs to destroy one of us, but this time it won't work."

The President-elect was dressed in elegantly tailored clothes in which he moved gracefully and easily. He was a smallish man, but with good shoulders. At sixty, he was in excellent physical condition. The Chancellor introduced Kandrof to Williams and Fred Jarvis, and then herded them all into a conference room where they sat around a mahogany table, a portrait of Adenauer staring serenely down at them.

Kandrof's first words stunned everyone. "I'm going to announce my resignation at five P.M. today. My staff has already contacted the television networks to set it up."

The Chancellor lunged forward, his stout body slamming into the table and pounded its surface. "You mustn't do that, Ulrich. That will be the most unforgiveable act."

"I'm destroyed anyway," Kandrof said lightly, but with sadness underlying his tone. "Whatever happens to those American hostages, I will spend the rest of my life answering questions about my, quote, treason, unquote, because some terrorists called me a traitor. My usefulness to the country is finished." He paused. "I must say it was most clever of Baader-Meinhof to libel me in their demands. The libel alone destroys me as a political figure."

Silence in the room. Williams said quietly, "But you must be hiding something, Mr. Kandrof."

Four shocked faces looked at him, and even Fred Jarvis seemed appalled. The Chancellor said, "Really, Mr. Williams, this is enough of a catastrophe without you tearing flesh—" but Kandrof only smiled wearily. "You see, already the distrust—from foreigners, not even German. But the question makes sense. The threats says explicitly I must reveal the facts of my secret treason, unquote. Conclusion: either the kidnappers are insane, or there are real facts to be revealed. All right, I'll tell you what they must mean, but only because it might save the American hostages. I've kept it secret for years." He drew in a breath. "It was scrubbed from the records by an anonymous supporter in Intelligence, but the fact is that when I was in Moscow with Chancellor Willy Brandt in 1972 I disappeared for eight hours. No one knows but myself what I did during those hours."

"What did you do?"

"I met a Soviet dissident who gave me a *samizdat* novel to bring out of Russia. But he's still there, so I'll never release his name. I also, if the truth be known, shared . . . champagne with a most lovely young Russian woman who wanted me to use my influence to help her get out of the Soviet Union." He paused. "My wife is unaware of this."

"Can what you did in those eight hours be proved?" Williams asked.

"Yes, by the *samizdat* writer and the woman. But I won't release their names." He paused, then said, "Unless the kidnappers tell me the names of the two Russians will save the hostages' lives. Then I don't know what I'll do."

The President-elect looked weary as he patted his forehead with a light blue handkerchief. "If that happens, I'll leave the decision up to the Chancellor, Mr. Williams. Kill five innocent Americans or send two innocent Russians to a Siberian prison camp for the rest of their lives. That's a choice I won't make without help."

"What doesn't make sense to me," Williams said, "is that the Baader-Meinhof people are leftists. So why would they become upset about your contacts with leftists in Soviet Russia?"

But there the other Germans were looking at Williams with European disdain.

"Baader-Meinhof hates Soviet Communism, Mr. Williams. They believe the Soviets have betrayed the working class. For years, Baader-Meinhof and the Red Brigade in Italy have been murdering Communist officials."

So much for that, Williams thought, as he changed the subject. "Just what is an ice house?" he asked.

The simple question seemed to startle everyone. Finally the Chancellor smiled. "To begin with the basics, they used to make ice in large blocks in ice houses. Trucks would take the ice to your home, and I remember in hot summers as a child how delicious it was to steal chips of ice from the wooden floor of a wagon."

"All right," Williams said. "What does such an ice house mean as a political symbol for terrorists? Any ideas?"

Everyone looked blank, so Williams turned to Kandrof. He was the linchpin of the demands—perhaps for reasons he didn't even know. He said to the President-elect, "The words in the demand against you are particularly venomous. It seems to go beyond any reasons you've stated here. Could it be the movie?"

"*The Secret Life of Hitler?*"

"Yes, that demand to destroy the movie comes right after the one calling you a traitor. Maybe they're linked?"

"Well . . . I'll be damned," Kandrof said. "I never thought of that. In fact, I did authorize the film to be made, after the Chancellor passed the recommendation on to me, of course. But my signature was more or less honorary."

He explained that a year ago the producer had requested the cooperation of the government for this anti-Hitler film. A bitter battle had broken out in the Bundestag, but finally they voted yes, and Kandrof signed the approval on behalf of the President, who was out of the country.

"Confidentially," Kandrof said, "it was the actors who swayed the vote in favor of approving the picture."

"What do you mean?"

"A year ago we were told by the producers that Jack Riley, Gail Edens, and all the rest would star in the film. Even the Bundestag members are movie fans, and were impressed by the special cast."

Williams was stunned. He was remembering Gail Edens receiving hate letters in America and telling him that it couldn't be linked to the movie because she was never even approached for the role until the day before. But the producers had been quietly using her name in connection with the film for a year. Even in Germany? Could that have significance? A secretary stood in the door. "A Mr. Jim Dilts to see Mr. Williams." Williams excused himself to see Angela Tuck's father.

Dilts was in the hall, a tall, immaculately tailored man, pacing up and down nervously. When he saw Williams he rushed over to him. "Did they trace the beeper?"

Williams said no, and Dilts's shoulders sagged in disappointment. "I've killed her," he said in a low voice. "They won't let anyone live who brought a beeper into the hideout."

Williams showed him into the Chancellor's office and Angela's distraught father could not stand still. He paced the room saying, "And the beeper isn't even the worst of it."

Williams asked him what he meant, and Dilts told him that the previous summer informers had told the Berlin police that an eighteen-year-old terrorist, Carl Ulbricht, kept a picture in his room of the American movie star, Angela Tuck. Apparently he had an adolescent crush on her. They had asked Dilts if his daughter would cooperate in luring the terrorist into a trap. All she had to do was to frequent underground parties, see if Carl Ulbricht showed up, then arrange a date in a certain hotel room.

"Well, she agreed to do it, and those trigger-happy German cops killed the kid. Angela was sick. And I was nervous. I knew she was going to do this film about Hitler in Europe."

"You knew that last summer? A year ago?"

"Yes. The producers had already spoken to her. And if Baader-Meinhof found out she was the one who arranged that rendezvous with Ulbricht, she would be killed while she was in Europe. So I sent her to security school, taught her how to use special devices and what to do if she's captured."

But Williams wasn't listening. Angela Tuck had also known of the picture a full year before it got underway. There must be an explanation for not telling Gail Edens ahead of time—maybe scheduling difficulties or other problems—but the significant fact was that all last year when the hate letters flowed in from right-wingers, it was known that the "Commie pinko" Gail Edens would play Hitler's lover. Nazis would hate that, all right, possibly enough to write those letters.

So why was she kidnapped by leftists, and not Nazis? Or was she? Williams interrupted the distraught father who had never stopped talking and pacing the room. "I don't have access to an American scrambler phone. Can you reach NSA in Washington?"

"Sure. I'll use the embassy scrambler."

"Okay. I want a second readout of the Arcon satellite." Arcon was the National Security Agency satellite that monitored telephone communications in the European sector, and was already searching for the calls to Berlin about the beeper. Dilts said, "You have *another* target?"

"Yes. I want a readout of all telephone calls from America to Germany in the last year in which the words *The Secret life of Hitler* were mentioned."

"But from Hollywood alone there must be hundreds of calls. It's been in production in Germany for three months."

Williams told the CIA officer to eliminate Hollywood from the readout.

"What?"

"Tell the computer to ignore all calls from Hollywood about the picture."

There was a silence, and then Dilts said, "I see. If somebody called Europe from a little two-bit town in the Midwest about a big Hollywood movie in Europe, it could be odd, right?" He paused. "Okay, I'll do it."

Williams told him about the hate letters to Gail in America, and Dilts said, "We had them here, too."

"What?"

"The U.S. Embassy received anonymous letters saying they didn't want an American Communist like
Gail Edens playing Eva Braun. We put them in the
file-and-forget drawer. But you're on the wrong track
there, anyway."

"Why?"

"The letters are from Nazis. But the demands from
the kidnappers ask for the release of Baader-Meinhof
prisoners, not Nazis. The Nazis and Baader-Meinhof
are blood enemies. Jesus!" he said suddenly.

"What's up?"

"I just remembered, I gave Angela a pill."

"Cyanide?"

"Blood."

"A blood pill? I don't understand."

Dilts stood by the desk. He drummed his fingers
lightly on its top as he said to Williams, "Mr. Williams,
I can't bear to think my daughter's in the hands of
those killers. I can't stand to know I've condemned her
two ways—the murder of a terrorist and now the beeper. If you don't mind, I'll keep the secret of the blood
pill to myself. I don't trust anyone anymore—not even
you."

3

10:00 A.M. Fourteen hours before the hanging.

On meat hooks in a cave in the Bavarian Alps, Angela Tuck hung limply, the blood pill in her mouth. Hans opened the door and saw that the unnatural stretching position had caused Angela's crimson minidress to ruck up, revealing shapely thighs. But in the circumstances, even Hans—at seventeen an adolescent yearning for sex—was not turned on by the sight of Angela's semi-bared body. She must be in agony. At dawn Hans had asked Helga if he could go into the room and take Angela off the hooks, but Helga had just smiled wearily at him and said brutally, "Your cock rules your mind, Hans. Let her stay up there long enough to wilt. That girl is full of poison for us."

Now as 10:00 A.M. Angela had been hanging for six hours. Hans couldn't stand it any longer. He opened the door.

Angela heard him enter and braced herself for his anger. She was feeling well. She had slept peacefully for hours on the floor; her wrists had been disengaged from their bindings within minutes of the guard's departure last night.

It was CIA's unreliable "Christopher Bent Wrist" escape technique, one she had practiced many times, that had saved her. Attributed to a former CIA agent in Iran, it was achieved by bending the wrist and stretching the outspread hand at the exact instant the knot was being tied. If you were lucky, the rope would be knotted over the artificially swollen juncture of the wrist. When you relaxed and straightened your hand, it could sometimes squeeze through the enlarged loop.

Hans, who had tied Angela's wrists, was a complete amateur—or maybe he had seen her wince with "pain" when he tied the knots. In any event, he had done a bad job. Her cuffed ankles precluded any hope of escape, so her only reward was sleep.

She had caught a few hours' rest on the floor below, lying in the fetal position, her ankles cuffed, wondering how to use the blood pill under her tongue, until she heard stirring outside and stood up. By tossing loops over the hooks, she had hoisted herself up until she presented herself again as a piteous spectacle.

But she knew that last act had been a complete waste of time. Hans saw the loose ropes on the hooks immediately. He shouted for Helga, roughly wrestled Angela off the hooks, and threw her down on the platform. "She sprung loose, Helga. I don't know how," he said to the blonde leader who stood at the door.

The color drained from Helga's face. In all her career with the Baader-Meinhof she had never faced a person like this little bitch, Angela. While Angela was supposed to be in agony, she had been peacefully sleeping. It was too much. The Colonel could not dare to question what she was about to do when he learned about this. The click of a knife snapping open echoed in the room. Helga advanced on Angela. Knife slashes across that so-called beautiful face would be a torture even this little bitch couldn't escape.

Angela saw Helga approaching and tensed.

Kurt Ollweg stood at the door. "Helga, the Colonel is on the telephone."

Helga had the point of the knife against Angela's cheek when Ollweg spoke. "Tell the Colonel to wait," she said.

But her mind was racing. In her anger she had forgotten that the Colonel planned to film the executions, and some other scenes besides. The film was supposed to put the final pressure on Ulrich Kandrof, the traitor, and a scarred and bloody-faced Angela Tuck might ruin the Colonel's plans.

Hell. She moved the knife from Angela's cheek to her neck, then sliced it lightly. Blood spurted from the side of Angela's throat. That scar the Colonel would have to hide with makeup. Helga had to do something to show this cunt who was boss.

Helga left the room to hear the Colonel tell her he was going to be out of touch with the kidnappers for a few hours. He had a personal mission to execute.

Helga said that she must know just what the Colonel intended to do. The Colonel said, "I'm a bit worried about the American investigator."

"So?"

"So I'm going to eliminate him and provide clues that point to the Reborn Eagles."

Helga said all right and hung up. She approved the Colonel's action. The neo-Nazi Reborn Eagles were the Baader-Meinhof's worst enemies. And it was not a bad idea, either, to eliminate that Williams character, if the reports she had heard about him on the radio this morning were true. If Williams was that good, there was a chance he might discover Helga Neff's identity from one of the witnesses in Berchtesgaden whom he would no doubt interview. The witness had seen Helga Neff three days before the kidnapping and might make the connection.

4

The German character, Williams was thinking as he and Assistant FBI Director Fred Jarvis flew in a helicopter above the Bavarian Alps. In some ways that character was so much like the mountains below: soaring and majestic. But it was also, like those same peaks and canyons, treacherous. Or was that a myth spawned by two world wars, into which America had been drawn to confront the people they called Huns?

What was there in that character which produced terrorist groups in the midst of unprecedented prosperity? What was troubling Germany? A sense of historical guilt that could not be washed way? Or worse, no sense of historical guilt at all, but a nameless craving for anarchy which obliterated everything?

The pilot banked above the Eagle's Nest that had been recreated for the film. To the original retreat, Hitler had often flown for rest as well as conferences. His cronies in the Eagle's Nest were called "the mountain people"—a name that signified they were the closest intimates of the Fuehrer. On its terrace walls Eva Braun had posed prettily in brief and fetching sunsuits, smiling at photographers and once, in a film

Williams had seen, executing joyous cartwheels while
Hitler and his generals laughed.

Was it wise to rebuild that very villa in such detail;
was it smart to produce a film on Hitler's life, no matter what the original motive—in a country of such an
unfathomable and mysterious character as Germany?

The answer was an obvious no, and now five Americans were caught in an internal political war from
which only a miracle could save them—Williams had
not much hope in eyewitnesses who told police they
had seen nothing but people in ski masks.

He looked down from a Plexiglas window to see
plunging forests, sharply edged peaks, and a jewel of
a lake shining placidly, and there—on a cliff overlooking blue water—was the chateau of Felix Bernhard,
the man who had been the host of the party where the
kidnapping took place. The helicopter settled for a
landing in the grounds, and he saw that one wall of
the house had been demolished and a tank was still
half-buried inside it. The police had asked Bernhard
not to touch anything until the investigation was completed.

Ducking out of the rotor blades' downdrafts, Felix
Bernhard appeared in a green blazer and white slacks.
With him was Max Weber, the producer of the movie,
whom Williams had met in New York, and a pretty
young woman in an orange suit. Her name was Laura
Doolittle, and she was the studio's European representative. After the introductions, Williams surveyed
the tank. He said to Bernhard, "How much trouble
would it be to install gears on a disabled engine?"

"Not much, I don't think. The gears had simply
been removed. Someone screwed them back into

place and attached a connection from the ignition to the button in the bulls-eye. Then he put in some fuel, and when the button in the bulls-eye was hit, it not only activated the dummy mechanism, it started the engine." He paused. "The only trouble is the mechanic who maintains the tank for me says no one got near the tank when it was in his garage."

"But obviously someone did," Williams said. He told Bernhard he wanted to speak to Mr. Weber and Ms. Doolittle about the film. This surprised the industrialist. "The *film*? Don't you want to spend more time examining the *tank*?"

Williams smiled. "If he left fingerprints, I'm sure your police have already got them." But Bernhard was nodding his head no. "Grease and muck was all they found on the engine. No prints."

Apparently he was somewhat disappointed in Williams, but courteously showed Williams, Jarvis, and the movie executives into a living room with spacious French windows, blue drapes, and rustic furniture with large blue cushions. A maid appeared, took orders for drinks, and then left as Max Weber said to Williams, "They want me to turn a thirty-two-million-dollar film into trash. I pay taxes, Mr. Williams. I'll hold the U.S. government responsible if this picture is ruined. . . ."

"If you want to sue, I'll help you, Mr. Weber."

Shrewd little eyes peeked at him from behind rolls of fat. "A deal? It smells already," he said. But Williams said, "I'm here to save the actors' lives and your thirty-two million dollars. Why don't we concentrate on that and maybe you won't have to sue."

But this only brought unhappiness into sharper focus on Weber's face. "The poor babies," he sighed.

"My children. These killers have got them. They'll never let them out alive."

"Which of them received hate letters?"

"Hate letters?"

Williams told him about the letters received by Gail Edens in America and Germany. "Oh well," Weber said, "only Gail got them. The right-wing nuts didn't like her playing Hitler's dream girl because of her pinko background. In fact, that's why we waited until almost the last minute before hiring her. We thought she might cause too much trouble. In the end, we decided she was such a great actress and so popular, we'd take the chance."

Williams thought, so that explained why Gail had told him she had just been approached for the role a day before she met Williams, and therefore hadn't believed the hate letters had anything to do with the film.

But Weber said that no other actors had received such letters, and Williams knew it must be a dead end. All four actors, not just Gail, had been kidnapped, and the others had received no hate letters at all. Weber said, "Funny thing, though. When Gail came to play her big love scene with Hitler, Jack Riley kept blowing his lines."

"What do you mean?"

"The very last day was a nightmare. We wasted that whole day's shooting. Every foot was unusable."

"What happened?"

"Riley was playing Hitler, in bed with Gail as Eva Braun. Everything was smooth except he kept calling her Alice. Over and over. And this is a pro. He never made a mistake before on the whole picture. All because of some groupie he's balling!"

Laura Doolittle filled in the background. "Jack has been seeing a young English girl in Berchtesgaden. But her name isn't Alice. That's what makes it even more puzzling."

But this didn't puzzle Mr. Weber. Rolling a cigar in a fat fist, preparing to light it, he said, "So he has a name for her in bed that isn't kosher."

But Williams said to Laura, "What was the English girl's name?"

"Judy. I didn't catch her last name when we were introduced. I only saw her once because Jack kept her hidden in a love nest someplace. It was against security regulations for him to be fooling around like that. I understand he had to give the guards the slip every night to see his girl."

And now Max Weber, his face in a cocoon of blue smoke, seemed annoyed. "How is it going to help find the kidnappers' hideout by looking for some groupie Riley was sleeping with?"

Williams said, "A strange young girl helping Riley break security regulations? Riley acting so oddly on the set, saying the wrong woman's name? Who knows what was going on?" He lit a cigarette. "Someone close to the actors must have kept track of the victims. The kidnappers knew ahead of time about the party because preparations had to be made. It could be the English girl was involved in that spying. She might be a Baader-Meinhof sympathizer."

Fred Jarvis said, "If she's young she could be a Baader-Meinhof type, all right. And she might know something, just by being in town and around the set. What do you think, George. Do we look for her?"

"I'd like to talk to her," Williams said. "See what she knows. Especially since her name *isn't* Alice."

Jarvis saw Laura Doolittle staring at Williams and smiled. "His mind works in odd ways," he said to Laura. "But things usually come out right."

Laura Doolittle smiled. "Well, I can help you find her. I've met her and know what she looks like. Let's just hope she hasn't skipped town since all this broke."

In a few minutes Williams was alone, waiting for the BFV Director to bring him the witnesses he would interview, while outside, with a whine and then a roar, the helicopter bearing Jarvis and Laura Doolittle flew over the house on its way to Berchtesgaden to find an English girl named Judy who might have caused Jack Riley to say, not Judy, but Alice.

A mission which, Williams thought, reflected his own desperation for clues. It was now 1:00 P.M. Eleven hours to the hanging, and his one real lead was two witnesses who, police said, had seen nothing and knew less.

And his own slim hope that he could lure the kidnappers into the open to attack him had failed. Williams had seen no one suspicious anywhere, and the Germans were blanketing him with so much security protection that no one would try.

5

In 1976, Franz von Werten went to the family cemetery where his ancestors were buried. The grave of his father contained only an empty chalice; Hitler's Nazis had not even let the family keep the ashes.

When he returned to Bonn, he met a retired General in the Officers' Club and told him about the visit. The General was in his cups. "Grand old man, your father. But I shouldn't think he'd be too proud of his son."

Franz said nothing, and the old, white-moustached General continued, "My boy, Hitler was a midget when it came to things military. But he had good enough ideas on what makes the German people great. If he had kept his nose out of our bailiwick and just concentrated on politics he might have carried things off."

"Why wouldn't my father be proud of me?"

"Because of blood! My dear, Franz, the Army expects its ranking officers to be superior in every respect—and that includes choice of wife. I don't believe your promotions are going to be coming along on schedule. Now I'm talking out of school here, but I'm doing it for your own good. Divorce her, Franz. Get back to your heritage."

At that point, Franz had been married to Sharon for less than a year. He was hardly surprised at the anti-ing, not since that sign "Kill the Jewish Parasites" on his door. But was anti-Semitism so deep that Franz, considered the most brilliant prospective General officer in Germany, would actually be taken out of the promotion chain? Would they go that far? In the late 1970s?

In March 1977, his name went on the list of officers eligible for promotion. In April the selections were made. Franz von Werten was not among them. Instead there were orders transferring him out of line-officer status into intelligence, where his "talents can best be utilized."

That night Sharon found her husband sitting at a kitchen table staring at the wall which held a calendar with a big crayoned X on this date. "Did you make it?" she asked.

"They passed me by," Franz said. "And that's not the worst of it. They booted me right out of the line into intelligence so I'll never have my own field division in the Army. They want me to squirrel away in little labs and produce the weapons they can use to make themselves proud." He swept his arm aside; a cup and saucer clattered off the table and crashed on the floor. "Oh, Franz," Sharon was starting to cry. "I'm so . . . sorry. It's all because of me."

And later when they made love it was no good at all. Franz's mind was on the injustice and the anti-Semitic animus, and Sharon said, "I'll leave. The Army is your life, Franz." But Franz had held bitterly onto her and now, years later, he was in Berchtesgaden inspecting a disassembled sniper rifle with a telescopic sight, *plastique* explosive in tiny balls, a Walther PK machine pistol in a holster, and two replicas of Hitler's wartime uniform, complete with brown belts and Nazi armbands.

None of these items was the subject of Franz von Werten's closest attention. He was fingering the gold chain with the locket of Hitler.

He was taking a chance using this particular locket because Hitler wasn't smiling in its picture. Somehow he could have obtained the authentic smiling photo of Hitler, the symbol of the neo-Nazi Reborn Eagles, all of whom wore such chains under their collars where they could not be seen. But Franz wanted to use this medallion with this picture, because of what it had meant to his wife.

And there really was no risk. When Williams was close enough to see the picture, he would die.

Franz took a wire and attached it to the medallion. He worked carefully, slowly, feeding the wire through a tiny loop between the chain and the locket. Then he took what seemed to be a cigarette lighter and attached it by the wire to the chain.

The "lighter" was a receiver with a difference. It not only received impulses to trigger an explosion, but contained a speaker. From a pocket in the suitcase Franz withdrew a transmitter only slightly larger than the receiver. He tested it, speaking softly in the room of a safe house in Berchtesgaden. Over and over, Franz said, "This is your clue, Williams."

The receiver picked it up perfectly.

The words would be the last George Williams would ever hear.

6

Jack Riley was showing the effects of the unending tension of the last twenty-four hours. He sat on his bunk against the wall, one hand manacled to a steel ring, his head on his chest, dozing. He was thinking of Judy Lipscomb, that young piece of English dynamite with whom he had spent two great weeks in Berchtesgaden. My God, English girls were the best. No inhibitions whatsoever. It was as if class gave them unrestricted license to indulge in any sexual fantasy that came to mind. But my God, he could hardly get it up that last night after Judy told him about her aunt.

The funny thing was that even when he was about to explode inside the beautiful young girl writhing beneath him, all he was thinking of was that sixty-two-year-old woman in England.

Alice.

"Jack!" A voice snapped him out of his reverie. It was Angela Tuck on the bunk near him, a rag around her throat where that sadistic Helga had cut her. Riley couldn't get over that kid's courage. Planting a beeper in the middle of this nest of gunhappy killers.

Hanging from the meat hooks for hours and never whimpering even when she was cut. But now, for the first time, she didn't look courageous. In fact, she appeared sad, even pathetic. Riley guessed that fear, which she had fought off so successfully, was now reaching her, too. "I'm frightened, Jack."

Riley had a reputation for being a wisecracker. He cracked jokes because he had always seen life in perspective, a rather grisly, comic affair in which people tried to find moments of happiness between car accidents, wars, diseases, and tragedies of every sort which inundated them continuously. Nevertheless, he found it hard to put his own situation right now in a psychological perspective. Like everyone with a philosophical bent, he was acting very human when the pain struck him in person. But at least he knew it. He said, "What's to be frightened about? They'll strike this set in ten minutes and we can go back to the hotel."

"Oh Jack," said the little girl whose mature beauty was now crumbling. At last, thought Riley, she looks like a real kid. She said, "I wish they'd let me sit next to you. If they're going to kill us anyway, what does it matter?"

"You want me to hold your hand?"

"Yes. And make jokes. Anything."

"You don't have another beeper up your ass?"

Angela, who had seemed to be about to cry, brightened at this. "You're so . . . funny, Jack. You're the greatest."

"Yeah. My death mask will have a grin," Riley said. "Anyway, I can't help you. Look, kid, after that beeper, they're watching every move you make."

All of this conversation was overheard by the guard, Kurt Ollweg, standing at the door, the machine gun in his hand. Ollweg was thinking, right on, Riley. We're watching. But Angela Tuck, for once, was not up to anything. All she said was, "I'm going to ask one favor and I think they'll let me have it. Before I die, I want one kiss from you."

Riley stared at her. A kiss? That sexy chick had passed the kissing stage since she was nine. Nevertheless, visions of Roman Polanski *did* dance in his head. He had made it a policy, since this picture began, to stay away from that gorgeous little piece, no matter how provocative were her swinging little hips and warm inviting eyes. And he had succeeded. Boy, had he succeeded. Angela had hardly glanced at him after the first day on the set—so shrewd she saw right through him and knew that nothing would happen between them.

Riley, before the English girl came onto the scene, had decided to make his standard on-location pitch at the formidable Gail Edens instead. Stuck on a set in a small village in the Alps, surrounded by security guards, what else was there to do but screw? That had been his argument to Gail—but she had laughed and then started telling him about some Washington bureaucrat she had met in New York and fallen in love with. Gail Edens—and a little Washington pip-squeak? Was that what she deserved? And the actress was really zonked on him, no doubt about it. In the boat when they were being kidnapped she had repeated his name like a mantra: Williams, Williams, Williams.

Thank God Judy Lipscomb had saved the day, or this location job would have blown his mind, and now little Angela Tuck had suddenly revealed that all along she had an eye for him, too. He might have dared take a chance in those days. Hell, she was no innocent baby, no matter what the law said.

Angela Tuck was resisting a temptation. The temptation was to crack a rock over Jack Riley's head. What could she do with such a stupid man to let him know she had an escape plan. Wink? The guard would be alerted in a minute.

And now, in an irony that would be comical were it not so dangerous, she saw Riley actually looking *hornily* at her. He believed it about the kiss. He probably had a hard-on. God. For the first time since she had been captured, Angela Tuck felt real despair. She needed a partner for the blood pill in her mouth to work.

Then she looked at Robert Morrison. She had believed that Jack Riley, the wiseacre, would be the quickest to realize that she had something in mind. Morrison seemed so straight. But now she regarded him more closely, sitting cool and quiet. Still waters ran deep, she had always been told. Maybe they ran fast, too.

The pill in her mouth was insoluble. One had to bite it sharply before it worked. But Angela couldn't do it because they would suspect her of a trick. She caught Morrison's eye and started to wave her free hand in strange patterns.

Morrison caught on right away.

Helga passed by and glanced through the window into the cell. Now what was Angela up to, waving her hands? She watched and decided it was harmless. Helga went back to the radio, whose reports still worried her. It had been arrogant and foolish to show herself to that man in Berchtesgaden. And the radio said that the American investigator, Williams, had now arrived in that village and was interviewing witnesses, just as she had feared.

Still, even if the man remembered seeing her, he obviously had not realized the connection. According to earlier radio reports, the witnesses had told police they saw no one's face.

7

The man who stood before Williams was stocky, with a rough-hewn face and broad shoulders. This was the security guard who had been in the limousine when the kidnapping took place. The chauffeur, a thin, red-faced man with a beaky nose and watery eyes, leaned against the fireplace. The guard was angry at the chauffeur. "If he hadn't driven over them, we might have escaped."

"Driven over what?"

"Micromines that blow up the underside of a car and stop it in its tracks." The guard detailed what had happened, ending with the gas grenade through the windshield. He said he had learned about the micromines at security school.

Two minutes later, Williams was talking by telephone to an instructor at that school, John Hansen, who said that micromines were so new they hadn't even been issued to the Army. They were still in Research and Development.

Williams asked him if any sophisticated weapons of that type had ever been used by the Baader-Meinhof before and was told no. "But that doesn't mean sophisticated weapons haven't been stolen. In the last three months, in addition to micromines, we've had a case of guns that spray knockout gas stolen, two drums of Tuflex-2, which is enough nerve gas to kill everyone in Berlin, both sides, and—this is the worst— the prototype of the first portable laser gun."

Silence. Williams could not believe what he had heard. He asked why those thefts hadn't been announced.

"It's the most sensitive secret we've got," Hansen said. "The government is afraid that people will panic if they know such deadly weapons as nerve gas might be in the hands of terrorists. I'm only telling you now because the micromines popped up in the kidnapping and the knowledge might help you find the kidnappers. But I beg you, Mr. Williams, hold the information to yourself."

Williams hung up just as a large man in a blue uniform, Captain Olking of the special antiterrorist department, entered the room. Williams told him about the conversation and Olking blanched. "Nerve gas?" Almost in a whisper he added, "My God, if Baader-Meinhof has nerve gas, the whole country will be at the feet of those insane kids."

Williams seemed nervous. Uncharacteristically, he paced up and down the room as Olking watched him. In front of the fireplace Williams turned. "It's worse than we thought, Captain. Much worse."

"What do you mean?"

"I smell grown men here, not Baader-Meinhof. And what's worse, I smell the Army."

"The Army?"

"The military. Air Force, Navy, Army, Intelligence, I don't know. But there's a pattern. Where do ex-college kids get access to helicopters to kidnap hostages? Where do they obtain sophisticated weapons like micromines? Who had access to all those weapons that were stolen? It feels like military to me, Captain."

But this statement angered the Captain so much he jumped up. "That's *crazy*. You think the Army has done the kidnapping? Why would military people want Baader-Meinhof prisoners released?"

"I don't know," said Williams. "But we'd better find out."

8

A cool breeze came off the Alps, clear and fresh, as they drove down the same mountain road that Gail Edens and her friends had ridden the night before. Williams got out of the car at the scene of the kidnapping. He could imagine Gail being dragged toward that ugly hole in the ground—and then stopped imagining and continued down the winding road, which gave, on cliff edges, a view of the lovely blue lake set among dense forests and mountains.

Williams had always loved the mountains. If somehow he got Gail back, perhaps they could build a little lodge in Vermont or upper New York State. . . .

"There it is," said Olking. They had passed through the private gate of Bernhard's property and now ahead of them on a two-lane asphalt road was a modest petrol station owned by the mechanic who had maintained the tank.

The station was smallish in size, three green pumps and a garage with a lift and space for three cars. On the lift now was a blue Duesenberg, an antique which must be worth one hundred thousand dollars. Seventy-year-old Johann Klaus, tall, bony, with gnarled hands, was underneath the car holding a grease gun and busily shooting lubricant into key bearings and niches as they approached.

When Olking remarked on the car, Klaus grunted that he only got the hard jobs. The real money was in the little cars that came in volume, but his station was too far off the main tourist route to attract them.

Pffft! Grease shot into an axle bearing. Klaus came out from under the lift and faced the investigators. "You'll get nothing from me," he said. "All I did was paint that tank, and check the spring under the dummy. I never even looked at the engine."

He went to a lever along the wall, pushed it, and the beautiful Duesenberg descended on the lift, as Klaus complained, "Been up all night. Reporters, television, police—a nightmare. And all for that fat Communist."

Silence. Williams and Olking looked at each other, and finally Olking said, "What fat Communist?"

"Herr Bernhard, who gives the party. What else could he be but a Communist? Who else would do such a thing, desecrate the memory of this country that way. For a joke at a party! General Goering as a dummy for people to laugh at? A disgrace!"

Williams asked him why he worked for Bernhard if he felt that way.

The mechanic drawled, "For money. Who has it? Jews and Communists, like Herr Bernhard. I heard Hitler say that's who would take over the country after he died—and he was right."

Olking tried to take control of the inquiry. Smoothly he said that, whatever the case, they were here to trace some kidnappers today.

But Williams interrupted him and said to Klaus,

"Where did you hear Hitler say that about Jews and Communists?"

Olking was annoyed. "A figure of speech, for God's sake, Mr. Williams. He heard him on the radio or—"

A hand on his chest stopped him. The mechanic was saying angrily, "Hitler was this close to *me* when he said it. To General Krebs. I was there."

"Where?"

"In the bunker, you fool. Where Hitler died. Where else? General Krebs told Hitler he was going to commit suicide and when he said *that*, Hitler told him the Communists and the Jews would take over Germany after he died, so the General had his permission to take cyanide."

Williams turned to Olking and asked him if he had a file on Klaus.

"On a mechanic in Berchtesgaden? No." Olking looked at the mechanic with new interest. "Were you in the Army? One of the guards in the bunker?"

"I was what I've always been. A civilian mechanic. Henschel and I ran the boiler room in the bunker."

Williams asked him how he had escaped the Russians.

"Henschel stayed behind. I didn't. I made the breakout with the third group. Bormann's group. Bormann was in uniform; so were the others."

The man shivered, his bony hands clutching the lift lever. "I still can't forget that night. No sir, gentlemen. That was a night the gods were crying."

But now Olking was so angry he pushed Williams aside. "Why are you wasting time on ancient history?"

Williams was thinking of the Nazi hate letters to Gail Edens. They seemed to have no bearing on the kidnapping, and yet—the threats had been sent, and now Gail was in trouble. And here in front of him was a genuine unreconstructed Nazi of the type who would send such a letter, if he could write.

Those were his thoughts, but all he said to Olking was, "He's the type of witness you can't hit hard with questions because he'll freeze. Let him loosen up."

Klaus had climbed into the driver's seat of the Duesenberg, preparing to back it off the lift, when Williams approached him: "Did Martin Bormann escape with you?"

April 30, 1945

Crouching, Klaus went forward. Ahead he could see the lumpy figure of Bormann hugging the side of a wall as he trotted toward the bridge. The others had spread out, dark figures under the moon, flitting over rubble—and all around the noise of exploding artillery shells and above, the sudden blinding glow of flares, dropping in parachutes, and causing the refugees from Hitler's bunker to hit the ground until the flares died out.

We'll never make it, Klaus thought. This is crazy. The Russians are around us in a circle. But ahead of him he saw the refugees heading for the bridge over the River Spree. If they could break out to the north they could eventually make it to Admiral Doenitz' headquarters—and the worst that could happen there was that they would surrender to the Americans instead of the feared Russians.

And then, just as they approached the bridge, they saw Soviet tanks rumble across it. A Russian lieutenant spotted one of the fleeing figures. "Who goes there?" he shouted in broken German. No answer from the man who dove for cover. And now the Sovi-

ets knew what was up; Klaus saw the cannons on the
tanks swerve toward them, and the next thing he
knew explosions tore the earth all around. He was
lucky because he was in the rear. Bodies flew into the
air, others were decapitated in front of him; they were
being massacred. But then he saw Bormann, shifty as
ever, the expert at personal survival, making off to the
south with Colonel Wilhelm. Bormann was now clear
of the cannon fire; the next day Klaus would hear that
Bormann and Wilhelm gave up the attempt to escape
and took cyanide—but Klaus never believed it. Right
now a flare pinned him; he froze in anticipation of
gunfire. None came, because he was too far away. He
went back toward the bunker and met a group of soldiers who were in Team Four. He told them about the
bridge and they stopped in their tracks. "There's no
hope," one of them said, "unless we split up and try to
get out singly."

"Who keeps the picture?" one of the soldiers asked.

"I'll keep it," said another, "and if I get through
alive you can come to my house in Ulm and borrow
it." They were referring to Hitler's favorite picture
that he kept in his bedroom in the bunker; it showed
him in close-up, smiling. The soldiers shook hands and
went off in all directions, looking for cellars in which
they might hide, take off their uniforms, and become
civilians. Klaus was already a civilian. He could blend
into the mobs of thousands of homeless civilian refugees in holes under Berlin. Which he did.

Olking said, "So that's where the picture came
from."

"What do you mean?" Williams asked.

"The Reborn Eagles . . . our neo-Nazi organization . . . the members all wear a gold locket with a
copy of a picture of Hitler smiling. That could be the
same picture."

"Who was the man who took off with the picture?"
Williams asked Klaus.

"I don't know. Just one of the last team of soldiers."

Williams said, "And there was no pact made under a
full moon to stay together forever, with Hitler's favorite picture as the symbol?"

The mechanic said, "You're making a joke of a serious thing. There was no pact made by us. But the picture survived, and the Reborn Eagles adopted it for
themselves."

He drove the car off the lift as Olking said to Williams, "Okay. We've been on this subject twenty minutes and what have we got? Nothing."

But Williams was checking the interior of the garage. Four windows, all with rusting screens, obviously untouched. That meant the people who tampered with the huge tank engine had to get inside
through the door somehow.

A taxi had wheeled up to the station on the outer
tarmac; a pretty brunette and a gray-haired man were
transferring from the cab to the Duesenberg. The man
handed Klaus some money off a large roll—then the
car was gone, the girl waving gaily, and Klaus was
spitting on the money. "Juden, Juden, Juden," he said.

Apparently one of the last of Hitler's bunker men
lived a life of agony, accepting Jewish cash, thought
Williams. He intercepted Klaus on the way back to his
little office. "You're a proud man, Mr. Klaus, and you
should be, with your experiences in the war."

Klaus's expression softened, but froze again as Williams said, "So why did you let people make a fool of you?"

"What are you talking about?"

"Your report to the police said you locked the garage every night and those locks were pick-proof—and never tampered with. I've looked around and seen rusty window screens which weren't touched either, right?"

Klaus nodded. Williams said, "So they made a fool of you."

"What?"

Williams said that the terrorists couldn't work on the engine during the day while Klaus was there, so they must have worked on it in his garage during the night. "But if the lock wasn't forced, and the windows weren't touched, how did they get into your garage at night?" He paused, "You had a visitor during the day who stole the key and had a duplicate made."

"But—but that's impossible," the mechanic said. "I would have seen them." He put a thin, twisted stogie in his mouth and lighted it, then said, "You know, those kidnappers aren't my kind—they're nothing but spoiled kids who should wear the letters COMMUNIST on their foreheads. So I want to help you. But no one ever hangs around my little station. I mean, what for? I don't even have a soda machine. So nobody at all ever comes to the place unless he needs his car fixed or—" he suddenly sat bolt upright—"the blonde."

"Blonde? A woman?"

"A woman. Yes indeed. A beauty."

"A blonde woman visited your station."

"Hell, no. I told you nobody did."

"Then I don't—"

"Her car had a flat. Down the road. She asked me to fix it. So I did it. It was only a block away."

"When was this?"

"Three days ago. Fifteen to twenty minutes, that's all I was gone." But the mechanic knew what they were thinking. "My God, while I was away one of her buddies snitched my key and went somewhere to have a duplicate made."

"Right."

The mechanic was thinking. "But then how did they return the key? I only fixed one flat for one blonde that day. Oh shit," he said.

"The blonde came back," said Williams.

"Yes, just stopped by before I closed to thank me for fixing the flat. Oh hell!" He stopped. No one spoke until the mechanic said, "She got out of the car to stretch her muscles. Said she'd been in the car sightseeing all afternoon since I fixed her tire. Somebody else came up for gas, and she could have flipped my key back into the drawer when my back was turned."

But even before he finished talking, Olking was on the telephone, ordering a police artist to come to the station to make a composite sketch of the blonde woman. Soon a young man in blue jeans and suede vest was in Klaus's office questioning him. Olking listened and turned to Williams.

"A woman about twenty-five, blonde, blue eyes . . . you still think you're tracking the Army, Mr. Williams?"

And when the composite was finished, Williams saw both Olking and the police artist stare at the picture. "Jesus," the artist breathed. "It's her."

"Who?" asked Williams.

"Helga Neff," said Olking. The artist nodded. "The Baader-Meinhof Princess. Four kidnappings on her record, all four hostages brutally murdered. Helga Neff, the killer. She stole the key; she's one of the kidnappers—and Helga Neff is *always* the leader." He slapped the desk. "Damn, I knew it. It's Baader-Meinhof all the way."

"You can't be certain from an artist's composite," Williams said.

But Olking told Williams to look at the picture more closely. "Under the right jaw."

Williams looked, and saw a small mole. Olking said, "Helga Neff has a flawless face—but one mole that's a landmark."

William said to the mechanic, "How did you notice such a small mole?"

But the feisty old mechanic had a sound reason to remember it. "I was sitting on the road fixing her tire and she was leaning over me. I kept looking up to see two great cantaloupes and the bottom of her chin."

So it *was* Baader-Meinhof, Williams thought. There was no question about it. The demands in the threat had indicated it was Baader-Meinhof, and now the first kidnapper to be identified turned out to be a famous Baader-Meinhof killer. My God, he had been off on this one, worrying about the military and Nazis who sent hate letters. Still he had one question. "Why did she do it?"

"Do what?" the Captain asked.

"Show herself. If she's so notorious, so easily identified, why did she show herself to the mechanic? Someone else not so well-known could have had a flat tire. She must have known the mechanic would be questioned after the tank acted up."

But there Olking once again revealed his knowledge of German attitudes so alien to Williams's experience. He told Williams that they had a picture of every Baader-Meinhof terrorist in the country on file, with a complete description—and the terrorists just laughed at the BFV. Why? "Because they know their middle-class friends will protect and hide them as they've always done."

And then Olking seemed to lose interest in Williams completely. He called in an aide and started issuing instructions. "The Baader-Meinhof terrorists have been able to evade us before because the middle class from which they come has closed ranks around them. But this kidnapping is so important a crisis it may make a difference. I want television to display Helga Neff's picture. I want every informer we have to see their contacts within the hour and make a special plea on this case."

When the aide left, Olking turned to Williams enthusiastically. "This time we just may make it. There's a chance. And at least we finally know what the god-damn Ice House Movement is. It's Baader-Meinhof on the rocks."

Williams told the bemused Captain he was going to the set of Hitler's villa to check footage from the movie *The Secret Life of Hitler*, a statement which earned him another tolerant smile. "No more Army, Mr. Williams? No crazed Nazi Generals plotting the fall of the Republic? Now you hope to find the real villains in a movie film instead?" He shrugged his head, smiling, so charged up with the break on the case that Helga Neff represented that he apparently couldn't calm down. "Excuse me, Mr. Williams. I am sarcastic, I know. But I've been in this business a long time—and I'm just a little intolerant of Americans who come to our country—and point right at the German military as the source of evil, and call them Nazis. You're still fighting the wrong war, Mr. Williams."

9

Gail wished she had been kidnapped from her home instead of from a party. At home she would have been dressed in jeans and boots or flat-heeled, comfortable shoes. The tight dress she had worn to the party was filthy and bedraggled. Her shoes had high heels, one of them half broken. That problem had been solved by kicking them off. She supposed she could rip off the tight dress, too, but kept telling herself to save that move for later. She still remembered that lusty look in the young guard's eyes . . . the guard they called Hans.

Unfortunately, ever since Hans's interested look, he had been removed from the door-guard shift, and the guard right now, Ernst Hinkle, the one who seemed most like a Nazi, stared at Gail with eyes filled not with lust but hatred. Cold, blue eyes glittered at her malevolently. Gail shuddered. This very night one of them could be standing on a trapdoor, a rope around his throat, waiting for the world to shift from under his feet and to drop down to eternity.

Would you feel pain? Gail's hand went to her throat. Oh God, why hadn't she listened to George? She should never have done this film; should have gone into hiding after those murderous letters arrived, as he had wanted her to. But no, she had to play the bigger-than-life movie star who couldn't be bothered with peasants, even when they wrote kill letters.

Gail turned to observe the other hostages. Angela Tuck was making hand gestures at Robert Morrison across the room. What kind of communication was that? Morrison was responding, when Gail caught on to what they were doing: sign language for the deaf. Gail knew that Hollywood had briefly been intrigued with manual signaling after politicians like Jimmy Carter and Senator Robert Dole had simultaneous sign translations for the deaf of their speeches on television.

What Gail didn't realize was that Angela did not know the sign language. When Angela had started directing fake gestures at Morrison she had discovered, to her encouragement, that he caught on immediately and pretended to answer her. They were waving meaningless hands and fingers when the door burst open and the guard who hated Gail came into the room. "That's all for the hands," he said to Tuck and Morrison. "No code."

Whatever Gail expected Angela to respond, it wasn't the little girl's next words, which gave her the biggest shock in her life. "I was just telling Bob that Gail Edens is sick."

All eyes turned toward Gail. No warning from Angela, no doubt because the cave was bugged. No preparation for a trick, which was what it must be. Gail was fatigued, beat, and hurt all over—but she wasn't ill. The guard with the hate-filled eyes came over to her. "Are you sick?"

A click in Gail's mind almost frightened her. With that click, she suddenly realized what to do. Their danger had been so terrifying that it had paralyzed her. So now she must forget it was real. In that case, the guard who had so frightened her was, in real life, just a big actor who would be on the unemployment line at the Highland Avenue office tomorrow. Imagine this is a set, she told herself, and the meat hooks are just plastic. Think that way and you might escape. "I feel terrible," she said. She lay back against the wall and actually felt the blood draining out of her cheeks.

Hinkle shifted his feet nervously. Helga Neff had said she didn't want to be bothered by petty gripes from the prisoners. Besides, what did it matter if the girl was sick or not. She was going to die soon, anyway. Still—

Angela said, "I can help her, I think. And you'd better let me."

"Why?"

"I think she has measles. Everybody in the cave, including the guards, will be infected."

"Shit," the guard said. He went to tell Helga, who said, "Anything Angela Tuck says is a trick."

"So what do I do?"

Helga wearily stood up and went into the prisoners' room. Gail Edens was slumped against a wall, white-faced, looking as ill as Angela Tuck had said. But Helga knew that Angela Tuck was a liar who was a cunning little enemy in their midst. She examined her and then said to Angela, "She has no rash." She felt her forehead. "No fever. Since when are you a doctor?"

"I'm a girl who had measles last year," Angela said.

"The whites of her eyes are yellowish. I saw her shifting around all over the place, as if she was covered with ants. That's how you feel just before the rash. And now she's feeling weak and sick." She paused. "Okay, forget it. But if she does have measles, you're *all* going to end up in the hospital instead of on the loose."

Helga Neff laughed. "Tuck, you're too good for this trick. The beeper doesn't work, so you try a little fantasy. What do you take us for, morons? Are you so stupid you expect us to listen to your chatter and, to protect ourselves from measles, release the woman so she can go to the police?" She shook her head. "You are . . . disappointing me."

But Angela's response surprised her. "Oh, no, you don't have to release her. I've got Theomycin. If she takes it before the rash appears, she'll be okay."

Helga Neff leaned toward Angela Tuck, her blonde hair falling over her face in two bells. The woman was really attractive, Angela thought. Put her on Sunset Boulevard in Hollywood at rush hour, and she would have been making movies herself by now—and possibly be a kidnap victim instead of a captor. Helga said, "I investigated the private parts of your body, didn't I? You have no pockets in your dress. So where do you keep a bottle of drugs?"

Angela opened her lips, and beneath her little tongue Helga saw a capsule. "Well, I'll be damned," she said. She removed the pill, cupping it in her palm. "Are you sure this isn't cyanide?"

"No sir. The doctors told me to keep a bottle of Theomycin pills in case there was a flare-up again. But that's not why I have a capsule with me now."

Helga asked her why she had it, and Angela said, "The doctors told me it has a temporary side effect. Acts as a pretty effective birth-control pill for twenty-four hours." She paused. "I've heard of rapes in these kidnappings, believe me. So when you all jumped our car I took that pill out of my purse and put it in my mouth. Just to be safe in case one of your people went crazy."

Helga believed not a word of it. Yet she looked at the pill. If it was cyanide, Gail Edens would die—but her death in that fashion would be the responsibility of Angela Tuck, not herself. Helga broke open the capsule; a powder was inside. She went to Gail and looked into her eyes. Damn, the whites of her eyes *did* seem to be yellowish, and the actress *was* squirming and looking weak. But it was impossible to tell for certain because the power of suggestion was working. The hell with it all. "Do you want to take this pill?" she asked Gail. Gail nodded her head, weakly. "Y-yes . . . please. God, I . . . feel terrible."

Helga had someone bring Gail a glass of water, and the actress swallowed the pill.

Angela Tuck didn't smile, but inside she was cheering. The broken capsule would start to work immediately; in a few hours its effects would begin. Which meant she had saved Gail Edens's life. And all of their lives—if Gail caught on.

Helga Neff went back to her desk to monitor the radio which carried nonstop news of the kidnapping investigation. Her mind was not on Gail Edens, but the Colonel. He was going to eliminate Williams. How? Williams must have squads of guards around him.

Then she froze. The radio reporter was excitedly announcing her name. That mechanic had realized what she had done. He had identified her to Williams.

The American investigator was fast. Fast! A few hours in this country and he had already pinpointed Helga. Helga sipped Polish vodka from an army mug. The Colonel had been right, as always. He must kill Williams. Now.

10

George Williams and the producer of *The Secret Life of Hitler* drove in a limousine up a winding mountain road toward Hitler's villa. Once, on this same mountain, Hermann Goering and Martin Bormann had built houses to be in closer proximity to their leader. The view was breathtaking; vistas of mountain peaks greeted travelers around every hairpin turn, as the road rose higher and higher to the Eagle's Nest where Hitler and his clique of political gangsters had spent so much time between moments of crisis.

Their limousine was preceded and followed by motorcycle police and guards in jeeps. The car itself was almost terrorist-proof with its cast-iron body and bulletproof windows. The German authorities were taking no chance that the visiting American official would be a terrorist victim.

In the limousine Williams had to listen to Weber's recurring lament. "I'm ruined, and the studio is kaput. The banks will call in every loan we have if we take a thirty-two-million-dollar bath on this crazy picture. I could kill Goldschmidt."

"Who's he?"

"Suede shoes. Pipe smoker. Typical writer idiot. He brought me the screenplay. And I went for it like a goniff."

Williams said nothing and the producer went on. "Who could believe it? The idea was so safe. Tell me one producer who lost money on a movie kicking Hitler in the balls. Tell me one. There is no such animal. So I raise my foot—and kick my own teeth in."

"What was the writer's original concept?"

"The original concept began with the idea of making money out of little Angela Tuck's adolescent ass," the producer said from behind a cloud of blue smoke. "This was a fourteen-year-old nymphomaniac who every middle-aged pervert was aching to screw. Such a girl," he said, pontifically, "should be exploited. A chance in a lifetime. At eighteen she'll be just another piece."

Williams found himself smiling for the first time in the last twenty-four hours. Gail Edens might die at midnight but how could you help being amused by these movie people? And they were Gail Edens's people, too. But how had she escaped that commercial syndrome? Williams heard Weber explaining, "So I have to give the screenwriter credit. He thinks of a way to exploit little Angela's best asset—in a picture that kicks Hitler in the groin. Two big plusses for the bankers right there. Hell, it's like double insurance. He comes in with a screenplay in which we see the whole story of Hitler through the eyes of a child. Angela is the niece of Eva Braun, get it? Can you see the new perspective? It was brilliant. To the little girl, Hitler is not a political monster at first—he's just a nice old uncle who bounces her on his lap and gives her toys. And then she gradually catches on that this nice uncle is evil, in fact the most evil man on earth. God, the concept was dynamite."

Williams, ever prosaic, asked, "Did Eva Braun have a niece?" a question which earned him a look of contempt from the producer.

"Who the hell cares? What a question!"

Williams smiled again. "I'm sorry. The concept does sound good. So what changed it?"

Weber told him how Hitler, at the political rallies, had an almost hypnotic effect. "It's unreal. I, a Jew, find myself cheering with the people. Hallelujah! The Saviour has arrived. Hitler is the greatest. Jesus!"

"But you must show the concentration camps and mass murders, too."

"We do. But somehow you don't care. It's like old news now, Auschwitz. But the *new* news is not only seeing Hitler at the rallies but like a human being, at home, treating a little kid nice, making love to a woman. I mean, just telling you makes me want to throw up. I was so dumb. I should have seen it would happen."

The projectionist, a slim bearded young man in jeans, waited for them in the villa. A screen had been set up in Hitler's living room. The producer went to a bar and made them some drinks. As he poured scotch for Williams he said, "Detective work ain't my business, but aren't you wasting your time watching our movie while the police are out looking for that Helga Neff and her buddies?"

"The German police can do a better job of tracking down Germans without me. They have the informants, the contacts, and the knowledge of the places to look."

Max Weber sank comfortably into the cushions of

Hitler's couch, sipping his drink. "Then why did you
come? If you're not going to help the police, why
didn't they send someone who would?" He turned on
Williams. "You think I'm funny. I see you laugh when
I talk. But this pickle I'm in is not funny. If those actors are killed and we have to scrub this film, it will
be the biggest financial tragedy in the history of Hollywood. Believe me. Marlon Brando in *Mutiny on the
Bounty* was peanuts compared to this. It might even
sink a few banks."

Williams said quietly, "The threat said the picture
was a scandal. I'm trying to find the kidnappers. I'm
still not one hundred percent certain it's Baader-
Meinhof, no matter whether Helga Neff is involved or
not. There's other evidence that more sophisticated
people are behind this."

He paused. "So I want to see why the picture is
thought by the kidnappers, whoever they are, to be a
'scandal.' That could give me a clue."

The producer shrugged and turned to the projectionist. "Put on some reels of those political rallies,
Jim. And then follow it with some of the human interest stuff where Hitler looks good." He turned to Williams. "Is that what you want? It's the most controversial stuff."

Williams nodded and the projectionist went to the
windows, closing the drapes, and suddenly they were
in a dark room, and white blinding frames with numbers were flapping through the projector: 4, 3, 2, and
never a 1, whatever happened to the 1's, Williams
thought, and then he stopped thinking because he was
staring into the face of Hitler, so shockingly real he
couldn't believe it, and the sound track was bellowing

his voice—and suddenly he was hundreds of yards above the crowds, looking down at masses of young German soldiers walled by white lights that reached into the clouds—and then side views of SS troops standing smartly behind the Fuehrer, close-ups of eager faces with a sense of wonder, roving shots down a white corridor catching rows of adoring young faces, and over all the thundering voice of Adolf Hitler, and the eyes of the people listening seemed to light more and more, to catch fire. And the camera exploded on a close-up of Hitler, arm shooting out in his famous wipe-it-away motion, then both fists from bent elbows pounding an invisible opponent, and his voice shrieking that Germany would rise and rise and rise and trample over everyone, *Deutschland Über Alles*, tumultuous applause, Wagnerian music rising to a crescendo, and that was not even it, that was not it at all, but the eyes of the people when Hitler finished, showing joy, adoration, happiness, exaltation—they loved the man, they loved the Fuehrer.

Williams found that he was coming out of a trance. He could hardly believe this wasn't a real documentary taken in the period forty years before. "They were extras?" he asked, the producer. "Just people off the street? How did they get those . . . expressions?"

The producer said, "Weller told me that the people needed no coaching whatsoever. He just put Riley up on that podium and started him speaking a real speech Hitler made—and he saw these extras looking like God had just come down from heaven. So he ordered second-unit crews to go around shooting close-ups while Riley was making his speech. And the expressions were real. Love, joy, ecstasy, for God's sake."

The projectionist meanwhile was threading new film and the lights went out and Williams was once again in Hitler's world. Berlin, 1938. Uncanny. Stock footage had been tinted and intermingled with new film so cleverly that Berlin came alive, and the open limousine on the streets with a uniformed, be-capped Hitler waving his arm to the shouting crowds was alive, too. Suddenly, the car stopped. A little boy holding flowers tore out of his mother's grasp, ran to the limousine, and held them up to the Fuehrer. The Fuehrer smiled, and the people went wild.

Reel 3. Hitler, looking smart, on a military platform, reviewing a parade of tanks and weaponry moving mightily up the Wilhelmstrasse, sometimes clamping his fists on his waist, at other times reacting jubilantly to something one of his Generals whispered in his ear—and then in reel 4, Hitler in this very villa at Berchtesgaden, striding around the room, talking to guests from Goering to Goebbels to Speer—

A crack of a shot! Then another! There was confusion on the balcony of the terrace and security men were shouting. Williams jumped up in the darkness and fought his way through unseen furniture to the door which opened on Hitler's terrace. Security guards were pointing toward a mountain peak slightly below them. "Some nut was shooting at this place, Mr. Williams," one of them said.

"Let's go find him," Williams said.

11

Phase one of the plan to execute Williams had been completed; Colonel von Werten knew the rest would follow flawlessly. Through his binoculars, from the protection of the underbrush, he had seen Williams come out on the balcony, with those stump-headed security guards pointing this way.

Franz had computed on a miniature calculator the length of time it would take the guards at Hitler's villa to reach this peak by car across the valley in between. He—and his driver—would be gone before the guards even approached the foot of the mountain.

But his own driver worried him. His behavior was an unexpected problem to Franz. Kurt Hurwirth was Franz's closest friend in the Ice House Movement— and the only one to whom he had confided his plan to kill Williams.

But almost as soon as they had reached the mountain peak before firing the shots, Hurwirth had been nervous. "I don't like it," he kept saying over and over as he saw Franz making his preparations on the little plateau across from Hitler's villa. "Look, let's forget this part of the operation," he said to Franz.

Franz told him to calm down. Every detail had been analyzed and computed. And it had worked. The shots had come as a surprise to the guards across the way. By the time the guards could traverse the small circuitous road through the valley between mountains Franz and Hurwirth would be back in Berchtesgaden having coffee.

And now as they sped down the mountainside in the jeep, all would have been well if Hurwirth had not panicked. A sharp curve loomed ahead, Hurwirth slowed, but not in time. Suddenly the jeep was skidding toward the precipice. Franz's hand shot out and turned the steering wheel in the direction of the skid, but there was no room on the narrow road to maneuver; the jeep careened toward the cliff edge and, as if in slow motion, Franz felt the rear wheels slide off the road into empty air and death, and he realized sickeningly that it was all over because of a stupid accident, and his last thought was not of his whole life, nor of the desperate plan that had brought him to this cliff and made everything so meaningless once again, but of the blue eyes of his young wife, saying goodbye to her husband, the only man she loved and trusted, kissing him with such sadness and compassion on the day of her own murder.

At the moment of his own death Franz wondered: did she have a premonition?

1978

Wilhelm Sartoff, the Director of Germany's version of the CIA, the BND, said, "That weapon you worked on. The nuclear mine detector."

"Yes."

"No one but Germany has it? It's still in R and D?"

"Right."

"The Americans arrested an Air Force officer who was giving secrets to the Soviets. The plans for our mine detector were among them."

Colonel von Werten couldn't believe it. Then a more awful truth dawned on him. "You suspect *me?*"

"No—but—"

"But what?"

"Your wife is the ex-wife of that U.S. Air Force officer, and they've been in communication. We intercepted the mail."

The words broke like a thundering wave across Franz's mind. He actually gripped the arms of his chair to keep himself steady. He never brought secret documents home, but Sharon did visit him in his office. Still—it was impossible.

Not to the BND Director. "We've suspected your wife for some time, Colonel. In fact, we've had her under surveillance, including mail cover."

His mind in a black impenetrable fog, Franz went home. His wife wasn't there. Neither was Elise, her daughter. He waited, pacing up and down the living room until she returned, laden with dry cleaning and laundry, the child grabbing at her skirt as she entered the door and laughed. "Franz, what brings you home in the middle of the day?"

"This," he said, brandishing a copy of a letter the BND had given him. "Read it."

She read a letter in which her ex-husband thanked her for the "information" he had received and said he would be in touch with her again. "Where did you get this?" she asked.

"The BND has you under a mail cover. This is a copy of a letter you received."

"A copy of nothing, I never got such a letter. Haven't spoken to that man in years. I didn't even know he went into the military after he left me."

"Is that his signature?"

"Y-yes."

The Colonel was thinking, my career wrecked because of my love for this woman, my life turned into torture because of anti-Semitism, and now anti-Semitism isn't enough—but espionage? "You're a Soviet agent," he said to her. "BND has no doubt. You may be arrested any day."

"Oh my God, Franz. Help me. It's a frame-up by my ex-husband. He's crazy and he hates me. He wanted to kill my baby when he found out she had Jewish blood."

He believed her because he loved her; he returned immediately to the BND Director and told him his wife had said it was a frame-up, and that she didn't even know where her husband was. Sartoff smiled wearily and called in an aide loaded with documents. "Your wife has been busy," he said. On top of the file were reports from BFV. His wife had written a newspaper article on BFV; Franz knew that. What he didn't know was that, for some reason of her own, she had asked to be shown a list of all Nazi party members on file in the country. And that wasn't all, said Sartoff. "The article on you and the German Army? Very interesting. She used your name to open doors and get access to some classified secrets. Never printed, of course. So why did she want them?"

But the Director went on. "That's just the fringe stuff, Franz. Here's a letter in her handwriting. You can verify it with her. It's to her ex-husband a month

ago, talking about his coming to Munich for 'new
business.' And a letter from him saying the trip will be
delayed until two weeks from now. Has your wife
mentioned that she plans to go to Munich at that
time?"

She had. An aunt was visiting from England, she
had said. And Franz didn't have to verify her handwriting; he knew it by heart, but he still held hope.
"Wait two weeks," he said. "See if the American Air
Force officer really comes to meet her. If he does, you
can move in and arrest them."

Two weeks later the BND Director called to inform
him that the U.S. Air Force officer was on his way to
Munich, and they had intercepted another letter from
him which made a date with Sharon at 12:30 in the
Osteria restaurant in Munich. And maybe it was the
use of the restaurant for their rendezvous, but it broke
Franz's defenses. For the first time he faced up to the
fact that he might have been had, that the KGB,
which had destroyed German Chancellor Willy Brandt
by planting an aide at his side, could also have used a
lovely young Jewish agent to steal secrets from a
naïve Colonel.

But then, on a rain-slick highway to Vienna, death
intervened before all could be known.

The shock of her death shattered von Werten completely; he could not function. He asked for leave
from the Army for a year. He took Sharon's little
daughter to her grandparents in England and then
went off by himself on a trip to he knew not where. It
was all a blur now. But he remembered once, in Jeru-
salem, bursting into tears when an old woman pressed
her cheek against the Wailing Wall and then, worst of

all, finding himself in the Osteria where he had fallen
in love with Sharon, and sweeping glasses off a table,
the proprietor rushing over, and later still blanking
out in a room—and the mental hospital where he
watched mutely, staring at the walls, ignoring the
nurses and attendants.

Three months later he was released from the hospital and went to fetch Sharon's child in England. Elise
was eight years old then, a pretty little dark-haired
girl with her mother's eyes. "I have something for you,
Daddy," she said.

It was a child's crayon-drawing on eight-by-eleven
paper. A man dressed as a colonel was throwing a
large pumpkin into the air, looking joyous, and a little
girl in a white dress was laughing. "What does it
mean?" the Colonel asked Sharon's daughter.

"Mommy always said if I ever felt sad to think
about someone throwing a pumpkin into the air. She
said that's the feeling you always gave her."

And the Colonel, in front of the child, had cried,
and then picked her up, and in some measure the little
girl had helped him regain his sanity, but not all.

For later he found out things he could not believe,
and they were all contained in a picture of Hitler that
was not smiling. Why wasn't he smiling? It drove
Franz crazy.

The jeep rested, rear wheels in space, the body of
the vehicle still on solid ground. Far below them was
the forest. Kurt moved—and the jeep teetered. Franz
said, "Wait, Kurt."

He looked down over the side. An extension of the
body above solid ground, one inch more than over the
edge, was all they would need. But who could calcu-

late one inch without a measuring device? If the jeep
was balancing on the exact middle, the lifting of their
weight as they attempted to climb out would so dis-
turb the balance that the jeep would start teetering
again in a fatal arc.

And when Kurt had merely shifted in his seat the
jeep had started yawing.

So they couldn't move, but they were not dead yet
if there was one inch in their favor. Franz said, "Re-
start the engine."

"What?"

"This is a special military jeep. Independent front-
wheel drive. If we have enough purchase on the
ground it might pull us forward. If not, it won't hurt
anything."

Kurt was in such a state of shock he could hardly
move or think. But he turned the ignition key, the engine roared, and he eased the shift into low gear and
pressed slowly on the accelerator. Pebbles and dust
spit from beneath the front wheels; a second later a
bump told them the rear wheels had lodged against
the cliff edge. "Harder! Press the accelerator to the
floor!" Franz said, and Kurt floored the accelerator.
With a lurch the jeep bounded high into the air as the
rear wheels crept up the cliff and then traveled
through empty space to land on the ground again.

"Into the woods," Franz said. "We'll abandon the
jeep."

Kurt turned off the ignition, then vaulted over the
side door and disappeared into the forest. Franz followed more slowly. The police would find the jeep
and would know where to start looking for the sniper.
But by the time they reached this spot Kurt would be
long gone.

Franz would not. He could never make it back to his room in the village in time to use the transmitter there. So he would stay nearby to execute the second part of his plan, the death of Williams using the portable transmitter.

He slipped into the woods, and began to do something few people other than Franz von Werten would have taken the time to execute in the circumstances.

He used a knife to nick his wrist. Blood flowed. He wiped it with a handkerchief, then threw the cloth on the ground. He cracked a twig above it. Then he moved through the woods, breaking limbs and underbrush, and splattering blood on the ground.

So much for bloodhounds, animal or human. He bandaged the wrist, then carefully moved at right angles away from the false trail, pushing, but not breaking any branches, his boots hardly disturbing the growth below.

He was climbing back toward the peak where the ambush for Williams was set.

One of the policemen in the first car to reach the abandoned jeep was Otto Schultz. He was a very special cop because he, alone among the security people racing to the scene, had a different reason for wanting to hunt down the killer.

The sniper must be Baader-Meinhof, and the private organization to which Schultz belonged, the Reborn Eagles, knew Baader-Meinhof was the enemy, no matter whether they used the name Ice House Movement or any other title.

Schultz and the other policemen stopped their car and four of them fanned out into the woods. Almost immediately one of them shouted, "Over here."

The policemen who went to his side saw him studying a bloody handkerchief on the ground. Ahead they observed broken underbrush, and started to follow the false trail.

Otto Schultz had an advantage. The Reborn Eagles' chief had alerted them all to be aware of the cunning of the enemy leader, as illustrated by the false beeper. If a handkerchief was left out in the open, Schultz thought, it could be designed to lead the cops in one direction while the sniper might actually go in the other.

Ten feet away, his heart almost stopped. There was a mark on the ground. He dropped to one knee and saw that bare dirt had been brushed over as if to cover an imprint. Schultz pulled out his gun and listened. No noise. No twigs cracking. Silently, he crept forward.

12

George Williams glanced across the valley, seeing the incredibly realistic re-creation of Hitler's villa perched on the peak high above them. Shots from this angle below could not possibly have struck anyone in the villa. So why the shots?

When they arrived at the peak he discovered Leuschner, the BFV Director, already there with two of his men.

The mountain road came to a dead end here. To their left, facing Hitler's Eagle's Nest, was a small plateau. A BFV agent was advancing toward the edge of the cliff, and Williams saw a rifle and something else that glittered on the ground. He called to the agent, "Don't touch anything."

Bent halfway over in the act of picking up the rifle, the agent froze. Leuschner, beside Williams on the road, was annoyed. "If you don't mind, Mr. Williams, I'll give the orders to my men."

"The rifle may be mined," Williams said, and this brought the full attention of the agents on him.

"Why do you say that?" Leuschner asked.

"Because they couldn't hit anything from this angle, so the whole attack was a fake—a ploy to bring us here."

Leuschner thought it over and decided on caution. "Okay. Karl, don't touch anything. But describe what's there."

Karl looked down at the rifle. "It's a World War Two Mauser rifle, Mr. Leuschner." He looked closer. "Serial number's been filed off."

"A World War Two Mauser?" Leuschner said. "An antique for a sniping mission?" He said to Williams, "You may be right—"

But Williams's attention was on the glittering object near the rifle. "What's that?" he asked Karl.

Karl carefully turned from the rifle and bent over the object. "It's a gold chain," he said. "There's a medallion on it. With a picture." He stood up and smiled at them. "Can you beat that? It's a locket with a picture of Hitler."

Williams was thinking of a boiler room mechanic in the ruins of Berlin. "Is Hitler smiling?" he asked.

"What?"

"Is Hitler smiling in the picture?"

The policeman leaned over, hands on his knees, then looked up at them. "No smile"—and just then a voice spoke from under the ground.

"This is your clue, Williams!"

"What the hell is that?" the sergeant said. Impulsively he reached toward the spot from which the sound was coming to uproot the hidden mike. Williams shouted to stop. "Let it go."

Too late. The detective had shoved the Hitler locket aside. A tiny wire broke, and a thundering explosion tore through the cliff. The body of the sergeant arched into the air, his arms flailing . . .

. . . and Williams was hurled off his feet against a boulder, where his head cracked sharply. . . .

Book V

TO THE CAVE

1

Franz von Werten crouched behind a tree and quietly replaced the tiny transmitter in its leather pack. He heard the policeman who had been searching the woods running away from him toward the scene of the explosion.

Now he should be safe. He was starting to move down the mountain when he heard a sound that froze him: the crackle of a bush. For some reason one policeman had not abandoned the pursuit, nor had he followed the false trail.

Franz screwed a silencer onto his pistol. The noise in the underbrush had stopped. The policeman, no doubt, was standing still, looking around. Franz had no time to delay. He stepped out from the protection of the oak tree, threw his gun on the ground, and said to the hidden policeman, "All right, I surrender."

Otto Schultz, the Reborn Eagle, emerged warily from the forest, his pistol outthrust. What he saw startled him. He had expected a crazy young Baader-Meinhof terrorist. Instead an Army Colonel in full uniform stood in front of him, smoking a cigarette, as if on a stroll.

"I'm too tired to scramble down a mountain with half of Germany's police force after me," said the Colonel. "We screwed the whole thing up."

Otto Schultz was trying to think. Not Baader-Meinhof but a Colonel? *The* Colonel. The one who, according to his superiors in the Reborn Eagles at the last cell meeting, had gone to England on the Reborn Eagle Fuehrer's trail? It must be—and if it was, then the Colonel's people, and not the Baader-Meinhof, were behind this kidnapping. And he, Otto Schultz, Reborn Eagles Party Member No. 011789, corporal in the reconstituted *Schutzstaffel* (SS), had the Colonel in his power. He could take him to his people; they would torture him until he told them the location of the kidnappers' hideout, and the Reborn Eagles would be heroes around the world.

But even as the thoughts whirled in his mind, Schultz knew he couldn't take the chance. His absence from the police patrol would be noticed—he couldn't afford any suspicious behavior that might alert the police to his connection with the Reborn Eagles. And especially not in *this* politically explosive case. The Reborn Eagles were innocent of any involvement in the kidnapping, and they were going to stay that way.

So the Colonel would die.

Schultz said, quietly, "You picked the wrong cop to bargain with, you shit," and his finger whitened on the trigger of his .38.

The stinging sensation in his throat surprised Schultz so much that he eased the pressure on the trigger. What was that? A fucking bee? Then his chest stung. What the hell was going on? He staggered back, firing wildly. Colonel von Werten calmly walked away. The poison in the microdarts from his cigarette was already doing its job.

2

George Williams had just regained consciousness when he heard the shots in the forest. He stood up, checking for broken bones. Blood from a cut on his forehead trickled into his eyes, and he held a handkerchief against it.

But even through the pain he was jubilant. He had done it. The kidnapping gang had come out into the open. And he had survived, and the shots meant the terrorists had not got clean away.

A mistake, Williams prayed. If only the terrorists left a clue in the heat of action—a policeman in a clearing in the woods was crouching over another policeman who lay with his arms outspread on the ground, blood seeping through his shirt.

Williams bent over and heard the crouching policeman ask, "Who did it?"

The man's lips opened painfully. Blood trickled from the corner of his mouth. "A Colonel . . . not Baader-Meinhof."

The interrogator was startled. "A Colonel? In the Army?"

But the face of the man fell to one side as if he were

unconscious. We need a doctor, Williams was thinking.
This policeman had actually seen the man who set the
ambush. He could describe him and that description
could lead to identification.

But no medical men were among the police who
had raced up the mountain to the sniper's nest. Williams knelt down beside the dying man. "What did the
Colonel look like?" he said, with no hope, but knowing he had to ask or forever punish himself with guilt
if it turned out that the man could have talked. But
the face remained in repose, the lips open, breath
gasping harshly.

The other cop had loosened the dying man's shirt.
Williams saw a gold chain under his collar. He tugged
and a locket broke loose from under the shirt. Williams opened it and saw a small oval photo of Adolf
Hitler, *smiling*.

The policeman was a Reborn Eagle. Williams did
something close to brutal. He slapped a dying man's
face. The eyes flickered open, and Williams held the
medallion in front of them.

"Is this the symbol of the Ice House Movement,
too?"

And for the first time he got a real reaction. The
eyes seemed angry. "No . . . Reborn Eagles innocent.
We touched . . . no one . . . not even Riley."

The reply puzzled Williams. Riley? Why was Jack
Riley special to anyone? He asked the dying policeman, but his question brought no reply. Williams saw
something shiny, a tiny metal sliver in the policeman's
throat, and leaned over the man. "You've been hit
with a poisoned dart. Only an antidote can save you.
Now talk and we may save your life."

"Poison?"

"Yes."

The policeman said, "Then hurry . . . get a doctor. Please."

"What did the Colonel look like?"

Otto Schultz saw a dark image which seemed to be moving away, then zooming in over and over. This was Williams's face, but Schultz saw no features, only shadows. My God, he was dying. Hadn't his cell leader told him, "The Colonel is our leading enemy, we want to deal with him in our own way, not the police." He shouldn't even have revealed that it was a Colonel who was here. He said, "Didn't . . . see . . . him . . . too . . . far away."

Williams was furious. The neo-Nazi policeman was protecting the man who had killed him. But still he desperately tried again. "He's here."

"Who?"

"The doctor. If you want to live, tell us everything you know about the Colonel, or we're walking away and leaving you to die."

Schultz's chest was on fire. His lungs burned so painfully that he couldn't breathe. What should he do? Life was more important than anything. He had to live. He said, "Riley knows . . . English . . . woman . . . who . . . is . . . dangerous. . . . So does . . . Colonel. . . . That's . . . all I . . . know."

Williams was stunned. An *English* woman? Could it be the one Jarvis was tracing in Berchtesgaden? Was she the key? The man began to die in front of Williams's eyes. Even if a doctor had arrived, he would have been too late to help. The Nazi shivered uncontrollably. Quickly Williams grasped his shoulders, and the other policeman helped him try to hold the convulsing man still, but they could not halt nor impede the tremors within him. Suddenly, with a great sigh, the man expired.

Leuschner had come down the mountain from the scene of the explosion. He walked over to the dead man, kicking small pebbles out of his path. Williams's mind was still on what the dying man had revealed. An English woman who was "dangerous" whom Riley knew. If only it turned out to be that girl in Berchtesgaden whom Riley was seeing, they would have a witness who actually knew—and could identify—the Colonel.

Leuschner looked down at the corpse with the medallion loose on its chest, "A Reborn Eagle? My God, right in the police. Those neo-Nazi bastards are everywhere!" He turned to Williams. "But in the picture in the medallion on the cliff, Hitler wasn't smiling. Why was that?"

"It was a phony. Someone hoped the locket would be blown to bits before anyone could see it wasn't the authentic picture of the Reborn Eagles." He paused. "If that's true, it gives the Nazis a clean bill of health on this case. Someone's trying to divert suspicion to them."

Williams walked painfully toward the road, only realizing now how much his head ached. The blood from the cut on his temple had stopped flowing. He would be all right. He would be better than that, if they found the Colonel in the forest below.

And yet—Williams's mind was on a beeper planted under a mattress in Berlin, on a medallion that was mined, on poisoned darts that killed the pursuing policeman. The Colonel was no ordinary man. He had acted like lightning to control the beeper emergency. He had concocted a clever ambush for Williams that would have diverted suspicion toward the innocent Reborn Eagles. And he had used ultrasophisticated weapons to kill, when necessary.

That Colonel would not be captured in a forest alive. He would escape, but somewhere in Berchtesgaden there was an English woman who might know him. And Williams would find her. He wouldn't quit.

3

3:15 P.M. Eight hours and forty-five minutes before the hanging.

Silence in the cave. Gail Edens couldn't figure it out. She was lying on her bunk, trying to look sick, but nothing had happened. What was the pill intended to do? She felt absolutely nothing.

Across from her, Jack Riley was playing a game with Morrison, throwing a pebble back and forth with one free hand. Riley missed and scratched a line on an impromptu scoreboard in the floor. Morrison said, "New game. If we get out of here alive, I'll own the rights to all of your income for the next ten years."

"No talking in there," said the guard through the little opening in the door.

"Oh, come on," Riley said.

Morrison said, "If you're going to kill us anyway, what threat can you use to stop us from talking? An earlier death? You're all sadists. What was your father—a guard at Auschwitz?"

Hans shifted his feet angrily. These arrogant Americans thought they could do anything. Now, under sentence of death, they were playing games and taunting him. Well, he would see how amused they were when the first neck snapped.

Riley said, "If you don't talk to us, we'll all shout. Right, fellows?"

"Right!" said Morrison. Then to Hans, "Do we talk?"

"And get your teeth smashed in," Hans said.

"Okay, people, let's yell a little," Riley said. And they started shouting in unison, Riley embellishing with choice profanity.

All of this time the only quiet hostage was Bernie Weller, the director. Since they had been thrust into the cave he had said hardly anything. It was as if an ancient curse had fallen on him. Try as they would, the others could not get a rise out of him. The all-powerful movie director was now a shrunken man, apparently convinced that he was doomed, and unable or unwilling to share the other prisoners' certitude that somehow, some way, they would get out of this crisis alive.

The door slammed open. Helga and another guard stood there. "I told them I'd smash their teeth if they talked," Hans said. "So they started to scream."

Helga looked at the prisoners with anger. "Him," she pointed to Weller. "He can talk!"

"Why should anyone—" Hans started to say, but Helga pulled him outside. "He'll build defeatism into them. Look at him and you see resignation and death. If they follow his lead, we'll have less trouble."

Hans went inside. Weller was already talking to the others.

"I suppose some of you are ashamed of me. You think I'm a coward."

The others said no, but Weller went on. "I lost my mother and father at Auschwitz. For decades I and my people have borne the burden of the question: Why did tens of thousands of Jewish prisoners allow a few Nazi guards to herd them to death? There is the implication of cowardice there, eh? Specific. Rarely spoken in polite company that includes Jews. But why indeed? I've asked myself that over and over again. Why did my people go so meekly to death?"

Hans was as interested as the others in what Weller had to say, but he kept his eyes fixed on the wall.

Weller continued. "We made a fundamental error, our fathers did. We failed to believe in bestiality. No one could imagine it would actually be done until the nozzles hissed and the cyanide gas filled the rooms and the children screamed. They couldn't believe any people would *do* such a thing."

He paused, then went on. "So I have given that problem much thought over the years. And now I, a Jew, find myself captured by Germans. And what is my reaction?"

No one spoke, and Weller said softly, "I believe. I believe in bestiality."

Silence filled the room. Hans felt nothing; the sins of his father's generation against the Jews were old news to him. He had only been interested in Weller's questions about the lack of Jewish resistance in the camps, and their possible cowardice. But Morrison said, "If you believe, then you must fight, not fall apart."

"I *am* fighting," Weller said. "I am fighting in my own way. You will see later." He paused, then said slowly, "This time the Jew will save the Gentiles."

And with that mysterious remark he closed his eyes as if to go to sleep, leaving Hans Ulbricht staring at him. What did he mean when he said he would save the Gentiles? The old Jew looked five-tenths dead, and nine-tenths frightened. Did he have a trick in mind, too? Even the old defeated one?

Jack Riley did a strange thing. He started clapping, a difficult feat with one hand cuffed. Morrison saw it and started clapping, too, but Gail still lay on her bunk, looking white and drawn.

Angela Tuck didn't clap. She had no faith in old Weller, much as she liked him. She felt he was only trying to draw attention to himself to buy time for the others. He was old. He would let them execute him first to gain at least one more day for the investigators to search.

That kind of thinking was baloney, Angela thought. The little child-actress with the lovely, mature face sat quietly, watching Gail. The pill Gail had swallowed should already be working. What was taking so long? Was it a placebo her father had given her? By now Gail should be writhing in agony.

Maybe when Helga Neff had broken the pill in the open air it had lost its potency. Angela shifted nervously. The pill was their very last hope. Otherwise they were dead, as she had sensed from the beginning. Last night in the hanging room she had overheard Helga talking to a guard outside. She couldn't hear every word but she had caught the drift, all right. Apparently one of the terrorists' demands was that the movie *The Secret Life of Hitler* be destroyed. If so, that clinched their fate more than ever. The only way to stop that multimillion-dollar film, if the demand were refused, was to kill all of the main actors.

Angela looked at the famous faces across from her. Irreplaceable and inimitable. This was a butcher's cave, and they were all doomed to those meat hooks that Angela had already experienced. But this time the rope would be around your throat.

So Angela reflected nervously as she waited for Gail Edens to show some reaction to the pill and realized with a dreadful sensation that something had gone wrong. The pill wasn't working. Their last hope to escape was gone.

Across the cave, Helga Neff ushered Ernst Hinkle into the hanging room. "The knot," she said. "It has to strangle. I've heard about men who hung there alive after they dropped."

Hinkle climbed on the platform and studied the knot on the first meat hook. He grasped the tough six-ply rope and slid the slipknot one inch along its bristly length. The knot worked smoothly. When the victim dropped through the trapdoor beneath him, the free fall would jerk the knot closed, breaking the windpipe and fracturing the vertebrae in the neck.

"Whoever feeds this noose, dies," Hinkle said.

4

3:30 P.M. Eight hours and thirty minutes before the hanging.

The local police headquarters in Berchtesgaden swarmed with more than a hundred BFV agents, anti-terrorist specialists, and regional police.

Leuschner had brought in a trailer with sophisticated electronic communication devices to assist the small village police station. And now Williams and he stood among teletype and video receivers watching the reports come in. No one had been found in the forest. The pursuers had been misled by false trails, one after the other. And the abandoned jeep could not be traced either. All the serial numbers on the engine and frame had been filed off.

Leuschner bitterly told his men to contact every military base in Europe for a missing jeep if they had to, no matter how far away. Then he faced Williams. "The bastard won't get out of Berchtesgaden on foot or any other way. We're not only combing every house in the village, but we have multiple roadblocks all along the roads. We'll get him, Mr. Williams."

But who was Leuschner kidding? Williams thought. Leuschner was pouring coffee from a Silex now with shaking hands. The strain was getting to him. Twice he had been foiled by the Colonel; the fake beeper and now a shoot-out on a mountain with a dozen policemen a few yards away. His job was precarious; his prestige was already at zero and falling. The BFV Director sipped his coffee. Williams had no time for sympathy for a German bureaucrat. He concentrated on what could save those hostages.

So far, the identity of Helga Neff had led nowhere. And as for the "English woman" mentioned by the dying Nazi, Jarvis had reported by telephone half an hour ago that they had found no trace of Riley's girl, Judy, in the village.

And that was it? The girl had vanished, too? End of clues? Williams stood up and poured a cup of coffee. One sugar. Touch of cream. No shaking hands. He was thinking. Something that he had requested in the fantastically hectic hours since he arrived in Germany. What? Oh, his interview with Jim Dilts, the father of the hostage Angela. He had asked Dilts to obtain a readout of all transcontinental telephone calls from any town in America except Hollywood in which the movie *The Secret Life of Hitler* was mentioned.

He called him at his office in Bonn, and Dilts exploded: "Where have you been? I have something for you, and I've been calling the number you gave me in Berchtesgaden for an hour."

"We were called away," Williams said. "I'm at a temporary police headquarters in Berchtesgaden now. What have you got?"

"One call. A transcript of a telephone call from a man in Birmingham, Alabama—Farley Smith—to Kurt Mueller in Berlin, recorded by the satellite."

Farley Smith. Williams knew his name from Justice Department files. The deputy commander of the American Nazi Party.

"Who's Kurt Mueller?" asked Williams.

"The leader of the Reborn Eagles in Germany. A lawyer. Brilliant. And a way with a speech. He goes from town to town and from campus to campus and he gets his cells formed. But this is what's important. The call was all about Gail Edens and Jack Riley."

Riley again. The one who the dying Nazi said was special? Maybe there might be a clue as to why he was special in this call.

A bell in the telex rang, as the machine started typing. Williams read the transcript of a telephone call made three days ago from the Deputy Commander of the American Nazi Party in Birmingham to the Reborn Eagles' leader in Berlin:

SMITH: Kurt, Farley Smith here. How's it going?

MUELLER: Nothing to report on your project. Gail Edens is guarded every minute. They have more guards around *The Secret Life of Hitler* than the Fuehrer himself had when he was alive.

SMITH: Well, hell, your people can handle that, can't they? We're not going to have a Commie playing Eva Braun. Hey, man, one cup of acid in her face and that's it.

MUELLER: Yes, well, you may get your wish in another way.

SMITH: What do you mean?

MUELLER: We've got spies in the Baader-Meinhof.

They're trying something themselves with the actors. I'm not sure myself what it is.

SMITH: (laughs.) Well, I'll be bull-screwed. What do they have in mind?

MUELLER: We're not sure yet. Anyway, the one who's got us really in a sweat over here isn't Gail Edens, but Jack Riley.

SMITH: Why?

MUELLER: He connected up with loudmouth. From England. She's sleeping with him.

SMITH: The English girl? You told me she was in Paris.

MUELLER: She was—until a month ago. Then she flits off to Berchtesgaden to see the great big movie—and no doubt give the actors some fun. God! She's like a plague. First the Colonel, now Riley. She just won't stop talking.

SMITH: I told you before, you shouldn't let her loose. Why are you guys so soft over there?

MUELLER: Well, it's too late now anyway. The damage has been done. The Colonel has already been to England to check out her story.

SMITH: Oh shit!

MUELLER: Don't panic. We don't know how much he found out in England. What proof could he get?

SMITH: Nothing, from what you told me. It had better be nothing.

MUELLER: All right. Don't call me again at this number.

SMITH: Why not?

MUELLER: If Baader-Meinhof does something to those actors, every telephone in this country will be tapped. Including mine.

SMITH: Oh, okay. How do you know it isn't tapped right now?

MUELLER: Our people sweep it every morning for routine stuff. But if the police get serious, they have sixteen hundred ways to tap a phone from satellites. So relax until I call you again.

SMITH: God. I hate to think of Gail Edens sleeping with Hitler, even in a movie. It's goddamned nauseating.

MUELLER: Yes, well, you just get on your knees every night and pray the movie is finished with or without Gail Edens. We have rallies planned all over the world; you wouldn't believe the responses we're getting. And that movie is going to bring in hundreds of thousands of new recruits. Maybe millions. It's no pipe dream—just the news of the movie has brought us kids from college campuses like we've never had before. They're sick of those lying, weak democrats that run the country.

SMITH: Okay. Heil Hitler!

MUELLER: Heil Hitler!

(end of transcript)

Williams read the transcript again. The English girl who had been dating Riley was the key witness, after all. She knew everything, including the reason the Colonel had flown to England.

So did the two Nazi leaders, both of whom had gone into hiding. Kurt Mueller had disappeared, after calling the Chancellor to say that the Reborn Eagles had absolutely nothing to do with the kidnapping, that the so-called Ice House Movement had already tried to pin the blame on them unfairly, and Mueller would drop out of sight for the duration to avoid further attempts at entrapment.

Farley Smith in America had also disappeared.

Which meant they just must find that English girl.

5

Judy Lipscomb didn't know what to do. She paced up and down the little Berchtesgaden room in jeans, her ponytail flying.

Jack Riley was in the hands of those Baader-Meinhof killers. Just two nights ago she had been making love to Jack right in this room. Now, within hours, he could be dead.

Of course, the rat deserved it. He hadn't even told her about the party last night—Judy at first was more angry about that party she missed than his kidnapping. But then she had read the threat and realized this was *serious*. Those Baader-Meinhof terrorists actually murdered people.

Judy had come right over to Jack's hideaway room in this inn. He had rented it just for their rendezvous, under the name John Barrymore, some dead movie star Jack adored. Normally he stayed in a hotel with the film crew, under guard. Judy felt that this little room belonged to Jack and her, sealed by the love that had taken place within its four walls

Jack. What was he doing? Was he handcuffed, stuffed in a closet? Were they torturing him?

She couldn't stand it. She had to get out of this village that had become so hateful to her. But if she went back to London she wouldn't be nearby if Jack needed her.

She looked into the mirror above a cheap maple bureau. My heavens, she looked awful. She needed a handkerchief, anything. She opened the top drawer and there was Jack's underwear. White jockey shorts. What the hell—she used a pair to dab around her eyes and then she pushed them back into the drawer, and stopped. There was a scrap of paper in the drawer.

She read it—and froze.

The son of a bitch. The bloody, coldhearted bastard. He had promised!

On the paper were words that read like a telegram— no doubt the draft of a real telegram. It read:

> MR. OLIVER PINCUS
> CMA AGENCY,
> BEVERLY HILLS, CALIFORNIA, USA
>   GREAT PROPERTY FOR NEXT FILM STOP ACTUAL HISTORY AND DYNAMITE FOR EXPLOITATION STOP LOCATED WOMAN NOBODY KNOWS WHO LOVED HITLER STOP FOR REAL STOP IN BED STOP SHE'S ALIVE STOP SUGGEST YOU FLY INSTANTER TO BERCHTESGADEN FOR CONFERENCE STOP AM SACRIFICING MY BODY EVERY NIGHT TO WOMAN'S NIECE SO THAT YOU CAN GET RICH

Judy threw the note back into the drawer and slammed it shut so hard the wood almost cracked. The *bastard*. Sacrificing his body was just the last twist of the knife. It was the rest of the telegram that really infuriated her. You just couldn't trust Americans. They were so greedy for dollars they would do anything.

Ever since she first read her aunt's diary a month ago—and learned the incredible truth—she had been entertaining a few people on the Continent with spicy details of her aunt's amour. It was too . . . precious not to tell anyone.

But the French and the Germans she had told were civilized. They might tell their friends, but they would never dream of rushing to the press. But this bloke— this American—was going even further: he intended to charge over to England with movie producers and agents and lawyers and descend on her aunt who didn't have any idea that Judy had read her diary.

God! Judy didn't spare herself in her anger. Why did she talk so much. Even Jack Riley had called her "motor mouth."

Fred Jarvis crossed the lobby of the Berchtesgaden Hotel, bumping into a matron with a flowered hat. The hat flipped off and a package she was carrying dropped with a crash. "My word," the woman said. "You Germans are blind."

Jarvis retrieved the hat and the package, and handed it to the American tourist with what he hoped was German disdain. The woman, without a thank-you, turned her back and went straight to the reservations desk. "My husband and I are leaving," she announced to the clerk. "We're not paying one hundred dollars a day to be part of a circus."

The clerk was pale, lean, and harassed. The kidnapping had caused unbelievable chaos in the hotel. Police all over the place, room searches, register checks, safe openings, and sirens outside periodically deafening him. And guests like Mrs. Lena Rhoades from Dayton, Ohio, U.S.A., were on his back all day. "I'm sorry, madame," he said. "But of course you understand "

"I understand, and I'm sorry for those American kids. You German brutes don't know how to raise your own children. But there's nothing I can do to save ours, and meanwhile—"

The clerk groaned. That tall, tweedy man with the pipe was gesturing to him from behind the nonstop-talking woman. What did he want now? He had let the man, who had showed him police credentials, pore over every name on the register an hour ago. Jarvis said to him, "May I use the telephone?"

The clerk shoved the phone across his desk, and Jarvis called Williams. "Good news and bad news. Across the street at the Lion's Head Inn we finally found a man who remembers a twenty-year-old English girl, blonde, beautiful, hair in a ponytail. Sounds like *her*."

But the bad news was that the man, a young ski instructor, had asked her for a date and got nowhere, not even her name. She had told him only that she was sharing a "free room" with a male friend already, and didn't "need any complications."

In the villa, Williams was thinking. The "free room" must be rented by Riley, but where? Not in his hotel—that wasn't allowed because of security. In fact, a star like Riley most likely would not use any hotel for a love tryst because he would be pestered in the lobby every minute.

"Forget the hotels," Williams said. "Recheck only the *pensions* and small inns. And look for crazy names that Riley might use."

"Crazy?"

"People who rent rooms for that purpose either use a common name like Smith—or a crazy name that strikes them as funny."

Jarvis groaned. His mind was already filled with pages of handwritten inky signatures. Now he would have to start again—and look at every signature even more closely to see if it was "crazy."

He went back across the lobby and told the news to Laura Doolittle, who was sipping a daiquiri she had conned a waiter into bringing her. She winked at Jarvis, and the FBI man experienced the same reaction he had when he first met her. Very competent. Very together. What they used to call "cool."

And sharp as a knife. When he told her of Williams's suggestion she said promptly, "Bavarian Inn, the little place three blocks from here on that crooked little street."

"How do you know?"

"I make movies. I jumped when I saw the name John Barrymore on the register, but we were looking for a woman at the time so I didn't say anything." She stood up. "That's it," she said. "That would be just the name Riley would use. He thinks he *is* John Barrymore."

Ten minutes later they were in an empty room, tearing through bureau drawers, and Jarvis handed Laura the note that Judy had found earlier. "Read this."

At that moment Judy Lipscomb was driving south in a Fiat. She had had enough of Germany forever. And American movie stars? They could stuff it.

She had made a mistake telling Riley, an American, greedy, exploitative type, about her aunt. But she might luck out. Riley might never get to talk.

In her anger, Judy felt she would not be unhappy if Riley were to die in the hideout. Ahead she saw a police roadblock, the third one she had encountered. My God, this was becoming too much. At the last roadblock, they said they were looking for a Colonel—and still every car was being painstakingly searched. But who would stop an innocent girl?

6

The little cobbled streets of Berchtesgaden were busy. Tourists mingled with police on the main avenues. Suddenly, on a side street, a bearded Colonel burst out of a door. Another Colonel with mustache and dark glasses followed with a pistol. "Stop that man," he shouted.

A policeman jumped—then started after the fleeing man just as two shots rang out and the Colonel on the run went down in a scrambling heap, groaning. The Colonel with the gun was on him in a minute, rolling him over. Blood trickled from the fallen man's cheek. The pursuing Colonel looked up at the policeman. "This is the man who tried to kill the American today."

The policeman saw that the army officer on the ground was near death. The first Colonel was trying to interrogate the dying man. "Why did you shoot at the American? Who is behind you?"

The man on the ground just groaned. Franz von Werten looked up at the Captain. "We have to see the American, George Williams, right away. Can you take us to him?"

"But if the man's dying—"

"The American has to talk to him while he still has a breath. Those are my orders."

"Who are you?"

Franz flashed a card, which identified him as a German Intelligence Colonel named Wilhelm Kohlesohn. "Have you got a police car?"

"Right over there."

"Help me get him in and we'll go right up to the villa."

The Captain helped Franz transfer the body into the police car. Ten minutes later they were through the last roadblock—and two minutes after that the police captain was unconscious and bound in the underbrush along the road. Kurt Hurwirth sat in the speeding car, patting his bloody cheek. "Nothing like a swan dive on concrete," he said.

Thirty miles away, at another safe house that had been prepared for just this emergency, they drove the car into a garage and closed the door. Inside the house they put on civilian clothes, and drove a Volkswagen toward Salzburg.

From there they would fly to the cave. It was all over now. The emergency had ended.

They had wasted hours in Berchtesgaden waiting for just the right moment, when one policeman was alone nearby. The lesson for the Colonel in the recent events was speed. No more tangential missions. The hostages must be executed on schedule—and nothing else mattered.

But even as he thought that, conditions in the cave were collapsing. The "uncontrollable" Baader-Meinhof terrorists were about to revolt.

7

6:10 P.M. Five hours and fifty minutes before the hanging.

Kurt Ollweg and Georg Freund stood tensely in front of Helga, who had removed the radio headset to listen to them. Kurt said angrily, "We've been duped, for God's sake. Don't you understand? The Colonel and his Army brass set up this whole thing to destroy us. The police may already be closing in."

But Helga said patiently, "The Colonel is an honorable man. If he hasn't called in, it only means he can't get to a secure phone right now. I assure you he'll be here before midnight, and then he and his men will take over the whole operation and you'll be free to run home, if that's what you want."

Her eyes—and her reputation for ruthlessness—cowed them briefly. "Now he hasn't phoned but in the meanwhile someone tried to kill the American investigator. The news was on the radio." She paused. "I'm sure he had to hide out for a while someplace."

The two guards were not satisfied. They withdrew, grumbling to one another that Helga was only prov-

TO THE EAGLES NEST229

ing at last that she was a *woman*. Maybe the Colonel
had a schlong six feet long, as Georg put it.

It was Georg who brooded the most. Sandy-haired,
squat, with the square, strong face and shoulders of a
footballer, he was the only one of the group who had
never attended a university and did not spring from
prosperous parents. All he shared with the others was
a passionate belief that the government had had it
and should be overthrown. But from the beginning he
had distrusted the Colonel, whom he had never met.
A Colonel in the Army? The very establishment that
shot Baader-Meinhof kids down like dogs whenever
they got a chance. Helga must be insane to take up
with an Army Colonel.

Still another hour passed and no call from the Colonel. My God, they had fallen into a trap, George
thought. A sudden hail of gunfire outside, a voice
shouting through a bullhorn, "Surrender!" and Georg
would be in prison for life and the hostages would go
free. He couldn't let that happen.

Georg's fingers caressed the butt of a Karpi machine gun, thinking the hostages were going to die anyway. According to the radio, both the German and
American governments had said "no way" in their response to the demands. So why should Baader-
Meinhof go on with this elaborate and risky venture,
with a Colonel who so mysteriously took off? He
heard a groan from inside the prisoners' cell.

Georg left his post to see what the commotion was
about. Hans had thrown open the prison door. Over
his shoulder, Georg saw Gail Edens flat on her back,
arms outspread, gagging and groaning. But that
wasn't the worst.

Even from here he could see red eruptions on her face and arms. A rash. She had the measles! For once the Tuck kid hadn't been lying. Now what should they do? One thing, obviously. Kill Gail Edens and bury her ten feet under.

He stood in the doorway listening as Helga and Hans discussed the situation. Then to his horror, he heard Helga say, "You and Georg take her down the mountain to the auxiliary cave." She was referring to a small cave fifty feet below which had been designed as a storehouse for ammunition in World War II. "Throw her in there with a thermos of water and a blanket, and seal the door." Helga went out of the door and brought back two World War II gas masks. "There are enough masks for all of us if we want to keep her here, but I don't know whether they filter out germs. And I don't feel like spending five days with a mask."

Five days. So she still believed the Colonel was coming, and his five-day plan of executions would work? A Colonel who had vanished on the very first day?

And that disappearance might signify a situation worse than they knew. It might mean the Colonel had been captured and interrogated, and, if so, the police were closing in right now.

In the prisoners' cell, Hans was unlocking Gail Edens's handcuffs when Georg suddenly pointed his machine gun toward them. "Helga, you're losing your mind completely. You're letting one of the hostages out of the cave. Suppose a police chopper spots us outside on the mountain. You're acting stupidly, Helga. But my life is on the line, too."

"Drop the gun, Georg," Hans said.

Angrily Georg stepped inside the prisoners' cell, slammed the door behind him, and locked it. Now only Helga and Hans were between him and the prisoners.

Georg said, "Get out of the way, Ulbricht."

Angela Tuck, who was listening, stiffened with surprise. Ulbricht had been the name of the Baader-Meinhof terrorist she had "murdered." And Hans did resemble him. Could he be his brother? He was in the same organization. It had to be him. Hans was standing right in front of Angela, holding his own gun on Georg. He said, "Listen to Helga, Georg. She's gotten us this far. I trust her."

"Well, I don't," Georg said, and suddenly swerved his gun so that it was pointing not at Gail, but at Hans. "Hans—get out of here, and Helga with you. I'm taking over this operation."

"No," Hans said, and moved his gun so swiftly that it frightened George, who dropped to one knee as if to avoid a shot, then pulled the trigger. Gunfire blasted, but Hans was not there. Angela had grabbed his wrist and jerked him sideways. The bullets plowed into the wall above Angela's head. Helga was on Georg like a cat, clubbing him behind the ear with a karate chop that felled him.

Hans had ended up on the floor beside Angela's bunk. He looked up at her. "Why did you save me?"

Angela said something that mystified him. "I owed it to you."

But when he pressed her for details she said nothing, and Helga was gesturing to him to help her carry Georg out of there.

Outside in the main cave Georg was placed on a chair and immediately fell forward on the desk, not even cushioning the blow with his arms. His face hit the metal hard. Hans moved Georg's head to the side so that his cheek rested on the desk top. He was thinking, Helga is a killing machine, all right. One karate chop and the man was out like this. Helga said, "She saved your life?"

"Yes, and she said she owed it to me. I don't know what she meant."

Helga Neff was thinking of the warning from the Colonel that Angela was dangerous, and remembering that this boy's brother had been lured to his death by an American girl working with the CIA.

"I think she's the American girl who helped kill your brother, Hans."

Hans straightened up. "That's just what she must have meant when she said she owed me one." But his mind was confused; he would be dead were it not for that same girl. "My God, Helga, I was lusting for that girl. You knew it—and told me to stop. And that isn't the worst part of it," he said. He looked toward the prisoners' cell and continued. "She has to be killed—or she'll haunt me all of my life."

"Why?"

"You've no emotion left, Helga. You buried it when your lover was killed. But I'm not a robot. I see flesh and blood and spirit, and that girl makes me vulnerable. I'm afraid of her."

"When she hangs she won't look so pretty," said Helga, brutally. The words were like ice water on Hans's face, and soon he was breathing normally and helping Georg come around, and even Georg was back to normal, too, as they waited for that telephone call from the missing Colonel. Where was he?

Ten minutes later the telephone rang. It was the

Colonel. All he said were four words: "Get target one ready."

The telephone clicked. Helga looked at Hans. Target one was Robert Morrison. He would be the first man to die. Morrison himself had decreed it when asked to select the first victim for the hooks.

Helga Neff was no motion-picture fan. She had never seen Robert Morrison act. Nevertheless, for the first time in her experience as a terrorist, she felt a twinge of pain about a necessary execution. There was something about Morrison that showed character, integrity, strength. He did not appear to be one of the typical Hollywood celebrities of lore, flashes-in-the-pan who were suddenly famous worldwide and milked their fame for every rotten cent. That was the way Helga saw the other actors. But Morrison she would hate to hang.

But then she had also hated to see her lover die. And both deaths were, Helga thought, a common thread whose color was bloodred in a corrupt system that Helga must change.

Helga glanced at her watch. 5:15 P.M. She willed the second hand to go around faster. She was becoming excited as the reality drew closer. Morrison's death would electrify the world. The German bureaucrats would be stunned; Americans would cry out in pain.

Book VI

THE DEATH OF
ROBERT MORRISON

1

It was all over, Williams thought. The Colonel had eluded the roadblocks, leaving an unconscious policeman whose information was that there were *two* Colonels, although one seemed in command. He also was working with a police artist but Williams had little hope there. He felt the Colonels must have used disguises because they hadn't killed the policeman, and these were men who didn't hesitate to murder when necessary.

And not only had the Colonels escaped, but the English girl had vanished, too. Still, Williams didn't give up. He studied Riley's note and the telephone transcript. Somewhere within them must be a clue to the identity of the Englishwoman who had slept with Hitler and who knew the Colonel. According to the telephone transcript the Colonel had gone to England to see the aunt. About what? Her romance with Hitler? Incredible, Williams thought. A love affair with Hitler forty years ago might actually have some bearing on this modern kidnapping? It made no sense. Who could care now?

Nevertheless, the Colonel had gone to see the

woman in England and then become involved in a
kidnapping. Why?

Williams's mind went back over the biographies of
Hitler he had read years ago. He had a fuzzy recollec-
tion that Hitler had enjoyed a romantic relationship
with a prominent English beauty in Berlin before the
war. But nothing sexual had been intimated in the his-
tories Williams had read. Perhaps the historians had
been wrong. He picked up the telephone.

"U.S. Archives in Washington, D.C. I want to speak
to John McNamara."

In Washington, Angry John McNamara was having
a good day. He had fired an employee, using the President's economy budget as an excuse, cursed a waiter
so loudly he had dropped a tray of glasses, and given
the finger to a sarcastic traffic cop. Angry John
smiled. He lifted a file of ancient documents and lov-
ingly extracted a yellowed sheet. Supposedly a letter
from Robert E. Lee to Ulysses S. Grant after the Civil
War. A forgery. Angry John would nail that woman
who brought this letter in—the telephone rang. "Mr.
McNamara."

The connection was thin, scratchy. "Who wants
him?" Angry John shouted.

"George Williams. I need some help."

Angry John thawed. He loved Williams. A smart-ass
all the way who thought he could mentally duel with
Angry John. Well, John had shown him in that nuclear
bomb case three years ago. Williams had insisted that
an ancient map be processed through the FBI lab,
even after Angry John had positively identified it as
authentic. "How you doing, big boy," he said. "I heard
you were in Europe trying to save some sinners."

Williams said, "We're looking into Hitler's love life. An Englishwoman, who's still alive, is supposed to have had an affair with him, There's a chance her first name is Alice."

"No soap, Williams," said Angry John, promptly. "No Alice in Hitler's life. Read the bios."

"I don't have time to read the bios," Williams said. "That's why I'm calling you."

"The English part figures," Angry John said. "One of Unity Mitford's crowd, no doubt."

"Unity Mitford?"

"In Berlin before the war, Unity Mitford was a blueblood playing kneesy with Hitler at dinner parties. Whether she got above the thighs we'll never know. But she ain't the one you're looking for because she's as dead as the Fuehrer himself."

Williams absorbed this information. "You think one of Unity Mitford's friends might have gone a little further with Hitler? To bed?"

Angry John wore white shirt sleeves with large blue rubber bands above the elbow. One of the bands was bothering him. He stuck a finger in it and pulled as he said, "Yes, sir. And I'm not surprised the biographers never heard of her."

"In forty years she never said a word?"

"Sure, Williams. If she was one of Mitford's friends, she's a lady. And if you're a lady who actually screwed Adolf Hitler because you were in love with him, would you admit it, even today?"

Williams said, "It just seems that somewhere sometime—"

A vein started to throb in Angry John's temple. Rage was building. "Jesus Holy Christ, Williams. Are you dumber than the last time I saw you, which I thought was the all-time low? Sure, she probably told a few friends she trusted, but they ain't gonna let that get out to any biographers, for God's sake. What is the lady doing now? Maybe she's the most sainted matron in the English countryside. Then the newspapers find out she once went down on Hitler—"

Williams stopped Angry John's sophisticated monologue by saying, "But if she was in Unity Mitford's crowd in Berlin, can you find her?"

"No problem," Angry John said. "Hold the phone."

Hold the phone? Angry John constantly surprised Williams who, a lawyer, automatically assumed hours of effort by legal researchers to find one vital fact. But John McNamara, beneath the bluff and vulgarity, was the brainiest archivist Williams had ever met. A photographic memory for names and details and, what was even more helpful, an instant knowledge of the correct reference work that contained the information he hadn't bothered to memorize.

"Setting up the microfilm, Williams," he said into the telephone. "Berlin *Zeitung* printed a piece in 1938 telling how England loved Hitler and naming some of the English types who were kissing his derrière at the time. Men and women both. My God, this stuff is awful. Listen to this, Williams."

"Headline May 14, 1938: 'Jews with Crooked Noses Hoard Gold.' And so forth. Yeah . . . okay . . . hold it." There was a silence and then, "Got it! 'The Fuehrer entertained the British Ambassador last night, a gala attended by all of the leaders of the ambassadorial world, as well as the highest members of the Third Reich. On the Fuehrer's right was Unity Mitford, looking charming in a green taffeta gown,' etcetera etcetera. We're into bullshit here, Williams; old

Streicher hired himself a society reporter for this piece. Okay, at last, the names of people who attended . . . Alice, Lady Portland. Ten women listed, one named Alice. I'll bet that's her."

Alice! Lady Alice Portland. Was she the "dangerous" woman in England? Williams said, "She must have married by now," but Angry John said, "So find yourself a Portland and trace her. There are plenty of Portlands around over there."

"How do you know that?"

"I know every noble name in England, Williams. Show me an àrchivist and I'll show you a man who spends half his time helping little old ladies trace genealogies back to English royalty. Sure they have to bend the truth a little now and then to bridge the gaps, but who will ever know?"

Williams said, "I want the most prominent in politics."

This surprised Angry John. "The most prominent in *politics* will be the hardest to approach. Why do you want him?"

"Because relatives of a politically prominent Portland would be the most likely to keep the Hitler connection secret."

"All right, hold it, Williams. We're into Blue Book stuff here. Okay, got it. Eric, Lord Portland, former MP, former Assistant Foreign Secretary, Knight of the Cross, etcetera. I have everything but his phone number. He lives in Knightsbridge, Sussex. Don't give him my regards."

"Why not?"

"If he's related to the lady in question he may have a nephew running around with a mustache."

Williams didn't know whether to shudder or smile.

JOSEPH DIMONA

He settled on the latter, thanked Angry John, and hung up. For a moment his hand rested on the telephone as he geared himself to speak to Lord Portland in England about a "dangerous" woman named Alice.

2

Lord Portland stood before a fireplace surmounted by elk's antlers. He swirled brandy in a large snifter, then put the glass down, picked up a billiard cue, and crisply struck the white ball. It rolled across green felt and collided cleanly with the yellow two-ball which scooted into the corner pocket. Lord Portland stood up in his den and smiled. The telephone rang.

A few seconds later there was a polite tap at the door. The butler said, "Telephone for you, my lord. A gentleman in Germany—"

"Germany?"

"He's an American investigator, sir, working on the kidnapping case of the American actors."

Lord Portland almost dropped his cue. What in the devil did he have to do with anything involving the kidnapping? He wouldn't let one of those Baader-Meinhof types in this house. He strode to a small eighteenth-century desk in a corner and picked up a telephone. "Portland here."

Williams said, "This is George Williams, sir. I'm in Germany investigating the kidnapping case, and I need to find a woman named Alice Portland—"

"Alice Portland?"

"That was her maiden name. Can you tell me where I can reach her?"

Maiden name? The lord relaxed. It was all coming clear. The American had mixed up names. "I'm afraid I know no one with such a maiden name, Mr. Williams."

Williams paused, then said, "A woman who was in Berlin in 1938 was named Lady Alice Portland. She's mentioned in the newspapers of the day. I thought you might be related to—"

"In Berlin in 1938? That's my *wife*!"

Silence, then: "Alice Portland is your wife? But you said—"

"Her *maiden* name was Alice Hodgkins. In 1938 she was married to me. We were in Berlin together because I was a junior coffee-carrier in the embassy there."

Williams said, "A press clipping in the Berlin *Zeitung* states that on May 18, 1938, Hitler gave a party for foreign ambassadors. Lady Portland attended. But you did not?"

"Attend that man's party? Not on your life, Mr. Williams. I hated that greasy little housepainter so much I couldn't stand the smell of Berlin, knowing he was in it. My wife liked those sorts of things, so she attended without me."

"Could I speak to Lady Portland, please?"

"Why dammit, no, man. This is . . . insufferable. Why are you asking about a party in Berlin in 1938? Are you investigating the Baader-Meinhof kidnapping or some ancient history?"

"I believe your wife may be able to give us some

information that may help us find the kidnappers, Lord Portland."

Lord Portland could not believe his ears. "My wife?"

Williams decided to take a chance. "Lord Portland, one of the hostages met Judy—"

"Judith Lipscomb? My niece?"

"Is she blonde, about twenty, and been in Berchtesgaden recently?"

"Yes, we had a postal card from her there three days ago."

Williams sighed. He knew now he had the right aunt. He said, "Please tell Lady Portland that Miss Lipscomb is involved in the kidnapping and may be in trouble unless I speak to the lady."

But his words were not being heard. Lord Portland's face was becoming red as it always did when Judith's latest peccadillo reverberated in his life. Since her parents had died in a plane crash in Jamaica, Judith had become his and Alice's responsibility. And what a handful she was. My word, it would be just like her to become entangled with those bloody Baader-Meinhof kids. For laughs, no doubt. He said to Williams, "I'll have Lady Portland contact you as soon as she comes home. I'm afraid I don't understand what a Berlin party in 1938 has to do with my niece's friends in Europe, but I'm sure you'll enlighten my wife."

"I will," Williams said, and hung up. Laura Doolittle was sitting sideways in an armchair, one shoe dangling from a shapely foot. Fred Jarvis was staring out of the great windows of Hitler's mountaintop villa, his back to the room. Williams picked up the telephone again, this time to call the German Secretary of Defense. The Secretary told him, "Not one Colonel is reported missing, Mr. Williams. But many of them are in the field on a training exercise, as I told you before."

"A most convenient exercise," Williams said.

"You really think they were both Colonels, and not just men disguised in uniforms?"

"I don't know for certain," Williams said. "But I've thought from the beginning that the military was involved in this crime."

"We'll do a head count," the Secretary said. "I'll stop the exercise right now. But it will take a full day or more to physically locate every Colonel in the German Army, Mr. Williams. In addition to the war games, there are Colonels on leave everywhere from Bermuda to St. Tropez."

Williams thanked him and hung up. He didn't have "a full day or more" to wait. According to the kidnappers' threat an American hostage would die in less than six hours. And a Colonel who used sophisticated weapons like poisoned darts and micromines would make sure that he would remain invisible. As would his associates.

3

7:00 P.M. Five hours before the hanging.

The great migration of the Ice House Movement members began. From a skyscraper in Frankfurt, a vice-president of a mining firm took an elevator down from the twenty-eighth floor, hailed a taxi, and went to a private airfield where a corporate aircraft was hangared. There he found three other men from the Movement waiting for him. One was an Air Force Major on leave, one the head of a small insurance company, the third a lawyer.

In Berlin, Bonn, Hamburg, and other great German cities, the scene was repeated. The aircraft took off at precise departure times in each city so that they would land in Salzburg at routine intervals.

Every year a World War II Veterans Reunion was held, sometimes in tropical resorts, other times in big cities. The choice this year was the beautiful Austrian city, Salzburg, a favorite of the Fuehrer's—although this was never stated in the brochures promoting the convention.

Austrian newspapers were calling it "the second coming," and there had been questions in the Austrian

Parliament, but in the end the tourism interests had carried the day. What harm could some beery, overage veterans do?

A band concert, banquets, and a uniformed ball had been scheduled as part of the festivities over the weekend. Salzburg would be crowded with veterans and their families, and the members of the Ice House Movement had decided to take advantage of the occasion to congregate in the area without special notice.

The members of the Ice House Movement met at one of three "safe houses" in Salzburg, a tall brick townhouse with gabled windows and a slanting tile roof. Some of the men were meeting each other for the first time. Talk was exchanged, occasionally nervous glances cast upward where Franz von Werten, who had conceived this project, was in an upstairs den on the scrambler phone to those young Baader-Meinhof guards in the cave.

Sitting in a leather chair in the den of Count Manstrasse, who had loaned Franz the house "for the duration," Franz told Helga his last call had been from a public telephone so he hadn't been able to talk at length. Helga sounded bitter. While he had been out of touch, she said, one of the guards had decided they were all being betrayed and had tried to kill the hostages right then.

"What happened?"

"He hit no one, but we had to knock him out. Now I have a surly guard, and a hostage with the measles, and if you don't get here in the next few minutes I'm going to fold this operation."

"Our men are here in Salzburg, Helga. It took longer than I estimated to get back to a secure scrambler phone. Just keep everyone in order for thirty more minutes and we'll be there to take over responsibility for the rest of the operation."

"All right. Everything is under control at this moment."

The Colonel's eyes were on a sculptured brass eagle, used by the owner of the house as a paperweight. "Oh, by the way, the case of measles. Which hostage is that?"

"Gail Edens. I had her taken into that little auxiliary supply cave and locked inside it all alone." She told the Colonel about Angela Tuck noticing the onset of the disease first. The Colonel's interest quickened.

"Did Angela Tuck offer her . . . medicine?"

Helga was surprised. "Yes. How did you know? A Theomycin pill. I thought it might be a trick so I broke open the pill, and it was a real one all right."

Colonel von Werten said quietly, trying to restrain his anger, "Bring Gail Edens back to the cell with the others immediately, Helga. You've been fooled. Angela Tuck gave her a blood pill."

"A what?"

"A pill that produces a rash, and convinces guards that someone is sick. And that auxiliary cave you placed Edens in is *not* escape-proof."

4

8:50 P.M. Three hours and ten minutes before the hanging.

On her last evening in the United States, George Williams had taken Gail to a movie in Georgetown. Afterwards they went not to one of the tonier places in Georgetown such as Clyde's, but to a little burger shop with a wonderful name: Christ's.

Gail had laughed when she saw the name in red on the window. "What do they serve? Christburgers?"

"Exactly." Williams smiled. "But they're so good even the Lord wouldn't complain about the exploitation."

The owner, Mr. Christ, turned out to be a fierce-mustached Greek with brawny bare shoulders in a T-shirt, laboring over charcoal in the kitchen. "Ah, Mr. Weelyums," he called out. "A live one with you. Oh my God. Magda. Magda!" His wife emerged from the back, looking worried. "What's the matter?" she asked.

"A movie star! In my place! Gail Edens!" He picked up a burger on a spatula, slammed it down on the griddle, then came around the partition to give Gail

TO THE EAGLES NEST

one of the greatest hugs she had ever received. "I a movie fan," he said. "Don't worry about my wife."

Gail saw a little Greek woman in a floured apron looking nervous, and laughed. "He's safe, Mrs. Christ." And Williams rescued her, and they had the two sinful-sounding burgers and crisp French fries and, on the house, a cup of coffee.

The owner never went to a telephone, only a few people left the restaurant while they were dining, and yet the news seemed to travel as if by jungle telegraph through Georgetown. Gail Edens, the famous actress, was in Christ's. By the time they finished, the little shop was bursting with people, some of whom thrust worn, gravy-stained menus before Gail's nose and asked her to autograph them.

She enjoyed it all. On one menu she wrote, "For Christ's sake, Gail Edens," and Williams laughed, and they escaped the crowd easily enough; no one followed, as they made their way to Williams's car. And Gail remembered how happy they had been that night, how charmed she had been in Williams's company; he really could be fun—Peggy DuPont must have drowned him with social stuff that wasn't Williams's style. But in Georgetown he was not only lively but comfortable to be with, ready to laugh and enjoy himself, and that night, her last in the U.S.A. before this nightmare began, they had made love, and Williams had joined her in a cigarette afterward, saying, "What a life you lead. How do you do it?"

"You mean the attention. The people staring at you and asking for your autograph."

"Right. You step outside, and that's it. You're the target." And that unfortunate word had brought an end to that line of conversation. Or almost. At the airport the next day Williams had alluded to the hate letters she had received. "We think it's the Nazis." he said.

Gail had looked at him as if he had gone mad. "The Nazis? How many of them *are* there? I thought there were just a few of those kooks in America!"

Williams said, "There are Nazis in every state. And the party is growing. It has to be them."

"Why?"

Because the letter campaign was organized, and there are only two large right-wing organizations, the Ku Klux Klan and the Nazi party. The Klan isn't in every state, but the Nazi party is."

"What about the John Birch Society?"

"Not the same. Birchers are mostly comfortable, rich, and old. They have no history of threats or violence. Of course, we're checking them, too."

And so Gail had kissed Williams goodbye and flown to Europe, and two months later—in a grotesque twist of fate—she was in a cave, condemned to death by left-wing Baader-Meinhof youngsters who, if they had lived in America, would be her biggest fans, and what she had to do was survive, somehow, some way, she *had* to survive. She must see Williams again, now that she had found him.

She groped along a wall in the dark. It was absolutely pitch black in this little stifling cave fifty yards down the mountain from the command post. The guards, upset by the shooting, had unceremoniously dumped her inside the cave, thrown in a blanket and a thermos, then locked the door. Outside the metal door that sealed her in was a second door made of stone, part of the mountain, camouflaged by underbrush, engineered to slide aside at the touch of a hidden button outside.

She was thinking, trying to put her head in order. Angela's idea had worked—the kid was like an Army General, as far as Gail was concerned—so cunning she got away with tricks even when every guard in the place knew she was up to something. That red rash had popped out on Gail's face and arms and Gail had almost jumped when she saw it, thinking Angela had given her a *real* case of measles just to further her plan, whatever that was. But then Gail had remembered she was immune; she had measles when she was twelve—so it must be a trick, and she had gone into her act, flopping back on the floor and flinging her arms out, one cuffed to the wall, the other sprawled lifelessly. Greta Garbo in *Camille* had been no more realistic.

But now she must try to think as Angela would. Angela knew measles would force them to separate Gail from the other prisoners. It would free Gail from the guarded cave. Furthermore, no guards would stay near her at all now, if they could help it. That was the beauty of the ruse. But what good was it, with Gail just scrabbling around in the dark in a sealed cave? How would that help them all escape a suicidal situation?

Her hand touched metal. What was that? A grille. Now both hands were on it, about five feet high. She pressed closer to it and felt a thin draft of air. An air vent? That might lead to the surface?

She tugged at the grille. It didn't move. No doubt it was rusted into place. She picked up the thermos bottle and banged it against the metal as hard as she

could, then put down the bottle, gripped the grille
with both hands, and pulled with all her strength.
Nothing. She banged the bottle on it again, swearing
to herself, cursing the producer who had got her here,
anything to divert her mind from the pain in her
shoulders and her panic in a pitch-dark cave with killers who used machine guns. Then she placed her bottle on the floor again, gripped the grille—and this time
it came loose so fast she tumbled back on the stone
floor, hurting her right shoulder.

She was bruised but ecstatic. She might get free!
She hoisted herself toward the opening, which was
eighteen inches wide; she could make it through that.
Her muscles were performing miracles with the inspi-
ration of terror; she hauled herself into the hole. Then,
flat on her stomach in the dark, she started to inch
forward through the small tube.

Five minutes later she saw it—the grille opening on
freedom. She pushed herself toward it, the sharp stone
floor of the tunnel cutting through her flimsy dress—
when suddenly whiteness burned her eyes. She threw
her arm over them, her heart beating fast, as a light
moved past. A guard had come down the path beside
the cave using a flashlight to find his way. In a minute he would enter the cave, notice the discarded
grille, and realize where Gail was. But instead the
light came on again from outside and then, to her horror, a face stared at her, inches away. She saw the cold
blue eyes of the guard, Ernst Hinkle, who had always
looked at her with such hate inside the cell. Of all the
guards to find her trying to escape! He said, "It's all
over, bitch. Go back down to the cave."

A few minutes later she was lowering herself into

the cave, when powerful arms wrapped around her thighs. A bristly cheek scratched her right buttock, bare ever since Helga Neff had ripped off Gail's panties. Now feeling his cheek on her, Gail Edens froze. Was it really hatred that she had seen in those eyes? Or was it lust? If it was lust, she might have a chance.

Ernst Hinkle lowered her to the floor. "We've only got a few minutes. But if you're good to me, I'll protect you in there." His flashlight was on the floor; the muscular guard was unbuttoning the fly of his jeans, and Gail was panicky. "Outside," she said. "I can't stand it in here any more."

Hinkle led her out of the cave and into the underbrush, and she was in the open at last. She needed only a knife, and she would be away, and Williams would think she was a hero, and the publicity would up her price to two million dollars a picture, and she would grandly refuse, saying she only wanted to devote her full time from now on to political and social causes, and oh God she was flat on her back, legs up, rough hands pushing her knees back against her chest and a nameless thug about to thrust himself into her, eyes wild, and like lightning she rolled away, and the man went sprawling, and she was up but too late.

Hinkle grabbed the hem of her dress and part of it ripped away, but her momentum stopped and he clutched her arm in an iron grip and leaped up so furious his eyes were actually rolling as if he were demented, holding her arm and saying, "I'll give you one more chance, whore." But Gail broke away and started running, and when Hinkle recaptured her he simply took her up to the main cave. But his angry words—

whispered breathlessly into her ear as he led her with one arm painfully bent behind her back—chilled her with fear and revulsion: "I guarantee that before you die you'll have my cock in your mouth."

5

9:30 P.M. Two and one-half hours before the hanging.

Judy Lipscomb was found by the German police at a roadblock and brought to Williams in the villa, kicking and launching a boot to one policeman's groin.

She was furious when she was shown into a room at the villa because the police had cuffed her hands behind her back. Williams said, "Take off her cuffs, please. I need her cooperation and I won't get it that way."

Judy Lipscomb liked Williams immediately. He was cool, not like those bloody German cops who mauled you the first minute.

But Williams's cool facade belied his inner tension. It was less than two and a half hours until the first killing, and this pretty little blonde with the vacant blue eyes could hold the key that would open the whole case, expose the identity of the Colonel and his associates, and perhaps even this motive. But once again he was stymied. Judy said she didn't know any German Colonels, although she might have "met some at dinner parties who were in civilian clothes."

Suppose her aunt replied in the same evasive way,

Williams was thinking. They would be lost. He threw
Jack Riley's note across the desk and watched Judy
bite her lower lip in dismay when she recognized it.
Then Williams told her about the dying Nazi's mention of an Englishwoman who had dangerous knowledge. "I think that woman must be your aunt, Judy.
And if it is, you can help save five innocent lives by
persuading her to talk to us."

"But . . . but what's the connection?" Judy said,
her lips trembling. "What in the world does my aunt's
affair in Berlin in 1938 have to do with what's happening now?"

"We don't know," Williams said. "But I think if we
find out we'll smash the whole case wide open in a
minute. Now you have to help us."

Judy paused, near tears. "But this will just . . .
destroy my aunt. She doesn't even know I read her
diary. Do you . . . have to speak to my aunt . . .
about that?"

"We don't have time to be . . . delicate, Judy." He
paused. "Besides, you already told Riley. The secret is
out. Did you tell anyone other than him?"

Judy wiped her eyes. "Yes . . . I'm afraid so. I talk
too much. Two months ago when I was packing to
come to Europe I found my aunt's old diary, written
when she was young. I don't think anyone but I had
ever seen it." She stopped "It was all in there. Even
. . . intimate details . . . Hitler naked . . . how he
looked, a trifle knock-kneed, hairy chest, dimpled
belly button, swarthy skin, pretty Z-shaped war scar
on his shoulder that he asked her to kiss . . . really
disgusting in retrospect—but she was so young then—
and anyway, it was all too juicy for me to hold to myself. I could cut out my tongue. . . ."

The telephone rang. Now or never, Williams thought. He looked at the telephone. On its other end could be a woman whose words might save Gail. Uncharacteristically nervous, he picked up the phone and an aristocratic voice asked with haughty irritation if this was a Mr. George Williams, please. When Williams said yes, Lady Portland said, "I hear my niece is in some sort of trouble. Please inform her that we'll do nothing to assist her this time. Eric and I are quite bored with bailing her out of every escapade she gets into in Europe."

"It's you, Lady Portland, who are important to us," Williams said. "Judy is all right."

"But you told my husband she was in trouble."

"She was, because she ran away from the police. But she's not running any more."

"Why was she running from anyone?"

"Partly to protect you, Lady Portland."

There it was, thought Williams. Silence in London. Williams could imagine Lady Portland putting together the earlier news from her husband that an investigator wanted to know about a 1938 Berlin dinner party with Hitler, and the new information that her niece was "protecting" her. But did her niece know? the lady must be thinking. How could she? Lady Portland said, "Mr. Williams, may I call you back in ten minutes?" Williams said yes and hung up. Judy said, "She's going to her own room to call you from there. I'm surprised."

"Why?"

"You don't know my aunt. She could have just hung up, you know. 'None of your business' sort of thing. Especially since you had told her husband it referred to Berlin in the old days."

"But you think she is going to help us?"

There was a tall thin vase in a corner of the room that contained six red roses. Judy was calming down. She pulled one of the roses out of the vase and touched it softly to her chin. "Auntie must be worried about something, Mr. Williams. My word, that diary must be important to somebody. Even today."

6

She glided over muted-colored Persian rugs, her eyes
taking in those Belgian tapestries she adored—how
kind Eric was to spend so much money on her slight-
est whim; he was always so generous, so supportive,
so loving, and now—since Colonel von Werten had visited her last month—Lady Portland had known absolute catastrophe was coming.

The Colonel, whose father she had so respected,
had been most polite at first, sitting in the erect military tradition, sipping tea from Wedgwood china on
her terrace under a perfect English sun. He had first
told her that he was in England on vacation and had
just stopped by to thank her again for her efforts, together with Ulrich Kandrof's, to save his father's life
so long ago.

Apparently he had found out about Ulrich Kandrof's role in that effort only recently. He asked her
how she had met Ulrich in those Berlin days, and why
she had chosen him to act as an intermediary between
herself and Hitler when General von Werten was in
trouble in 1944.

She had told him how she met the young university student Kandrof at an opening night of a university production of *King Lear*. Hitler had attended also; it was quite a gala occasion—and Kandrof had been the hit of the evening in his lead role as the King, even gaining the approval of Herr Hitler himself. In fact, Hitler, in a moment of expansiveness toward the youths around him, had told Kandrof if he ever needed a favor to remember his Fuehrer. In Berlin in 1938 the guests had been impressed by that statement.

Lady Portland had become friendly with Ulrich and so, years later, when the war between England and Germany was raging and she couldn't approach Hitler directly when General von Werten, her friend and Eric's in those Berlin days, was in such trouble, she had remembered Ulrich Kandrof, who was now a soldier, and reached him. He was in East Prussia somewhere, at a place called Wolfschanze. "I asked him, as a favor to me, to ask Hitler for the favor *he* had promised. Wouldn't have done it if I knew the poor chap was going into politics some day. He wasn't even a member of the Nazi party; he was just a child who had nothing at all to do with Hitler's gang, and because of me he now has a meeting with Hitler on his record."

The Colonel said, "You know, my family's never even known what he did."

"Why not?"

"His meeting with Hitler isn't in any historical files. And Kandrof's never mentioned it to the press."

"Well, I think he's being overly cautious. What he did on that occasion was heroic. And anyway, the German people don't hold that sort of ancient history against politicians anymore, do they? You even elected a Chancellor a few years ago who had been a

registered member of the Nazi party back then. Ulrich was nothing, just a nonpolitical soldier when I
asked him to do that favor."

Later she had added, "I was quite fond of him in
his student days. I was only twenty, myself, then.
Used to have tea with him at the Adlon Hotel—he was
quite amusing."

And so the conversation with the Colonel had
passed pleasantly, no doubt a smoke screen for the
Colonel because he suddenly said words which struck
her to her heart, and she knew that was the real reason he had come to see her.

"You were a friend of Unity Mitford in those Berlin
days, right?"

"Of course."

"A friend of mine is researching a book about Hitler's romance with Unity. I wondered . . . did you
keep a diary back then?"

Lady Portland had colored. She didn't know what
to say, nor even what to believe. Only her few closest
and most trusted friends knew of the existence of the
diary—not even her husband had ever seen it. Now
this young German Colonel with the fair skin and
friendly eyes was implying that he *knew* she had a
diary. Lady Portland was no fool.

She said, "I do have . . . some notes of those days,
Colonel von Werten, but I'm afraid I resent your asking about them."

"Resent? Why? I'm sorry if I offended you, Lady
Portland. . . ."

"The notes were written when I was a young girl.
Its details are personal. Even embarrassing now, con-
sidering my husband's position. You must remember
that Unity and all of her friends, including me, were

quite taken at first by the young and dynamic Hitler. We couldn't know then what the future would bring. Poor Unity put a bullet in her brain when Germany and England declared war."

Even as she spoke she was seeing not a pleasant Colonel in front of her but a slim, blonde, elegant beauty who took Hitler's heart by storm. Unity Mitford conquered Hitler, all right, no matter how the historians and biographers covered up their affair.

Unity was so young, so lovely, yet so tart-tongued; Hitler roared at her quips about his pompous stooges, and laughed even harder at her jokes against the even more stuffy English elite. And Unity could laugh at herself, too.

My God, Unity had been adorable. Brain-twisted, yes. Even Lady Portland, equally smitten by the Fuehrer, never swallowed the Nazi idea as Unity did.

And then, on one terrible day, Eva Braun had caught Hitler embracing Unity on a chaise longue on Frau Wagner's terrace, and that simple peasant girl Eva went out of her mind—one would not have thought she had intelligence or spunk enough to do it—and Unity thought it wise to leave for England for a while, and the next day Adolf Hitler said he wanted to see Lady Portland.

The glory of those days! Hitler knew so much about drama; no politician in the world had ever equaled him since.

The ride to Berchtesgaden was heavenly. Pure theater all the way. A limousine with a transcendently handsome young chauffeur picked her up at her hotel and drove her through glorious mountains until they reached the most lofty of all in the Obersalzburg, Hitler's mountain. The limousine moved slowly up a winding road along which were smartly uniformed SS troops at roadblocks, and when the car passed the last gate she saw Goering's and Bormann's chateaus nestled in trees. And then higher and higher, until they reached a cave, guarded by a squadron of armed troops, which was a parking garage carved out of the inside of the mountain. When the limousine came to a halt inside, she debarked, went to a private elevator paneled in mahogany, pushed a button, and glided up as if in a dream to the highest point, and when the door opened she found herself in a spectacular living room on the top of the world with the most feared man on earth, the Fuehrer, waiting to serve her biscuits and tea against a heroic backdrop of blue ice-topped mountains that caught her breath. . . .

In front of the window was a twenty-foot-long table on which Hitler sometimes spread war maps. In the corner a raised area led to a charming fireplace, with armchairs placed around a glass-topped round table. This was a favorite spot for Hitler, she knew. Here he listened to operettas and snatches of Wagner, surrounded by paintings which reflected his various tastes. The might of empire: a lovely landscape of Rome by Panini; architecture: a portrait of King Henry, "the founder of cities," by Eduard Steinle; women: a Bordone portrait of a lady with a naughtily voluptuous bosom, and a priceless Titian of a reclining nude.

That day Hitler was nervous. Dressed in a brown coat and black trousers, he was scheduled to meet with his Generals in the afternoon.

"Alice," he said, "I would ask your help."

"Anything, Herr Hitler."

"I must not see Unity again. Eva insists, and I cannot allow any of my time and energy to be dissipated on quarrels between women."

"But Unity has gone home."

"She'll return. I would like you to . . . intervene, if you will. Be . . . diplomatic. Tell her I think highly of her, but I need someone like Eva who is just a toy, a pastime, not an intelligent woman who might question or even divert me. I think if you put it that way you might have success."

Hitler was right. She did put it to Unity that way, and Unity understood. Unity returned to Germany that fall, but thereafter her relationship with Hitler was no longer intimate.

In that time Lady Portland had taken her place. More than once she literally swooned in Hitler's arms; the memory of the experience never left her. Hitler was too dynamic for Eva Braun. He quickly tired of her coy, kittenish manner; he craved real women and yet he feared them, too, as Unity had discovered.

But Alice was married. Their affair was sex alone. She never bothered with Hitler's politics, until she learned, too late, what the political Hitler was doing. . . .

When war broke out, Alice did not kill herself. Instead she returned to England feeling a cloud lifting from her mind as the dynamism of Hitler's personality no longer hypnotized her.

And now, after all those years, like a genie from the past came the General's son, not with gratitude but with unpleasant references to a diary, and she had known there would be trouble. After the Colonel left she feared it with all her heart, and now an American investigator was asking about those Berlin days, and what else could it be? The secret was out. She and her husband would be disgraced. . . .

7

"Mr. Williams."

"Yes."

"This is Lady Portland. I suppose . . . I'm ready to answer your questions. But if it's about Berlin in the late thirties—"

"Lady Portland, I'm only interested in the present." Williams took a deep breath before asking, *"Do you know a German Colonel?"*

"Colonel von Werten, do you mean?"

The name! He had it! Williams clung to the phone almost numb with relief. "We don't know his name but we have reason to believe he might know you."

"Why I saw Franz just a few months ago. You see, I knew his father, and he stopped by on a friendly visit."

Even as she spoke she thought, I won't tell Williams the real purpose of the Colonel's visit—to find out more about her love affair with Hitler.

"I helped his father during the war," she said. "It didn't help. The General died on a meat hook."

A meat hook? Williams's memory was jogging back to the past even as Lady Portland said, "General von

Werten was one of the brave officers who tried to assassinate Hitler on July twentieth, 1944. They failed, and Hitler hung them on meat hooks and photographed them in agony, don't you see."

"And Colonel Franz von Werten is his son?"

"Yes. Is he connected to the kidnapping somehow? I can't believe it. He's too much of a . . . gentleman."

"If it's the same Colonel, he tried to kill me this afternoon, Lady Portland." But even as he spoke Williams was thinking. The son of a General who was hung on a meat hook? In an ice house? The kidnappers called themselves the Ice House Movement. Was this the genesis of the Movement, a group connected to the assassination of Hitler? But that had been in 1944—decades and decades ago.

Lady Portland was saying, "I used an intermediary to try to save General von Werten's life. My husband and I knew the General personally. He was a very civilized man. And when that terrible event happened on July twentieth, I couldn't intercede directly with Hitler, whom I knew. It would have been terribly awkward for my husband at that time, if it got out. So I needed an intermediary, and I thought of Ulrich Kandrof."

"Who?"

"Ulrich Kandrof. He was the man who brought my message to Hitler in 1944 in an attempt to save the General's life."

Williams's mind jolted again, this time almost dizzyingly. From the beginning of this case they had concentrated on Ulrich Kandrof's possible Communist leanings, including his trip to Moscow. His files had shown a man who didn't belong to the Nazi party, and whose military career was spent as a humble nonpolitical soldier in Poland and Russia. Now, if Lady Portland was right, he had been so close to Hitler in 1944 that he had acted as a personal intermediary to Hitler for a message. Williams said, "Are you certain? His record shows he was only a foot soldier in Russia at that time."

"Well, he was."

Williams's head was spinning. "He *was* a soldier in Russia?"

"East Prussia, as I remember. A place called Wolfschanze. But the troops were *fighting* Russians." She paused. "Oh dear, I'm afraid I'm giving you the wrong idea. You're thinking that Ulrich was a Nazi and a friend of Hitler's or something, is that right, Mr. Williams?"

"Right."

"Nothing could be further from the truth. The Ulrich Kandrof I knew was a devout anti-Nazi. Hated Hitler's politics all the way. But he had a path to Hitler no one else had for an intermediary."

"What was that?"

Lady Portland told how she had met Kandrof when Munich students put on a private performance of *King Lear* for Hitler and his guests, and how she used him, Ulrich, years later as an intermediary with the feared Hitler. "A brave man, Ulrich. Can you imagine his courage pleading for mercy for one of Hitler's assassins?"

But Williams was only wondering why Kandrof had never mentioned the incident. Was it because it might be political death to show any kind of a relationship with Hitler, even if only as a drama student the Fuehrer admired? Lady Portland had one answer. "A gentleman, Ulrich. I asked him never to reveal my role because it would be . . . embarrassing. People might start asking questions about my own relationship with Hitler."

Williams said, "Still, he could have left your name out of it, and just put in the record his attempt to help one of the July twentieth heroes."

But Lady Portland then said something Williams had heard over and over again since he came to Europe nine hours ago. "You don't understand Germany, Mr. Williams. To a great segment of the German people, those July twentieth officers were traitors, not heroes. And many others feel that revolt is one thing, but an assassination of the leader when the country was at war was treachery. Ulrich took his own life in his hands, I now know. When he saw Hitler at the Wolfschanze, Hitler's command headquarters in East Prussia, Ulrich was called into Hitler's presence, made his pitch, got nowhere, then was sent right back to oblivion—and I'm sure he's thought it politically wise to keep my errand quiet all these years. It was a little incident in which nothing concrete was gained anyway. The General was hanged despite my plea.

There was a pause, then she added, "They came so close."

"Who?"

"The July twentieth conspirators. We found out later that the bomb almost killed Hitler and while he was unconscious von Werten's people took over in Paris—and would have taken over in Berlin, too—if not for Goebbels. He was down to his last SS Major—the officer in charge of the guard battalion—all the others had gone over to the anti-Hitler forces—when Goebbels managed to get a telephone call through to Hitler himself, and convinced that last Major that Hitler was alive, not dead. That was the end for von Werten and all of those brave men."

Williams knew that history but hearing it from the lips of a woman who had known Hitler made it more poignant. But he couldn't spend more time on the past. He asked, "Do you know if Colonel Franz von Werten is still on active duty?"

"He was in uniform. I'm sure it will take just minutes to find him." She stopped and then said, "And Mr. Williams, as to my own . . . involvement with Hitler . . . I turned against him when I discovered what a rotten man he was. I do have your assurance that you'll be . . . discreet."

"Perfect assurance," Williams said; then he added, "You may have saved five lives, Lady Portland."

But sixty seconds after he hung up he wasn't so sure. Colonel Franz von Werten was on the training exercise at the NATO war games. His aide said that a General had been furiously trying to find him because of a military problem, and the aide had finally ignored the rules of the exercise and disclosed the location of the intelligence post that the Colonel was supposed to be manning. But Colonel von Werten had not been at the assigned post all day. He had disappeared. And two hours later he knew the worst. Fifteen sons and nephews of the July 20, 1944 conspirators had also vanished. Their families said they had been told only that they would be away for five days: the precise time named in the threat to kill the five hostages.

In his whole lifetime Williams had never felt such despair as he did when he heard that news. To identify the Colonel, and the whole Ice House Movement, which sent the threat, and still be nowhere?

8

11:00 P.M. One hour before the hanging.

Jack Riley was a man who had been around. His life in the Navy before he came to Hollywood had introduced him to the seamier edges of human existence, replete with drugs, sex, even murder. Then his amazing success as an actor had catapulted him into a new—and in some ways even stranger—orbit, the life of a superstar. Amazingly enough, he had found it filled with the same three ingredients: drugs, sex, and even murder—although the murder was less brutal and more inclined to be death in slow stages by humiliation, if your talent or luck ran out.

But Riley had never lived in Germany, and he was not exactly politically aware. So he was absolutely startled, and could draw no inference of any kind, when a German Army Colonel and some older men arrived in the cave and apparently took over the whole kidnapping operation from Baader-Meinhof. Helga and the young German guards now stood around in the background as the Colonel took charge. Who in the world were the newcomers? He watched them moving around the cave, and hope bloomed in his heart. They were men in their late thirties and early forties, adults like himself, not wild-eyed youngsters. Surely these men could be reasoned with and, even more certainly, they would not murder innocent hostages.

The illusion lasted only until the Colonel who seemed to be in charge approached Robert Morrison.

"Mr. Morrison?"

"Yes."

"I'm afraid it is definite. You will be the first."

Morrison was ashen-faced. "My God, you look like a civilized man. I can't believe you're actually going to do something like this."

"You're not a person to us, Mr. Morrison." The Colonel's slate-blue eyes were cold. "In this sad situation you are a pawn in a game of great political stakes," he said. "A martyr."

"I don't want to be a goddamned martyr," Morrison said angrily. "I want you all to wake up to what you're really doing. Re-establishing what everyone else in the world thinks about Germans. That you're savages. Whatever your cause, that will hurt you."

The Colonel didn't react angrily. Instead, he said something absolutely baffling to Morrison. "You may be right. We'll think about it," and withdrew.

Morrison was so stunned he couldn't speak.

Gail said, "Can you believe that? 'We'll think about it'!"

For the first time in hours, Bernie Weller, the director, spoke. "Do whatever they say, Robert."

Riley turned on Weller angrily. "That's what got your people incinerated by the damn Huns in World War Two." He mocked Weller. "Do whatever they say! I'll be damned if I'm going to do whatever they say. If they tell me my number is up, I'll kick every ball in the room."

But Weller was unperturbed. "Listen to me, Robert."

The door clanged and guards came over to remove the handcuffs from Robert Morrison. "What's up?" Morrison asked the guards. They merely shrugged and led him out of the room.

Five minutes later the guards came to get Riley and uncuffed him also. But this time they met resistance. "So Morrison talked himself out of it and now I'm the first, eh?" He kicked at the guards. One of them grabbed his wrist, bent his arm behind his back, and said into his ear, "Relax, Riley. Morrison is still the first to go down."

Outside in the main cave Jack Riley was startled to see a miniature movie set. A camera and lights had been installed in the far corner and Morrison was sitting on one of two high stools. The guards escorted Riley to the other stool.

"What's up?" Riley asked Morrison, who said, "I don't know. They told me if I cooperated only one person would die. So I said yes. At least it might save the others."

Riley turned to the Colonel, a shadowy figure behind the lights. "What's going on, Colonel?"

The Colonel's words didn't reassure him. "Mr. Riley, this affair isn't pleasurable for any of us. But there are things that must be done. If you don't cooperate, we may decide that you will be the first one to hang."

Well, what the hell, thought Riley. "Look straight in the camera, please," a voice spoke from the blackness behind the camera. Riley and Morrison looked ahead, grimly.

Then Riley saw the Colonel approach them with a makeup kit. "Now hold it," Riley said. "What's with the powder puff stuff?"

"Let's say I need to know which one of you should make the rest of my film. You played Hitler in the movie, Mr. Riley. Perhaps Mr. Morrison should be first choice for my own film."

Riley watched while the Colonel went to work on Morrison's face. He was thinking, who were these loony birds—this Colonel and those so-normal-looking civilians who had taken over the cave? They were crazy, that's what they were. At least with the Baader-Meinhof kids you knew where you stood. But the insanity of the older men struck Riley as even deeper than the Baader-Meinhof version. They should *know* better. The powder puff touched his face; he jerked his head, but a guard held him still.

He suffered while cream and powder were applied, and then the mustache, as he, too, was made up as Hitler. Morrison had been more difficult to turn into the Fuehrer. His nose had a slight, though not unseemly, break, his face was lightly freckled, his hair was red. But with putty to Morrison's nose, a black wig, and shadow to his cheekbones, powder, eyeliner, dark eyebrows, and the mustache, Morrison had become Hitler too.

The Colonel checked the picture through the lens himself. Twin faces of Hitler stared back at him. One more lie to Riley and this all-important film would be completed.

He ordered the camera to roll again and when the scene was finished, he said, "Mr. Riley, you win. Mr. Morrison, that's all for you. Guard, take him to the washroom and remove the makeup. Mr. Riley, I have one more job for you."

As he spoke the lights were being dismantled and brought to a room marked OFFICERS' QUARTERS where the photography would take place. The Colonel approached the prisoners' cell. Gail saw him enter their room, a handsome blond man—but weren't all German military officers handsome, as a generation of war movies, in two of which she had appeared, had convinced her? He said, "Miss Edens, we are making a little film. If it's successful, only one of you will die. We believe the film will force the government to yield to our demands. If you cooperate, you may save the others' lives."

"What do I have to do?" Gail asked nervously.

The Colonel paused before answering to light a cigarette, inhaled, and only spoke after smoke was curling to the ceiling. "I understand your last day of shooting was devoted to a love scene with Hitler. I would like you to re-create that scene."

Gail knew she had to stall. She was not going to undress again in front of these German pigs and give them a peep show no matter what their phony promises. She said, "But the last scene we shot was ruined."

"What?"

"We had to scrap the footage."

"Why?"

"Because in the middle of the love scene Riley kept calling me Alice."

The cigarette in the officer's hand actually trembled. She realized with surprise that she had shaken the Colonel, completely. It was a full minute before he spoke: "Why did he say the name Alice?"

Gail said, "He said he never dated anyone by that name—and he just didn't know why he kept saying it."

The Colonel made an instant decision. "Then we'll do the scene exactly as it was done on the set. With Mr. Riley saying Alice."

And he turned away as guards came to uncuff her. The Colonel's mind was racing. Somehow, some way, Riley must have stumbled onto Lady Portland's secret. Riley was in a bedroom undressing when the Colonel approached him. "I understand you said the name Alice by mistake during the shooting. Why did you do that?"

Riley thought it over and then made a decision of his own. "I'll make a deal with you. I know the niece of a woman who was screwing Hitler years ago. The lady's still alive. If you let us out of here I'll not only lead you to her, but if a film is made I'll cut you and your people in on the profits. I'm telling you it will be millions."

For the first time that day the Colonel smiled. He was thinking how Lady Portland would respond to the motion-picture exploiters from Hollywood. She had jumped when Franz merely mentioned the diary. "You've a very enterprising young man, Mr. Riley. But this is a political crisis for me, not financial. Nevertheless, you've given me an even better scene than I was planning. Please try to do it exactly as it was done in the shooting yesterday."

"And what do I get out of it?" Riley flared.

"Your life, Mr. Riley."

A few minutes later, Gail Edens came into the room, barefoot, her dress torn. "How can I play Eva Braun like this?" she asked the Colonel.

"Was there nudity in the footage you shot?" asked the Colonel.

Gail's expression told him it was so.

"We'll shoot only from the waist up, Miss Edens. I am not making this film for pornographic purposes, believe me."

Riley was already on the side of the military bunk. Gail dropped onto the bed beside him and said, "What did he tell *you*?"

"He says if we cooperate only one person will die. Now even if he's lying, we have to take the chance, right?"

Gail thought it over. "Right. But he made a condition, 'if' the film is successful." She paused. "If he sends this film out I'd hate to let the world know that instead of fighting we were degrading ourselves to the end for these creeps."

The Colonel was beside them. "Take off your shirt, Mr. Riley. Riley gave him a look of hatred, then ripped off his shirt. "Turn around," the Colonel said. Riley did so, and the Colonel used a wax cosmetic pencil to create a scar on Riley's right shoulder. "We must be historically accurate," he said.

Then they were ready for the scene, Gail still trying to make up her mind whether to go through with it or not. The last image of her in people's minds would be of a coward, slavishly putting on a porno show for her German captors. Should she do that? But the damnable problem was that it might actually save some hostages' lives. What would Williams do? She didn't know. What would Angela Tuck do? She knew. She took off her dress and prepared to play the scene.

Damn, she wished she still had her panties, but she couldn't complain about the Germans' discretion.

They all turned away except for the camera operator as she slipped into bed, while Riley stood nearby and said to the Colonel, "In the original she was reading a book, and I took it from her and threw it aside."

The Colonel said, "Very good, Mr. Riley." He went outside and returned with a military book. "We'll start with a long shot so the viewer won't be able to read the title. Now proceed."

9

Adolf Hitler stood naked. Eva Braun didn't even notice; she was lying on her side in bed, facing away from Hitler, reading an illustrated popular novel. She had borrowed the book from one of Goebbels' film stars, a tome that had somehow eluded Hitler's ban on "pornographic filth." It was called Lady Chatterley's Lover, and right now the heroine was draping wild flowers around a gardener's privates. Delicious!

Or so the bemused smile on Eva's pretty face seemed to say as a hand caught a bare shoulder and rolled her on her back. "You are a real slut, Eva," Hitler said. He removed the book from her hands and threw it blindly across the room. "You have the Fuehrer in your bedroom and you read manure."

Eva giggled. Adolf was so old-fashioned. She found that trait in him endearing. He slipped into bed. And Eva knew that soon, through her skilled ministrations, she would reduce this "god" whom Goebbels feared, before whom even the mighty Goering trembled, to an ordinary little man writhing and begging in the same tones, and on the same level, as a common clerk.

.. *The only problem was that this time, in a seeming transport of passion, the Fuehrer called her "Alice."*

And this time the director, who was the Colonel, said not "Cut" but "Could you reverse positions, Miss Edens? We'll only shoot from the waist up, and only briefly, just to see the position."

No people were more formal than the Germans, thought Gail, even when they were committing pornography, kidnapping, and murder at the same time.

"What do you say, Jack?" she said to Riley, who thought a minute, then said, "In for a penny, in for a pound."

Gail lay on her back and Jack rolled over. It's odd, she thought, how your mind flashes images in a time of terror. And not of a Colonel who, despite his calm demeanor, was obviously crazy—nor the Baader-Meinhof killers outside this room who were so quick to explode into violence—nor even of Riley, so close to her, but of good old Henry Kissinger, of all people, along with some cabinet officers and three heavyweight political columnists at a dinner party to which Williams had taken her. He wanted Gail to see close up the Washington power structure that she had heard about—and spoken against—because he felt that Gail was too cynical of government, *too* down on its people, and what you had to do, as the people she had met did, was *try* to make the system work.

The idea impressed Gail; it was true she had spent most of her adult life railing at the government and never looking at the flip side, as her musician friends would say, the positive approach. And here was Kissinger and there the Secretary of Defense and they seemed intelligent and normal and concerned and, most surprisingly, human. Gail had always seen them as symbols—oh hell, what was she doing here, disgracing herself in a cave, lying on her back half-naked for an insane man who meant to kill poor Bob Morrison, and why had she left Washington at all, why had she not listened—Gail Edens found herself crying. But that was all right because the lights had been turned off, the scene was ended, and a guard was bringing her dress.

10

11:30 P.M. Thirty minutes before the hanging.

An old chandelier cast a glow on papers strewn on a desk. Behind the desk in Colonel von Werten's office in Munich a wall safe was open. A frightened Army captain, the Colonel's aide, stood by the safe regarding the visitors, George Williams, Fred Jarvis, Laura Doolittle, and Paul Leuschner, the BFV Director.

Every second ticked like a bomb in Williams's mind: all hope had been lost when they discovered that the search for fifteen of the sons and nephews of the anti-Hitler conspirators of 1944 had begun too late. Other relatives who *were* found at home professed to know nothing of the Ice House Movement and thought the name was a "coincidence." They were being brought into police stations for further interrogation.

Williams looked at his watch. 11:32 P.M. In twenty-eight minutes one of the hostages would hang. Williams surveyed the office. It was furnished in Victorian style, deep carpets, heavy oak furniture and, most surprisingly, the chandelier. Noticing his expression, the Captain told Williams, "The antique furniture belonged to his grandfather, a General under Bismarck."

11:33 P.M. Williams riffled through the documents in the Colonel's safe and felt frustrated. All in German, of course. If there was a clue on paper, Williams would never be able to find it. Leuschner said, "We'll get these translated in minutes."

But Williams had a thought. He said to the Colonel's aide: "Do you have access to the safe?"

"Yes, sir. I use it all the time."

Williams said to Leuschner. "Then I think we're wasting our time here. If there's anything in his papers about the Ice House Movement it would be kept secret, most likely in his home and not his office."

11

11:40 P.M. Twenty minutes before the hanging.

They entered the Colonel's modest brick home at 19 Konnenstrasse. Once again the Colonel's tastes surprised them, for this house was furnished in a modern style: light Danish furniture, throw rugs, bloodred abstract paintings. Laura Doolittle said, "An eclectic."

The Colonel was a widower with a stepdaughter. Upstairs they found two bedrooms, one with toys and children's drawings tacked to the walls. The Colonel's bedroom had a picture on the table by his bed of a dark-haired woman of serene beauty. "Jew," said the BFV Director.

"What?"

"His wife was Jewish. That's why he's a Colonel and not a General. Never get the Combined Staffs to admit it, though. I met her once."

"You did. Why?"

All the while they were talking quietly by the Colonel's bed, the BFV agents were ransacking the rooms of the house, looking behind oil paintings, under mattresses, and behind doors. No papers at all. Nothing. The BFV Director said, "I met Madame von Werten two years ago. About six months before she died in a car crash on the autobahn. She wanted to interview me for a Viennese newspaper. That's how she met the Colonel originally, incidentally. She came to Germany as the Vienna *Zeitung* correspondent."

Leuschner said that the wife of the Colonel continued writing for Viennese newspapers and magazines even after she was married. "Most flattering piece she did on us," said the BFV Director. "She naturally compared it to the SS and Gestapo days, and found us to be a spot more civilized. She wanted to see our files on the Nazis of today, to see how we're making sure it doesn't happen again. I gave her a peek, but only on condition she keep the information off the record. She respected that. First honest journalist I ever encountered."

He paused, thinking, "Well, it was a tragedy, that car crash. I wonder if her death had anything to do with what her husband's up to now."

Williams was startled. "I don't see the connection."

"Something damned funny about that accident that killed her," said Leuschner. "A link in the steering chain broke. Snapped right in two. Now how could that possibly happen? The police department said they'd never seen a heavy link like that snap in all of their experience."

"You think it was sawed through ahead of time? That she was murdered?"

"That's what's even more baffling. The link had no ragged edges that a saw-toothed blade might make. It was just . . . cleanly snapped, in two." He paused. "We told the Colonel about it. Had to. Poor chap."

Williams said, "I'd like to see that link."

"No problem. It's at BFV headquarters, close by. What good it will do you I don't know." He glanced at his watch as if it were the enemy. "Christ, 11:45. We should be charging a hideout with guns, and we're standing in a bedroom talking about a car accident two years ago."

Williams and Leuschner left the bedroom and saw a ladder leading to the attic. "I wonder what's up there?" said Leuschner. They climbed the ladder, pushed up the trapdoor, and found themselves inside the Colonel's secret office, complete with scrambler telephones, one red and one green.

But the desk drawers contained no papers, and there were no files. Williams imagined the Colonel on these telephones, sitting at his desk, relaying the order to plant a false beeper in Berlin. He pointed to the scrambling devices. "This was it. This was his head-quarters."

But there were no clues there. The phones led to the hideout, but what secret number connected it? They didn't know, so it was useless. They went down-stairs to the living room to find Laura Doolittle stand-ing in front of an abstract painting, trying to figure out its meaning. She said, "Something's funny."

"What?"

"The picture in front of you, signed by the artist, Otto Golenstern is an abstract, right?"

"Yes."

"Otto Golenstern never painted an abstract in his life. He was one of Hitler's favorite artists, and Hitler hated abstract painters."

Williams turned to Leuschner. "Is the artist still alive?"

"The artist?" said Leuschner. "How the hell do I

know? We don't have files on artists unless they're in their twenties and smuggling cocaine."

"If he's alive I'd like to talk to him."

Leuschner tried not to look irritated. He tapped the watch on his wrist. "It's 11:50. In ten minutes an American is going to be executed. And you want me to start tracking down a senile artist who painted for Hitler forty years ago."

Williams said, "This painting wasn't done in Hitler's day. It's recent."

"How do you know that?"

"I don't know anything about artists, but I know a lot about FBI laboratory analysis of paint. This painting is done in acrylic. Artists didn't use that in Hitler's time. So let's find the artist."

12

"It's 11:52 and this is CBS in New York. It seems as if the whole world is watching Germany tonight, the country where four American actors and actresses, who are considered the very top in their field, are being kept hostage, along with a director whose name is a legend in Hollywood. Truly astounding developments in the last twenty-four hours have kept the tension mounting, as the investigators have made surprising progress in an all-out effort to find the hideout and rescue the prisoners.

"George Williams, the Justice Department's Chief of the Criminal Division, is the President's personal liaison man with the German police authorities. Earlier today a sniper tried to kill him, and there are reports, unconfirmed, that the kidnappers may not be the Baader-Meinhof at all . . . that, instead, an Army Colonel and his associates are the leaders of the gang.

"What this means, no one in a position of authority has said. It flies in the face of the fact, earlier revealed, that Helga Neff, a renowned Baader-Meinhof killer, had definitely been established as a member of the kidnapping team.

"In a dramatic television appearance one hour ago, the Chancellor of Germany made an appeal to the kidnappers, and incidentally addressed himself to the demands of the kidnappers for a statement from Ulrich Kandrof, the President-elect. Here's part of that speech, as recorded by Station KLWD in Berlin:"

The Chancellor:

"Tonight I address myself to the kidnappers. Do not spill needless blood. All can be negotiated. But within reason. This government cannot release fifty-eight Baader-Meinhof prisoners, many of them convicted of brutal murders. This government cannot afford to unjustly lose the services of one of its greatest and most popular statesmen, Ulrich Kandrof, because of unfounded and general accusations. This government cannot demand that a private American corporation destroy the footage of a thirty-two-million-dollar motion picture.

"But we can reason with reasonable men. Come to us with your grievances. Specifically, the people of Germany—and the world—want to know: what *are* your grievances? Aside from an unspecified charge that one of our government leaders is a traitor, your two other demands amount simply to a 'do this—or we kill' threat.

"This government will not bow to the demands of random terrorists. We would lose the support of the people if we yielded blindly to such threats. But the blood of innocent people should not be shed. So we urge you tonight: Delay. Think. Gather your people, whoever they are, and consider the consequences."

The film ended and a correspondent stood on a lawn in front of the Chancellery building in Bonn, harsh white light from television lamps etching his

face. "This is Morgan Rollins in Berlin. As of this minute"—he looked at his watch—"11:55 P.M., there has
been no response from the kidnappers to the Chancellor's moving plea. The excitement in this city has been
tremendous this evening, particularly as revelations
have come which seemed to lift the kidnapping out of
the normal Baader-Meinhof terrorist incident into
something even more frightening. Police are said to be
tracing certain Army officers, but will give no details
as yet. But the implication of Army involvement has
sent a shudder down German spines. A report that
could not be confirmed said that various sophisticated
weapons have been stolen from Army bases in the
past year by the officers, and if this is so, it could pose
an even greater threat to the country. But the Army's
high command swiftly denied the report and said that
no sophisticated weapons are missing. . . ."

13

11:58 P.M. Two minutes before the hanging.

Laura Doolittle had not won her high job in the motion-picture industry without knowing men, inside and out. She felt she was expert in sensing their vulnerabilities, and absolutely the best at exploiting them. And even better, as far as she was concerned, she could see a man whole, analyze almost at once what motivated him, made him tick.

These were the thoughts that went through her mind as she watched one of the most unusual men she had ever met, George Williams, walking up to the doorway of a Bavarian-style cottage in Munich. This was the home of the artist Otto Golenstern, who had surprisingly painted an abstract in acrylic when his lifelong reputation was of an artist who hated abstracts and used only oils.

What made Williams so unusual was that he was so calm. Laura knew—and was a trifle jealous—of Williams's relationship with Gail Edens. In less than two minutes Gail, the woman he loved, might be dying. And what was Williams doing? What he had done all day, patiently and doggedly moving ahead on his investigation and never showing any sign of panic or any personal concern for Gail.

But he didn't have one more day, or two, or five, to finish his investigation. Her watch moved to 11:59. He had one minute. And even this phase of Williams's investigation was being blocked. The house was dark and empty. The artist Otto Golenstern was away. No clues would come to him in time to save an innocent life.

George Williams turned away from the door. Before him were Leuschner, two other BFV agents, Fred Jarvis, and Laura Doolittle. Williams saw none of them. Instead Gail Edens's face was in his mind and the knowledge that he had lost, that someone would die because he had failed, that the missing Colonel and his associates were in the hideout for the duration and he would never find them outside of it before all five hostages were killed, and where was that artist?—and Williams did something that endeared him to Laura Doolittle forever. He showed he was human after all. He picked up a whitewashed boulder along the path to the artist's door and threw it angrily through a window. It was 12:00 midnight.

12:00 midnight. 0 minutes before the hanging.

A cell in a cave in the Alps. Robert Morrison prepared to die. He was alone in the ice-house room with the Colonel. The Colonel had been good enough to excuse the Baader-Meinhof guards and his own associates from the ceremony. So at least he wouldn't die with goons watching him.

Morrison had made tearful farewells to the other actors and to Weller, who kept saying, "I was wrong. I was wrong." Apparently, from the beginning of their stay Weller had seen the brand-new meat hooks installed in this cell and guessed that their real captors were associated in some way with the July 20th conspirators, and would therefore be, as he said, "gentlemen, not savages."

But now this strange Colonel, this alternately mild and corrosive man, was actually conducting the execution by himself. Morrison closed his eyes and prepared to die. He thought of his wife—where was she now? And then a picture of his ten-year-old son flashed through his mind. Would he grow up twisted because of this bizarre tragedy which had befallen his father?

The first five minutes in this room he had argued with the Colonel, trying to get through to him, but the Colonel had only busied himself adjusting the trapdoor and then the camera with which he would record the macabre scene. At 12:03 A.M. the Colonel went over, adjusted the noose around his neck, and spoke briefly to him. The camera was already rolling. Then the Colonel, without saying a word more of warning, released the hinge of the trapdoor. Morrison screamed, and the first man had died.

Across the cave the prisoners heard Morrison's cry in shock. "Oh, my God," said Gail, her hand against her mouth. "Oh, sweet God." A minute later they heard the door to the hanging room open, and the Colonel's order to his guards. His voice was calm, as always. "Place the body in the rubber bag."

Book VII

THE REBORN
EAGLES MOVE

1

12:32 A.M. Colonel von Werten went over to Bernie Weller sitting on his bunk in the prisoners' cell. "Old man, don't be afraid."

"I'm not."

"Good. I want to talk to you outside."

The Colonel ordered a guard to unshackle Weller, then led him out of the cell. In a few minutes they were standing outside the cave, Weller breathing the fresh mountain air in big gulps. The Colonel told him what was to happen next, but that neither the Baader-Meinhof nor his fellow prisoners must know. "The young people in there," he said, referring to the Baader-Meinhof guards, "are dangerous."

"I know," said Weller.

"I'm going to separate you from the prisoners. You stay in the Ice House with the body, and wait. I'll tell Helga Neff to give you special privileges."

"Will she go along with it?"

"Why not? I've given her the blood she wanted."

Silence for a moment. The sky was filled with stars. Weller hated to go back inside that cave. "Why are you giving me special privileges?"

"I married a Jewish woman. From Vienna."

Silence.

"She died in a car accident. Some say she was murdered."

Weller said, after a pause, "I'm sorry."

The Colonel leaned over, picked up a pebble, and threw it high over the cliff. It landed, soundless, in the forest below. "I never even knew a Jew before her," said the Colonel. He looked at Weller. "Why do you Jews always cause so much trouble—for thousands of years?"

"The trouble comes to us," Weller said. "My family didn't die in a car accident. They were massacred at Auschwitz."

"And you survived? And went into frivolous movies, and live a frivolous life in Hollywood? After Auschwitz?"

"We Jews know most of all how to survive. My own talents you may consider frivolous, but they are only my method of surviving."

"I see." The Colonel stood up, a strong figure in the moonlight, but with sick eyes, thought Weller. Yes, that was the impression of the Colonel that had struck him from the first. He was sick. Von Werten said, "You're a good man, Mr. Weller. May God somewhere shine on my wife. She betrayed me, I think. But I love her just the same."

"You *think*? You don't *know* she betrayed you?"

"I don't know." The Colonel said nothing for a moment and then, almost apologetically, said words that frightened Weller. "Whatever happens from now on, know that I am a friend of the Jews who are so hated and despised, and will only do what I must—but never out of malice toward you and your people. Von Stauffenberg died because he cared for the Jews, you know."

Weller remembered reading about Colonel von Stauffenberg, the handsome and brilliant young war hero, blinded in one eye and lame from combat wounds, who headed the July 20th conspirators and planted the bomb that almost succeeded in ridding the world of Hitler. Von Werten said, "He took an inspection trip for the Army in 1944 and saw the death camps, Auschwitz, Buchenwald, Dachau. After that trip, he planned the July twentieth assassination of Hitler, no matter what risk."

At that point the door of the cave opened, and one of von Werten's associates called to him. "Time to go." And ten minutes later Weller, survivor of Auschwitz, sat in an ice house near the hated meat hooks, a corpse in a rubber bag beside him, thinking of a sick, dangerous Colonel. . . .

The Colonel and his men flew back to Salzburg, leaving the Baader-Meinhof on guard. The Colonel would have his film processed, and send it to a television station with a message while the rest of his associates would disperse to safe houses and await the reaction to the film, and their demands.

2

1:30 A.M. in Munich. The artist had not been traced. George Williams said a prayer for the hostages. He had failed. His instincts during this whole day had fluctuated between optimism and pessimism. When he had found that the Ice House Movement was an organization of sons and nephews of Hitler's enemies, his spirits had sometimes lifted. These would be civilized men, he knew. They wouldn't kill hostages in cold blood.

But the revelation that Colonel von Werten's wife had died in mysterious circumstances had shaken him. Suppose the Colonel, a man who had married a lovely young Jewess—a strange move for a German military officer right there—now believed, as the BFV Director did, that his young wife was deliberately murdered. Could this account for his insane actions? Or was there really some political danger so urgent that a rational man of mature years would turn to terrorism?

The telephone rang.

"Well, it's in," the BFV Director said. "They hanged Robert Morrison."

The phone felt cold in Williams's hand. "How do you know?"

"A film," Leuschner said. "X-rated, too."

"What do you mean?"

"It's a three-segment job. First we see Jack Riley and Robert Morrison being made up as Hitler."

"Morrison too?"

"Right. Then we see Hitler—can't tell which one of the actors it is because they look so much alike—making love to Gail Edens in a bed."

"What?"

"That's right. Erotic as hell, I might add from my middle-aged standpoint. Finally we get to the violence to complete the application for the X-rating. A long shot of Morrison standing on a trapdoor with a loop around his neck from a meat hook. Then the trapdoor goes, Morrison drops to his death, and we end on a hanging man, eyes bulging. Horrible."

Williams said nothing, and Leuschner went on. "It all came in a package in a film can delivered to a TV station in Munich, KGYX. In it was a note: 'This film is dedicated to the traitor Ulrich Kandrof. Tomorrow, at midnight, another hostage will die because of his treason. Our demands must be met!'"

Kandrof! The Colonel and his men were *obsessed* by Kandrof. It was obvious to Williams now that the most important of their original three demands centered on that German politician.

"Oh, incidentally," Leuschner was saying, "there was a tape with it. The actor playing Hitler says, 'Alice' just as in the bloody film they shot at Berchtesgaden."

Williams was thinking of the three-segment film, and a light was trying to force its way through the darkness of his mind. A bald-headed little man in a white smock was standing in front of him. "You are a smart man, Mr. Williams." He held a black X-ray negative in his hand. "There is something under the acrylic in Colonel von Werten's abstract painting."

Williams had ordered the painting X-rayed. Now the technician held the X ray up to the light so Williams could see it. Laura Doolittle and Fred Jarvis crowded behind him as they looked through the upraised negative and saw what seemed to be a rectangular object in the middle of the painting.

Five minutes later in the laboratory the technician used a knife to scrape away the thick paint at the center of the work, and plastic emerged from beneath the paint, with a document inside it. Williams ripped it free. The plastic contained a map of the Bavarian Alps. An X marked one mountaintop, and on it was printed PROJECT VALKYRIE.

Leuschner said, "Project Valkyrie was the code name of the July twentieth conspiracy," and Williams thought, here, hidden by the Colonel, was a map with the name Project Valkyrie indicating one mountain peak in the Bavarian Alps. He said to Leuschner, "I want to see the film the kidnappers sent."

A few minutes later Williams and the others were watching the footage showing two actors being made-up as Hitler, then Hitler making love to Gail Edens, then . . . in a horrible cut . . . the execution of Robert Morrison. When the lights went on, Williams said, "Okay, the background cinches it."

"Cinches what?"

"The background of these film scenes is obviously the walls of a cave. The Colonel's map shows a mountain, and this film shows a cave. I think the hideout is a cave in that mountain on the map."

BFV agents were smiling as they left the room to be driven to a police heliport. This time, Williams was thinking, the Colonel would not wriggle loose. Williams wouldn't let him. In the back of the police car on the way to the heliport the BFV Director was jubilant. He shook Williams's hand. "We've broken this case, Williams. We've broken it! We'll pull that cave apart in thirty minutes."

3

In 1975 ten presidents of major German corporations flew to the Bahama Islands for a conference, ostensibly to discuss worldwide marketing problems. Once installed in the Princess Hotel, they got down to business. The real reason they were conferring was patriotism. As they saw it, dramatic steps must be taken. The United States, in the post-Vietnam trauma, had abdicated its role as the world's policeman. The Soviet Union would be quick to seize advantage. In all parts of the world, from Africa to Indochina, they would use satellite forces such as Cuba and Vietnam to expand Communism into countries formerly allies of the West.

But the peripheral expansion, disturbing as it was, was not the most important concern for the German businessmen. What worried them was the next phase of Soviet expansion they foresaw: directly into Europe, using Communist parties who would call themselves "independent" and pretend not to be under Soviet influence to lure the voters. Only after they were in office would the Communists come out into the open, as Fidel Castro had done so long ago, laughing at an embarrassed U.S. State Department that had considered him a democrat.

In the opinion of the ten industrialists in the room—and more than twenty other corporation presidents who agreed with them but could not attend the Bahamas conference—Soviet Russia would take over Europe quite easily as the stresses of inflation mounted and Germany approached financial depression, always the breeding ground of Communist revolutions.

The German industrialists saw this inflation as a direct result of Zionism. It was their opinion that inflation could be controlled, a deal could be made with the Arab OPEC nations to limit oil prices. But always it was the Jew who stood in the way. Perhaps this attitude reflected the background of the industry presidents. All the chosen few had been members of the Nazi party in Hitler's time.

And now, because of the Jew, Germany faced a peril. If inflation spawned a financial crash, it would be a choice of right-wing or left-wing dictatorship if Germany were to survive.

The industrialists opted for right-wing control and the Reich Emergent party was born. Within weeks of its birth, a very rich industrialist had called a brilliant young politician, Kurt Mueller, into his office and made him a proposition: to head the Reich Emergent party.

"We'll get you everything you need to grow. The top brains in this country will be working for you. We've already found a name for the organization that will appeal to the young people."

"What is it?"

"The Reborn Eagles."

Mueller had sat back. Good. Better than good. A great name. The industrialist was going on. "This will be a secret but major undertaking, Kurt. One: a computerized communication system throughout the world. Every corporation will have a secret room with a computer terminal. Two: identity symbols for image. Gold-plated chains with a medallion of Hitler for every member. Three: television used in a clever way. Commercials for the novelty and even the toy industry which will gear up with Nazi planes and insignia and tanks, even uniforms for public participation. Four: public actions: Our legal department will push for rallies and parades all around the world, even in America. And a military arm—"

Mueller raised his hand. "Military?"

"Commandos," the industrialist said. "We're training them with the P.L.O. in Lebanon right now. It won't be the old S.A., Kurt. These will be men living their regular civilian lives who will be militarily trained if we need them. Understand? For whatever happens. We don't know, Kurt. The world is fluid, dangerous. The Soviets are at their height now."

And so Kurt Mueller had been installed as the head of the Reich Emergent party which, the public believed, was simply a new conservative party that could gain nothing against the entrenched political establishment. What newsmen couldn't understand was why one of the brightest young politicians, Kurt Mueller, had accepted such a hopeless post. It was a political dead end.

No one made any connection when a Jewish businessman in Munich was found mysteriously murdered. He was one of the leading financial backers of a So-

cial Democrat candidate for Chancellor. Nor did anyone see a connection when some Israeli businessmen
complained that certain German multinational corporations were raising "red tape barricades" all over Europe to deprive Israel of vital imports.

What the newspapers *did* notice was that the Reich
Emergent party was growing in every corner of the
nation. To the ten industrialists who had journeyed to
the Bahamas in 1975 the success was even swifter
than they had dreamed. Every day was in their favor,
as inflation grew and the fear of a financial crash
heightened. Soon, very soon, the time would be ripe
for their move to power.

Now Kurt Mueller and two of his lieutenants in the
Reich Emergent party sat in a secret office in Bonn,
waiting for a radio call. As far as Mueller was concerned, the Colonel's mad escapade that was happening this moment would catapult the party even faster
into the leadership of the country.

Mueller smiled. That poor, pathetic, little Colonel
and his fellow officers with their dreams and plots.
Didn't they realize the Reborn Eagles were all-
powerful? Didn't they know that the Eagles could easily infiltrate a spy into the Baader-Meinhof kidnapping team, and thereby monitor the kidnapping from
the first minute? As they had done.

Ernst Hinkle, one of the guards in the cave, was
their spy. Already on one of his lookout watches outside the cave he had used a small transmitter to confer
with Mueller.

There was a time when Mueller and his Nazi broth-
ers had feared von Werten more than any man in Germany. He was a future chief of staff whose father had
been killed by Hitler! He was a violent anti-Nazi who

would bring all of his anti-Nazi friends into the top echelon of the Army, where they could monitor and quell the rise of the Reborn Eagles.

But that had been easily taken care of, and now the formerly feared Colonel was just a sad little man shunted off into a military dead-end job. And look what the pathetic reject had done. His kidnapping scheme would hand the Reborn Eagles the acclaim of the world. The moment the first hostage was killed, the Reborn Eagles would move into the cave, take it over, and rescue the remaining hostages. And what the world would see were men in black uniforms who were not, as the Jewish media said, evil and violent but the real protectors of law and order in Germany. For the first time a new Nazi party would win respectability around the world, thanks to the Colonel.

One hundred skilled commandos were in Salzburg now, waiting the call from the spy in the Baader-Meinhof gang. A helicopter was at the airport to transport a squadron of them to the mountain. The rest would remain in reserve in Salzburg. Mueller poured himself some fine cognac. Colonel von Werten had trapped himself. By waiting until the Colonel's men had killed the first hostage, the Reborn Eagles would show how brutal, illegal, and violent were von Werten and his associates. And whatever von Werten had to say about Ulrich Kandrof would be discredited as the words of a kidnapper and killer.

And if that didn't silence von Werten, Mueller had other ways. He could tell von Werten the whole truth about how and why his wife had died, if that were needed. The Reborn Eagles knew everything, and why not? They controlled Germany. It was just that Germany didn't realize it yet.

4

2:10 P.M.

Winston Churchill laughed. He bent from the waist, peered at the crowd, then plunged a cigar into his mouth. Blue smoke wreathed his features, then he removed the cigar with one hand and goosed General Eisenhower with the other. Eisenhower, mincing like a pansy, jumped away as Churchill said, "Forget the second front, dear General. I prefer the first rear."

Hundreds of voices roared in laughter. The great hall in Salzburg was crowded with German war veterans and their families sitting at tables enjoying—as in the old days—the famous Berlin political cabaret.

Franklin D. Roosevelt was wheeled onto the stage. But this was a Roosevelt no one would recognize. He had a hooked nose, and a sign hung around his neck just in case anyone missed the point. The sign read: JEW. Roosevelt said to Churchill, "You always told me that instead of a second front you preferred a soft underbelly. Now the only General I can suggest for that fetish is a German: Hermann Goering."

The crowd laughed again. Later the curtain descended on a high-kicking trio of Josef Stalin, Winston

Churchill, and Charles de Gaulle, with Roosevelt at the climax rising from his wheelchair and showering dollar bills over the threesome. The curtain went down to applause.

"Just like the old days," said a stout red-faced bürger, veteran of Germany's Fifth Panzer Division in the great Kursk tank battle, receiver of two medals, including the Iron Cross.

"God, we had good times then," said a little man with a wooden leg, amputated after he stepped on a mine planted by Tito's insurgents in Yugoslavia.

Franz von Werten was not there. He was in a safe house in Salzburg, keeping in touch with Helga Neff and the guards by scrambler telephone.

His associates were staying at nearby safe houses, with orders not to show their faces in public. Franz had checked with his military aide a few moments ago and received a sharp surprise: "The BFV is looking for you, sir. I shouldn't tell you this, but I'm absolutely certain you're not involved—"

"Tell me what?"

"They say you're involved in the kidnapping, sir. And all the sons and nephews of the July Twentieth Movement, sir."

For a moment Franz had gone numb. How had Williams found out his name? How had he discovered the identity of the whole Ice House Movement? Had the cop Franz had killed talked before dying? But what did the policeman know?

In a minute he was calling the three other safe houses. The first two checked in and said everything was normal. But at the third house the telephone rang and rang, and the Colonel was in despair. Those officers had gone out against instructions. They could be found by the Reborn Eagles, or the BFV.

Four of Franz von Werten's associates sat at a table in the cabaret, three drinking schnapps, a fourth drinking vodka. The impulse to slip out just briefly to see the festivities in town had been too urgent to deny.

But now a veteran passing their table recognized Kurt Hurwirth, son of General Hurwirth, executed by Hitler. The veteran went back to his table of friends and said, "The piss-ass traitors are here."

"Which traitors? The Reich was full of them," said another.

"The swine who tried to kill Hitler. I saw the son of General Hurwirth—and I'll bet those fags with him are all of the same stripe."

But a minute later a German band struck up a barrelhouse theme, and steins of beer were waved in strong old fists as voices were raised, and the traitors were forgotten. On the dance floor a pretty girl hiked up her dress, showing beautiful legs, and launched into a series of acrobatic splits while her partner, fifty-nine-year-old Karl Askling, wounded at Antwerp in 1940 by a British machine gunner, then again at Warsaw by a handmade bomb thrown by a Jewish resident of the ghetto, huffed and puffed to the jeers of his fellow veterans.

"Look at the fat one! He can't move!"

"I'm sure he can't get it up, either," roared another voice.

Kurt Hurwirth had found a pretty girl of his own. He mingled in the crowd, watching the dancers and laughing with the rest. His girl said, "You know, I'm working."

Hurwirth looked into the demure face of a brunette with ice-cold blue eyes.

"I'm a working girl. I only play for pay," she said. "I didn't want you to waste your time."

Kurt laughed. "And out of all these people you picked me as the perfect client for a prostitute? I'm flattered."

The sweet little hooker smiled. "No, I came to you to get away from some rough trade."

"Trade?"

"That's what we girls call the violent ones."

The music whomped, a fat musician in a red-striped shirt nearby loudly squeezed an accordion. Hurwirth was thinking he would have to give this "working girl" a pass, not because he minded paying her—at his age he was not surprised to be asked for money by strange young girls who appeared in the middle of a cabaret and offered love. But Franz had ordered them definitely to remain inside the safe houses and they could just stay out for a few minutes—

The girl said, "I hate Nazis."

Hurwirth looked at her with real interest for the first time. "What do you mean?"

"I told you. The rough trade. I saw the gold chains. They're Nazis."

The Hitler medallion? Hurwirth said, "Point out the Nazis."

The girl looked around, and then turned back to him in disappointment. "They were at that table but other people are sitting there now. I guess they've gone to the mountain."

"What?"

"When I first got near their table I heard one of them say, 'Thirty minutes and we're off to the mountain.' And when I talked to one of them about 'business' he said he only had a half hour and we'd have to do it in his room across the street, and he'd have to whip me. That's when I spotted the medallion chain. They wear it inside their collars, but every German knows you can see the ridge the chains make. He and his friends were Nazis, and that's bad news. Hey, wait. . . ."

But Kurt was already on his way back to his comrades. Nazis had left for a *mountain*? Which mountain? Could it mean—?

But he had no chance to consult with his friends. The German band had struck up *Deutschland Über Alles*, every veteran in the place was standing, beer stein in hand, singing the mighty anthem—except for the table where Kurt's friends sat. There a fight was in progress. Veterans at nearby tables, noticing that the others were not standing, started cursing and jeering. Then one man rushed the table and shoved one of Kurt's friends so hard his chair toppled over, and a melee was underway.

Kurt Hurwirth didn't wait. He rushed outside, hailed a cab, and raced toward Franz von Werten's safe house. He didn't see a man from the cabaret follow him out, jump into a car, and start after him.

5

In the cave Ernst Hinkle, the guard who was the Re-born Eagle spy among the Baader-Meinhof kidnap-ping team, approached Helga Neff. "Can I relieve Hans, Helga?"

Helga looked at her watch. One guard was always posted outside the cave as a lookout. Hans's tour had fifty-eight minutes to go. Hinkle said, "I'm going crazy inside here. I need some fresh air."

"Ask Hans," Helga said. "If it's all right with him, you can take over for him early."

Hinkle went to the door. A guard was on the inside facing the main room in case the prisoners somehow got free from their cuffs and made a break for it. Now he turned, inserted a key in a lock, and the outer doors slid open. Hinkle went outside, spoke to Hans, who was lying against a boulder, staring out over the moonlit mountain peaks. "Christ, it's beautiful," Hans said. "I'd rather stay outside myself."

But Hinkle told him he was going crazy inside the cave and asked him, as a favor, to allow him at least half an hour of fresh air, and Hans said okay. He went back to the cave, gave the secret knock, and the doors opened.

When they closed again, Hinkle was alone in the night on a peak of a majestic mountain. The air was chilly at these altitudes, but clear and sharp in his lungs as he inhaled. He stood up and moved fifteen feet around the mountain, then knelt down and started scrabbling at the earth with a penknife. A tiny radio was revealed where Hinkle had buried it on his first watch. His orders were to transmit as soon as one hostage was killed. Now he spoke softly into the transmitter: "Reborn Eagles, all clear. Come on up."

Hinkle's voice crackled over static in the cockpit of a helicopter already circling the mountain in anticipation of the call. This was a troop-carrying helicopter, and the soldiers appeared to be from another war in another era. They all wore black uniforms, and the death's-head insignia of the SS on their caps. The Reborn Eagles were in formal dress.

The helicopter swooped low, its pilot straining his eyes through the darkness. Then he saw a pinpoint of light, the hooded flashlight of Ernst Hinkle outside the cave.

The noise of a helicopter's engine might be heard inside the cave. The pilot avoided that problem by dropping far below the cave. He was searching for a plateau cropping out from the mountain, and found one. A minute later the helicopter was on the rock surface, and the Nazis, holding machine guns, were filing in orderly fashion out of the aircraft. Soon a line of men in Nazi uniforms toiled upward through undergrowth and scrub pines until they reached the plateau outside the cave.

Hinkle, upon seeing them emerge, said nothing. The plan had been outlined long before. As soon as he saw the troops were armed and ready, he went to the door of the cave and knocked sharply on it in the code: three raps, then one, then two. A moment later the door swung open.

Young Hans Ulbricht's face appeared. "What do you want? You just went out there a few minutes ago."

Those were the last words he would ever utter. A vicious chatter of machine-gun fire, and he was cut in half, doubled over in agony, his hands grasping bloody flesh and cloth, and the Reborn Eagles were charging into the room, seeing at a glance that there were four guards inside the main room and no hostages, and the Baader-Meinhof swine were raising their guns, but too late. The Nazis forced them to drop their guns and kick them into the middle of the floor, then without more ado the Baader-Meinhof youngsters were taken into a side room, faced against a wall, and each was killed with a silenced bullet through the head.

The other Nazis freed the stunned Americans who had looked up to see black-shirted troops break into their cell. Nazis! In the uniform of World War II! Jack Riley said: "What the hell—"

But even Bernie Weller could not deny the fact that it was Nazis who were taking off his handcuffs and saying, "You're free. We've saved you."

Outside in the main room, in front of the line of desks with World War II equipment, Ernst Hinkle was tugging the Captain's elbow. "Captain. Something's wrong."

"What is it?"

"The Baader-Meinhof leader, Helga Neff. She's disappeared."

"Disappeared? How could she? There's no other exit from this cave, is there?"

"None that I know of."

"Then she must be hiding in one of the rooms." He shouted orders, and the Nazis started to open doors and charge into side rooms with guns ready. One of them opened the door to a room with meat hooks, and saw Morrison's corpse in a rubber bag on the floor. "Hey Captain, look at this. Here's Morrison's body." He knelt and pulled down the top of the bag. Morrison's chalky face emerged, eyes open. "Christ," said the soldier. The Captain said, "No time for that. Help the others, Gunther."

But in fact the Captain didn't care that much about Neff. The Baader-Meinhof bitch had escaped. So what? So she could tell the police that in rescuing the hostages the Reborn Eagles killed the kidnappers. Would that make anyone angry in Germany, killing Baader-Meinhof terrorists? That would add to the appeal.

He went to the telephone on the desk in the communications area and dialed a number in Munich. Kurt Mueller answered, and heard the words: "We've got them, my Fuehrer."

"Good. Bring the Americans out. Were there any problems?"

"One of the Baader-Meinhof people seems to have escaped. Helga Neff. How she did it, I don't know. There's only one door to this cave."

Mueller didn't like it. "Don't move until you've

found Helga Neff! She has to be in that cave some-where if there's no other exit."

"But why worry about *her*? What can she say?"

"I don't like loose ends," Mueller said. "Find Helga Neff. Now!"

6

Pitch dark in the rubber bag. Helga Neff clutched a corpse. The Nazi who had opened the top of the bag had missed her head by an inch. What would happen now? Would they give up the search? Or, when they freed the prisoners, would they realize as soon as they picked up Morrison's body that another body was in the bag?

She clutched the stiff corpse, realizing her ruse wouldn't work. They would know she was inside the cave, because there was nowhere else she *could* be. They wouldn't quit until they found her. Her arms ached from clutching the body. She adjusted herself to lessen the pain in her arms in such a way that the side of her head jammed against the chest of the dead man.

Christ!

His heart was *beating!* Was it her imagination? She listened in what seemed to be thunderous silence, her ear against a cold chest, and heard boom, boom, boom. Or did she? No, she didn't. My God, she was going crazy! She had to get out of here. Now.

"Careful," a voice said.

If ever Helga Neff achieved extraordinary self-
control, it was in the next instant when she didn't
scream. Nevertheless, her own heart almost stopped
functioning as she realized a corpse was hugging her.

"It's okay," Morrison said.

Helga had a hundred questions, but there was no
time to ask them now. All she knew was that, for some
reason, the Colonel had faked the hanging of Morrison. Now she realized why he had asked Helga and
the Baader-Meinhof guards to stay outside the execution room when Morrison was hanged and why he had
assigned Weller to sit by the "corpse." The Colonel
had betrayed them. He had never intended to kill the
hostages. He had lied to Baader-Meinhof.

Morrison whispered, "The Nazis are going to rescue
the hostages, right?"

"Yes."

"I'll go outside and show them I'm alive. Then
maybe they won't look again at what they'll think is
an empty bag in the corner and you can escape."

Helga wanted to ask why the American would rescue someone who had intended to kill him, but then
remembered that Morrison didn't know it was the
Colonel alone, and not Helga, who had saved his life.

Morrison pulled down the top of the bag. In the
outer room, they would hear voices. "The septic tank,"
Hinkle was saying. "She could be hiding down there."

Three of the Nazis went back to the water closet
and shook their heads. The toilet door was bolted on
the outside. Helga Neff was not below.

The Captain was becoming irritated. "So one
Baader-Meinhof bitch got away. So she's hiding in a
secret closet. I'm going to call the Fuehrer—"

But sudden shouts caused him to jerk his head around. The American hostages all had terror-stricken expressions on their faces. The Captain turned to see what they were looking at, and almost cried out himself.

The corpse of Robert Morrison was staggering into the room, white-faced, one hand holding the side of the door as if for support.

Then he smiled. "You've been tricked," he said.

7

Mueller, in his secret office, checked his watch. 2:15 A.M. They should have heard from the Captain again by now.

As if hypnotized, the other two men in the room stared at the telephone, waiting for it to ring.

But no call. Had Helga Neff gotten away?

Mueller's orders for the rescue mission had been specific. Plan Able was to rescue the American hostages unharmed.

Plan Baker, to be implemented if something went wrong and endangered the Eagles, was to kill all the American hostages immediately and leave evidence to show that the Ice House Movement had committed the executions.

The telephone rang and an excited voice exploded over the wire. "My Fuehrer, we're still in the cave. We need instructions."

"What's happened?"

"Robert Morrison is alive."

For the first time in months, Mueller's composure forsook him. Robert Morrison alive? How could that be? The film of his hanging had been on television only an hour ago. Morrison alive? It didn't make sense.

"Dr. Mueller, are you there?"

But Mueller was thinking and then, Oh my God, he saw it all—the whole plan of Franz von Werten—and Mueller, so confident with the massive Reborn Eagles organization behind him, so sure of himself that he mocked the pathetic little Colonel, had walked right into the middle of it. If the Reborn Eagles hadn't intervened, the Ice House Movement "executions" would have taken place, one hanging after another, all evidenced by film on television, and pressure would have risen to an incredible height. And then, at the end, with the eyes of the world riveted on him, the Colonel would produce all of the actors miraculously alive. What a sensation that would make when the world thought they were all dead! And at that spectacular press conference, against the backdrop of those live actors, he would state to a stunned world his reasons for calling Ulrich Kandrof a traitor. And those reasons involved the Eagles and could destroy them.

Mueller was still smoking. In the blue cloud he saw the face of Colonel von Werten, and he realized for the first time the depth of genius of the enemy he faced. And what the Colonel had already done was not even the problem. What Mueller must reckon with now was that the same genius who planned fake hangings would have *another* plan IN CASE THE NAZIS *DID* INTERVENE. As they had.

The Colonel must die, Mueller thought in fury. He must die. But meanwhile, he must think fast—the fate of the entire Reborn Eagles Movement could be involved. What would the fantastic Colonel's plan be if the Nazis intervened? Would he anticipate Mueller's Plan Baker, to kill the hostages and leave evidence to show it was done by the Ice House Movement? Even if the Colonel did, how could he stop the Nazis from killing the hostages? The Eagles were in the cave with the hostages in their power, and Mueller's spies had assured him the Colonel was in Salzburg more than one hundred miles away.

He said, "Execute Plan Baker immediately. Don't wait one minute."

The contact almost stammered. "K-kill all the hostages?"

"Yes, you fool," Mueller said angrily. "We're in a war. Now get that message to the Captain. At once!"

He hung up, his mind on the cave. In minutes Morrison would know what it was like to die for *real*. And the four other Hollywood people, those stupid tools of Zionist America, would hang, too.

He stubbed out the cigarette angrily. The Colonel had thrown him off his stride and he had backslid into the attitude which Hitler hated more than any mistake: defeatism.

Mueller had a growing party; the Colonel had nothing but a few sons and nephews of traitors. Mueller had the real Germany behind him—not just the old-timers, but the young people with new ideas seeking a change for the better in this country, along with the Establishment, the powerful men of industry. Mueller had everything, and yet he was letting one man defeat him? Never. Think like the Fuehrer, he told himself. Go on the offensive.

The telephone rang. Gauleiter Schulz was calling.

"We found the Colonel's safe house in Salzburg," he said. "One of his drunken friends led us to it. The Colonel's right there."

Mueller was elated. The Colonel had made a mistake, after all. He was human. He said to the Gauleiter, "Take all your commandos and kill the Colonel!"

8

Kurt Hurwirth found Franz playing three-level chess. Franz looked up angrily. "You shouldn't have left the safe house."

Hurwirth ignored the rebuke, quickly told him what he had heard at the cabaret, and Franz snapped to attention. "The Eagles know the hideout? They must have a spy in Baader-Meinhof." He picked up the scrambler phone to call Helga Neff in the cave. It rang, but for the first time there was no answer.

Hurwirth paced the room nervously, a big man with wide-swinging arms. "My God, everything's falling apart," he said to Franz. "And we're deep in murder. That wasn't the way we planned at the beginning."

"I told Baader-Meinhof not to kill any guards when they kidnapped those people. And I'll take full responsibility for the ambush of Williams. Now stop charging around the room like a lion in a cage. Everything's under control."

Hurwirth stopped at this remark and looked at Franz. "You told us everything was under control a few hours ago. And now look what's happening!"

But Franz was on his way to a closet below a book-case. He knelt down and opened the door. Hurwirth saw what seemed to be electronic "black boxes" inside the closet. On a shelf was a small portable unit the size of a cigarette pack. Franz removed it and hooked it to his belt.

Franz stood up and spoke quietly but firmly to Hurwirth. "From now on, the Ice House Movement has ended. Spread the word to our associates. Whatever I do from this moment on is on my own. You will have no responsibility."

Hurwirth suddenly felt his manhood was being challenged. "Well, now wait, we went into this to-gether—"

"I've held back facts from you," Franz said. And then he added words that mystified Hurwirth. "I've held back facts from myself. Now go. Tell the others. That's my last order to you."

"But what are you going to do?" The expression in Franz's eyes frightened his friend. "You're . . . you're not going to kill more people?"

"I'm telling you nothing. Now go."

Hurwirth hesitated, then shook the Colonel's hand sadly. They had come so far, and now they had failed—defeated by the Nazis again as their fathers had been—and now Franz was going to make it worse. It could be frightening to have a man like Franz loose, with all his knowledge of weapons. Hurwirth said, "Franz. Think. Don't do it."

"I have to," Franz said.

Hurwirth left. Outside, the street was empty. No taxis. He walked toward the center of the city. In an alley close by, two figures waited. When Hurwirth passed they leaped on him, big hands smothering his face, an arm around his windpipe. They dragged him into the darkness of the alley and held a knife to his throat.

9

Gail Edens watched Nazi stormtroopers in black uniforms conferring in a corner of the room while she and the other American hostages stood by nervously. The series of shocks to their systems had escalated rather than lessened. The Nazis had suddenly seemed to become cold and ominous. One of them had herded the hostages to a corner of the cave at gunpoint while his superiors discussed what to do.

"You damn fool," Riley said to Morrison. "If you had stayed put we would all be out of here."

Gail tried to lighten the atmosphere. "He's an actor. He couldn't resist that entrance."

But Morrison wasn't happy himself. "I guess I was grateful to that Colonel for sparing my life. He told me if anybody tried to take over the cave to come out of the bag and tell them they had been tricked. So I did it." He paused, then said in a whisper. "Listen. Helga Neff's alive."

"She is! Where?"

"She was in the bag with me. In the meat hook room. If these Nazis try anything, maybe she can help us."

But just then a square-jawed Nazi came over to them.

"Stand at attention. That's it. You too, Riley. Arms at the side. I must inform you that you are now our prisoners, you have been tried in a *pro forma* military court, and the sentence is death. By hanging."

Then he snapped out his arm rigidly, "Heil Hitler!"

Even in her renewed terror and despair, all Gail could think was, an imbecile! At least the Colonel had brains. Now they were in the world of the mental dwarfs. Then her attention was diverted to an amazing sight. Little Angela Tuck at the end of the line of prisoners was shooting her arm out stiffly also. "Heil Hitler," she said.

Gail Edens drew an instant conclusion. The Baader-Meinhof terrorists had been warned about Angela, but the Nazi bullies might not have heard of her or her CIA father. Indeed her ploy had taken the SS man completely by surprise. He said, "You're not one of us."

"San Marino, California, Chapter 427," said Angela. "Look it up. You'd better check before you execute one of your own."

A guard remained near the actors, who were still standing at attention, while the SS Sergeant went back to confer with his superiors. Klaus Burger, the Captain, said, "If she was a member the Fuehrer would have known. He never mentioned it."

"With all respect, the Fuehrer doesn't know every member of every American unit," said the Sergeant.

Captain Burger looked at him, then slapped a glove on his khaki knee, smiling. "Oh, you are a lusty one, Sergeant. Your eyes tell me all. You want to eat the delicious little one. For supper, correct? But the orders are that all of the hostages must be executed at once. If we spare your little one she will tell the authorities that the Reborn Eagles executed the Americans, not the Ice House officers."

He walked over to the group, with the other SS stormtroopers following him. Gail Edens's mind was numb. She was remembering a documentary in which she had seen American Nazis. How pathetic they were when out of uniform. Truck drivers in T-shirts with beer bellies, garage mechanics, hard-hats, construction workers, talking about taking over America from the Jews and the niggers.

But in this cave the men in uniform seemed different, even as the Americans had changed from potbellied hard-hats to frightening symbols when dressed in their Nazi regalia. But whatever she thought or did was apparently insignificant to the Captain. He was staring at the demure and sweetly sexy Angela Tuck. "You want me to check out your membership, liebchen?"

"Yes."

"Come into the commandant's office," he said. Then to the guards: "Handcuff the other prisoners and bring them to the scaffolds. The executions will take place in ten minutes.

"Ten minutes!" The Americans were thrown into a turmoil. Riley said, "The Colonel and his men will tell the world that you killed us—for no reason."

But the Captain only smiled. "My dear fellow, the outside world doesn't even know who is inside this cave right now. They do know the Colonel and his men kidnapped you. When they enter the cave, the police will find the evidence we've planted that the Ice House Movement executed you. We came prepared with documents. Our Fuehrer is just as clever as the Colonel, and our movement has master forgers." He paused. "But who will even question it? The American, George Williams, so brilliantly established that the Colonel is the mastermind and has already killed Morrison."

All through this monologue he had been smiling, but now his expression suddenly turned cold. He turned to the guards and said, "Hang the Jew first."

In the almost unendurable tension of the last hours Gail had held onto her control, even when she thought Robert Morrison was being killed. But now, as they were taken into the room which held meat hooks all along its walls, and saw the lengths of rope, she faced for the first time her own immediate death.

And suddenly—it could not be happening—Gail was shoved onto a pedestal with a trapdoor under her feet, with some goon in a black shirt placing a real rope loop around her neck . . . and the other hostages were similarly placed beside her, and Gail started to tremble all over. She thought she would be sick. "My God," she wanted to scream, "*Let us out of here. . . .*" And then she saw the black rubber bag in the semi-darkness across the room. Helga Neff was inside it. She was a killer. But she had no gun.

In the private office the Captain had commandeered, little Angela Tuck wasted hardly a minute after the Captain suggested he just might let her live. Her sweet little fingers unzipped the Captain's fly. Her cool hand encircled him, and a monster grew. Expertly, she trailed her fingernails and the Captain was squirming. "Oh my God," he said. "Kiss it. Kiss it."

"Not yet," said Angela, who appeared to be breathing hard. The Captain found himself looking down into the most beautiful face he had ever seen, and he was lost in her eyes while tormenting nails scratched, then a hand cupped him gently while he grew so hard and so large, and he knew he would kill her anyway afterwards, but my God he would hate to do it. . . .

A knock on the door. "Verdammt!" the Captain said. Impulsively, he pulled Angela to her feet and gave her a kiss. The Sergeant outside said, "The prisoners are ready."

The Captain straightened out his uniform, then said to Angela, "Stay here, little one. I'll be right back."

"You didn't check," Angela said.

"What?"

"You said you were going to check whether I'm really a member of the party."

"But . . . but I'll do that as soon as I'm finished." She gripped his hand. "Don't go!"

"Why not?"

"I'm afraid of your men. They don't believe I'm one of you. I want to stay with you."

But the Captain would have none of that. "You stay right here, and I'll be back in a few minutes. That's all it will take." He went out of the door and closed it. Angela waited a moment, then went to the door and cautiously opened it a crack. She peered through the opening. Damn, one guard was posted by the outside door of the cave. He would see her if she broke out of here. On the other hand—she stepped out of the door. "Guard!" she said.

"What's the problem?" the guard shouted from the door.

Angela walked boldly toward him. God, she had to hurry. Those Nazis were in there right now, ready to hang her friends, and what she needed to do was somehow get that gun away from one young guard. She could do it.

"Stop!" the guard said. He had the machine gun pointing toward her chest. And she was still fifteen feet away, just even with the door to the hanging cell. "Don't make one move until the executions are over."

Four Americans, with hands cuffed behind their backs and rope loops around their throats, stood on trapdoors above eternity. When the Captain had entered the room, Gail Edens's last hope had died. Even Angela Tuck had failed.

But they would have one moment's grace. The Captain wanted to say something to Weller, "You, a Jew, have the gall to come to this country. Hitler tried to rid us of parasites like you—yet, now that Germany has money again, you come to grab it, eh? And you even dare exploit the Fuehrer in a movie."

Weller said with dignity, "The picture, against my wishes, turned out to be favorable to Hitler. You have no complaint with me."

"As a director, no. As a person, no. But as a Jew?" He spit in Bernie Weller's face.

Weller said, "And I say this to you fat slobs who dress up in uniforms and think it changes vermin into soldiers. I have a present for you, a gold tooth. Your people used to extract these at Buchenwald and Auschwitz."

The Captain was skeptical. "You have no gold tooth," he said. But he looked closer. Weller spit right into his eyes. Drool ran down the Captain's cheek. The Captain bawled and leaped backward, scraping at his eyes with his sleeve. "You . . . you *filth*! Hang him, Otto! Hang him now. Let the trapdoor go!"

And before the horrified eyes of the Americans, a black-shirted Nazi bent over the platform, pulled a lever, and the trapdoor dropped. Weller's neck snapped with a horrible, audible crack. He hung in space with his head tilted grotesquely to one side, face turning purple, blood trickling from the corner of his mouth.

"Oh you . . . bastards," Gail cried. "You horrible beasts!" She was sobbing uncontrollably now. Even Riley was crying.

Morrison said, "You sons of bitches will pay for what you just did."

In the commotion there was a knocking on the door. A Nazi opened it and Angela bolted into the room, sobbing, "Captain, your guard tried to kill me."

The Captain pushed her away, but too late. Angela had his gun from the holster and threw it toward the corner. "Helga!" she shouted. The gun skidded across the floor of the cave into the corner as the startled Nazis whirled to see a hand thrust out of the bag, grab the gun, and loose a fusillade of bullets in one motion. Helga was rising out of the rubber sack, the gun firing, and the Nazis were diving every which way to land on their bellies. Helga hit one guard in the shoulder; he dropped his gun; another was killed instantly by a bullet through the head. And then withering machine-gun fire from all directions tore through Helga's body, jerked her against the wall, and the gun dropped.

The groans of the wounded Nazi filled the room. Smoke made it almost impossible to see. The Nazi Captain was furious at Angela. "String her up!" he shouted, and Nazi guards roughly threw Angela onto a scaffold, tore the rag off her throat, revealing the fresh scar, and replaced it with a bristly rope.

"Attend to the wounded," the Captain said. A guard went to the man with the injured shoulder while the Captain rolled over the dead Nazi, seeing the man's temple half shot away. "Swine," he said. In a fury he went to the corpse of Helga Neff and kicked it once, twice, three times. Then he went back to the handcuffed hostages with the ropes around their throats. "Now you will all suffer!" he said. "You little girl, will be impaled on the meat hook, not hanged. And you also, Morrison, because you knew Neff was alive. Prepare the hooks."

Guards stepped behind the two prisoners. The rope was removed from the meat hooks, and the hooks lowered until they were halfway down the backs of the victims.

"Lift them up!" the Captain commanded. And the guards raised the two victims while the other guards behind them started pressing the razor-sharp points of the meat hooks into the bodies of Angela Tuck and Robert Morrison.

Morrison felt first the fabric of his shirt tearing, then the bite of the hook. At any second the guard behind him would thrust the fatal hook forward while the others let him drop onto it. Gail watched, almost fainting, and then she threw her handcuffed body against Morrison's so that the hook was dislodged. The guards shouted at her angrily and the Captain stepped up and screamed into her face, "Move again and you will get the hook through *your* body!" And at that point, in a shuddering silence, a voice boomed through the cave: "ATTENTION, REBORN EAGLES. ATTENTION, REBORN EAGLES!"

10

The Nazis were looking everywhere. Where had the spectral voice come from? Now it continued. "I SUGGEST YOU ALL TAKE COVER, INCLUDING THE PRISONERS, BECAUSE AN EXPLOSION WILL NOW TAKE PLACE AT THE DOOR."

An instant of indecision. Another, and the Captain starting to move toward that door—WHOOM! A thunderous, earsplitting roar, smoke and chips of stone flying, as the Nazis dropped to their stomachs. The prisoners, in the side room, were unaffected.

Now the sound of rumbling filled the cave. The Captain, flat on the rock floor, raised his head. Part of the cave was intact. All of his men were alive. But the outer door—where was it? Huge boulders and rubble now sealed it to the top—the explosive had been planted above the door to the cave in the side of the mountain. My God, if they couldn't move those boulders, they were trapped. The voice over the hidden speaker sounded again:

"I advise you to remain as still as possible until further word from me. I have planted nerve-gas mines in glass ampules in the walls of the cave. And I am now activating them. The glass will break at any undue vibration of any kind. Any attempt to cut through the wall of the cave, or smash aside the boulders at the door will cause instant death to everyone inside the cave. As a demonstration I will release tear gas from a sample mine." A hissing sound immediately transfixed the Eagles. They stared at the far corner of the wall and saw a wisp of acrid smoke appear as if from nowhere. The voice said: "That small amount of gas, only a tiny puff, would kill all of you instantly if it were nerve gas. I am entering final negotiations with the German government for your release, and then you will all be freed. If any hostages are harmed, the Reborn Eagles will be pinpointed as the murderers." The voice stopped.

"Oh, sweet Christ!" said one Eagle.

Another walked to the corner of the room and sniffed the gas. He started choking, and ran back toward them. "The bastard isn't kidding," the Eagle said. His eyes were running; he pulled a brown handkerchief from his pocket and wiped them. "Captain, we have to get out of here. Some way."

But the Captain was already picking up the telephone to call the Fuehrer and report. Standing on a trapdoor with her hands cuffed behind her back, a rope bristling her throat, Gail Edens heard the Captain shout loudly on the telephone. "Some sort of a remote-control device caused a cave-in over the door and the boulders look like they weigh two tons. And the rest of the cave, he says, is mined with nerve-gas bombs. . . . Some voice from a loudspeaker, it must be the Colonel. . . ." Then his voice quieted. "Is that so? . . . You're on your way to the Colonel's house. You've found him? . . . Good, good. Torture him un-

til he shows our people how to turn off these
mines. . . . Yes. . . . Oh, my Fuehrer, one more
thing. The Jew is dead. But not the others. . . . We
wait? . . . How long? . . . Until the Colonel's
death. . . . Better what? . . . Better dead, if there's
a crunch. I understand, my Fuehrer. I will wait to
hear from you."

He hung up the telephone. The guards made no
move to release the hostages from their nooses. Instead they milled softly around the cell and the main
room of the cave with their machine guns, talking nervously in low tones. Two of them could be heard by
the boulders outside, seeing if there was any way to
move them without vibrations. From the remarks they
made, it would seem hopeless.

The Captain vetoed everything. "The bastard told
us any vibration from now on will break the glass ampules filled with nerve gas. No, we stay put, gentlemen. Let the Fuehrer handle it on the outside."

Book VIII

BATTLE TO THE DEATH

1

In his safe house in Salzburg, Franz von Werten calmly readied himself for his last mission. Vest. Belt. Electronic equipment. Microdots in a tiny plastic envelope. One machine pistol, a second specially designed gun, and secret killing devices ranging from a phosphorous handkerchief to explosive coat buttons to various innocuous-looking poison-dart launchers. He was a mobile death machine.

The others in his Ice House Movement now must fade back. They were, in the end, unequipped to take the strain. No doubt some of them were sorry, as Hurwirth had implied, that they had embarked on such a perilous enterprise, even for the highest of political principles.

Franz would not fade. He would win. He had his alternate plan all prepared and the nerve-gas ampules would hold the Nazis in control. A muted roar on the street caught his attention just as he was about to step out of the room to the secret underground passage in the house that would lead him to freedom—and the climactic phase of his revenge.

He went to the window, pulled the drapes aside,

and saw a mob with torches advancing toward his
house. The fiery light showed fists raised, and he
could hear ugly shouts.

Some people in the mob wore parts of uniforms and
medals; they were the war veterans assembled in Salzburg for the World War II reunion. Someone was leading them to this house.

Kurt Hurwirth must have talked. Or maybe he was
made to talk. Franz knew he must leave at once—but
something held him glued to the window. Torches at
night on the streets—Hitler's great theater when he
cast himself as a god on a pedestal above thousands,
or sent torch-bearing mobs into Jewish ghettos to
burn and loot and kill.

But what hurt Franz von Werten was not the memory of Hitler's past theater or murders of the Jews—
but that these men who were advancing to kill him
were *his* people. Many of them no doubt had fought
under his father's command. They belonged to, and
would always be part of, the army which Franz still
loved.

But now men alone were sprinting ahead of the
mob, and Franz had to leave. A few minutes later he
was in the basement, turning the handle of a rake.
The handle concealed a tiny radar transmitter. Its signal, activated by the twisting motion, caused a section
of the basement wall to slide open. A crashing noise
and heavy footsteps above told Franz the mob was
already in the house. He stepped through the opening,
taking the rake with him, then closed the wall again.

No one could ever open it now.

2

Through the night, on their way to the cave, search-lights from the helicopters probed the great dark mountain range below, illuminating, then passing over, bare, harsh, granite summits whose trees below drifted down into blackness toward untouched valleys. George Williams sensed the grandeur of history as he had never done before. In ancient times a Carthaginian General named Hannibal had led elephants and troops across the most awesome mountains in the western world and surprised mighty Rome. The people of this continent had lived with a sense of thousands of years of historical experience. It gave them, as he had been told over and over again, a different mental attitude that was difficult for Americans to grasp.

And here he was, in a frail aircraft among impenetrable mountains, trying to extricate Gail Edens and her fellow Americans from the middle of Byzantine European political conflict in which great forces were locked in battle to the death for reasons he didn't even know.

Unless the Hitler medal he now carried had something to do with it. The medallion the Colonel had left at the site of the bomb explosion when he tried to kill Williams had been recovered partially shattered.

No less than five police helicopters were flying to the cave that had once been the doomed command post for the gallant officers of Valkyrie, now enclosing five hostages guarded by young Baader-Meinhof terrorists known for their ruthlessness. With them, acting in a dangerous alliance, was a German Army Colonel and other sons and nephews of the Valkyrie officers.

The speaker above the pilot's head crackled with dialogue between the pilots. Now Williams heard through the static, "Okay, we've got it. Three hundred yards range at two o'clock."

All searchlights focused on a lone mountain peak, indistinguishable from the others but marked clearly on the map made from Colonel von Werten's original. Closer and closer, and they could see, half camouflaged below it, a helicopter.

They had found the hideout.

Antiterrorist specialists in William's helicopter were strapping on bulletproof vests, and checking ammunition in their machine guns. They would drop from the helicopters onto the mountain peak, surround the cave, and use loudspeakers to command the kidnappers to surrender.

If no reply came, they would mine the door with explosives and blast their way in.

But suddenly the voice of the pilot of the lead helicopter was heard. "Something's wrong." Nothing but static, and then the voice said, "There seems to have been a cave-in," and the searchlights brilliantly lit tumbled boulders and fresh cuts in the mountainside.

Then a new order came over the loudspeakers in the helicopters. "We'll execute a holding pattern around the cliff. One-fourth mile each leg, and follow in order. The Director will notify you when landing operations begin."

Williams's chopper swung to the south, its light pinning the giant rubble which sealed the cave. What was going on? Williams wondered. Was it a natural cave-in, perhaps caused by the chopper that had landed there earlier and was still to be seen, sitting placidly under hastily thrown pine limbs on a plateau?

Then he heard Leuschner's voice for the first time over the loudspeaker. Leuschner was in the lead helicopter. "I've contacted headquarters. They've just had a communication from Colonel von Werten in Salzburg. He is not in the cave. He states that the cave has been sealed by him by remote control and there are nerve-gas mines implanted in the walls. Any undue vibration by police trying to cut through the walls will cause instant death for all inside."

3

The helicopters flew in a pattern around a spotlighted cliff, green and red running lights blinking as Williams leaned awkwardly into the pilot's cockpit holding a mike. He was speaking to Leuschner in the lead helicopter. "You say your men have *found* the Colonel?"

The static from the loudspeaker so close to his ears almost deafened him, but then Leuschner said, "They've got a thousand war veterans marching on his house. We don't know how they found his address."

"Well, let's get back there," Williams said. "We can't do any good here."

"Okay, but just in case, I'm landing some of my men here to stand guard. Then we'll get back to Salzburg."

So Williams had to wait while his chopper followed others into a hovering position just above the ground, and the antiterrorist troops jumped out—and then they were away, and Williams heard Leuschner say on the radio, "He's gone. The house is empty."

The pilot of William's helicopter heard this and swore. "Goddamn, I thought we had those babies free!"

Williams was thinking, where would von Werten go? To another safe house, and hole up? But he would think that if the address of one safe house were known, all of the safe houses would be compromised. As indeed they were. Leuschner said, "The police had an anonymous call giving them the addresses of two other secret houses."

"Two other safe houses?"

"Right."

"Then his associates may be in them. They might be willing to talk now."

The helicopters, with their troops disembarked, flew west toward Salzburg while Leuschner communicated with his deputy on the scene. Then he was on the air to Williams. "Okay, they've all disappeared— maybe afraid of the veterans. But there's a wounded man in a hospital, Kurt Hurwirth. He was found beaten up and stabbed in an alley."

"Can he give us a lead?"

"Yes. He says he wants his friend von Werten to end this madness now. He says von Werten has a helicopter parked at the Salzburg airport. Von Werten's a pilot. I'll call our people and make sure that chopper doesn't leave the ground."

"No need," said Williams, seeing the lights of Salzburg Airport's clearly defined green and red runway lamps just ahead. "We're there."

The police helicopters swooped down from the sky. To the right of the terminal, private planes were parked, among them some helicopters. But most of the area was in darkness; the only light came from the partially opened doors of a hangar. Searchlights from the helicopters clicked on and the whole scene was illuminated in spectral white, with sharp shadows from the aircraft. No one moved in the area.

Williams said to Leuschner, "Put me down next to the helicopters. The rest of you stay in a hovering position over the area in case I fail."

"What? Let's just move in and take him."

"If I know von Werten, he has the remote-control device on him that controls those nerve-gas mines. And if he's cornered, he'll press a button."

Static while Leuschner thought that over. It was true that the Colonel had used a remote-control device to seal the cave and activate nerve-gas mines. And if Williams failed, they could still move *en masse*.

"Okay," he said, "but . . . be careful! The man knows eighteen ways to kill, including poisoned darts."

But just then the pilot's startled exclamation made Williams jerk his head around. Below them to the right, one helicopter's rotor blades had started turning. Von Werten had been inside the helicopter when they arrived. "Put me down right next to it," Williams said. The pilot complied, swerving at the last minute as the wind from the grounded helicopter's rotor blades caught his own aircraft's belly. It tilted—the tips of the blades crumpled on concrete. The helicopter thumped down and Williams was opening the door on the high side of a broken helicopter, seeing von Werten in the cockpit straight ahead. Von Werten thrust his arm out of a window and fired at him. Williams ducked, jumped down, and headed for the other side of von Werten's helicopter, out of the pilot's line of sight. He made for the door of von Werten's aircraft. It was locked. The wind from the rotor blades was a vertical hurricane, pile-driving him into the ground. His hand slid from the door handle; he fell onto the helicopter skids, and the helicopter took off so swiftly Williams was thrown to the left and instinctively wrapped his arms around the skid. In a moment Williams was clinging to a helicopter skid hundreds of feet above the ground.

Salzburg's lights far below; they were now at three thousand feet. Williams, buffeted by the rotor blades' downdraft, fought for his life. He swung his leg and hooked it around the skid. There. Immediately he felt more secure. He rolled his body leftward, once almost losing his grip completely as the helicopter lurched in an updraft. Then he was lying precariously balanced on a five-inch-wide metal skid, arms and legs wrapped around it.

In this position he was looking forward, seeing lights of houses on rolling hillsides, as they left the high mountains behind. They were heading north.

Searchlights from behind crisscrossed the helicopter's path. The police aircraft were convoying von Werten to wherever he was going. Where could that be?

And then Williams saw a vision he would never forget. For a minute he thought his nerves had inspired a hallucination in his mind.

Ahead of him were the ruins of Berlin, untouched since 1945 when Hitler and his last desperate men lived under them in a bunker. Fragments of great buildings thrust toward the sky; broken walls of houses, apartments, and office buildings stood alone above an ocean of rubble. The city was blacked out; only the moon cast its glow.

Where was this city? Berlin was thriving today, a

modern metropolis—Williams, on a helicopter skid thousands of feet high, caught his breath. Just beyond the ruins of Berlin was a brightly lit city. And this was Berlin, too, only of another, earlier historical period. The Wilhelmstrasse, the main artery of Hitler's glittering city in 1940 before the bombs came, was awash in brilliance. The great glistening Chancellery, the Luftwaffe building, the Foreign Office, all marched along the great avenue to the gutted Reichstag which had never been rebuilt after the fire.

And Williams knew all, realized what he was seeing as the helicopter suddenly dipped down, and a third area now became visible, containing guard towers, wooden barracks, and high barbed wire—a great concentration camp named Auschwitz—and Williams could see they were flying above the movie set erected for *The Secret Life of Hitler*.

Ahead of them was a high tower, like an observation post, which thrust up at the epicenter of the three different sets, and the helicopter stopped its forward motion and dropped swiftly.

When it was three feet off the ground Williams jumped out and waited. Von Werten had shot at him at the Salzburg airport; Williams had no gun now. He watched as von Werten stepped out of the door in a blaze of light from the police helicopters above, his gun in hand, swerving it toward Williams.

The Colonel said, "Do you want to live longer than the next second?"

"Yes."

"Get on the radio in the helicopter. Contact those people above and tell them I have this." He opened his coat and Williams saw what seemed to be a radio transmitter hooked to his belt. Von Werten's finger touched a button on its top. "If I press this, everyone in the cave—including the Americans—dies."

"And your own people, too?"

"They're out of it, Williams. The Nazis have taken over the cave."

Williams was startled. The Nazis had the prisoners as hostages? How had that happened? But he went to the chopper radio, twisted the dial until he heard the pilot's channel, then pressed the button on the mike and relayed von Werten's message to Leuschner.

Von Werten was in the cockpit with him. "Tell them to clear out, Williams. Even if I'm killed instantly, the nerve-gas mines are automatically timed to detonate at four A.M. That's sixty-five minutes from now. Only I know how to deactivate them, and it isn't any simple button push either."

"What do you intend to do? You know they won't let you out of here alive."

"Let me worry about that, Williams. Do as you're told. And tell them at 573 Mohrstrasse in Salzburg, in a safe behind a painting in the bedroom, is a tape recording with my final demands."

"When did you make that?"

"Ahead of time, Williams, in case something went wrong."

Williams relayed the instructions over the radio. Leuschner said they would swing their helicopters to the edge of the motion-picture location, but not out of sight, and if the Colonel refused he could blow up the cave and take his chances. Leuschner was angry. The Colonel smiled. "Not too intelligent, the BFV man, eh? Not like you, Williams. You, I must kill. I've known that from the beginning."

The Colonel still had the gun trained on him. Williams turned and looked at him. "Why aren't you doing it now?"

"I may need you as a hostage for a while. Let's go."

Above them the choppers were swerving toward the perimeters of the movie set. Williams knew what he must do. Overpower the Colonel and force him to reveal how to deactivate the mines in the cave.

But if he failed, and the Colonel managed to push the button—

"Into the elevator, Williams," and Williams saw an open-grille elevator that climbed the side of an observation tower fifty feet high.

"What's up there?" he asked.

"That's where the movie director plays God. And he has some good machines," Franz said.

Franz followed Williams into the elevator; they reached the top, and everything might have been all right, all lives might have been saved, Gail Edens could have returned to him, if a frustrated, angry Leuschner had not thought he saw his chance with von Werten pinned inside an elevator, and sent his choppers in with machine guns blazing as soon as Williams left it to enter the tower.

Bullets flew through the grille and struck right beside Franz; his hand flashed for the transmitter on his belt. Williams grabbed him by both arms and pulled with all his strength, and von Werten flopped inside the cabin, hand pinned beneath him, and gunfire flashing under the tower and then stopping, as the helicopters swerved away again.

"The bastards," von Werten said angrily. "The bastards."

He got to his knees. Williams didn't even know whether he had pressed the transmitter button. The

Colonel stood up. Williams said, "Did you press the button?"

"No."

"Why not?"

"I want Ulrich Kandrof," von Werten said. "And I need the hostages alive to get him."

They waited on the tower, the darkened ruins of Berlin in 1945 directly before them, lit by a strange artificial glow from lamps that simulated a pale moon; next to it, in contrast, the dazzling floodlit promenade of prewar Berlin; and beyond them, in the glare of harsh lights on poles, Auschwitz, a death camp.

Ten minutes later, von Werten's demands were read over the radio.

4

To the German people:

My associates and I are the sons and nephews of the German patriots who tried to rid the world of Hitler on July twentieth, 1944. We have now risked our lives and careers in a cause which we call the Ice House Movement. The plan was to kidnap prominent Americans in Germany, but not to harm them. The execution of Robert Morrison was staged. He is alive and well. We planned to use fake executions to bring the utmost pressure from the American government on the German administration to accept our demands. We even enlisted the Baader-Meinhof to assist us.

Why did we take such desperate measures? Because we, the sons and nephews, are in a unique position in German society. We instinctively smell what others ignore. And that stench is Fascism, rising again. But if this were just a general instinct we would of course never have risked so much.

People of Germany, you know the Reich Emergent party is growing. It is a neo-Nazi party. You have read it has a brilliant new leader, Kurt Mueller. But that is not correct. He is not the real leader. The new Nazi

TO THE EAGLES NEST

Fuehrer, in an irony of history that is catastrophic for this country, is the President-elect of this country. Imagine. The secret Nazi Fuehrer is President of Germany.

I have the proof. I now drop all my demands except for the one in which Ulrich Kandrof reveals his treason. I want him to be brought to the movie set of *The Secret Life of Hitler*. There in the gas chambers of Auschwitz, I will confront him with my evidence.

And I demand that he be joined at that confrontation by five of his many secret allies in the Nazi cause, all rich industrialists and powerful people in the conspiracy that is out to destroy this nation.

Their names are:

Egbert von Bachmann, President, KAL Steel Corporation

Hans Polterberg, President, GFR Telephone Corporation

Karl Heinrich Aschenbach, President, Frankfurt Coal and Oil Corporation

Erwin Schwager, President, Consolidated Computer Corporation

Heinrich von Hoffmann, President, BFK Automotive Industry

5

Auschwitz lay in semidarkness. The railroad siding
from which hundreds of Jews debarked believing they
were going for a stay in camp; the gates where they
checked in; the outside area where they were forced
to undress and stand naked and cringing before hard-
eyed, swaggering SS troopers; the extermination
chambers, which bore the sign in German "Shower"
and into which the naked men, women, and children
entered, having been told that, as a matter of sanitary
routine, they were going to take a shower before
going to their barracks . . . and then

HISSSSS!

A glance up. What was that? A vapor? From the
ceiling? What? No water but vapor? A gas? And suddenly the first wisp drifted into a face; a scream, and
then another, and the cloud thickening and bodies
falling and a stampede, a rush, a force to escape, to
get out of here, to live—but you couldn't move, bodies
were jammed together, inch by inch, only those on the
outer fringe could bang helplessly on the door, trying
not to breathe, remembering the ice-eyed SS guards,
and realizing now, no, no, no, no, no—they were

dying. For what? And then dead, and into ovens on slabs, and ashes where there had been human beings.

Now, years later, part of the camp had been re-created in exact detail, and George Williams looked down from a tower and saw not an old railroad train with Jewish victims but a modern limousine with five rich German industrialists and the President-elect of Germany pull up to the gate.

Franz was looking through binoculars at the limousine. He saw the industrialists and Kandrof exit from the car, shielding their faces from the tower where they knew Franz was watching.

"Hide," Franz hissed at them. "Fat good that will do you."

"Why?"

"I've studied them all, Williams. Their lives are in my files, with pictures."

"Is Ulrich Kandrof there?"

"He's hiding his face from me, too."

Williams thought that was strange, but said nothing. His arms ached from the wire the Colonel had bound him with, cutting into his wrists. He watched the backs of the industrialists as they entered the extermination chamber.

To Williams's surprise, the Colonel was, for the first time, jubilant. "It's working, Williams," he said. "I think I'm going to make it. They can't stop me now."

"What are you going to do?"

"Go into that chamber and confront them with five microdots."

"Five what?"

"Five microdots. A sample of the documents which prove Kandrof has been a Nazi all his life and he's their Fuehrer today. Documents which show how

those five industry leaders—and others—are in a conspiracy that will take Germany back to the Dark
Ages."

But Williams still didn't see. 'You're going to hold
microdots up to their faces? I don't understand."

But the Colonel was staring at the gas chamber below. "No, Williams, this is a movie set, remember.
There's a sound stage on the perimeter. I'll get the microdots thrown onto a large screen there."

"So why send the industrialists into the death chamber?"

"I wanted to give the bastards some of their own
medicine," Franz said. "Let them stand in the gas
chamber and see those openings in the ceiling above
them like the Jews did, and start thinking. Maybe that
will do some good, too." He paused. "So I'll go down
there, take you as a hostage for extra protection in case
the BFV try the sharpshooter routine, confront those
rich Fascists, and take them to the sound stage—"

"I wouldn't waste my time," said Williams.

"What?"

"They're *not* five rich industrialists. They're BFV
agents. That's an agent playing Kandrof, too."

The Colonel's eyes were snapping. "How do you
know?"

"Because I know how policemen think, Franz. It's a
perfect decoy setup. And I know it's true because
Kandrof hid his face from you. Now why would he do
that? He'd want you to know he's following your demands to the letter." Williams paused. "You weren't to
know until you were in a death chamber with six
agents with guns. And they wouldn't kill you—they'd
torture you until you told them how to deactivate
those nerve-gas mines."

Franz stared at him. "Why are you turning against the police, Williams? It doesn't make sense."

"Because I know you, Franz. You would have found some way to push that button. You wouldn't quit until those mines went off, no matter what they did to you. If I let you walk into that trap, the lives of the Americans would depend on a duel between some German police agents and you. I'd rather have the responsibility."

6

In the gas chamber, six policemen in expensive business suits nervously shifted their feet; they were forbidden to talk or act suspiciously for fear that a hidden camera or microphone was installed for communication with the movie director in the tower.

Each of them clasped in his side pocket a leather-handled iron blackjack. As soon as that outer door opened they would be on von Werten, swinging. When he revived they would apply fire to his scrotum—knives, nails, hoses, anything. They'd get the truth out of him.

But if he came in the door with his hand on the button? Their orders were—go for him anyway.

HISSSSS!

A glance up. What was that? A vapor? From the ceiling? What? No water but vapor? A gas? And suddenly the first wisp drifted into a face; a scream, and then another, and the cloud thickening, and a body falling, and a stampede, a rush, a force to escape, to get out of here, to live—

And the cloud was all around them as they

slammed frantically at the door, pulled it open, and stumbled into the air.

Franz watched them through his binoculars, seeing gasping men, choking from the harmless gas he had released into the hut with the special-effects machine. Williams had been right; they were BFV agents; not one industrialist had shown up, and most definitely not the traitorous Ulrich Kandrof.

Because no one cared. The government thought nothing of his demands. They only wanted to kill one man who created a small problem, Colonel von Werten. And then all would go on smoothly as before, only this time with Kandrof as President. And only gradually would people realize, as they had only gradually realized so long ago, that von Werten had been right; this was not just another new President in a democracy, but a Fuehrer in a revolution in which democracy would suffocate, and by then it would be too late.

Below them in the area where the BFV agents had run out there was confusion. Guns were pointing toward the tower. A helicopter that had been among those patrolling the perimeter now swooped directly toward them.

Franz sat down on the floor. "It's all over, Williams. Your friends in the cave die."

"But why? They're not Nazis. Gail Edens has even been called a Communist. And Morrison never made one political statement in his life. They're innocents."

Behind Franz's back, Williams saw a sniper leaning from a helicopter. A shot, and a bullet plowed through the waist-high wooden walls of the tower. Franz said, "It's a hundred to one that I won't get out of here alive now, Williams. And if I die, nothing,

JOSEPH DIMONA

nothing will have been accomplished. The actors will go free and finish the movie. The people will talk about their amazing escape from the lunatic Colonel. And that will be the end of Valkyrie II—disgrace for patriots, and the Nazis taking over the government."

He paused. "But if they die, and the Reborn Eagles with them, *that* will be remembered. Mass death is the only answer, Williams. Who would remember an obscure charlatan like Jim Jones if he hadn't taken nine hundred bodies with him? I don't have nine hundred, but I have five of the most famous people in the world—and if they die, the people will want to know why, and they'll investigate and probe and investigate and probe and they'll find out about Kandrof and what he did."

"What *did* he do? Tell me in case they kill you."

"It's in the microdots, Williams." He took a glassine envelope out of his pocket and emptied five tiny black dots into the palm of his hand.

"Watch me, Williams," and he swallowed the dots. "If I die, Williams, you be there at the autopsy. But if I live, I want to be the one to use the information the way it should."

Whingggg! Another bullet whined through the tower. The sharpshooter's chopper was moving cautiously closer. Williams saw Franz extract a strange-looking gun from a second holster. Instead of a regular muzzle, an aluminum tube two inches in diameter surmounted the grip. Wire was coiled around it. Franz uncoiled the wire, looked for an electric outlet in the baseboard of the tower platform, and plugged in the wire. "Only limitation so far, Williams," Franz said. "Batteries won't work."

Crack! Crack! Two more bullets flew through the tower. Franz raised his head and saw the helicopter not forty feet away, its side facing the tower, a surprised sniper seeing the face of the Colonel emerge. Then Franz pressed the trigger of his gun. A light beam flicked across the forty-foot space. The body of the helicopter, the sharpshooter in its door and the head of the pilot seemed to glow and tremble—and then flame erupted and the helicopter exploded and disappeared toward the ground.

"Jesus Christ," said Williams.

"Portable laser," Franz said, "but it's only portable if you have an outlet nearby. So far. We've been working on it at the lab. Okay, that will hold them off for a while. I'm leaving. Say goodbye to your friends, Williams. I'm sorry."

Williams saw his hand move to the button which would shatter tiny glass cylinders in a cave miles away and release nerve gas that would kill everyone instantly, and all his efforts were for naught, the tracking of Alice, the ride hanging on to the helicopter skid, even the saving of the Colonel's life when he stopped him from going to the death-chamber ambush.

He said, "You're a liar, Franz."

The hand stopped. "What do you mean?"

"You come here saying you're going to kill five innocent people because you're so worried the Nazis will take over Germany again, and it's a lie, Franz, and you know it. And your friends in the Ice House Movement know it, and you can't do it."

"What do you know what I—"

"You're not doing this for political reasons, Franz.

Yes, Kandrof may be a Nazi. Yes, the Nazi party's growing under a cover name, but that's not why you're here; that's not why you broke away from the Ice House Movement to try to kill me to make sure you succeeded." He paused. "You're doing this for personal reasons, Franz. You're obsessed for personal revenge. I saw the link."

Silence. Franz looked at him.

Williams said, "The police couldn't figure out how that link on the steering chain in your wife's car was cut, Franz. They said it was too strong to snap and yet there was no jagged edge that would have been made by a saw. But they didn't think of a laser, Franz. You cut that link yourself."

Franz was kneeling now, staring at Williams.

Williams said, "The newspapers said your wife died in a car accident. The police found this link and think she was murdered. You went almost crazy after her death, Franz. And no wonder." He paused. "You murdered your own wife."

Franz's eyes watered. "You bastard, Williams. You bastard."

"I know you did it because of the laser cut."

"I didn't kill her, Williams. *They* did. The Nazis killed Sharon.

"But the laser—"

"They stole the laser and used it themselves, Williams. Then they made sure the police got the link. To blackmail me, Williams. In case I ever came up with anything against Kandrof, they'd use the link to say I murdered my own wife."

"God."

"But in a way I did kill her, Williams. At the last

minute Sharon decided not to go to Munich because I
seemed so upset, and I talked her into going because I
wanted to know once and for all. I didn't believe her,
Williams. And because I didn't trust her the bastards
were able to kill her."

"What did you want to know, once and for all?"

"The truth. That she was a Soviet agent."

"You believe that she was?"

He faltered. "That's the worst part for me, Williams.
She *was* a Soviet agent, and she used me. Still, I
would never have killed her. I loved her too much."
He paused. "The BND showed me the proof against
her. Her ex-husband was an agent, too."

"Who was her ex-husband?"

"An American Air Force Captain. He's involved in
an espionage trial in New York right now. BND
showed me correspondence between them two years
ago—they had monitored her mail. He was coming to
Munich to see her on KGB business. He was a Communist spy, Williams."

Williams's mind was whirling. He was again in a
Federal court in New York at a trial of an Air Force
Captain, watching a government attorney holding up
a grapefruit-juice bottle, and speaking to FBI Director
Casey later. . . .

"What was the Captain's name?"

"Draper. John Draper."

"My God, Franz. You were tricked all the way."

"What do you mean?"

"Whatever that Captain is, he's not a Soviet agent.
He's a Nazi. In England he attended Nazi meetings."

Silence. Then: "But that can't be."

"The FBI Director told me so just two nights ago.

The FBI believes the Soviets were framed by a Nazi,
and they're dropping the whole case."

"The Captain isn't a Soviet agent?"

"His father was in the Ku Klux Klan. The son wrote
right-wing articles as far back as high school. In England he attended Fascist meetings. It's in the FBI
files, Franz. My God, he was no Soviet agent, and
that means your wife wasn't either. The Reborn Eagles set you up. The documents the BND had were
forged; even the Captain's trip to Munich was laid on
to coincide with your wife's visit to her aunt."

And now Franz clutched his fists. "I knew it. I
knew it. Oh God—"

"How did you know?"

"After Sharon died I went to her family in England
and they showed me her possessions. Among them
was a pile of junk that had belonged to her husband.
He had left so fast he hardly packed, and among the
knickknacks was a medallion with a picture of Hitler."

"The one you left at the bomb site?"

"Yes, but it wasn't the real Reborn Eagles' medallion, Williams, because Hitler wasn't smiling. So I supposed it was just a sarcastic gift he had given her after
he found out she was Jewish. I was so obsessed with
the suspicion that he and my wife were Soviet agents,
I didn't catch on that he could be a Nazi—"

"You caught on, Franz. You caught on."

"Why do you say that?"

"Because I have the medallion in my pocket. It survived the explosion. Take it out, Franz."

With trembling fingers, Franz removed the medallion from Williams's right pocket. It was bent almost
in two, the picture of Hitler partially shattered but
still visible. "What does it say on the back, Franz?"

Franz said angrily. "I know what it says. I've read it a thousand times." He was holding the medallion with its back toward him. Engraved in gold were the words:

In memory of Unity Mitford.

Williams said, "You didn't know what the medallion meant when you first saw it, but later you found out that Unity Mitford tried to commit suicide by swallowing a Nazi brooch identical to this, and that this particular medallion is worn by members of the Reborn Eagles in the English branch of the party. And when you found that out, you knew Sharon's first husband was a Reborn Eagle and a Nazi, not a Soviet agent—and that they had tricked you into helping murder your wife, the woman who loved you with all her heart, who never did one thing wrong. And you swore revenge against the Nazis, and that's why I'm here, and your associates are in trouble, and innocent people are in a cave waiting to die. . . . It's monstrous, Franz. You can't keep taking innocent lives for your own revenge. . . . We didn't murder your wife, Franz. You did. . . ."

Franz stood up, obvious of the risk of gunfire from helicopters that might see the target. He was not looking at anything, really. His eyes were opaque. And then the ice-cold technician broke. Tears rolled down his cheeks. He took the transmitter off his belt and tossed it onto the floor. "Have the police take . . . it apart, Williams. Dismantle it and the mines won't go off. . . ."

Then he went to the special-effects control board, moved the dials, and stepped into the little elevator. "You're right, Williams. They killed my faith in my wife. Then they murdered her in cold blood, and tricked me into helping them do it. Then they planted evidence to hang me with her murder, in case I talked. That's the Nazi party, Williams. That's the way they work." He paused. "But I'm going to beat them, Williams. I'm going to make the bastards pay. I won't quit. Now more than ever."

His eyes were tearful as he moved the elevator control and dropped down the tower, seen by helicopter pilots who had kept a respectful distance since the laser gun attack.

And it was 3:50 A.M. and Williams was calling the police on the radio for assistance. But would they get here in time? Only ten minutes to go before the nerve-gas mines in the cave would automatically detonate.

3:51 A.M. He couldn't wait. With his hands wired behind his back, his fingernails scratched at the screws on the remote-control device. Nothing. No opening. He couldn't do it alone.

7

Franz von Werten was halfway down the tower before the first shot sounded. More shots rang out, before the elevator touched ground. Williams, hands cuffed behind his back, unavailingly scratching at screws, helplessly observed the drama below. He saw the Colonel crouching near the tower as a wave of police who had been restrained at the perimeter of the set swept toward him with guns. But suddenly an explosion erupted in front of them. Bodies of policemen catapulted. Dirt and stone and wood flew; fragments of buildings crumbled. What was happening? The police stopped the pursuit in confusion, many lying wounded and groaning.

Williams knew instantly what had occurred; the Colonel had activated the "battle" special effects on the control panel before he left, but Williams could not take time to play with those controls now. It was 3:55. Even as his eyes took in the spectacle below, his hands continued to work on the screws of a little box which, if dismantled, would prevent five Americans from dying. . . .

. . . and below him, in the ruins of Berlin, with
fearful explosions tearing the rubble, the Colonel fled
as, so long ago, the members of Hitler's bunker elite
had run into the ruins among Russian shells . . . and
this was Götterdämmerung more vivid than even Hitler's men had experienced. On the nearby set of untouched Berlin, Hitler's voice could be heard shouting
of victory in gutteral German, from loudspeakers
above glittering buildings on Wilhelmstrasse to the
roar of the crowds; fervent *Heil Hitler*'s responding in
jubilation to news of the fall of Paris. And on the
other side of the set, Auschwitz, mighty explosions
tore through the gas chambers and barracks to simulate that day of dread discovery . . .

. . . and now civilians burst out ahead of the police
who had stopped after the explosions, and Franz
knew who those civilians were, so determined to destroy him that they would run ahead of the police into
an area studded with mines: Reborn Eagles out in
force to kill their hated enemy.

Franz crouched against a fragmented jagged stone
wall. Three months ago he had asked Intelligence to
forward him a copy of the screenplay from the German
authorities who were working with the producers, and
he knew that the movie was going to reproduce the
breakout from the bunker of Martin Bormann's team.
Mines to simulate artillery-shell explosions would be
planted on either side of the well-known route that
Bormann had taken that fateful night. If Franz took
the precise route and did not stray, and if the mines
were planted correctly, he would be safe. So Franz
ran directly along the path the cunning Bormann had
once trod, and ahead was the bridge where the fight
with the Russian tanks had broken out, the fight that

Bormann had somehow survived, but then he had
taken cyanide—or so went the legend, and who would
ever know if it was true—but all Franz was interested
in now was how to survive that battle himself, and he
raced toward the bridge, the Nazis pounding along
behind him, and got by the battle site safely. But
some of the Nazis were not so fortunate. When they
reached the location where the World War II fight
had occurred, unearthly explosions suddenly ripped
and tore the ground beneath them. The Nazis
screamed. Their bodies flew in spumes of dirt and
rubble, one explosion after another—Whoom! Whoom!
Whoom!—and then the survivors were cowering
breathlessly in the ruins, frightened to move, and
Franz knew he might be safe, knew he might reach
the sewer conduit built for this film down which some
of Hitler's bunker troops were supposed to have escaped . . .

. . . and my God, he was free, he had made it! Far
off he heard the shouts of police, but they were too
late. He would live to fight those Nazi germs again,
the filth who murdered the woman he loved, and he
crouched over a manhole and opened it. Rungs led
down into the escape tunnel: he threw the manhole
cover aside, placed one foot on the first rung in the
escape tunnel, and then another below it. Could he
make it? Could he get away? One more step and he
was safe. There! His heart was beating fast as a
crouching Nazi aimed his rifle and squeezed the trigger. A .45 hollow-nosed bullet smashed through his
back, hurling him to the ground. He was dying, but
he must not die. He must not let them win. He rose
from the ground like a wounded lion, the most dangerous killing machine in Europe, firing at phantom

shapes who went down, and amazingly escaping their return fire.

But they came in waves, and it was useless for a man alone, and as the Nazis shouted in triumph, machine-gun bullets from all sides finally cut through him, jerking Franz into a dance of pain, much as his father had twitched in agony on Hitler's meat hooks so long ago.

The bullets ripped open his stomach. In the gush of blood the microdots with the only evidence vanished into the earth, never to be found.

8

3:58 A.M. Two minutes before the nerve-gas mines would erupt in the cave. Handcuffed, Williams had broadcast for a technician to dismantle the transmitter, but the call had been useless. The police had been stopped by the explosions. Now, at last, he saw a technician moving toward the tower. But would he make it?

3:59 A.M. Never. The man had not even reached the elevator. By the time he arrived and started to remove each screw . . . the second hand swept inexorably toward 4:00 A.M. and death for all in the cave. Williams stepped to the railing of the tower. If he dropped the transmitter, it might smash. But Williams remembered that the ground was soft beneath the tower. Could he smash it here on the floor of the tower? His foot hit a wire and he almost tripped. The wire from the outlet to the laser gun on the floor.

3:59 and 45 seconds. A heartbeat. Williams knelt down, dropped the transmitter behind him, and fumbled for the laser. He had it! He tried to aim it at the transmitter while looking over his shoulder, but couldn't see, and pulled the trigger anyway. A blinding laser beam shot out behind him, and Williams was thrown headfirst against the console as a sheet of fire tore through the whole tower.

"Holy Christ!" a voice said. Arms pulled him, and he was on the shoulders of a man on an elevator beside a fiercely burning tower. The elevator dropped quickly.

In a cave in a mountain in the Bavarian Alps, tiny glass cylinders containing Tuflex-2 nerve gas trembled as their activators came to life, then became still as the signal abruptly stopped. It was 4:01 A.M. The hostages would live.

Book IX

EAGLE ONE IS INNOCENT

1

Gail Edens, nude, stretched up her arms in bed. Last night had been heaven, if heaven allowed sex, a proposition on which Gail was not prepared to speculate one way or the other.

She and the other American actors had been flown to Bonn where, amid an explosion of television camera coverage, they had all made statements, shock still on their faces and in their minds. Gail's appearance in the tattered dress and barefoot, as she first debarked from the helicopter, had drawn applause. And then, in an impulsive gesture that mystified the newsmen, the actors had lifted little Angela Tuck, whose throat was trapped in a towel, high in the air.

Almost immediately the newsmen had swarmed around Angela to learn the reason the other actors had saluted her. And Gail had seen George Williams.

Williams and his friend from Washington, that tweedy tall man named Fred Jarvis, pushed their way toward her, preceded by policemen. She ran into his arms and he picked her up, smiling, flashbulbs popping.

* * *

Within an hour of the time German police had blasted their way into the cave, Max Weber, the motion-picture producer, had announced that shooting of his epic *The Secret Life of Hitler* would begin again in two weeks.

"It is now an important picture," he had announced, using the word Hollywood loved more than any other—important. "It is relevant. It speaks to the times. It must be made."

Williams had taken Gail to the guesthouse provided by the Bonn government for the visitors, where she had ordered a divine breakfast for two, and then suddenly the world had seemed to tilt and she had fallen fast asleep.

She had not awakened until 4:30 in the afternoon, to find scores of messages from reporters pleading for interviews, congratulations from her mother and father and friends in America—and a note from Williams saying he was "away on business."

At 5:00 P.M. Jack Riley had bounced into her room in chino slacks and a T-shirt. "Hey, babe, I broke the case."

"You did?"

"Yeah, when I said 'Alice' in the movie. Your old man, Williams, took the hint, tracked down the broad, and found the Colonel under the rocks."

He told Gail about Judy Lipscomb and the aunt who had balled Hitler. "I was so excited about the secret, and the idea of making a picture about Alice, that the next day on the set I kept calling you Alice." He threw himself down on the bed. "I'm laughing and dying, too," he said.

"What do you mean?"

"Old Bernie Weller. What a sweetheart he was. Those Nazi pricks."

Gail was sitting on a chair in red shorts and a white blouse, lovely long legs resting on the dressing table. She looked fetching, but Riley didn't even see her. He was staring at the ceiling.

"You know what I'm thinking?"

"Sure," said Gail. "Aren't we all?"

"I'm not going to play any Hitler in that movie. Let every studio in Hollywood sue me. No court in America would make me do it after what happened."

"I'm not going to finish that picture either," said Gail. "They can't call me Eva Braun any longer."

And Riley made her laugh when he rolled over on his elbows and said, "I never did . . . Alice."

Now, lying in bed the next morning, Gail remembered when Williams had returned to her room after Riley left last night, looking so exhausted—he had never caught up on his lost sleep. And what she had done was undress him, thrust him under a shower, and then they had made love for three straight hours—with occasional breaks.

In a way it had been funny. Gail, using fingers and nails and lips, had aroused him to a truly gargantuan effort, a delicious bout with him thrusting and Gail's long legs wrapped around his body, and then the tempo had increased, and she had smiled in anticipation, and then the smile became open-lipped gasps, she with her head to the side, hair tousled over her face—and he had exploded inside of her just as she climaxed, in ecstasy, feeling a tingling clear down to her toes.

And she had kissed him a hundred times on his cheeks and forehead, looking deep into the calm blue eyes of the man she loved. And then, in the sweet aftermath of climax, she realized that Williams, who had not slept for forty-eight hours, was doing so now.

She raised herself on one elbow and regarded him. Straight nose. Nice medium-heavy eyebrows. Good bone structure. Firm jaw. Trim muscled body.

And a mind, too. She had decided to let him sleep awhile, and turned on the TV with the sound low, and there was an excited announcer talking over a picture of a helicopter. Gail knew enough German to understand most of what he said. "The American Justice Department official took a hair-raising ride . . . (the camera cut to a close-up of the helicopter skid) . . . on this skid in an epic of heroism that is the talk of Germany today. He held on as the helicopter flew thousands of feet high, and thus was on hand to confront Colonel Franz von Werten when he landed."

Gail looked at Williams sleeping quietly on his back. He had done that? Her man? No stuntman, no process shots, no rearscreen projection? He had actually clung to a helicopter by his arms when it flew high in the sky?

My God, thought Gail, a little awed. And then she smiled and thought, he did it for me.

Fifteen minutes later she had decided he had had enough sleep and nestled into bed beside him, her hand seeking him out. He started to grow hard and he wasn't even awake yet. She helped him rise to the occasion with a teasing tongue, and this time he groaned and she was rewarded when he woke and rolled over her again, and soon ecstasy was rebuilding in her heart.

Williams felt as if he were in a dream. Throughout the search he had pushed personal thoughts of Gail out of his mind, knowing it might hamper his ability to concentrate on the investigation. But he had yearned for her, and now . . .

Thirty minutes later, Gail was smiling, watching him sleep again. This time she showered and hummed a happy tune. And when she emerged, rubbing herself with a big nubby towel, she turned on the TV again, and this time that crazy, wonderful little Angela Tuck, whose sex drive could solve the energy crisis, was being interviewed. The towel around her throat had been replaced by a small bandage.

"No," Angela said. "I never was really frightened."

Gail's jaw didn't drop. She *believed* Angela.

"But you were cut, you still have a bandage over it. Was that because the kidnappers discovered you had a beeper?"

Angela looked him right in the eye. "I don't know anything about a beeper. What *is* a beeper?"

Gail laughed aloud, watching the newsman's expression. The police had obviously told him the little girl bravely carried a beeper into the cave, and now she was, well, lying. On camera.

"Miss Tuck," he changed his voice to a formal tone, "the police announced when you were in the cave that you had an electronic device with you. It's no secret anymore. What our audience wants to know is, where did you hide that beeper so the kidnappers didn't find it immediately?"

The camera cut to a close-up of Angela's face. Gail was dying. She knew Angela well by now, and knew what she wanted to say to this man's audience: "I cannot tell a lie—right in my twat, sir."

Instead Angela smiled and said, "I just can't discuss it. I'm too young for any intrigue," and left the newscaster with his mouth open.

In the middle of this there was a discreet knock on the door. Gail answered it and found a government official. "Please, Miss Edens, we are overwhelmed with people from the media. Now I know you made a statement at the airport, but if you could just hold one small press conference we could then tell them this is it and get them off our backs. The others have all done so."

Downstairs more than a hundred newsmen crowded a press room. They clapped when Gail entered.

"What do you want to know, ladies and gentlemen?" Questions bombarded her. Apparently the other actors had filled in the newsmen on most of the details of the nightmare. . . .

"What was the most frightening moment for you?"

Head down, flat on her belly in a small tunnel suddenly seeing a face against a grille, blue eyes of a guard filled with hate. . . .

Gail shuddered. It wasn't an act, and her discomposure was noticed. The room quieted.

Gail said, "There was a moment when one of the guards decided to rape me. In every movie I have ever made, I would fight off such a rape and escape."

The silence was absolute. Gail smiled.

"You will be pleased to know that in this case, life did imitate the cinema." A sigh, and then applause as Gail added, "But just barely, and I don't mean that as a pun."

But to the questions about more facts, Gail shook her head. The detailed memories of the night in the cave were still too fresh and painful.

"Are you joining the other actors in refusing to do the movie?"

"Yes, sir. I've seen our Nazi friends, and I don't like them. I did like the Colonel, after I found out what he intended to do."

Silence.

"You know he's dead, Miss Edens?"

Gail hadn't known that. She said, "I slept for about twenty hours, and I've just picked up bits and pieces about what happened in the outside world while we were in the cave. But as I said, I liked the Colonel, and the men with him, especially as we learned later that they never intended to harm any of us."

This brought a murmur from newsmen still trying to sort out the heroes and villains in a crime that had begun as simply another Baader-Meinhof terrorist incident and ended as a clash between the neo-Nazi party and some sons and nephews of the July 20th conspirators.

Gail's press conference finished with the question: "Are you going to marry George Williams?"

Laughter.

"The gentleman hasn't asked me." She paused, then said, "I've heard he took a helicopter ride last night holding onto a skid. If he doesn't ask me, he'll get another ride just like it, and this time a foot will kick him off it."

Everyone laughed and Gail went back to the room. George was awake and this time they had dinner with champagne, and she told him of the question about marriage at the press conference.

Williams said, "I like it."

"You do? Is that a proposal?"

"We'll talk about it later." Williams smiled. "You're

so high now you don't know what you're saying—or accepting."

Gail laughed. "You're right." She paused, then said, "God, I could sure use a hit."

"A hit? Cocaine?"

"Yes. I only indulge once in a while. Is that a crime?"

"Yes," said the Justice Department's Head of the Criminal Division. "It *is* a crime." He paused. "My new wife may be my first personal arrest."

"By God, he called me his new wife," Gail said, punching his bare shoulder. "But knowing you, the proposal will come wrapped in a subpoena."

Now, the next morning, she stretched, tingling all over. God, sex was great. Coke was the last thing she needed.

George was enough of a kick. He was great, but where was he?

The Chancellor, in his high-ceilinged office with massive oak furniture, looked at Williams. "Well, Mueller is dead."

The body of the new Nazi Fuehrer had been found stretched out in his bathroom, a pistol on the floor beside him. The police had called it suicide. All the documents in his files at home and at the office had vanished.

"They killed him," Williams said. "The Reborn Eagles murdered him to save the real Number One man."

The Chancellor was irritated. "You *still* believe the Colonel's"—the Chancellor wanted to say "fantasy" but restrained himself—"theory that Mr. Kandrof is the Fuehrer of the neo-Nazi party, and that the presidents of great German industries are also in that party?"

"I do."

"But the Colonel unfortunately died without any proof."

"I wouldn't say that," said Williams.

For the first time the Chancellor jolted to attention. He had been humoring Williams's efforts, ever since the hostages were rescued, to convince him that Kandrof was part of some sort of Nazi conspiracy. The absurdity of such a thought seemed to elude Williams. Kandrof was the President-elect. He didn't *need* Nazi thugs. He didn't even need any rich industrialists. He was *in*. The next President.

So Williams had discovered Kandrof once met Hitler at a theatrical play, and acted as an intermediary for a Lady Portland. So what? That was history. The lady herself, when reached by telephone by the Chancellor, told him in strident tones that Kandrof had been anti-Hitler, as were both his parents whom she also knew.

And it turned out that the surviving members of the Ice House Movement had no proof, either. The Colonel had kept the microdots in a hidden place, not trusting anyone, even his own associates.

Since all the facts about the Colonel had been made known, the Chancellor had breathed a sigh of relief about Ulrich Kandrof. It was obvious that the Colonel was deranged by the death of his wife. He had told Williams that the Reborn Eagles had killed her—but everyone in Germany knew that his marriage to a Jewess had wrecked his military career, and Intelligence confirmed that von Werten had suspected that she was a Soviet agent. How could anyone give credence to anything such a disturbed man, driven for revenge, said about Kandrof or anyone?

The Chancellor, in the last twenty-four hours, had checked Kandrof's record in every tiny detail as far back as he could do. War record spotless. Soldier in Russia, serving as personal courier for General von Kraus, now dead. Voting record since he entered the Bundestag even more innocent. Liberal democratic on every single vote. So what were all these charges and implications of a Nazi connection? If Kandrof was a Nazi Fuehrer, they had received absolutely nothing for their financial backing.

And yet, there were the sensational charges blared throughout the world by a man who died for his ideals, and what could the Chancellor do? In the end he had come up with a suggestion that could resolve the situation. He had said to Kandrof yesterday, "Make a television speech and tell everything to the last detail about your past relationship with Hitler. Don't leave anything out. Then we'll hold a referendum throughout the country."

Kandrof had liked the idea, although he had still been angry. He knew, he told the Chancellor, that his position as President-elect had made him a pawn in a war between two lunatic fringe groups—the Nazis and the anti-Nazis. Von Werten's people had needed a symbol of the rise of Nazism and so they had decided to show that *the President of the country had once known the evil Hitler, and had hidden that fact all of his life.*

"I'll tell the people everything. Even how Hitler held a teacup with shaking hands when he screamed at me after I intervened for von Werten's father. Every detail I can remember. Then let the people decide whether I've been libeled as a Nazi by some deranged man who was using me to make a point."

Now Williams had just startled the Chancellor by saying he had proof that Kandrot was, after all, a Nazi?

"What kind of proof? The microdots are gone. And so are the documents in Mueller's file."

Williams said, "Mr. Chancellor. I'm not here to hound Ulrich Kandrof. I'm not here to influence your political process in any way. But I feel an obligation to the Colonel. He died trying to prove something. I owe it to him to try to see whether his charges were real, or—"

"Or what?"

"Or if he was just obsessed by something personal, as I told you. He might have dragged Kandrof's name into this affair only to make his friends help him in his personal revenge against the Nazis."

The Chancellor's pudgy stomach stopped rumbling. He put plump hands, palms down, on his desk, almost as if he were balancing himself. "Which is exactly what I believe."

Williams said, "If you could arrange for me to see Kandrof with a friend."

"Who's the friend?"

"Lady Portland," said Williams, and the Chancellor reacted with surprise. "I think she holds the key to the mystery."

2

Lady Portland was beautiful. At sixty-two her face was fine boned, her eyes deep and lovely—not at all the prudish matron Williams had imagined in their telephone call. This was the woman who had made love to Hitler; the thought still bothered Williams, even though she was here now in Kandrof's house, gracious and charming as she glided across the room toward Ulrich Kandrof, both arms outstretched.

"My dear Ulrich," she said, "I'm so sorry for all you've been through."

The President-elect took her hands warmly and smiled. "I have a very estimable gentleman here who is convinced that I'm a new Hitler."

At which Lady Portland turned to look at Williams. "Extraordinary. I heard the most . . . gallant remarks about you today. But why must you torture Ulrich? I was in Berlin in 1938. I knew Hitler's friends. Unity and I were in the inner circle. Ulrich was just a boy. He would never even have seen Hitler again if I hadn't foolishly dragged him into the July twentieth affair."

They sat down. A maid brought them drinks and

Ulrich said to Williams, "It is of some interest to me that Franz von Werten never seemed to mention in his libelous remarks a most interesting point."

"What?"

"My later involvement with Hitler, consisting of one meeting, was for the sole purpose of saving his father's life. Why no thanks from the Colonel? Was he there in the Wolfschanze headquarters in East Prussia when Hitler heard me ask for mercy for a general I had never even met? Did he see Hitler jump to his feet in fury, shrieking, 'An eye for an eye, a tooth for a tooth,' and storm around the room so livid I was sure I would join the General on the meat hooks?"

"It makes you wonder," said Williams. Neither Kandrof nor Lady Portland liked that answer. Eyes flashing, the lady said, "You've made up your mind, sir. So what good is it to have this meeting?"

"Do you know how they make microdots, Mr. Kandrof?"

"What?"

"Do you know how they make microdots?"

Kandrof thought, then smiled. "Actually, I don't. How do they make the damn things?"

"Well, it's simple, actually. They reverse a microscope above a document, then photograph it through the reversed scope. End up with a dot." Williams paused. "Franz von Werten had five of the dots. Claimed they were documents linking you to the Reborn Eagles."

"So why the technical description of how to make microdots?" asked Ulrich Kandrof.

"Because it occurred to me that the same technical device might be used to *find* the microdots."

Kandrof sat up straight. "I don't understand. You

mean the microdots von Werten swallowed? They were washed away in his blood, weren't they?"

"But we know the exact spot to the inch. And I have a team of BFV laboratory specialists with microscopes searching every inch of the ground. What seems to be a speck of dust to the naked eye will show up as a document with writing under the microscopes. You see? Simple."

Kandrof regarded him levelly. "And you have found the so-called microdots and the documents?"

"Not yet, I'm afraid. But we will."

Kandrof stood up, furious. "In that event, Mr. Williams, I suggest you go to the area yourself and stay there until you find the microdots. I *want* you to find them. And when you discover the documents are innocent letters that only the Colonel's tortured mind could assume were guilty—"

Williams stopped him. "Why do you say the Colonel had a tortured mind?"

"Well . . . uh . . . look at what von Werten did, for God's sake. Kidnapped. Killed. He was more than tortured. He was insane—"

"I have a microdot," Williams said.

"What?"

Williams pulled out a small glassine envelope. Glued to a piece of white paper within it was a dot.

"What's that?" Kandrof asked. "Where did you get it?"

"From an abstract painting done by Otto Golenstern who never paints abstracts. But he had painted one for Franz von Werten to hide the map of the Valkyrie cave. It occurred to me that the Colonel might have used the painting to hide other secrets as well. So yesterday I tracked down the artist. Very interesting old man. He told me that microdots *had* been hidden on the painting by von Werten."

"And this microdot was one of them?"

"Yes. There probably were four others, but when we chipped away the paint earlier to find the Valkyrie map, we lost them."

"What does the microdot say, Mr. Williams?"

But Williams apparently was not ready to tell him. Instead he held his drink and looked over the edge of his glass as if into space. "Golenstern was in the July twentieth conspiracy. The Reborn Eagles don't know that to this day. So Franz used him, after he had gone to England and found out some facts from Lady Portland. He said he suspected Kandrof was a Nazi and could Golenstern use his past reputation as Hitler's court painter to get inside the Reborn Eagles' inner circle and photograph some documents." Williams paused; his audience was enrapt. "Golenstern did better than that. Mueller, himself—the Fuehrer—was enchanted when Hitler's personal artist suddenly showed up at his office and offered to paint the new Fuehrer in oils just as he had done Hitler."

Williams put the glass down on the table. "The rest is easy for you to imagine. One day during a break Mueller left his office, and Otto was able to photograph five documents in his briefcase before Mueller returned. And that's how von Werten got his proof that ended up on the microdots—and on a tower in Berlin."

"And one microdot survives?" Kandrof said, sarcastically. "Let me read this magic document which will no doubt spell out my reasons for hiding the fact I'm a Nazi all of my life."

Williams said, "The one that survives is interesting,

but not fatal, Mr. Kandrof. I'll show it to you, but there's really no need. It's a letter from you to Mueller, hand-carried by messenger, in which you state that the war on Zionist Jews should be intensified in all fields, beginning with the commercial aspects, and guaranteeing that, once Eagle One is in office, very effective steps will be taken to aid our Arab friends destroy the Jewish state of Israel which is destroying the world."

Kandrof was smiling, "Oh my," he said. "That's beautiful. Of course, I never heard of such nonsense, in or out of a letter. I suppose there's a forged signature, too."

"Not even that, Mr. Kandrof. Your name isn't on it and that's why the document isn't fatal. No signatures. It was simply addressed from Eagle One to Eagle Two."

Kandrof's jaw had opened in amazement. "What? The so-called incriminating document, the proof, the microdot doesn't even have my name on it? What is this? An inquisition in absentia? This is monstrous."

And then, almost as suddenly, his mood changed. He was laughing. "My God, it's a frame-up. That's what it is, pure and simple. I've finally figured it out." He was so exultant he actually swung his arms, striding around the room. For a moment Williams thought he was going to dance a jig as the Fuehrer had done outside of Paris. "I can't tell you what a burden this lifts from my mind, Williams."

"The letter was not from you?"

"My God, of course not. No sane politician anywhere in this country would ever write such a disastrous letter. Show it to German politicians and see.

They'll roar with laughter at such . . . naïveté." He stopped in front of Williams. "Mr. Williams, the Colonel hated me, so when he finds documents from some obscure Nazi politician he attributes them to me although my name isn't even on them. Incredible!" He paused. "Mr. Williams, tonight I'm going on television to tell the complete story—such as it is—about my contacts with Hitler: once as a drama student at one theatrical evening, and the only other in his Wolfschanze headquarters, lasting fifteen minutes. Period! If you like, I will show this famous letter, and let the people decide whether I wrote such comical garbage." He paused, so high with enthusiasm he could hardly bring himself under control. "Mr. Williams, my party is the Social Democrat party. This is the party to which this country's leading Jewish citizens belong. Do you think they would support me if I had not shown them by the way I voted over the years that I was their friend?"

"Why did he hate you so much, Mr. Kandrof?"

"Who? Von Werten?"

"Yes. You said it yourself," said Williams. " 'He hated me.' And before that, you said you tried to save his father's life and he never thanked you."

But Kandrof had the answer to that. "Because the Reborn Eagles are growing dangerously, and now I'm the President-elect, and the Colonel saw Nazis under every bed. Here I was, a man who had hidden all mention of my contact with Hitler. Why had I hidden it? I must have been a Nazi all along—or so his perverted mind would think."

Williams sipped his drink. He hated Kandrof. Lady Portland spoke up. "I find you a great disappointment, Mr. Williams. I don't know how you view justice in America, but in Europe we have some standards." She paused. "And I have come all the way from England for nothing. Did you think my appearance in the flesh would cause Ulrich to collapse and start shouting, 'Kill the Jews! Long live Hitler!' or something? You're really . . . incredible!"

Williams looked at his watch. "I do have one or two questions for you, Lady Portland, but I'm waiting for someone—"

"Now what?" Kandrof said. "You didn't tell me you had other people coming."

"Mr. Kandrof, two nights ago when the hostages were in captivity, the Colonel sent us a film. It was dedicated to you."

"The so-called death of Morrison. Yes, another incredible dirty blow by that man. Why dedicated to *me*? I never even met Morrison. And, speaking of technical tricks like forgery, look how the man staged that so-called hanging scene."

The doorbell rang. In a few moments the maid came to the door. "A man with a projector and film, sir. He says Mr. Williams told him to come."

Kandrof regarded Williams angrily. "What lengths won't you go to?"

"I'd like to show the Colonel's film to you both and point out some features you may have missed."

"Show it where? In here? I don't have a screening room."

"The projectionist has a screen. Bear with me on this film, Mr. Kandrof, and then I'm going. If it will relieve both of your minds I have an eight o'clock flight to Washington, and you'll never see me again."

Kandrof said to the maid, "Send him in, please." To

Williams he said, "The film shows no evidence that will lead you to call the police and arrest the President-elect?"

"No, it doesn't."

And this time Lady Portland interrupted. "Then what—"

But the arrival of the projectionist cut off all conversation. He set up the screen and threaded the film through the projector. When he asked Kandrof to cut the lights, Kandrof did so, then pulled the drapes and the room was dark.

Colonel von Werten's film, shot in the cave, started.

3

Jack Riley and Robert Morrison stared angrily into
the camera in close-up. Then the Colonel's hand appeared and started to apply makeup to Morrison.
Magically before them the face turned into Hitler.

Riley was seen talking to the Colonel who was offscreen, then the hand started to apply makeup to Riley's face. Soon he was Hitler also.

Two Hitlers, in close-up, stared from the screen.
Then abruptly the film cut to Adolf Hitler in his bedroom, taking a book from Eva Braun's hands, tossing
it aside, and getting into bed with her. Gail Edens
was naked from the waist up. But the film sequence
did not end with Riley saying "Alice." Instead it continued with Riley rolling on top of Gail.

"Stop the film," Williams said. The film froze.
"Zoom into a close-up of Riley's right shoulder."

The projectionist twisted the lens and Riley's bare
right shoulder moved toward them until it covered the
screen. There on the shoulder was a Z-shaped scar.

"My God," said Lady Portland.

"I don't understand," said Kandrof.

But Williams said, hotly, "You *do*. The film was addressed to *you*." To the projectionist, he said, "That's all. Turn on the lights."

The projectionist stepped to the wall and flipped the switch. The light showed Lady Portland looking sick.

"But that's extraordinary," she said. "The man made him up with the scar."

"What about the scar?" Kandrof said. "Really, Mr. Williams, I don't understand, no matter what you think."

"Lady Portland, I must be blunt. By now you know your niece read your diary. In that diary you described the Z-shaped scar on Hitler's shoulder, correct?"

"Right."

"Hitler had no Z-shaped scar on his shoulder."

"What?" cried Lady Portland. "You're . . . insane! I saw it!"

"You kissed it, according to your diary. And to the few friends you told over the years when they wanted details about Hitler. Franz von Werten obviously heard about it, too, when your niece was spicing up everyone's dinner parties in Europe."

"But what has the lady's lovemaking to do with me?" said Kandrof.

But Williams spoke only to a white-faced Lady Portland. "Lady Portland, in 1938 you *didn't sleep with Hitler*. You made love to Ulrich Kandrof, the drama student whom Hitler took under his wing, the theatrical student who showed Hitler how effective makeup can be—even in a lover's darkened bedroom—and gave the Fuehrer a real laugh about you, and got himself a new job."

He turned to Kandrof. "You, Ulrich Kandrof, earned

yourself a unique position in the Third Reich. You were Hitler's double. You appeared in public places wherever there was a danger for Hitler. That's why von Werten purposely made up two Hitlers and dedicated that film to you."

Kandrof stood up to object, but then remained frozen as Williams said, "I spent part of yesterday afternoon in a cell with a captain in the Reborn Eagles who's now accused of the murder of Bernie Weller. I made a deal with him. I'd speak to the Chancellor and see if he could get favorable treatment in the trial process if he would cooperate. So he told me he was a low-ranking party member and didn't know the names of any politicians working with the party. How about businessmen? I asked him. He said the president of the KAL Steel Corporation in his area, who had been named by von Werten, was a member. So I went to the president and he didn't know anything either, wasn't even a member of the party, couldn't imagine how the Captain had ever said such a thing."

Kandrof and Lady Portland waited. Williams went on: "So I said to the president of KAL Steel, 'I know your own connection with Eagle One,' just throwing the code name at him, and the president turned white at the code name. The BFV Director and his boys then had a talk with the president, and we ended up at a computer terminal. The president said the Eagles have a computer network, using the facilities of corporations that aid them to communicate throughout their party. But the president insisted that he never touched the computer, that party people would come in, punch out their messages, receive their replies, and disappear. So I got tired of arguing and just sat down before the computer terminal and punched in the name Eagle One."

Silence in the room. Williams said, "I requested from the computer all documents in which the code name Eagle One was mentioned. There were only two. The Eagles are very circumspect on the computer where Eagle One is concerned. But the two were interesting enough. For one thing, Mueller, who was supposed to be the Fuehrer, really wasn't the leader at all. He was only the Number Two man, as von Werten had said."

Kandrof had taken his seat again. He held his glass as Williams continued. "One of the documents was very recent—two days ago. It merely said, 'All contact with Eagle One to be broken off until further notice.' In other words, lie low until the kidnapping crisis is over. The other document was dated two months ago. I have a copy." He extracted the document from his briefcase and handed it to Kandrof, who read:

From: EAGLE TWO
To: ALL GAULEITERS

Von Werten went to England to see Lady Alice Portland. Considered extremely dangerous for Eagle One if Eagle One's double role in 1944 is discovered, particularly as von Werten is son of General killed after July 20th conspiracy, and knows all details. When Lady Portland contacted Eagle One in July 1944, he was already stationed at Hitler's Wolfschanze Headquarters in Rastenburg, East Prussia, not on the front lines in Russia as a soldier as his files show. If Lady Portland told von Werten Eagle One was at Wolfschanze in

July 1944, von Werten may have drawn the correct conclusions. July 20th officers have always
wondered about the Fuehrer's telephone call
from Wolfschanze to Berlin when the explosion
had rendered him unconscious. Eagle Two directs
von Werten be terminated soonest, and will coor-
dinate this mission with commando leader
Burger.

Williams said, "I took that copy to Kurt Hurwirth,
another son of a General killed after the July twentieth uprising, and he said von Werten had that information about the double role and the telephone call
from Wolfschanze on one of the documents that was
lost. And he told me just what that 'double role' meant
and why the telephone call was so important." He
paused. "Why didn't von Werten thank you for trying
to save his father's life? Because you betrayed all of
their fathers. When Hitler was wounded by von Stauffenberg's bomb so badly he was in a coma, the July
20th officers went into action in Berlin and Paris, taking over all key command and communications cen-
ters. Goebbels was the only top Nazi official in Berlin
at the time. He knew that even if Hitler recovered it
would be too late; the July twentieth officers would
have already seized power, and the Hitler gang would
be out. So Goebbels thought of you, Kandrof."

"Me?"

"Hitler's double, standing by as always, at the
Fuehrer's bidding in Wolfschanze. And so he called
you and set up the fraud—and when Major Otto Re-
mer, in charge of the Nazi guard battalion, went to
Goebbels' office to tell him he was going over to the

other side, Goebbels put through a telephone call to Adolf Hitler to show the Major, in person, that the Fuehrer was not only alive but completely in control. Only the man he spoke to wasn't Hitler. It was you, Hitler's double, a common actor, mimicking Hitler's voice—or should I say shriek—and you did your greatest impersonation so successfully that the Major snapped to attention in awe, convinced that his Fuehrer was really in command. And he turned around and started arresting the July twentieth officers; four of them were shot, including the brave von Stauffenberg, in the courtyard within minutes—no trial, of course—and the SS started hanging Generals on meat hooks, and Germany's last chance was over. From then on it was blood and ruin because no nation would enter peace negotiations with Hitler, and Germany was overrun by the Soviets, who kept half of it and built a wall to divide the nation forever. That wall is the heritage of the President-elect, Kandrof. *Your* heritage."

Silence in the room. Then Kandrof said. "An incredible story, Mr. Williams. But fantasy times twelve. I was a boy of twenty in 1938—"

"Your specialty was makeup," Williams said. "You played King Lear at twenty. Hitler—and Lady Portland—saw you."

Williams reached into his inside coat pocket and passed something to Lady Portland. "Lady Portland, this is a picture of Hitler's back, taken from his medical files. The German historical archivist says Colonel von Werten asked to see it three weeks ago." He paused. "You will note it shows no scar on the shoulder."

"Oh, my word," said Lady Portland. "This is so . . . embarrassing."

"Mr. Kandrof, I would ask you to take off your coat and shirt."

And for the first time, Ulrich Kandrof broke. He put his palms up. "No. I will not."

"Not even to prove that I'm lying?"

"N-no. I will not do that," said Ulrich Kandrof.

Williams stood up. "Then explain it to the BFV. The Director was kind enough to obtain a picture of your back taken at *your* government physical examination, a picture which von Werten also had requested to see. You *have* a Z-shaped scar on your right shoulder, Mr. Kandrof. You were Hitler's double at the height of his powers. Do you think you should include *that* news in your television address tonight. Hitler's double is now the President-elect of Germany? And he is Eagle One in the Reborn Eagles?"

Lady Portland stood up, and for the first time addressed Williams with some warmth. "Mr. Williams. I think we should be leaving together."

Outside, the lady offered Williams a ride in her limousine. "That beast!" She was trying to pull herself together. "After forty years it would be silly to slap someone but I almost did it there. So Hitler had a long laugh about me, did he? While I thought I was in love. Oh yes. I never told anyone *that*, not even my diary." She paused, lips trembling. "And they were using me for a joke!"

But Williams was thinking only of a hectic day in Berlin, von Stauffenberg reporting the explosion in Hitler's headquarters, and heroic but frightened men, in a land controlled by the Gestapo, risking their lives to come out into the open against Hitler's murderous regime, and the man they had just seen disguising his voice on a telephone from Wolfschanze to deceive a Nazi minion in Berlin—and turning the pivot of history on a wheel of agony still going around.

4

That night Williams flew back to Washington with Gail. The next day he was in the Oval Office when news came that the Chancellor had announced Kandrof's resignation "for reasons of health having nothing to do with the recent charges."

Later that afternoon, Williams entered a jewelry store on Connecticut Avenue to buy an engagement ring for Gail, but faltered on his way out when he saw a little heart-shaped pendant with the name *Elise*.

He bought the ring for Gail and the pendant for a Colonel who had lost everything. He was thinking, "For reasons of health?" The Chancellor, no doubt afraid of repercussions, had decided to cover up the facts on Kandrof and the Nazi party? No doubt he was putting pressure on the July 20th sons and nephews who were held on kidnapping charges. If they made a pledge of silence, they would be freed.

All those deaths in Germany, and the Nazis would now emerge unscathed and regroup with their powerful backers? And their American associates, who wanted to kill Gail Edens, would gain new momentum and arrogance? Because of a timid Chancellor who wanted to keep everything quiet and smooth? Williams couldn't let it happen. The Chancellor was blind. A man was clutching his elbow. "Mr. Williams, you're wanted back at the White House."

Cardinals on the White House lawn, a gardener pruning roses. In the Oval Office, the President said, "I took your advice and called the Chancellor. He didn't like it."

"What did you say?"

"That I couldn't stop you from telling all of the facts about Kandrof and his Nazi backers to the public press, including Kandrof's connection with Hitler. That you told me you'd resign, if you had to, in order to get out the truth about how powerful and dangerous the Nazis are, no matter what the Chancellor thinks. But that wasn't the clincher, George. I told him what the Nazis are doing here."

The President reached into his desk and threw a packet of envelopes on the top. "Movie stars are one thing, but Cabinet officers? Here are anonymous death threats, forty in all so far, all identically worded, all from different states—just like Gail Edens—to the Secretary of HEW. If he doesn't resign immediately, his wife and son are going to be murdered. The Secretary is so frightened, he's not even coming into the office. In effect, they're controlling part of my government. And when they see how successful they are, they'll move against other government leaders." He paused. "The neo-Nazis are too damned dangerous to ignore and sweep under the rug. That's what I told the Chancellor, and he began to wake up."

Williams was thinking of Gail, who was already the

target of threatening letters from American Nazis. The President said, "So he agreed and he's going on the air in a few hours to tell the facts. All of them. And I think that calls for a celebration."

Williams followed the President to the Rose Room and then recoiled, because there, beneath a portrait of Thomas Jefferson, were dozens of White House staffers, and Gail Edens. A cake and champagne were set up. "Give her the ring, George," said the President gruffly. "Don't faint now."

The President beamed as Gail, looking radiant, opened the little package and saw a sparkling diamond nestled in a slim gold ring. The Secret Service had obviously followed Williams when he left the White House angrily after his first visit that day. Gail affectionately punched him in the side and said, "Hooray for us," and kissed him, and the President told everyone that Gail would have FBI guards until "we stamp those Nazi goons out, which we're going to do." And who knows, maybe it could be done, thought Williams. All it took last time was a World War.

But the merriment rose, the champagne poured, and two hours later, after the Chancellor's speech in Germany, Williams's mood was changing. The report that the new President of Germany had been Hitler's double during the war, and was now the Fuehrer of the Reborn Eagles, broke across the world with a fury. The industrialists whom the Colonel had named as Nazi party backers were brought back before television cameras, and for the first time subjected to skeptical and even bitter questions from a press which had tended to think that the Colonel was deranged.

And in this country Williams had released the transcript of the telephone call between the Deputy Commander of the American Nazi party, Farley Smith, and Kurt Mueller in Germany, in which the two Nazis calmly discussed murder—and throwing acid in the face of a woman—and Nazi gauleiters across America found themselves sweating in the glare of public revulsion.

And by ten o'clock Williams felt so good he took Gail dancing and later escorted her to a restaurant she had remembered in a dark cave in which she was almost raped and killed. The proprietor with the totally unforgettable name, Mr. Christ, shouted happily, "You're back! You're safe! What's that?" as he saw the engagement ring, and then, overcome with excitement, closed his doors for the night and opened some Greek wine, and invited the few customers in his little place to join the party with a "beeg movie star."

While in Bonn a man with a scar on his right shoulder contemplated a Luger held in his right hand. In the bunker, the Fuehrer had told him how afraid he was that he might have a failure of nerve, while attempting to shoot himself in the temple, and miss. So he would take the cyanide pill as insurance. That conversation was just before Hitler gave Ulrich Kandrof his favorite picture, showing the Fuehrer smiling.

Kandrof studied the picture now, the Luger in his hand.

Exciting Bestsellers by
ROBERT LUDLUM

☐ **THE GEMINI CONTENDERS** (12859-5) $3.25
A desperate hunt ensues for a dangerous ancient document
that could alter the course of history!
"A breathless rollercoaster ride!" —*John Barkham Reviews*

☐ **THE OSTERMAN WEEKEND** (16646-2) $2.50
"The shattering action of MacLean, the spy machinery of
Le Carre, the flawless intrigue of Deighton . . . THE
OSTERMAN WEEKEND will cost you the night and the
cold hours of the morning!" —*Cincinnati Enquirer*

☐ **THE RHINEMANN EXCHANGE** (15079-5) $3.25
Featured in a three-part serial on the popular NBC
Bestsellers Series, this Ludlum masterpiece portrays a top
secret American agent and a beautiful young widow—and
their roles in the most sinister deal that two nations at war
ever made with each other . . .
"Breathless!" —*Cleveland Plain Dealer*

☐ **THE SCARLATTI INHERITANCE** (17638-7) $2.50
An international flavor envelops this gripping drama about
a woman who attempts to save the world from the plans
of her handsome, brilliant, incalculably dangerous son.

At your local bookstore or use this handy coupon for ordering:

Dell | **DELL BOOKS**
P.O. BOX 1000, PINE BROOK, N.J. 07058

Please send me the books I have checked above. I am enclosing $_____
including 75¢ for the first book, 25¢ for each additional book up to $1.50 maximum
postage and handling charge.
Please send check or money order—no cash or C.O.D.s. *Please allow up to 8 weeks for
delivery.*

Mr./Mrs._____

Address_____

City_____ State/Zip_____

JOSEPH WAMBAUGH

author of *The Choirboys*

THE BLACK MARBLE

Joseph Wambaugh's "best novel yet!"
New York Daily News

Five Months on The New York Times Bestseller List

The Black Marble is Wambaugh's fifth bestseller and first love story! It tells the story of two unforgettable characters: Sgt. Valnikov, a damned good cop who turns far too frequently to the warmth and solace of Russian Vodka, and Natalie Zimmerman, an energetic woman detective determined to preserve the sanity and order of her division and to avoid at all costs the bad luck of the Black Marble. Together they fight crime, boredom, and each other and find more than they had ever hoped for!

A Dell Book $3.25 (10647-8)

At your local bookstore or use this handy coupon for ordering:

Dell	**DELL BOOKS** The Black Marble $3.25 (10647-8) **P.O. BOX 1000, PINEBROOK, N.J. 07058**

Please send me the above title. I am enclosing $_____
(please add 75¢ per copy to cover postage and handling). Send check or money order—no cash or C.O.D.'s. Please allow up to 8 weeks for shipment.

Mr/Mrs/Miss_____

Address_____

City_____ State/Zip_____

When the Wind Blows

A chilling novel of occult terror!

John Saul

author of *Suffer the Children*
and *Punish the Sinners*

To the Indians, the ancient mine was a sacred place. To the local residents, it was their source of livelihood.

But the mine contains a deadly secret—and the souls of the town's lost children. Their cries can be heard at night, when the wind blows—and the terror begins.

A DELL BOOK $3.50   (19857-7)

At your local bookstore or use this handy coupon for ordering:

 DELL BOOKS   WHEN THE WIND BLOWS $3.50   (19857-7)
P.O. BOX 1000, PINEBROOK, N.J. 07058

Please send me the above title. I am enclosing $ _____
(please add 75¢ per copy to cover postage and handling). Send check or money order—no cash or C.O.D.'s. Please allow up to 8 weeks for shipment.

Mr/Mrs/Miss _____

Address _____

City _____ State/Zip _____

SOLO

by **JACK HIGGINS**

author of The Eagle Has Landed

The pursuit of a brilliant concert pianist / master assassin brings this racing thriller to a shattering climax in compelling Higgins' fashion.

A Dell Book $2.95   (18165-8)

At your local bookstore or use this handy coupon for ordering.

| **Dell** | **DELL BOOKS**
 P.O. BOX 1000, PINEBROOK, N.J. 07058 | **SOLO $2.95 (18165-8)** |

Please send me the above title. I am enclosing $ _____
(please add 75¢ per copy to cover postage and handling). Send check or money order—no cash or C.O.D.'s. Please allow up to 8 weeks for shipment.

Mr/Mrs/Miss _____

Address _____

City _____ State/Zip _____

Bestsellers

☐ **THE RING** by Danielle Steel $3.50   (17386-8)
☐ **INGRID BERGMAN: MY STORY**
  by Ingrid Bergman and Alan Burgess $3.95   (14085-4)
☐ **SOLO** by Jack Higgins $2.95   (18165-8)
☐ **THY NEIGHBOR'S WIFE** by Gay Talese....$3.95   (18689-7)
☐ **THE CRADLE WILL FALL** by Mary H. Clark $3.50   (11476-4)
☐ **RANDOM WINDS** by Belva Plain $3.50   (17158-X)
☐ **WHEN THE WIND BLOWS** by John Saul $3.50   (19857-7)
☐ **LITTLE GLORIA . . . HAPPY AT LAST**
  by Barbara Goldsmith $3.50   (15109-0)
☐ **CHANGE OF HEART** by Sally Mandel $2.95   (11355-5)
☐ **THE PROMISE** by Danielle Steel $3.50   (17079-6)
☐ **FLOWERS OF THE FIELD**
  by Sarah Harrison $3.95   (12584-7)
☐ **LOVING** by Danielle Steel $3.50   (14657-7)
☐ **CORNISH HEIRESS** by Roberta Gellis $3.50   (11515-9)
☐ **BLOOD RED WINE** by Laurence Delaney....$2.95   (10714-8)
☐ **COURT OF THE FLOWERING PEACH**
  by Janette Radcliffe $3.50   (11497-7)
☐ **FAIR WARNING**
  by George Simpson and Neal Burger $3.50   (12478-6)

At your local bookstore or use this handy coupon for ordering:

DELL BOOKS
P.O. BOX 1000, PINEBROOK, N.J. 07058

Please send me the books I have checked above. I am enclosing $ _____
(please add 75¢ per copy to cover postage and handling). Send check or money
order—no cash or C.O.D.'s. Please allow up to 8 weeks for shipment.

Mr/Mrs/Miss _____

Address _____

City _____ State/Zip _____